"In her delightful and descriptive style, author Laurie Alice Eakes has once again crafted a story that will capture readers' hearts from the first page. Her tales are both exciting and tender, and her characters speak to us right where they are, despite the different cultural and time settings. *Heart's Safe Passage* may well be her greatest offering to date."

—**Kathi Macias**, author of *Deliver Me from Evil* and *A Christmas Journey Home*

"I'm still thinking about the characters in *Heart's Safe Passage*, the new novel from Laurie Alice Eakes. Her turn of phrase and twist of a plot had me smiling long after th̶ ̶ ̶age was turned. Eakes has crafted a do̶n̶'̶ ̶ ̶ ̶ ̶e̶!"

—**Kathleen Y̶ ̶ ̶ ̶ nt ̶ ̶ k**

"In *Heart's Safe Passage*, La̶ ̶ ̶ ̶ ̶ ̶ ̶ ̶ readers on a heartrending high-se̶ ̶ ̶ ̶ ̶ ̶ pack to the 1800s, where they'll smile and cry, cheer for the good guys, and boo the bad guys. Make room for this one on your 'keepers' shelf!"

—**Loree Lough**, author of *From Ashes to Honor*

"*Heart's Safe Passage* is the finest kind of fiction. Not only does it take the reader on a high-seas adventure, it also explores the bounty and suffering of the human heart. I loved it!"

—**Victoria Bylin**, 2010 ACFW Carol Award finalist; author of *The Outlaw's Return* and *Marrying the Major*

"A book that will move you deeply, a love story that rises and falls with the turbulent seas, and two people wounded by life who need God's healing before they can embrace the love melding their hearts together. Adventurous, moving, and passionate, Laurie's books never disappoint!"

—**MaryLu Tyndall**, Christy Award nominee and author of the Surrender to Destiny series

Books by Laurie Alice Eakes

The Midwives

Lady in the Mist
Heart's Safe Passage

The Daughters of Bainbridge House

A Necessary Deception

The
MIDWIVES

BOOK 2

HEART'S SAFE PASSAGE

A NOVEL

LAURIE ALICE EAKES

Revell

a division of Baker Publishing Group
Grand Rapids, Michigan

© 2012 by Laurie Alice Eakes

Published by Revell
a division of Baker Publishing Group
P.O. Box 6287, Grand Rapids, MI 49516-6287
www.revellbooks.com

Printed in the United States of America

Library of Congress Cataloging-in-Publication Data
Eakes, Laurie Alice.
    Heart's safe passage : a novel / Laurie Alice Eakes.
        p.   cm. — (The midwives ; bk. 2)
    Includes bibliographical references.
    ISBN 978-0-8007-1985-2 (pbk.)
    1. Title
PS3605.A377H43 2012
813'.6—dc23   2011034160

Scripture is taken from the King James Version of the Bible.

Published in association with Tamela Hancock Murray of the Hartline Literary Agency, LLC.

12   13   14   15   16   17   18   7   6   5   4   3   2   1

To Carrie, Debbie Lynne, and Gina
for all the marathon phone calls that kept me grounded
to the real world. Your friendship is a treasure.

And I will give them one heart,
and I will put a new spirit within you; and I
will take the stony heart out of their flesh,
and will give them an heart of flesh.

Ezekiel 11:19

As concerning their persons, they [midwives]
must be neither too young nor too old,
but of an indifferent age, between both;
well composed, not being subject to diseases,
nor deformed in any part of their body; comely
and neat in their apparell; their hands small and
fingers long, not thick, but clean, their nails
pared very close; they ought to be very chearfull,
pleasant, and of a good discourse; strong,
not idle, but accustomed to exercise, that they
may be the more able if need require.

Touching their deportment,
they must be mild, gentle, courteous, sober,
chaste, and patient; not quarrelsome nor
chollerick; neither must they be covetous,
nor report anything whatsoever they hear
or see in secret, in the person or
house of whom they deliver. . . .

As concerning their minds, they must be wise
and discreet; able to flatter and speak many fair
words, to no other end but only to deceive the
apprehensive women, which is a commendable
deceipte, and allowed, when it is done,
for the good of the person in distress.

William Sermon,
seventeenth-century physician
and clergyman

1

Williamsburg, Virginia
October 4, 1813

"You want me to go to sea with you?" Phoebe Lee stared at her sister-in-law as though she'd sprouted whiskers and pointed ears between supper and this midnight invasion of Phoebe's bedchamber. "In the event you've forgotten, we're at war."

"Of course I haven't forgotten." Pain distorted Belinda Chapman's features, and she twisted her fingers through the fringe of her silk shawl. "If we weren't at war, my husband wouldn't be a prisoner in a barbaric English hulk. And I can't free him if I can't get to England."

"Go to England? Free him?" Phoebe stared at her deceased husband's sister with eyes wide and jaw sagging. "You must be—" She stopped speaking and made a circuit of the pink-flowered carpet of Belinda's guest bedchamber, her slippers silent in the lush pile, her blood roaring. She must not tell Belinda that she had certainly become a raving mooncalf to consider traveling on water as far as Norfolk, let alone across the Atlantic.

Silence filled the bedchamber. Belinda watched Phoebe, saying nothing. Outside, a carriage rumbled up the roughly paved street, and laughter soared into a crescendo.

Inside, Phoebe inhaled the too-sweet air of Belinda's townhouse and tried to remember what her teacher, Tabitha Eckles Cherrett, would do under similar circumstances—remain even-tempered. Speak in a slow, calm voice.

"Bel, my dear, you can't simply step onto a packet and sail across the ocean, land in an enemy country, and demand they free your husband. That is—" She dropped to her knees before Belinda's chair and drew the younger woman's hands away from the tangled knots they'd made of her shawl fringe, sending more reek of lavender oil into the air. "I'm devastated with the news of George's capture." The news had sent Phoebe racing from Leesburg to Williamsburg in a heartbeat. "And I can't imagine how awful it must be for you. But this is outright war, and we're losing on land."

"But not at sea." Belinda's round chin jutted out at a pugnacious angle. "In the last year, George has taken six prizes just with his little sloop. His investors were ecstatic."

And now he was the prize. Something too obvious for Phoebe to point out.

"We're all very proud of him." The twisting of the truth tasted a little sour on Phoebe's tongue. "And you for bearing up so bravely while he's gone. But, my dear girl, we can only pray and trust God to take care of George. We can't take matters into our own hands."

"Of course we can." Belinda's lips curved. She suddenly resembled Phoebe's cat after a nice bowl of cream. "I've already made the arrangements. That's why I asked you to come here."

Phoebe's stomach knotted like Belinda's fringe. "What . . . sort of arrangements could you have possibly made to get to England in the middle of the war?"

"Privateers are crossing the Atlantic all the time," Belinda said. "I've simply taken berths for us on one of them."

Phoebe shook her head. "You are not thinking clearly, Bel.

No American privateer captain would allow two women aboard for that kind of journey. No scrupulous captain, that is."

"Who said anything about an American?" Belinda tossed her head of ebony curls. "An American ship couldn't get close enough to land us in England."

"Then how——?" Phoebe couldn't finish the question. She feared the answer.

Belinda inclined her head as though Phoebe had spoken the right conclusion aloud. "We're sailing on an English privateer."

"Impossible." Phoebe rose and stalked to the window, beyond which the night glittered with lights from plantations and boats on the James River, flickering sparks like fallen stars, like earthbound dreams. "It's too dangerous. I won't go with you. It's—well, it's treachery to consort with the enemy."

Belinda's flawless white forehead puckered. "Not if we're freeing an American, surely."

"Yes, surely. And I won't let you commit treason."

"You can't stop me."

Belinda spoke the raw truth. Short of reporting her to the authorities and having her arrested, Phoebe couldn't stop Belinda. She was three and twenty, three years younger than Phoebe, and her husband had left her in charge of their considerable fortune in his absence.

"I'll take the risk of being considered a traitor whether you accompany me or not. But—but—" Belinda faltered for the first time since making her announcement. "Phoebe, I need you to come with me."

"You need someone to go with you, yes, but not me." Phoebe turned back to face her sister-in-law. "You need a guard, a protector, half a dozen strong, well-armed men. I can write to Tabitha and Dominick. Dominick has powerful connections with the British still."

"That will take too much time, and I don't need his help."

"You don't need the help of someone my size either."

"You're a midwife," Belinda broke in. "That's why I need you."

"Belinda, you're not—"

But she was. Even as Phoebe protested, Belinda shoved her shawl off her shoulders. What the silk wrap and flickering candlelight had concealed since Phoebe's arrival just before supper, the fine muslin of her nightgown revealed.

Belinda Lee Chapman was expecting a baby.

"When?" As her heart joined her stomach somewhere around her knees, Phoebe's mind raced to the date of George's last visit home. She didn't know for certain. He slipped in and out of the Chapmans' home in Williamsburg, and months had passed since Phoebe had seen Belinda, let alone her privateer husband.

"At least five months, as best I can estimate."

"Are you certain?" Phoebe reached out her hands. "Let me examine you. You look further along than that."

"I know when my husband was home." Belinda's voice held an edge.

Phoebe scrutinized Belinda's middle with narrowed eyes. "Do you?"

"Of course." Belinda wrapped her shawl around herself again. "I had a midwife confirm my condition when I began to suspect."

Phoebe ground her teeth together and counted to ten to stop herself from shouting that she was a midwife, a well-trained one, who wanted nothing more than to practice, if only the ladies of Loudoun County would see her as more than a wealthy marriage prospect for their brothers, sons, nephews . . .

"If you don't want me as a midwife," Phoebe managed with remarkable calm considering how her insides boiled, "then why do you want me to accompany you on your madcap journey?"

"Well, I want you for my midwife once we're at sea, but not here. It's just too embarrassing to have my sister-in-law examine me. I mean, I don't eat at the same table with my midwife."

"Then maybe you should take a different midwife with you."

"I can't." Belinda sighed. "She has a family she doesn't want to leave. And I didn't think you'd mind leaving Leesburg."

Phoebe couldn't disagree with that part. After all, she'd packed up and departed for Williamsburg the day she'd received Belinda's request.

"But I don't want to leave on the ship of some enemy and possibly be tainted in this country."

"He can't be a real enemy if he wants to help free American prisoners." Belinda smiled serenely. "We could be there and have George free before my confinement."

"Or end up in an English or even an American prison ourselves," Phoebe muttered. Rubbing her suddenly aching temples, she tried another tack. "Bel, this is the worst time for you to travel. All the jostling, the bad food, not to mention the danger of attacks from the French or our own ships . . ." She gave her head an emphatic shake. "You could miscarry or even die."

"What I can't do," Belinda said, "is leave my husband to rot in the hulk and condemn my unborn baby to never knowing his father."

"Of course you can't." Phoebe resumed pacing, concentrating on treading only on the pink flowers in the carpet and avoiding the violet blossoms or green leaves. "I've prayed every morning and night for George to be safe and freed, and I know it will happen."

11

"Of course he will, because this opportunity presented itself."

"Presented itself?" Phoebe spun toward Belinda, her right foot squarely in the middle of a violet. "How?"

"I don't really know." Belinda closed her eyes. "A man came to see me one night. He said his name is Rafael Docherty—Captain Docherty—and he told me of George's capture, then he said he could help me get George free if I'd sail to England with him. It was like an answer to prayer. I'd been feeling quite desperate about my dear George being a prisoner of war and how awful things are. His investors . . . well, they may want their money back, especially Mr. Brock. Then this man appeared like a message directly from the Lord."

Phoebe sighed. "I don't think the Lord meant childlike faith to be childish faith, Bel. But that's what you're demonstrating—downright irresponsible—no, don't cry. I know you must be upset by George's imprisonment. It can't be easy. But no Englishman who would take a female across the Atlantic in the middle of a war is up to any good."

"I don't care what his reasons are." Belinda drew a handkerchief out of her reticule and dabbed at her eyes. "If he helps me get George free, it's worth every bit of risk."

"Is it a risk George would want you to take?" Phoebe asked.

"Yes. Well . . ." Belinda dropped her gaze. "Maybe not, but it doesn't matter now. It's too late."

"For what? Bel, before you do anything rash, we should tell your father—" Phoebe stared at her sister-in-law as she rose and trotted to the door of the dressing room.

A heartbeat before Belinda turned the handle, a floorboard creaked in the adjoining chamber. Phoebe caught the sound, then a scent, a tang of damp wool, salt air, tar. She bolted for the hallway door and the sensible servants beyond. Her hand closed over the latch, lifted. The door clicked.

12

Behind her, the dressing room door clicked. Footfalls trod on the carpet, silent but heavy enough to feel. Phoebe yanked open her portal. Arms closed around her from behind, pinning her arms to her side. She parted her lips to scream. A hand as hard as boot leather clamped over her mouth, stifling her scream but freeing one arm.

Kicking out with one foot, she swung her freed arm up and back. Her fist connected with flesh. A man grunted, grabbed her wrist, growled an oath.

Phoebe had never deliberately harmed anyone in her life. Now she twisted, turned, lashed out with her feet. And only managed to bruise her slippered heels. Prayers for deliverance and vows of revenge raced through her mind. She opened her mouth and bit hard into the calloused palm over her mouth.

Her captor gasped. "Can ye lads no' help me? She's a wild woman."

Belinda let out a whimper. "Don't hurt her."

Too late for the minx to think of that.

Phoebe gritted her teeth and tasted blood. The stranger's blood. Gagging, she spit. His hand jerked away. Before she could scream, another hand closed over her mouth and nose, cutting off her air.

"I need her well." Belinda's protest was the last thing Phoebe heard before the world turned black.

✺

Chesapeake Bay, Virginia
October 5, 1813

Legs braced against the pitching roll of the deck, Captain Rafe Docherty held the night glass to his eye and scanned the horizon. Nothing showed save the inverted view of sea bulging in ever-increasing waves against the flat gray expanse of the sky. Not a single British patrol or American privateer ready to waylay him—the former a risk to his crew, the latter a nuisance, both an interruption he couldn't afford.

On the other hand, the cutter hadn't returned either.

He shoved the glass into the binnacle rack and turned to the helmsman. "If they're not back within the quarter hour, we'll have to be leaving them behind."

"But, sir," the man protested, "we'd be down by three of our best men, not to mention the cargo."

"Better that than losing all of you to a man-of-war or Yankee privateer."

Except perhaps not. He needed the cargo, the female whose presence would help to lure his quarry out of hiding.

He retrieved the night glass and began to pace the width of the quarterdeck. Five strides to windward. Five strides to leeward. A pause to scan the horizon before he turned on his heel and repeated the circuit. With each view of an empty sea, he felt his gut twist a wee bit tighter. All his planning, all the risk of sailing to the mouth of the harbor at Norfolk, for naught. His first mate, Jordy McPherson, had warned him the flibbertigibbet of a female would ruin Rafe's scheme.

Five minutes. Ten. Jordy was likely cursing Rafe's name and saying, "I told him so," while sighing relief that for once, Rafe Docherty wasn't going to get his own way.

No, not for once. If he'd gotten his own way nine years earlier, he wouldn't be riding at anchor much too close to the shore of Virginia on the eve of a full moon, awaiting three of his best men to return with the wife of one of the most important merchants in Virginia.

All of them about to commit treason.

Another lap of the deck. Two. A scan of sea and sky. Rain began to patter onto the planks, cold for October.

Another circuit. Midnight was nearly upon them. His men had been gone for four days, leaving him riding vulnerable at the mouth of the Chesapeake, or hiding out as best he could in inlets during the day.

Rafe paused at the quarter rail and opened his mouth to give the order to up anchor, then heard the creak of rigging, a muffled command, a thud felt more than heard.

The cutter had returned.

Rafe leaped to the main deck and ran to the entry port, one hand on his dirk, the other on his pistol in the event the arrivals weren't his crew and passenger after all. They hadn't hailed him.

He gave the challenge. "Who goes there?"

"'Tis I, Captain Rafe." Though low-pitched, Jordy's voice rolled up from the boat, unmistakable with its highland burr.

"And well past time you got yourselves here." Rafe dropped the rope ladder over the side. "We were about to leave you."

"Aye, weel, you'll be wanting to leave soon enough, I'm thinking." Jordy headed up the ladder, his face a pale blur in the phosphorescent glow from the sea, their only light. "We had a time of it with the two of them."

"Two?" Rafe stepped back as though struck. "What are you saying, mon?"

"More'n you want to hear." Jordy landed on the deck, then turned back to assist the next man.

Derrick, a full head taller than Rafe and half again as wide, rose through the port with a burden on his back. With a sigh of relief, he set the bundle on the deck and descended the ladder again, muttering, "I'll fetch t'other one."

"Other?" Rafe stared at the package at his feet. It looked like a bulging burlap sack, but it moved. It let out a squeal, which, though wordless, conveyed protest, objection, and outrage in a handful of notes.

"What—did—you—do?" Rafe gave each word a distinct enunciation as he dropped into a crouch and reached for the bag. The scent of lavender rose from its folds, and he wrinkled his nose.

"It couldn't be helped." Jordy ran his words together in his haste to talk. "Mrs. Chapman said she wouldn't come without her, but she didn't want to come with us, so we had to bring her along like this or she'd have raised the alarm."

"She who?" Rafe slit the sack open with his dirk.

A fair face and gossamer hair emerged. The squeals increased, and she drummed her bound feet on the deck.

"Mrs. Phoebe Lee," Jordy said. "She's Mrs. Chapman's sister-in-law."

Rafe hadn't sworn in front of a lady since he was fifteen and said something unacceptable in his mother's hearing. Though he'd been twice her size already, she grabbed him by his hair queue and dragged him to her boudoir, where she proceeded to wash his mouth out with lavender soap. He had been vilely sick, to this day couldn't bear the scent of lavender, and watched his tongue around females of all ages and social rank.

Until that moment.

The words slipped out unbidden, not repented. More crowded into his throat. He swallowed them down and clamped his teeth shut to stem a surge of burning in his throat.

"It couldn't be helped," Jordy repeated. "You said to ensure Mrs. Chapman didn't change her mind about joining us, and she said she must have this one with her."

Another thud hit the deck. Rafe glanced toward the source, brows raised in query.

"Along with her cabin stores," Jordy added. "Should I be taking this one down to your cabin?"

"Aye." It was all Rafe dared say.

He rose and turned his back on the boat crew and their cargo. If he counted to one hundred—nay, one thousand—he might not toss his first mate overboard. He might not assign the other four men to the worst duties on the brig—scrubbing decks and cleaning bilges.

No, that would take counting to two thousand.

With a measured gait, he paced to the prow, stood gripping the forestay for balance. At that moment, he could have ripped it away from its belaying pins and yards with one twist of his wrist.

"Phoebe Lee indeed." He ground the name between his teeth.

Mrs. Phoebe Carter Lee, widow. Wealthy widow with a somewhat cloudy reputation because of how she'd spent the past four years of her life. When Rafe had slipped ashore in Williamsburg to find Belinda Chapman, more than one man in the waterfront taverns mentioned the Chapman lady's sister-in-law, who had likely driven her husband to his death, then allied herself with some interesting people on the eastern shore. One interesting person in particular. Possibly the one person in America Rafe feared.

No amount of counting drove away his desire to send Jordy McPherson sailing headfirst off the crosstrees for coming within ten yards of Phoebe Lee, let alone trussing her up like a Christmas goose and hauling her aboard his majesty's privateer *Davina*. Counting did, however, afford him a measure of control. He managed to uncurl his hand from the stay and stride aft.

"Winch that cutter aboard, then up anchor," he directed the men on watch. "Set course for the Atlantic. This storm is going to get worse, and we need to be out of the Chesapeake before daybreak. And keep Mel and Fiona below until I say otherwise."

He didn't wait to see if his orders would be obeyed. He took the companionway ladder in two steps and shoved open his cabin door.

Light from two swinging lanterns blazed into his eyes. He closed the door behind him and leaned his shoulders against it. "Are you going to offer her to Cook to cook up for tomorrow's dinner, Jordy, or cut her bonds?"

Across the cabin, upon the comfortable bunk he intended to give up for the voyage for Mrs. Chapman's convenience, the still bound and gagged Mrs. Lee met his glance with green eyes that blazed like sunlight through stained glass. Green eyes, hair like moonlight reflected in gold.

Rafe's stomach seized up, and he ripped his gaze away to settle on Mrs. Chapman. "Are you a'right, madam?"

"Yes, but I want him to free Phoebe." Mrs. Chapman huddled on the window seat beneath the stern lights. She wore a woolen cloak large enough to fit two of her, and her dark hair tumbled around her shoulders, giving her the appearance of a girl of ten rather than a woman of—what? Twenty?

Rafe smiled at her. "I apologize for your companion's rough treatment. Jordy, free Mrs. Lee, then see to navigating us out of the bay."

"Do you think I should, Captain?" Jordy looked dubious. "She gave Watt a black eye when we took her. And she kicked me hard enough to make me lose my dinner the first time I set her free aboard the cutter so she could be more comfortable."

Rafe gave Mrs. Lee a sidelong glance. "Shame on Watt and you for getting in the way of such a little fist and foot."

She pounded the little fist, along with the companion to which it was attached, on the mattress.

"And bit a hole in Watt's hand," Jordy added.

"Let us trust she's not rabid."

She squealed like she might be.

"Aye, you may have at Mr. McPherson if you like." Rafe stepped away from the door. "When I'm through with him."

"Don't harm anyone." Mrs. Chapman started to cry. "I told your men Phoebe wouldn't want me to come and would try to stop me if I gave her a chance, but I couldn't come without her. I just couldn't."

"You should have warned me." Rafe chose to remove the gag first. He could exact a promise of no violence if the woman could speak. "I need to untie the kerchief."

He needed to be close to her despite the abhorrent aroma of lavender. He moved her hair to untie the kerchief. The pale gold tresses lay across her shoulders and over the coverlet like a cascade of silk thread. He tried to brush it aside with the back of his hand. The strands clung and coiled and tangled in his fingers.

Perhaps dropping Jordy headfirst from the crosstrees wasn't punishment enough.

Rafe extricated his fingers from the woman's hair and slipped the sharp edge of his dirk between her pale skin and the kerchief.

"Don't hurt her," Mrs. Chapman cried.

Mrs. Lee lay still and quiet. He would have too with a dirk at his throat.

A few deft strokes split the linen kerchief. It fell away, and she spit out the handkerchief gagging her mouth. "Water." It was a mere croak.

"Phoebe, your voice! What happened to your voice?" Mrs. Chapman leaped from the window seat. The *Davina* twisted down the side of a wave, and Mrs. Chapman flew forward.

Rafe caught her shoulders before she struck the deck. "Have a care, madam. You do not have your sea legs yet."

"Nor will she get them." Raspy, Mrs. Lee's voice still held the bite of venom.

19

Perhaps providing her with water for her probably parched throat was a poor idea. Who knew what she would sound like with her voice clear. Sound like or say.

Rafe guided Mrs. Chapman backward to one of the chairs bolted to the deck around the table. It had arms and would hold her better. "Stay here until someone can help you."

"But Phoebe—"

"I'll see to your friend."

But not as he liked. He couldn't risk putting her ashore.

He patted Mrs. Chapman's shoulder, then returned to the bound woman. "I am going to cut your bindings now, madam, but do not get violent."

"I am not a violent person," she whispered.

"Aye, and Watt walked into your fist?" Rafe lifted her hands and slit the ropes, then crouched to do the same with her ankles.

The ropes fell away, revealing red marks and a few bleeding sores marring the creamy smoothness of her skin. He must tend to them. No, he would allow Mrs. Chapman to tend to them. Having an unattached and beautiful female aboard was bad enough without adding touching her to the bargain.

He turned his back on Mrs. Lee and crossed to the table. A carafe of fresh water crouched between the fiddle boards slotted perpendicular to the tabletop to keep beverages and cups from sliding with the vessel's roll. He poured water for Mrs. Chapman first, then carried a second cupful to Phoebe Lee.

She lay huddled on the bed as though the ropes continued to bind her. If possible, her face—at least what he could see behind the spill of her hair—had grown paler, and her breath rasped between her lips.

"Are you ill then, lass?" He crouched before her, the cup in both hands.

"Phoebe, you can't be seasick," Mrs. Chapman protested. "I need you well, and I feel perfectly fine."

"I'm all right." Mrs. Lee's voice sounded a bit stronger. "Just . . . my hands and feet. I can't feel them."

"Oh no. Let me." Mrs. Chapman started to rise again.

"Sit down before you fall." Rafe waved her back.

He braced the cup of water between his knees and the chest beneath the bunk and lifted one of Mrs. Lee's hands. A small hand as smooth as porcelain and just as cold. He began to chafe it between his palms. His calluses, earned from nine years at sea, grated on her delicate skin. He winced with each scrape. She didn't move. Her fingers warmed beneath his. He grew warm. He started on her other hand. Their eyes met through her curtain of hair. His mouth went dry, and he released her fingers.

"That'll do. You can manage your feet yourself, no?"

She nodded and pushed herself upright. "May I have that water first?"

"Aye, of course."

He needed the water. Gallons of it in him. Over him.

He handed her the cup, then backed away, half expecting her to throw it at him.

She drank several dainty sips. "Thank you. That's much better." Her voice proved as light as sea foam and sweet as ripe peaches.

Rafe took another step backward, closer to the door. "Let me fetch some ointment for your wrists and . . . er . . . ankles."

"Do you have any comfrey?" she asked.

Rafe started at the question, then remembered she was a midwife, a healer. Not so odd for her to ask what sort of salve he had, or for Mrs. Chapman to want it if she fell ill.

Or were in need of a midwife.

He nearly groaned aloud. The brig pitched and rolled through the next wave, and Rafe's stomach joined it. Surely not. Surely she wasn't—

He glanced at Mrs. Chapman. He couldn't tell beneath her cloak and with her well-fed physique. And no matter if she were expecting Chapman's bairn now that the dice were cast and this friend of a well-connected man had come aboard. He couldn't let either of them go and just might find the lady's condition useful to his plans.

A prickling started in his middle. Not his conscience. He didn't have one of those anymore. Not that he knew of.

But the smell of lavender reminded him of his mother, so he maintained courtesy. "Aye, madam, 'tis a comfrey salve."

"I'm surprised." Phoebe Lee glanced toward the wall, where a rack held a sword, two pistols, and a selection of knives. "Or maybe I shouldn't be."

"Nay, madam, you should not be surprised we can manage wounds here. We're part of this war." He grimaced. "These wars."

"Which is why you have no business having Mrs. Chapman aboard."

"He needs me to free George," Mrs. Chapman said.

"Ha." Mrs. Lee looked him in the eye, her glance shards of green ice. "You shouldn't lie to an innocent like Belinda, Captain. You don't need her help to free her husband. In truth, I doubt you have any intention of freeing her husband."

"Of course I do." Rafe fingered the hilt of his dirk.

Mrs. Lee curled her full upper lip. "Because you're such a kindhearted man? Because you're on the side of the Americans after all? Do please tell me of your altruism, sir."

"Phoebe, be nice." Mrs. Chapman had paled, and her knuckles gleamed white on the arms of the chair. "He may change his mind if we're unkind to him."

"No, he won't. He holds all the cards in this game." Phoebe Lee skewered him again. "Don't you?"

"Aye, I suppose I hold a winning hand now that I hold Mrs. Chapman."

"What—what do you mean?" The young woman licked her lips. "I thought I—I was going to help somehow."

"You will, lass." Rafe gave her his best smile—a mere tilting of the corners of his lips. "After he's freed, you will ensure his good behavior until I get what I want from him."

"I thought as much." Mrs. Lee bared her teeth. "You have no scruples, do you?"

"Nay, madam, I do not. I lost them on the deck of a Barbary pirate's boat nine years ago." He backed to the door and grasped the handle. "Of course, once my mission is complete, Mr. and Mrs. Chapman may have a long and prosperous life together. Now, if you'll be excusing me, I'll fetch that comfrey salve."

"Wait." Mrs. Lee shot out a hand.

"Aye?" Rafe arched his brows in query.

She took a hobbling step toward him, lost her balance, and grasped the edge of his desk a mere yard from him.

Did the woman bathe in, wash her clothes in, and wear bags of lavender?

Rafe's nostrils pinched. "What?" His tone was sharp.

"I insist you set me ashore and allow Belinda the same courtesy."

"You're not in a position to do any insisting, madam." He gave her a mocking bow. "Now that you're here, you must be my guest. I can't release you to tell your friend Lord Dominick Cherrett anything of me."

"Ah, so you know of him."

"I've stayed alive knowing such things, and 'tis too possible Cherrett's uncle the admiral in the British Navy will work out who I am and have my letters of marque removed. And no woman, especially not one your size, is going to make me a pirate."

"And no Englishman is going to make Belinda and me traitors to our country."

"I'm no Englishman, and I don't want you here any more than you want to be here, but now that you are, you're going all the way to England with us."

2

"You can't keep me aboard." Phoebe's breath rasped in her throat.

"Aye, but I can." Docherty's nostrils pinched as though he smelled something foul. "I have no choice."

"Of course you have a choice." Phoebe dug her fingers into the desk so she didn't gouge them into his eyes. "You can set me ashore."

"Nay, lass, I cannot risk it." He started to turn away.

"If you don't set me ashore, I—I'll—" She snatched a penknife from its rack on the desk.

Docherty caught her wrist. "Do not you dare, madam."

"Phoebe, no," Belinda cried from her chair. "I need you."

"Not aboard this brig."

"Let go of the knife," Docherty repeated in a burr rolling like distant thunder. "If you harm me, my crew will lock you in the hold until the end of this voyage. Do you like the notion of being a prisoner of war?"

Their gazes met, locked, held.

Phoebe's knees sagged, and she leaned her hip against the carved mahogany edge of the desk. Going back to the bed and feigning illness seemed like her best escape. No, not feigning. She felt ill—knotted stomach, spinning head, a brain that must have lost its powers of reason.

She couldn't look away from the man's eyes. They were

gray. Not blue-gray. Not hazel. Just pure gray like the sea on a stormy day. They pierced into her eyes from beneath straight dark brows that contrasted with the red of his hair. Rich, dark red like garnets. Like blood. Though wind-tossed, it hung to his shoulders and swung forward against the plains of his cheeks in a sheen of satin without a hint of curl.

Her hand itched to reach out and smooth the glossy locks. Out and up. She barely came to the middle of his chest. He was too tall to stand upright in the low-ceilinged cabin. And he appeared strong enough to lift her in one arm and Belinda in the other.

A man she could best only by trickery, not combat.

Slowly, she adjusted her stance, balanced on her own feet, and backed away. "I think . . . I think I need to sit down."

Before she sagged in his hold or was sick down the front of his damp boat cloak.

"Please." The single word nearly choked her.

"The wee knife, madam." His gaze pierced her like shards of gray ice.

She shivered but didn't let go. "You're forgetting that I've seen some of your crew. I prefer to remain armed."

"Apparently your fists are more than sufficient. Let it go before you get yourself hurt." His tone, though low, cut like honed steel.

"Phoebe," Belinda whimpered.

The captain's hold tightened. Phoebe gritted her teeth, braced for pain, for the twist of her wrist bringing agony or the vice of hard fingers that would crush her wrist bones, or at the least numb her fingers into dropping the blade.

Behind parted lips, Docherty's white teeth looked clenched. Slowly, with strength that required no application of pain to enforce his will, he drew Phoebe toward him a half step, a whole step. Scents of ginger and tar, nutmeg and salt-wet wool assailed her nostrils. Heat washed over her, through her. His face loomed so close to hers she could have counted his whiskers. She needed to let go, surrender to his greater strength. But she'd done that once too often with her husband. No man would treat her like that again.

She tightened her hold on the knife.

A gleam, a flash of silver, shot like lightning through Docherty's eyes. "Aye, you're a strong-willed lass, aren't you?"

Phoebe kept her focus on his eyes. "I've had to be to survive."

"You're going to get yourself hurt." From her stance by the table, Belinda sounded more petulant than frightened. "And I need you more than you know."

With the same kind of abruptness he'd employed when he grabbed hold of her, he let Phoebe go. "A'right then. Keep the wee knife. But if you use it on me or any of my crew, you will pay the consequences same as any enemy combatant aboard this brig." With a grace and speed surprising for a man who had to stand with his head bowed, he spun on his heel and stalked from the cabin.

Phoebe tensed, expecting the door to slam. It didn't. The latch click proved inaudible above the roar of sea and creak of rigging.

But the bolt sliding home on the outside sounded like a gunshot.

Like the clang of prison bars.

Phoebe dropped to her knees and tucked her face into the crook of her elbow. "God, what have I done? What are You doing bringing me into this?"

"Don't blame God." Belinda let out a sob. "God wants me here and I brought you along. If you need to shout at someone, shout at me. I told you that on the cutter."

Phoebe lifted her head and shook back her tangled hair. "I never shout at anyone."

Except for her husband Gideon—once. Once too often.

"I am a calm, reasonable lady dedicated to bringing life into this world and preserving the lives already in this world." Her fingers tightened on the knife.

Belinda's gaze dropped to the blade. "Then what's that for?"

"Self-protection. No one says I have to let myself be ravished aboard this pirate ship."

"They're not pirates. They're—"

A thud and a string of curses pierced through the deck head.

Phoebe rolled her eyes upward. "Then what are they? Knights Templar upholding Christendom and glory—or whatever they stood for?"

"They're British privateers. No different than my George."

"George," Phoebe said, pulling herself to her feet, "never abducted anyone."

"Neither have these men. I came willingly and I asked them to bring you along. So I suppose that makes me the abductor."

"I suppose it does."

But she couldn't shout at Belinda now any more than she could on the cutter during the short periods in which they had removed her gag so she could eat or drink, times when not another vessel ran near enough to hear her cry for help. Belinda acted without thinking through the consequences— like a child. Shouting at Belinda was like shouting at a puppy for chewing up shoes. Puppies chewed shoes in their path. Belinda swept people along in hers.

Phoebe sighed. "I'm not going to shout at you now either."

"Good. George never shouts at me." Belinda glanced around. "Do you think you can find me something to eat? I'm quite famished, even if that isn't ladylike to say."

"Oh, Bel." Phoebe laughed. "Let me see if I can find anything in your boxes."

28

And take her mind off the bulkheads and deck beams closing in on her.

"I want a cup of hot tea."

"I can't help you with that." Phoebe tucked the small-bladed knife into her bodice. Without losing her balance on the tilting deck, she held on to the desk and then the chart table and made her way to the stack of Belinda's cabin stores she had also insisted Docherty's men bring aboard. Each crate appeared marked with its contents—linen and notions, tea, coffee, raisins and currants, preserves, bread.

"You didn't expect this to last the voyage, did you?" Phoebe tugged one box away from the others. The aroma of freshly baked bread wafted to her nose. Her stomach growled, then seized up like a fist.

"I thought we could set it out and dry it when it gets stale."

"In the humidity at sea, you're more likely to end up with nothing but mold. But we may as well eat while it's edible."

"Yes, let's." Belinda rubbed her stomach. "I think the baby is hungry too."

The baby, of course.

Phoebe released the crate and turned to Belinda. "When did it quicken?"

Belinda shrugged her shoulders. "I don't really know."

"A month ago? Two?"

"I said I don't know." Belinda's tone rose with impatience.

"You must let me examine you," Phoebe insisted.

"No, no, I'm all right." Color tinged Belinda's fair skin. "I don't like being examined. And I've told you not by you especially."

"Then why did you ask me to come along with you?" Phoebe planted one hand on her hip as she glared at her sister-in-law. "Why did you force me to come with you?"

"Well, um . . ." Belinda bit her lower lip, then the tip of

29

her forefinger. She paled in the lantern light. "In the event my lying-in happens while we're aboard."

"It's not likely to take us four months to cross the Atlantic, if we even do, though the return—"

"Oh, Phoebe." Belinda let out a wail. "I lied to you. I'm at least seven months along."

Phoebe's heart pounded so hard it threatened to bruise her ribs from the inside. She couldn't breathe. Spots danced before her eyes. The hand on her hip curled into a fist, and the nails of her other hand dug into the table. In half a second, she just might start screeching at Belinda after all, saying things she would regret before the words left her lips, declaring truths about Belinda's parents—how they'd spoiled her and how they'd never condemned, if not outright condoned, her deceased brother. No one else needed to, or should, know the ugly truth of the Lee family. Belinda had George, and she was harmless—mostly. And Phoebe knew how to keep her mouth shut—mostly. Life with Belinda's brother had taught Phoebe how to use that half second to control her tongue. The consequences with him had been immediate and painful. With Belinda, they would likely result in hysterics, which was not good for the baby.

Phoebe dropped to her knees beside the box marked BREAD and said a quick prayer for restraint before she began to pry open the lid.

"I suppose that was unkind of me." Belinda's high, rather breathy voice filled the stillness inside the cabin. "Not telling you, I mean."

Phoebe said nothing, still not trusting her tongue. She concentrated on using the little knife she'd taken from the desk to push the lid up enough for her to get her fingers beneath and tug.

"I—I was afraid you'd find a way to keep me from coming and rescuing George."

Phoebe grasped the edge of the box lid and yanked. With a screech of the thin nails, the slatted wood covering flew off. The aroma of bread already going moldy overpowered the odors of the ship and vied with Belinda's abundant use of lavender oil that seemed to cling to everyone who came in contact with her. Phoebe's mouth watered, but not with anticipation of eating one of the fragrant loaves. If she took one bite of the bread, it would not stay down, if it even reached her stomach.

She hadn't felt queasy on the cutter crossing the bay. She'd sailed before, and farther, like the time she traveled to Seabourne to visit her aunt and uncle to get away from Leesburg, away from the gossip after her husband's death. Despite her recent brush with death then—from a blow, a fall, her baby being born too early and stillborn—she felt no indisposition. On the contrary. She'd felt healthy again upon her arrival on the eastern shore. Upon the water, she'd never experienced anything like this outright nausea. If this was the effect of sailing on the open sea, then she had another reason to get off the brig immediately.

"This is barely edible now," she told Belinda.

"I still think I can eat the whole thing," Belinda declared.

"You don't have any sickness?" The midwife in Phoebe took over her tongue now. "Not in the morning or afternoon? Not from the ship's motion?"

"I haven't been ill at all. Everyone says how one gets dreadfully sick, but I haven't ever."

"That's a relief." Phoebe began to work on the box marked PRESERVES. "I hope you stay that way, if you insist on remaining here. Of course, if you eat moldy bread, I can't guarantee you will."

"I'll pull off the moldy bits. And of course I'm staying. Captain Docherty needs me." Belinda held out her hand. "Do hurry. I'm so hungry I almost feel sick."

Phoebe refrained from saying Belinda should have brought a maid instead of a midwife. Phoebe hadn't been much different when she'd gone to stay with her aunt in Seabourne. Pampered and petted all her life by everyone except her husband, she had to learn to cook, clean, iron, even pin up her own hair. When she apprenticed with Tabitha, she had to learn more—how to do often unpleasant tasks for other women without showing revulsion. She could do all proficiently now.

But Belinda was pampered and petted by everyone, including her husband, and could do none of those tasks. She would never survive alone on a brig for weeks, even months. And if she was far enough along in her condition, she might go into labor at sea. If she wouldn't allow Phoebe to examine her, she surely would object to one of the sailors delivering her child, if anyone knew what to do. If trouble arose . . .

No, she must get Belinda to agree to go ashore, once Phoebe figured out how to get them ashore. If Belinda refused, Phoebe would return the favor Belinda had done her and force the younger woman onto a boat or into the water itself.

The roar of wind and surf suggested the idea of going into either boat or water lacked good sense now. As though remaining on the brig of the enemy was sensible. They were likely headed straight out to sea, away from the mouth of the Chesapeake, away from the last spit of land.

Then Phoebe must find a way to turn them around.

She wrestled the lid off the box of the jars of preserves and selected one marked PLUMS. Her little knife wouldn't do for slicing bread, and Belinda hadn't thought to include utensils or cutlery in her cabin stores. Phoebe rose and glanced around in search of something with a bigger blade. Her glance landed on the rack of weapons hanging from one bulkhead. Cutlasses, rapiers, an ornate sword hung there—

Behind an iron bar with a prominent lock.

32

The penknife would have to do for cutting the bread and spreading the preserves, and one vague notion of how to get away would have to go. She could only gaze upon the blades rather than employ them for good use, rather like Tantalus in the myth always thirsting for water but unable to reach it.

Phoebe set the bread and preserves on the table and tore off a hunk of the former. "This will make a mess, but we do have water."

"I want something hot too." Belinda had turned petulant again. "Why can't they prepare me something hot?"

"I believe they douse fires in a storm. You'll have to wait for the sea to quiet."

"And sleep." Belinda yawned and picked up the bread and preserves bottle. "I don't care if it's messy." She snatched up Phoebe's knife and used it to break the wax seal over the end of the jar and scoop out some of the jellied fruit. Much of it slid onto the table. Enough landed on the bread to apparently satisfy Belinda, for she began to devour the repast.

With a bit more grace, Phoebe spread plum preserves on her own bread. Her stomach would stop hurting once she ate something, and she loved plum preserves. These had come from her in-laws' plantation. They would taste like ambrosia.

They didn't smell like ambrosia. Before bread and jam touched her lips, Phoebe's nose wrinkled at the stench of rotten fruit.

"This jam has gone bad." She started to set the bread aside. "I'll find some—"

"It's not bad. It's delicious." Belinda tore off another chunk of bread and doused it with more preserves. "If I had a spoon, I'd eat it right out of the jar."

Phoebe's stomach clenched. She'd eaten little since she'd been forced aboard a tiny ship's cutter, overcrowded with men, Belinda, and her, tossed about in the Chesapeake as they evaded other vessels and pretended to be innocent fishermen. Her stomach had hurt then too, outrage, apprehension, fear tearing at her insides. Not eating made it worse. She knew that. She must eat to think.

She lifted her hunk of bread to her lips, took a bite. The sweet and tart flavor of the plum preserves burst on her tongue, burned in her throat. The bread tasted like glue smelled. She tried to swallow, gagged, raced for the stern windows to jerk back the latch, and slammed the panes aside.

"Phoebe, what are you doing?"

Phoebe gripped the sides of the window frame and leaned out as far as she dared. Sea spray slapped her face like icy palms. She gulped in cold, wet air, tried swallowing again. The bread remained stuck in her throat.

"Phoebe, shut that window at once," Belinda cried. "You're getting soaked, and it's cold."

The brig twisted itself into the trough of a wave. Phoebe's stomach twisted in the opposite direction. She groaned. Involuntary tears spilled from her eyes, hot against her chilled cheeks.

"I can't be seasick. I can't."

The stern slammed onto the water. The bread went down. Stayed. She wasn't seasick. She inhaled the fresh air—and took in a mouthful of seawater. She coughed, choked, rather welcomed the frigid blast.

Behind her, Belinda raged. Her words made no sense, but the tone was clear. She sounded like her deceased brother when he'd been in a temper, when he'd been thwarted, and Phoebe's shoulders tensed, her back muscles rippling in anticipation of a blow, a kick, a pinch at the least.

No, no, not Belinda. She threw tantrums like the spoiled child she too often still was, but she never inflicted pain. At least not with her fists. She preferred cutting words. Physical pain was Gideon, and he was dead, dead, dead. But if Belinda continued to rage, the captain would return.

Phoebe started to draw back inside the cabin to tell Belinda to be quiet, let her enjoy the storm in peace. But the lavender and mildew combination in the cabin sent Phoebe's stomach roiling again, and she leaned out of the window for tangy, briny air.

But Belinda did grow quiet as though someone had shut her into a box and sat on the lid. Hands clamped on Phoebe's waist. Belinda come to help? No, large hands held her, pulled her away from the sea, lifted her off the window seat.

"Don't." Her voice sounded like a mewling kitten's cry.

"Do not what?" He sounded amused. "Do not let you tumble on your head into the sea? Do not let you catch your death soaked as you are?"

"Don't help me." She kept her eyes closed so she didn't have to look at him, see contempt or mockery for her weakness. "If you won't let me off this brig, you'd better just let me die. I'll likely hang anyway."

Belinda gasped from somewhere nearby. "Phoebe."

"I thought better of the great Phoebe Carter Lee." His burr rolled over the R's in her maiden name, a purr to her whimper.

Had he not cradled her in his arms, she would have curled up on herself like an overcooked shrimp, hidden her face so he couldn't see her any more than she would look upon him.

"'Tis a wee bit of the mal de mer, no more." He set her on the bed. "Get yourself into dry things while I fetch you something to drink."

"No, not mal de mer." Yet inside the cabin, with the windows closed, the merest suggestion of sustenance set her off again. With her eyes still closed, she tried returning to the window. "I need air."

"But you're getting everything wet letting the water and rain in like that."

"No, please, I can't—" A sob of pure mortification broke from Phoebe's throat.

Rafe Docherty handed her a basin and held her head.

Phoebe burned with shame, shivered with cold. Sobs of mortification choked her so she couldn't say what she was thinking. *If one can die of humiliation, I'll be dead in minutes.*

"No, you will not die of the humiliation or the sickness." The sonorous voice held a hint of laughter. The hand that brushed her hair away from her brow held tenderness despite rough calluses.

So she had spoken her thoughts aloud.

She curled up as tightly as she could and wrapped her arms around her knees. The door latch clicked. No bolt sounded.

"That's revolting, Phoebe," Belinda said. "I'm not even hungry anymore."

"So sorry." Phoebe began to shiver. "This cabin is so small. It's like—"

But it wasn't. Though low in height, the chamber wasn't much smaller than an average bedroom. If she continued to tell herself that, she would be all right. Surely.

"Will you fetch me some dry clothes, please?" she asked.

"I don't know where—oh, all right."

Rustling, snapping, the creak of hinges followed. A few moments later, Belinda brought Phoebe a nightgown reeking of lavender. Her throat burned, but she was done for now. With Belinda's aid, Phoebe exchanged wet things for dry, then snuggled into the quilts on the bunk, covers smelling of sea air and sunshine and oddly calming.

A knock sounded on the door. "May I come in, ladies?"

"Of course." Belinda tucked a stray curl behind one ear with one hand and gripped a chair back with the other. The smile she granted Docherty was positively coy. "You're being so kind to my friend."

"I like my carpet in here." His tone was brusque, chilly as sea air. "Drink this, Mrs. Lee." He crouched beside the bunk, slipped his arm beneath Phoebe's shoulders, and lifted her enough for him to hold a cup to her lips.

Ginger tingled in her nose. Ginger and—

She jerked back. "You're trying to drug me."

"Aye, there is a wee bit of poppy juice in there." His clear gray eyes met hers with a gentle compassion that made her own eyes sting. "'Tis the best way. 'Twill calm you without incapacitating you." One corner of his mouth quirked up. "Believe me, I ken how you are feeling."

Ginger, of course. She'd smelled it on him earlier.

"Odd you'd choose to be a sailor," she murmured.

"I did not choose it." The harshness returned. "Drink. I have not all night to play nursery maid."

"Then take it away. I am not seasick."

"Indeed?" His brows arched. "Seems I have seen evidence to the contrary."

"No, no, it's the cabin, the smell."

"Aye, the lavender." He grimaced.

"What's wrong with lavender?" Belinda sounded belligerent. "It makes me happy."

"It makes me ill," Phoebe muttered.

One corner of Docherty's lips twitched. Their eyes met in a moment of understanding.

"Drink the ginger water," he said. "'Twill help whatever the cause."

"I don't want my brain to be as useless as mush." She glared at him. "However you want it to be."

"Considering Mrs. Chapman's condition, I do not want your brain like porridge either, but I do not wish you suffering from the sickness either." He held the glass to her lips. "Drink."

"Considering Mrs. Chapman's condition," Phoebe countered, turning her head away, "a reasonable man would let us go."

"Aye, but you are presuming I am a reasonable mon."

She opened her mouth for further protest, and he tipped the contents of the glass between her lips. She could choke, spit it all over herself and perhaps him, or swallow. She swallowed and prayed he spoke the truth about the poppy juice being a small amount.

"Ver' good. That should calm you." His glance of approval was almost warm.

Nothing felt warm about the speed with which he departed from the cabin. The slam of the bolt on the outside of the door felt like an icicle through her chest.

"See, I told you he was kind." Belinda had resumed consuming bread and jam and licked her fingers between words.

Phoebe didn't shudder when she looked at her sister-in-law this time. For that she did owe him a debt of gratitude. He'd been kind about her sickness, even if he thought it was mal de mer. He'd drugged her in his kindness, a fair treatment for sickness like hers. And a way to keep her quiet until they sailed too far away for her to get Belinda and her back to land? No, he'd claimed not enough to incapacitate her, and in those moments of his gray eyes compassionate upon her face, she believed him.

Dangerous, that kindness in him. She must never forget that he was not any more altruistic about making her survive the voyage than he was about getting George out of prison in England—he possessed some ulterior motive for that too, or she wasn't a fully qualified midwife.

A midwife not all that far from her teacher if they hadn't left the Chesapeake yet. Not all that far from her teacher's still well-connected husband. If she could find a weapon . . .

If she could get her brain to clear and her limbs to work . . .

"No." She fought against the poppy juice. It dragged her down like anchor chains. She shook them off and used the bulkhead to pull herself upright. "No, no, no, he isn't kind. He's a devious scoundrel, a cur—"

Belinda's eyes widened with shock. "Phoebe, that isn't very Christian of you."

"I don't feel particularly Christian toward him." Phoebe flopped her leaden legs over the side of the bunk. "He's a—a rogue, a louse, a—"

She didn't know, or at least wouldn't use, worse epithets for him than she'd already applied. Name calling got a body nowhere. She needed action, a clear head, and a lot of help from God.

Her conscience twinged that she would ask for God's help after heaping uncomplimentary appellations upon a fellow being and while planning to be what she claimed she was not—a violent person.

"I won't have to do anything violent if he cooperates." She didn't realize she'd spoken aloud until Belinda surged to her feet.

"What are you going to do? Do you want to get us locked up in the hold or something?"

"No, I'm going to get us set ashore." Phoebe dropped her head into her hands. "If the cabin will stop spinning."

"But I don't want to—"

"Do you want one of those men delivering your baby?"

"If necessary, yes, if that's what I must do to go to England."

Phoebe groaned. "I should have guessed."

She tried to stand. Her legs gave way beneath her. On hands and knees, she crawled to the desk and opened the bottom drawer. A pile of thick leather-bound books rested within. Logs. Perhaps interesting reading, if she were to re-main aboard the privateer.

"But I won't," she vowed between her teeth.

"What won't you do? What are you doing?" A glance back showed Belinda sticking the penknife into the jar of preserves and licking it off.

Phoebe's stomach protested. She closed her eyes and con-centrated on her task—searching. She didn't look at Belinda. She didn't answer her. She slipped her hand inside drawers, beneath paper and books, quills and wax wafers. She felt along the sides of the drawers and on the bottoms of the ones above. She used her hand to measure, seeking a hidden compartment.

"You know that's rude," Belinda said.

"Abducting someone is rude." Phoebe scowled at the desk.

No more drawers. No results. Nothing as interesting as a hidden compartment. So where could it be?

She scanned the top. A fiddle board kept an inkwell, a pen holder, and a box of sand in place. She braced her hand on the fiddle board as she staggered to her feet. It didn't move in its slot on the desktop, and yet . . .

She yanked the board from the desktop with a screech of protesting, swollen wood.

Belinda gasped and knocked the plum preserves onto the floor. It rolled with the tilting of the ship but didn't break and stain the plush carpet.

"You're destroying things." Belinda was white.

Phoebe stared at her. "Are you frightened of these men? If so—"

"Not these men. You. I thought you'd understand. I thought you'd want to come. I thought you'd stay with me no matter what." Huge tears began to roll down Belinda's round cheeks. "You were so faithful to my brother, even if—

but you're going to make something horrible happen, and then George won't get free."

"Oh yes he will. If we get free, we can go to Dominick, as I wanted to in the first place."

"He can't help."

But Docherty had confirmed that Dominick, son of a British peer, could. If he still held enough influence to get someone's letters of marque revoked, he held enough power to get a prisoner free, despite being married to an American lady.

"We'll get him free without subjecting ourselves to this." Phoebe swept out one hand to indicate the cabin. It happened to be the hand holding the fiddle board. It cracked against the bulkhead and split down the middle without the screech of rending wood.

Belinda screeched, though. Phoebe smiled, for a shining brass key lay on the rug. If only it proved to be the right one.

She sank to her knees to snatch it up. The brig dipped and twisted. Phoebe took long, deep breaths, thought about aromatic ginger water.

And a gray-eyed man smelling of eastern spice.

A shiver ran over her skin. She curled her fingers around the key. If this was what she hoped it was, she would be rid of the man whose presence, whose voice, whose moments of tenderness raised gooseflesh on her arms with the merest hint of memory.

"Phoebe, please tell me what you're doing." Belinda wasn't whining, pleading, or commanding. The quietness of the question drove a spike of ice through Phoebe's middle.

"I'm doing what I must to get us off this brig." She hauled herself to her feet. Her head spun from the opiate in the ginger water, but her stomach cooperated. She could manage a spinning head. "I won't let you risk George's baby like this, with a stranger we have no reason to trust, if he thinks nothing of alienating us to our countrymen."

Belinda didn't respond. Her dark eyes wide, she stared at Phoebe as she dragged and stumbled her way across the cabin, shoved aside boxes of provisions and trunks of clothing, and fetched up hard against the opposite bulkhead.

The one with the array of weapons. The locked-up weapons. But Phoebe held a key. If it fit . . .

She slid it into the lock. It turned. Tumblers fell into place. The lock clicked open.

Phoebe curled her fingers around a dagger with a six-inch double-sided blade and lethal point. Then she turned back toward the door.

And found Belinda right behind her. "If you don't put that back right now, I'll scream to get the captain or someone down here."

Phoebe smiled. "Go right ahead."

3

Guided by the distant glow of lantern light through canvas walls, Rafe prowled between the double row of muttering, sighing, snoring men sleeping in hammocks suspended from the deck beams, and pushed open the door to the source of the light—a cabin beneath his own quarters. The chamber was made up of no more than canvas walls and a wooden post frame, too flimsy a shelter for two beings he wished to keep out of harm's way as much as possible aboard a vessel that could and did go into action at a moment's notice. But not on this run, not with noncombatants aboard, however much that annoyed the crew hungry for prize money. He didn't like vulnerable people exposed to more danger than necessary. Even this canvas room would not do for long for its inhabitants. They needed to be back in their own cabin, now that he had had a good look at the Americans and deemed them harmless.

Not that he had intended to welcome two Americans aboard.

Grinding his teeth over the unwelcome passenger, he knocked on the door to the temporary cabin. In response, a high, clear voice called, "It's unlocked."

"Why?" Rafe turned the handle.

The instant the door latch clicked, one of the beings went into action. She sprang up from the lantern-lit hammock and charged toward him, tiny legs flying, mouth open in a joyous grin.

43

"Do not leap on me, you wee beastie." He scooped the black-and-white terrier into his arms.

She proceeded to lap her miniscule tongue across his chin.

"She doesn't like being stranded down here any more than I do." The disembodied voice rose from the depths of the hammock.

"Why was the door unlocked?" Rafe emphasized his earlier query.

"As if a lock would stop anyone from breaking in. The walls are canvas. Rip." A hand emerged from the hammock and sliced through the air. "They're to hold me hostage. Which sounds rather intriguing."

"You would not think so if you had it happen to you."

"It must be better than being stuffed down here like cargo. 'Tis stifling and boring."

"You have your books."

One of the tomes thudded to the deck. "Stuffy and boring." A head emerged from over the edge of the hammock. Dark red hair gleamed in the glow of the lamp.

Dark red hair that should have hung in a braid at least a foot past thin, childlike shoulders. Except it now swung in a tangled, ragged mass to just above those shoulders.

"What . . . did you do . . . to your hair?" With care, Rafe set the dog on the deck and closed the yard and a half distance between door and hammock. He curled his fingers around a hunk of the ruined hair and glared into the child's green eyes. "Answer me, Mel."

"I cut it." A round chin jutted. Mel's full lower lip protruded. "It was heavy and ugly, and I'd have cut off more if Jordy did not stop me. Now I look more like you."

"I don't want you to look like me. I've told you 'tis not safe."

"Only if we lose a fight." Mel rolled off the hammock and

44

scooped up the dog. "Besides, I have Fiona here to protect me."

Rafe set his hands on his hips and scowled. "She's a wee dog. She cannot protect you against a horde of bloodthirsty Frenchmen or Americans. If they think we're related—"

"They'll treat me with courtesy and kindness." Mel chuckled in a voice surprisingly rich for a child of barely twelve years. "What did that one broadsheet call you? The scourge of the English Channel?"

"You should not be reading such nonsense."

"Why not? You're a hero."

"Nay, I'm no more than a legalized pirate making a profit off this war with France."

"And now America." Mel rubbed grimy hands through the dog's black-and-white fur.

Fiona wriggled and made noises that sounded as though she were trying to purr like a kitten.

"See, she thinks so too." Mel grinned.

Rafe sighed. "You're both daft. There is naught heroic in war. I'd like to see it all end."

"But how will you make money if the war ends?"

"I have more than enough."

More than enough to provide a fine home. More than enough to return to most of the life he'd had before evil men ripped his world apart. More than enough to see Mel educated and clothed properly and himself made respectable.

But not enough to get him what he really wanted until he'd made landfall in Southampton in July and visited his usual haunts, sought out his usual informants. One sent him to the Nore, to a prison hulk rotting with its human cargo in the Thames, to one of those prisoners aboard, then across the sea to lands he'd avoided since Great Britain and America went to war the previous year.

He didn't want to fight Americans. Their complaints against Britain held merit. They didn't deserve to be destroyed.

Except for one of them.

Who would take one look at Mel and use the child as Rafe was using Mrs. Chapman—bait to draw his quarry from hiding, draw him into surrender.

"I'm retiring after this voyage," he announced.

Mel stared at him, horror registering in big green eyes. "You cannot. We'll have to live on land then. I'll have to dress properly in front of people."

"Aye, shoes and stockings and no cutlass in your waistband." Rafe frowned at the unsheathed weapon.

Mel set Fiona on the hammock and removed the cutlass. "I thought perhaps I should be carrying it with strangers aboard."

"They are two harmless women." He thought of Watt's black eye, of hands that appeared too delicate and smooth to have inflicted such damage, and added, "Mostly harmless." If he thought little of her hands, her eyes, her fairy-tale-princess hair. "And one has the seasickness."

Reduce her to nothing more than the crumpled, retching stranger, and she wouldn't haunt him so.

"Ugh." Mel grimaced. "I don't have to do any cleaning up, do I?"

"Nay, but I'm thinking you can make me more ginger water for her."

"More?" Mel gave Rafe a sidelong grin. "We're running low on ginger. What happens if she drinks up all your ginger water?"

"We'll stop in Bermuda and buy more ginger." He turned toward the door. "And get a proper barber to undo as much damage to your hair as possible. Until then, wear a cap when on deck."

"I can go on deck?" Mel grabbed Rafe's arm. "I'm not one of the prisoners?"

"You were never a prisoner, you imp. You had the lock and were supposed to use it until I assured you all was well up top."

"I did stay down here with Fi, and I am always obedient."

Rafe snorted. "I wish I were that good at raising you. But now that you have mentioned obedience, obey me in this: keep out of the way of our guests."

"I thought they were not dangerous."

"Aye, weel . . ." Rafe drummed his fingers on his thigh and gazed up as though he could see through the deck. At that moment, he couldn't hear through it either. The ladies either slept or remained nearly motionless. "I do not trust the one to not be up to some tricks. She is not happy about being here." He reached for the door and caught sight of the book still lying on the floor. He stooped to retrieve it.

Mel dove in front of him, snatching it up first. "I—I still need to do my work in this."

"You threw it on the floor." The bantering tone left Rafe's voice. His muscles tensed. "You threw your Bible on the deck."

"I did not. I dropped it. I—" Mel's chin jutted again. "I saw you throw one overboard once."

"Aye, weel, one thing you should have learned aboard this brig is that I am not the best example for a child."

"But you are." Bible clutched in one hand, Mel laid the other hand on Rafe's arm and gazed up at him with limpid eyes. "Do not be angry with yourself for me being here. You are the best teacher in the world. You make certain I can read well and write a fair hand and do my sums better than any of those schools you sent me to."

"But they taught you Scripture."

"And you don't beat or starve me."

Rafe's muscles relaxed, and he tweaked the end of Mel's nose. "Nay, I simply expose you to danger every day."

"'Tis still better than being alone on land."

"You would feel differently if you suffered from the sea-sickness."

"Like you do?" Mel's eyes twinkled.

Rafe responded with a narrow-eyed glare. "Insolence will get you naught but a caning."

Laughing, Mel scooped Fiona off the hammock and darted past Rafe, out the makeshift door, and into the darkness of the lower deck. "Bring the ginger water to me when you've made it," Rafe called softly to the retreating figure, "and then you can recite your lessons to me, if you cannot sleep."

Mel would stay with Rafe and recite. Neither of them ever slept during a storm. Mel didn't remember why, having been but three years old when a storm ripped through their lives, but Rafe did. So he ensured they knew how to spend the wakeful hours in the dark and wet, in the heaving seas and lashing winds. Mel recited lessons and Rafe concentrated on listening, correcting, teaching until the sun returned.

The sun should return with the dawn. Already rain fell only in spurts, though the waves loomed before the prow and white-rimmed mountains climbed and slid down the other side.

Rafe's stomach rolled with them. He'd never gotten used to heavy seas, never lost the nausea that kept him surviving on ginger water and ship's biscuit for days on end. Unlike he had done for the lady below, he never dosed himself with the merest hint of poppy juice. He needed his head completely clear. A drugged privateer captain meant death for himself and his crew at the hands of the enemy.

The enemies.

He sighed as he climbed to the main deck and strode aft

to the quarterdeck ladder, his boat cloak flapping around his legs in the gale, his hair catching on his wet cheeks and eyelashes. He disliked the notion of Britain fighting more than one country at a time. War with America was a mistake. They were only a generation removed from being Englishmen, Scots, Welshmen, and half a dozen other nationalities. Yet if the Americans hadn't declared war on England the previous year, he might never have found out how to run James Brock— merchant, politician, murderer—to earth with a scheme so unscrupulous, so craven, he couldn't do enough to make up for his actions of the next two months, if he acknowledged a conscience.

He preferred to keep that suppressed. A conscience had brought him nothing but grief.

And his latest actions had brought him another enemy. No doubt James Brock had learned something by now, might even be considering an action against the captain of the *Davina*.

And in a moment of weakness, he'd allowed Mel to come aboard.

Loneliness, like a conscience, was no good for a man's safety.

Rafe grasped the taffrail hard enough to nearly rip it from its bolts. "You will pay for that too." He glared at the distant lights gleaming from the eastern shore of Virginia, a sign they were out of the Chesapeake. His breathing eased. In a few hours, the chances of them running into trouble with an American vessel would come close to disappearing. Mrs. Phoebe Carter Lee and her powerful friends on shore would be of no danger. He just needed to get through the night, through the storm, beyond where the woman would think he would dare set her—onto land anywhere this side of Bermuda.

He strode to the wheel, where Jordy held the *Davina* on a

steady course east. "I can take the wheel for you if you want to seek your bunk."

"I'd rather be here till we're far from land." Jordy spat to leeward. "I do not trust those Americans not to chase us down and pick a fight at dawn."

"Let them try." Rafe rested a hand on the binnacle. "We're not fighting the Yankees on this voyage."

Jordy snorted. "Aye, and how do you plan to let them know that? Or our own lads, for that matter. We've not taken a prize in three months, and they're growing restless."

"Greedy, are they not?" Rafe tried to laugh.

His mirth fell flat. Restless men on a privateer spelled potential danger. They didn't know what their captain intended, and they wanted to fight, accumulate more wealth, perhaps buy vessels of their own. No one got wealthy sailing back and forth across the Atlantic, risking life and limb, enduring cold, damp, and bad food for no purpose. He would have to compensate them somehow, or be worrying about mutiny.

"No Americans," Rafe said. "'Tis like fighting our cousins."

"Aye, but—" Jordy stopped.

Feet pattered up the quarter ladder, and Mel appeared from the gloom, Fiona clicking behind. "I have the ginger water, Captain Rafe."

Rafe flinched at the sobriquet his crew had adopted from Mel. He didn't mind it from the crew; he disliked it from the child. He wasn't Mel's captain, for all he demanded obedience while on board.

"Are you feeling poorly, sir?" Jordy asked.

"'Tis not for me." Rafe took the tankard from Mel and did consider drinking it himself for a moment. "Mrs. Lee has not taken to the sea so well as her sister-in-law."

"Hasn't she now. I had no notion of it aboard the cutter."

Jordy leaned over the wheel, staring at the binnacle compass. "We're getting pulled to the north. Can we get a man or two up top to set some sail? The wind is dropping."

Rafe shook his head. "As much as I'd like to be away from the coast in a trice, I'd prefer no more sail until light. We'll not be that far off course that 'tis worth the risk. And with an ailing passenger . . ."

"Why would she not be sick aboard the cutter?" Mel asked. "It bounces around like a cork in boiling water."

"And when have you been boiling corks in water?" Rafe tugged Mel's shorn hair and frowned. "I told you to wear a cap on deck."

"I cannot find one."

"Ha. You're going to regret doing this."

"Aye," Jordy agreed, "I said it deserves a thrashing."

"Ha." Mel tossed back the ragged locks. "Neither of you ever did such a thing to me."

"Aye, and it shows. As for Mrs. Lee not being sick aboard the cutter, the weather was not so bad until right before she came aboard. And speaking of the lady, I should see how she fares."

"Do you think you should go down there alone?" Jordy lifted one hand from the wheel and rubbed his belly.

"Ah, yes, she got you too?" Rafe pictured those small, high-arched feet curving into delicate ankles.

Abraded ankles.

"Mel, fetch the comfrey salve. Jordy here tied Mrs. Lee a wee bit too tightly and she has some scrapes that need tending."

"Aye, sir." Mel executed a perfect acrobatic flip despite the canting brig and landed on the main deck.

Jordy grimaced. "That bairn is going to break a limb one of these days."

"Or give me an apoplexy before I'm five and thirty." Holding the tankard of ginger water, Rafe paced across the quarterdeck, his body shifting to the roll of the brig, until he reached the skylight. It was closed to keep out sea and rain, and the glass was colored green for privacy, but light glowed through from his cabin, a reminder of Phoebe Lee's eyes glittering with suppressed emotion despite her calm exterior.

He understood her illness, the roiling of rage and frustration suppressed to make the body sick. Absently, he sipped at the ginger water and listened, one hand on the taffrail for balance. No sound rose from the chamber below, nothing loud enough to penetrate deck planks and creaking timbers, or the roar of the sea and whistle of wind through rigging.

Quiet didn't mean all was well. She might sleep, but he hadn't dosed her earlier draught with enough opiate to guarantee sleep. She might very well be awake, plotting, scheming, trying to work out a way to escape.

There is none, my dear lass.

As if in reassurance to him, the last glimpse of light from shore winked out behind a wave. When the *Davina* lifted to the crest of the next swell, the horizon remained a line of black between sooty sky and phosphorescent sea. Gone. The threat of Phoebe Lee's friends vanished beyond the waves.

But Rafe remained tense, ears straining for sound, nostrils flaring for a scent wrong amidst the effluvium aboard a vessel, eyes straining for the darker bulk of a ship or schooner swooping out of the night to challenge his presence so close to the coast of Virginia, or engage him in a fight.

At that moment, a fight sounded grand, gun smoke and powder flashes to wipe out the sight of her green eyes and tumbled golden hair, her silken skin and warm cream voice. For a moment, while she sobbed from the discomfort and humiliation of seasickness, he considered setting her ashore.

But he couldn't risk it, couldn't take the chance of her reaching Cherrett too soon for Rafe.

Nothing must stop Rafe. No one must warn James Brock that his years of pillaging in the name of the privateers in which he had invested, like George Chapman, neared their end.

Scampering footfalls sounded on the deck. Rafe turned back to find Mel and Fi leaping up the quarter ladder.

"Can you carry all this, old man? Shouldn't I go down to protect you?"

"I do not need the protection of a wee bairn. Now, either get yourself to your cabin or be prepared to recite your lessons."

"But I want to see the ladies. Watt says the one is ever so bonnie, even if she is a virago."

Rafe took the jar of salve from Mel. "'Tis no way to speak of a lady."

"If she's a virago, she's not a lady."

"Mel."

"All right then. Is she pretty?"

"If you like them as substantial as spindrift." Rafe headed for the companionway. "If you wish to do your lessons by the binnacle light, you may. The storm is abating."

Mel said nothing.

Let the child sulk over being thwarted. Rafe needed the reassurance that the ladies below were settled for the night, not to concern himself with the wants of an adolescent.

Balancing the salve and tankard of ginger water in one hand, he turned the key to the cabin with the other. Beyond the panels, someone exclaimed and the other one responded, the words indistinct above the creak of timbers.

"Is it a'right if I come in?" he asked before lifting the latch.

"Of course, Captain." Mrs. Lee's sweet voice responded from close to the door.

Too close to the door. Before he stepped over the coaming, Rafe knew he should have taken Jordy's advice. But two unarmed females were harmless against nothing more than his size and strength, not to mention the dirk he kept in his belt.

Except they weren't unarmed.

He noted the missing fiddle board from the desk, slammed the jar and tankard onto the mahogany surface, and spun. His hand dropped to his knife—too late. A blade slipped through his hair and beneath the collar of his cloak to lie with its point against his jugular vein.

4

The brig rolled beneath Phoebe's feet, and she grasped the captain's shoulder for balance. She kept the flat of the blade against his neck so she didn't slice him open by accident. She needed him alive and cooperative until she got her way, or lost her nerve.

Or just got sick, though she felt considerably better with the door open.

"Tell your men to turn this brig around and take us back to Virginia." Phoebe kept her voice low, calm despite her pounding heart.

"Or you will be slitting my jugular?" Docherty snorted. "And where will that be getting you, lass? Tossed overboard, I'm thinking."

Phoebe nodded, though he couldn't see her. "A risk I've calculated. But you'll still be dead."

"I don't want to be dead," Belinda whimpered from where she'd retreated to the furthest end of the window seat. "I want to stay alive."

"No one will harm you, Bel." Phoebe tightened her grip on Docherty's shoulder. "Will you?"

"Not a lady with a bairn coming." His hand still rested on the hilt of his dirk. "I'd prefer not to harm any lady."

"You've already done that by bringing us aboard an enemy ship."

"I am not your enemy."

"Then drop the knife." Phoebe hardened her voice.

"If you insist." He drew the dirk from its sheath.

Phoebe tensed. The top of her head didn't even reach his shoulder, and with one flick backward, he could gut her like a trout.

He tossed the knife onto the desk, his head turning to follow the trajectory. The blade slid into the slot cut to hold the fiddle board. "Foolish of me not to remove the key. Clever of you to find its hiding place. But you're not clever enough if you think that one wee lass can get a whole crew of fighting men to do her bidding."

Phoebe tossed her head and laughed, a little too high, a little forced. "Only if they don't care for their captain."

"At present, they are not so happy with me." He sighed, the motion pushing the folds of his damp boat cloak into Phoebe's face, smothering her with aromas of wet wool and tar, salt and man, a dizzying bouquet of scents.

She breathed through her mouth so she couldn't inhale the aromas, and closed her eyes so she couldn't see the sway of the lantern light. "Maybe they're unhappy with you because you abducted two ladies."

"Nay, 'tis because I have not let them take a prize for the past three months and will not let them take one for another two."

"Until we rescue George?" Belinda asked.

"Aye, 'tis so."

"See, Phoebe, I told you he is a good man."

"Me being aboard this brig says he is not a good man." Phoebe slid her left hand toward his neck, grabbed a handful of his hair, thick and soft and so warm beneath that she realized she'd been chilled until that moment. "Give the orders, and all will be well."

"You said you were not a violent person. Which leads me to something to ponder. Either you are too kind to harm me and thus this is naught more than a ruse, and your word is good regarding that, or you will slit my throat and take the consequences, and your word is good on that. Which is true, madam?"

Bile choked Phoebe like the words she could not speak. Of course the former was true. If she spoke the truth, she wanted to rest her head against the broad, strong back in front of her and weep, pleading for him to take her ashore, let her go to Tabitha and Dominick, who would surely be able to welcome her back after a year, take her to freedom to practice midwifery and be a useful female.

But pleading with men only got a body hurt.

She swallowed the bile. "Are you willing to take the risk that the latter is the truth?"

"Aye, I do believe I—" He broke off on a muttered oath as a tapping sound rattled in the companionway.

"Get her, Fi," a child's voice cried.

Belinda screamed. Phoebe jumped and dropped the dagger. With a swirl of fabric like mammoth wings, Docherty's cloak sailed through the air and around Phoebe's shoulders. And around, trapping her in a cocoon of warm, damp wool.

"Fi, do not—"

Docherty's command came too late. Growling, a black-and-white dog no larger than a barn cat sank its teeth into the hem of Phoebe's gown and through to her ankle.

To her shame, she screamed too. The lantern light blurred, blackened before her eyes, then flared brighter than ever. She sagged in the enveloping cloak, in Docherty's supporting arms. "Stop it." She croaked the command. Tears of pain and mortification spilled down her cheeks.

"She only listens to me and Captain Rafe." A youth of

perhaps eleven or twelve trotted into the cabin, crouched, and disengaged the dog from Phoebe's ankle. "You're a grand girl, Fiona McCloud."

"And you're a disobedient imp." Docherty's tone was dry. "I told you to go to your cabin."

"Aye, sir, and I had to come down here to do so, and I could not help but listen in the companionway." Grass-green eyes in a too-thin face glanced up. They twinkled. The full lips curved into a three-cornered smile like an elf. "And 'tis a grand thing I did or you'd be eating your dinner through your gullet 'stead of your mouth."

Phoebe blinked down at the child. "You not only force innocent women aboard, you force children too?"

"He did not force me." The lad rose and planted his hands on his hips. "I came aboard of my own free will and stay of my own free will."

"If not mine," Docherty muttered. "But if you do not vacate this cabin with that wee beastie, Mel, I'll be putting you ashore first chance I'm granted."

"Virginia can't be far off," Phoebe suggested in dulcet tones.

Docherty's arms tightened their imprisoning hold. "'Tis not close enough for going back. And I would not leave the la—the lad on enemy soil."

"We're not enemies to children." Belinda made her way forward, gripping a chair then the desk for support. "You should be our cabin steward for the voyage. I'd like that."

"I would too." The lad rose with the dog in his arms.

Phoebe's ankle throbbed at the mere sight of the little mouth of the beast, but she felt no warm trickle of blood, only the nauseating ache of the impact of teeth through her gown and onto her flesh. She rather welcomed Docherty's supportive hold. Without it, she might be spinning with the cabin, the swaying lantern light, Belinda plump and smiling in her lavender-soaked gown, the child and dog shifting with the motion of the deck. Spinning. Spinning. Darkening—

"Do not faint on me, Mrs. Lee," Docherty said into her ear. "You'll be disappointing me."

"With all reverence, God forbid I should do that." Phoebe blinked hard, tried to move her arms.

The cloak held them captive. Her lungs felt compressed with air too difficult to breathe. She gasped.

"She's gone all funny colored," the elfin child cried.

The next moment, the cloak fell away. One hand pushed her onto the window seat. Another pressed on the back of her head, lowering her face to her knees.

"Breathe," Docherty commanded. "Mel, get that cur out of here, and if I learn you taught her to bite, you'll be spending the voyage below deck with Mrs. Lee."

"I needed some kind of protection." Mel sounded sulky. "And it worked. She saved you."

"As if I need a wee dog to rescue me from a wee lass." Docherty crouched before Phoebe and nudged her chin up.

For a moment, their faces hovered mere inches apart, close enough for her to feel his warm breath on her lips. Close enough for her to see her reflection in his gray eyes.

"You're looking better." That odd tenderness had crept into his voice again, a compassion that belonged in a pastor or friend, not the captain of a privateer who had allowed her to be abducted.

Her insides quivered like a plain of quicksand. She straightened but didn't look away.

"She's still a funny color," announced Mel, the child with the vicious dog.

That dog now rested in her master's arms as limp as a fluffy toy.

"You can't continue to be sick," Belinda protested. "You're here to take care of me."

"But you're not ill." For the first time, Phoebe realized that the lad bore the same burr as the captain.

And the same red hair.

She glanced from one to the other, noted the cheekbones, the straight noses, and the shape, if not the color, of the eyes. "A young relation?"

"Aye, for my sins." The glance Doherty cast Mel held pure affection.

Phoebe managed a smile. "Which are numerous."

"Like the stars in the heavens, no doot." He rose. "Mrs. Chapman, will you tend to your friend's injuries?"

"Me?" Belinda paled. "I've never done anything of the kind. Blood makes me ill."

"There's no blood." Phoebe started to hold out her foot, realized she would be displaying her ankles to a man, and tucked her toes inside the folds of her gown. "I can manage myself." She started to rise.

Fiona raised her head, muzzle twitching.

"Take that menace elsewhere," Docherty commanded Mel.

"But—"

"Do not argue with me. If she bites anyone else, she'll be going ashore."

"Lucky dog," Phoebe muttered.

At that moment, with Docherty's kindness still radiating around her, slipping out of the stern windows and swimming ashore sounded like a fine idea and the only way to make up for her horrendous behavior. Unless scrubbing decks or cooking meals for the crew would serve better.

Or staying aboard to tend to Belinda, regardless of the fact it made her a traitor to her country.

God, what would You have me do?

More shame burned through her. She'd acted without praying, had taken the human way to obtain their freedom. Not the first time she'd done something so foolish. This time, the results weren't half as bad—yet.

Maybe she could simply slither under the table until he departed. Better yet, ask to spend the voyage in the hold unless Bel needed her so she didn't have to look at him.

Outrage, anguish, a hint of despair clawed at her belly. Phoebe drew her knees to her chest and wrapped her arms around them.

In front of her, a hand on the lad's shoulder, Docherty spun him to the door. "Scoot."

"Aye, Captain." Mel trudged from the cabin.

Docherty turned back to Phoebe and held out his hand. "The key."

"It's still in the lock." Fatigue washed over and through Phoebe. Speaking seemed like too much of an effort. She put her head down on her knees and closed her eyes. "Just let me get wherever you want me below and let me sleep."

"I'll let you sleep here." The lock to the weapons snicked closed.

"You forgot the dagger," Belinda said.

"Aye, so I did." He returned to Phoebe's side of the cabin, taking up the open space, filling it with his scent, with his heat.

Phoebe tightened her arms around her knees.

"The storm is abating." Docherty spoke right above her. "You should rest easy now, but there's more of the ginger water on the desk, should you be needing it."

Phoebe managed a muttered, "Thank you."

For what felt like forever, he didn't move away, then suddenly, the cabin felt larger, colder, and the door latch clicked. The lock grated.

"God is certainly smiling on you tonight." Belinda joined

Phoebe on the window seat. "The captain could have stopped you in a moment."

Phoebe nodded. Of course he could have. He'd been toying with her, letting her think she controlled the moment. Of course she hadn't. She couldn't have hurt him. Not once had he been in real danger from her, and he knew it. All she'd done was make a fool of herself.

And she was completely in his control, locked in like a prisoner, sequestered with Belinda. Phoebe was at her beck and call too. Nothing forced Phoebe to do her sister-in-law's bidding. Experience told Phoebe that giving in turned out easier than living with the consequences of refusal.

Oh, she was going to need that ginger water. Though the waves no longer felt like the brig sailed through the peaks and valleys of the Blue Ridge Mountains, the cabin door remained firmly in place, and her stomach began to flip and churn again.

She rose and took the tankard from the desk. "Go to bed, Belinda. You need your rest."

"I am tired." Belinda stumbled to the bunk and slipped beneath the quilt. "This isn't big enough for both of us."

"You should have thought of that before you forced me to come along." Phoebe sipped at the ginger water. The aromatic herb began its ministrations on her middle. "But never you mind. I'll manage on the floor."

Except she was cold. She hadn't been warm aboard the brig except for those moments when Rafe Docherty had wrapped her in his cloak.

She began to search for another coverlet, a blanket, a cloak. A chest beneath the bunk proved to be locked, but the window seat lifted to reveal a second boat cloak of fine black wool. She wrapped it around herself, inhaling the sweetness of the chest's cedar lining.

"You shouldn't be going through his things," Belinda muttered into her pillow.

Phoebe curled her upper lip. "He should think of my comfort."

But of course he was. He hadn't stuffed her into the hold or even forced her below deck. He'd given up the comforts of his cabin. He hadn't hobbled her in any way, except for that locked door, which she mustn't think about. He'd brought her ginger water and comfrey salve.

And she'd repaid him with a knife to his jugular.

A vein in the neck he'd known the name of, oddly enough. Phoebe knew it. Tabitha insisted she know things like that, read and memorize important veins and muscles and bones from medical books. But an ordinary man wouldn't know such a thing.

Rafe Docherty was no ordinary man.

A shiver ran through Phoebe, and she wrapped herself more tightly in the cloak. "I'm going to blow out the light now."

"What if we need to see in the night? I'll fall over something in the dark."

"It'll be light before you need to get up again." Phoebe removed the second pillow from the bed and wedged herself between the window seat and another locked chest at the foot of the bunk.

Above her, Belinda began to snore lightly like a cat. Higher up, someone paced the quarterdeck. Back and forth. Back and forth. Restless. Monotonous. The motion of a caged wolf.

Or a sentry.

Phoebe went to sleep with the image of a wolf guarding prison gates.

She woke to the rhythmic slapping of waves against the hull and a field of blue—from robin's egg to indigo—blazing through the stern windows, blue sky meeting bluer sea and not a speck of land in sight. Finding the cabin stuffier than the night before, Phoebe rose and opened the stern windows for a blast of cold, fresh air.

"Close the window," Belinda grumbled from the bed. "It's cold."

"I need the fresh air."

"Revolting. How will I get my breakfast?"

"Maybe you can bang on the door and get someone down here."

"That would be so vulgar. I should wait for someone, don't you think?"

"I don't care what you do." Phoebe curled up as best she could in the narrow space on the floor. "I want to sleep some more."

But a knock sounded on the door, and the child called out for permission to enter.

"Of course, my dear." Belinda sounded awake and cheerful. Phoebe moaned.

The lad entered, bringing the tannic aroma of tea and the buttery fragrance of toast.

"Uh-oh." A thump sounded from the region of the table. "I'll fetch my—the captain."

His what? Uncle? Brother? That they were related was obvious. Regardless, Phoebe didn't want him near her.

"Don't." She sat up. "I'll manage some tea."

"It helps, I can assure you." The lad's eyes twinkled. "Captain Rafe suffers from the sickness sometimes too. It'll go away."

"If I don't die first."

No sense in saying the sea didn't bother her, the locked door did. They would think she lied to get her freedom.

Belinda scolded.

The lad laughed and scampered from the cabin, ragged hair swinging, long legs flashing. Long legs ending in curved calves, slight ankles, and dainty feet. Rather too elegant and petite for a boy of even eleven or twelve.

"Lad, my eye." Phoebe struggled to her feet.

Belinda stared at her from where she sat at the table, no doubt waiting to be served. "What are you talking about?"

"Our friend Mel. Do you want jam on some of this toast?"

"Yes, and I hope they bring us more than tea and toast. I usually have sausages and eggs."

"This is a ship. They don't have sausages and eggs."

Thank the Lord.

"I'll starve." Belinda's lower lip protruded.

Phoebe ground her teeth to demolish the words trying to reach her lips. She would get nowhere and nothing but grief if she told Belinda she looked in no danger of starving. Indeed, even with her condition being more advanced than she'd originally told Phoebe, Belinda appeared to have gained a great deal of weight since they'd last met in April. No doubt she was getting no exercise. Phoebe would have to see to that. A daily walk made delivery easier.

A daily walk aboard a ship? Not if they remained locked in. She would have to talk to Docherty about that—and a number of other matters. One in particular.

"I'll fetch out some of your stores." Phoebe spoke a little too loudly to drown out her own thoughts. "Some raisins? Some dried meat?"

"Yes, both."

Phoebe served Belinda her breakfast because she and everyone else had always served Belinda. Because serving her proved easier than listening to her complain. She seemed totally selfish, yet she risked her life, risked being tainted a traitor, to accept the word of a stranger, the enemy, in an effort to save her husband.

She'd been that devoted to her brother too. George might be worth the danger.

Phoebe prepared a meal for Belinda and began to organize the boxes of provisions to keep herself busy, to keep herself from thinking of Belinda's brother, of the confinement of the cabin, of her own queasy stomach, of her current circumstances.

She couldn't avoid those. Through the skylight, she caught the rumble of Docherty's voice, the lilt of his young relative's, others'. Locks surrounded her—on chests, on the weapons rack, on the cabin door.

The lock on the door clicked as Phoebe dug sewing materials out of a box for Belinda. Phoebe straightened and faced the portal, expecting the captain with orders as to what he intended to do with his recalcitrant prisoner.

Instead, Mel entered bearing a copper jug from which steam emerged. "Hot water. And I'll bring you more ginger water, Mrs. Lee. But you really ought to eat something."

"I know." Phoebe dropped onto the nearest chair. She knew what she needed to ask, but the words lodged in her throat.

"Are you all right, Mrs. Chapman?" Mel asked.

Belinda swallowed her mouthful of raisins. "Never better. But I'm used to sailing. My husband took me on his schooner up to Baltimore and down to Norfolk many times. Phoebe prefers to ride."

"If God wanted us on water, he'd have given us fins." Phoebe forced herself to smile. "Thank you for serving us, Mel. Is your—is the captain leaving our care to you?"

"Aye, mostly. He says you will do me no harm."

"He's right." Belinda cast Phoebe a hard glance.

"Of course." Phoebe took a deep breath. "Will you ask him

if I may please speak to him? I . . . I'm . . ." She swallowed and looked around the cabin. "Alone. That is, without an audience."

"Aye, I'll ask him." Mel handed Phoebe the ginger water, then crossed the cabin to one corner. There she set the can of water on the deck, balanced between her feet, and pulled a shelf from the bulkhead. "You have a washstand now. Fold it up when you are finished with the washing up."

"That's so clever." Belinda sprang up and made her way to the corner. "Where's the—ah, you keep the bowl tucked behind."

Clever indeed. Phoebe glanced around. Did other sections of the paneling conceal hidden compartments with less mundane cargo than a washstand and basin? More than likely. She would seek them out, if Belinda let her.

For the moment, she remained motionless, uninterested, as though nothing but her ginger water lay on her mind. Which was close to the truth for the time being.

"I will talk to Captain Rafe about you wanting to talk to him," Mel said.

Phoebe nodded and watched the child strut from the cabin.

In the corner, Belinda happily splashed in the water, washing up as best anyone could with a basin, soap, and a sponge. The aroma of lavender bloomed through the cabin. Unless she found something else, Phoebe would have to use the lavender soap too, and she was already weary of Belinda's excess with the fragrance. She didn't have any of her own things except the handful of gowns she had packed for what she thought was a mercy trip to Williamsburg. She still huddled in Docherty's boat cloak.

Belinda poured more water into the basin. Phoebe roused herself enough to request she save some for her.

"I will, but you'll have to pour out what's in the basin. It'll take two hands, and I might fall."

"Which is one reason why you shouldn't be on a brig this size. The risk—"

"Never you mind the risk. I'll be careful, and it's worth it. Will you help me cut out some clothes for me to sew for the baby?"

"Yes, of course." She might as well. The hours, days, weeks stretched ahead without much hope of a change.

At least Phoebe hoped for no excitement, as that would likely mean a gun battle with another vessel, maybe even an American.

She shuddered and drank more ginger and awaited her turn to wash. When it came, she made quick work of it, wrinkling her nose at Belinda's lavender soap, frowning more at the wrinkled state of her gown. Her hair proved hopeless. She gathered it into a ribbon and tied it atop her head. The effect likely made her look like a chrysanthemum, that flower she'd seen once on a journey to Philadelphia with her husband, but at least her hair was confined away from her face with little trouble. If Docherty would see her outside the cabin, she wouldn't be embarrassed.

Not that she should be. He was the enemy, a man who stood for everything she abhorred. But she must talk to him. She'd wronged him too.

She finished readying herself for her first full day aboard the brig and gathered up the fabric Belinda wanted to sew. It was of the finest lawn, soft enough not to irritate a baby's skin, and the color of fresh cream.

"Do you have patterns?" Phoebe knelt on the now gently rolling deck and began to spread out the fabric.

Belinda raised her head from a book she'd been reading. "Pattern? Somewhere, I think. Wasn't it with the fabric?"

"No." Phoebe returned to the box.

The door lock grated. She froze, every sense alert like a dog's pricked-up ears, to see who would enter.

Mel again, this time with the nasty little dog in tow. The former smiled that elfin grin. The latter sat and glared at Phoebe.

"If she bites me again," Phoebe said, "I'll toss her overboard."

"That's what Captain Rafe says." Mel grimaced. "But he doesn't mean it. He loves Fiona."

"Which doesn't speak highly of him," Phoebe muttered.

"You should be nice to him," Belinda said. "He didn't lock you in the hold last night."

"And he says I can take you up top," Mel said. "Mrs. Chapman too, so we can clean in here."

"Thank you." Phoebe's stomach settled. It should remain that way on deck—she hoped. If she got sick in front of him again, she'd lock herself in the hold.

She gathered up his boat cloak, realized she shouldn't be using it without his permission, and started to put it down again.

"You'll want that." Mel drew Belinda's from the back of a chair. "It's cold out there, even in the sun."

So Phoebe wrapped herself in the cloak that dragged on the deck behind her like a train, and followed Mel, Fiona, and Belinda up the companionway and onto the main deck.

Wind like the blast from an icehouse slammed into her face. She gasped and braced herself against it, turning her face away. Belinda squealed and tried to retreat.

"Nay, madam." The mate called Jordy appeared down the quarterdeck ladder and took Belinda's arm. "The captain says you're needing exercise, and I'm to walk with you to hold you steady."

"Why, that's so kind of you, sir." Belinda batted her long eyelashes at him. "Such a handsome escort."

Jordy was attractive, with his silver-gilt hair tied in a queue at the back of his neck and his strong, regular features, but *handsome* seemed a bit overdone, and Phoebe glanced away to hide a grin. She met Mel's eyes, and they laughed.

"Jordy will get tongue-tied if she keeps flirting like that," Mel whispered.

"'Tis good for him." Docherty appeared at the quarter rail. "You wish to speak with me, Mrs. Lee?"

"Yes, I—" She looked down at the borrowed cloak.

"I do not care if you wear my boat cloak. Come up if you like, Mrs. Lee. Mel, you and Tommy Jones go clean up the cabins."

Mel's fine features tightened. "Not Tommy, please. He— he's so unpleasant to be around."

"Is he now." Docherty's face hardened. "To you?"

"He says naught to me. 'Tis what I dislike above all things. He just grumbles and mutters . . . stuff."

"What sort of stuff?" Docherty's tone was so cold and hard that Phoebe took a half step backward and caught her heel in the extra length of the cloak.

"I will go with our imp here." His black eye now turning all sorts of colors from green to yellow, Watt leaped from the quarterdeck and rested a hand on Mel's shoulder. "Tommy has a bee in his bonnet about doing women's work."

"No work aboard a vessel is women's work." The chill remained in the captain's voice. "Set him to scrubbing the lower deck if he won't clean cabins."

"Rafe—er—Captain—" Watt began, then stopped, nodded, and started forward.

"Scoot, imp," Rafe said to Mel in a gentler tone.

"Aye, aye, sir." Mel gave him a salute so exaggerated it verged on insolent.

Docherty sighed. "There's no disciplining the lad."

Phoebe climbed the quarter ladder so she stood at least

close to level with the captain and looked him in the face. "No lies between us, sir, please. It's obvious to me that's a girl."

"Aye, I should have known you'd work it out this quick. 'Tis too obvious." He leaned against the rail and scrubbed his hands over his face. Beyond him a dozen feet away, the helmsman looked on with concern. "'Tis more obvious since she took the notion to cut her hair so she cannot braid it and stuff it down the back of her jacket. I do not ken how that is possible."

"It's softer, perhaps." Phoebe's hand twitched, wanting to reach out and touch him. Wipe away a trouble he shouldn't have if he didn't have a child aboard a brig in constant danger. She grasped the rail with both hands behind her, for she no longer felt like giving him comfort. "This is scarcely the place to raise a child, let alone a girl."

"You tell Melvina that." His lips twisted.

"What do you mean? This is your ship."

"Brig."

Phoebe flipped one hand in the air. "What does it matter? It's a vessel of war. You're the captain. Put her ashore."

"You ken naught of it." He turned on Phoebe. "What do you want from me other than set ashore?"

Words of apology slipped from Phoebe's mind. She set one hand on her hip and willed her temper to be obedient. "You are irresponsible keeping that child aboard. What if an enemy took her, harmed her? Could you live with yourself knowing you were responsible for something awful happening to—who is she? A relative, that's obvious. Your sister? Do you want your flesh and blood—"

"Madam," Docherty interrupted in a voice as low as that of a growling feline, and just as hair-raising, "state your business or get off my quarterdeck."

"I, um, I—" Phoebe gulped. She turned her face away from

him. The bracing bite of the wind steadied her, took away the last of the malaise in her middle with the clean, open air. "I'm sorry. I care about children."

"And you're thinking I do not?" Though still low, his voice had gentled. "Believe me, you are wrong in that. I care about two things in this life, and Mel is one of them." He hesitated a beat, then took a breath loud enough to hear over the wind and surf. "She's my daughter."

5

In less than ten hours, Rafe had learned one thing about Phoebe Carter Lee that Williamsburg gossip hadn't taught him—little left her speechless. His announcement of Mel's parentage did. It left Mrs. Lee wide-eyed, gape-mouthed, and, above all, silent.

One corner of Rafe's mouth twitched upward. "Something surprises you, madam?"

"I—well—" Her pale cheeks grew rosy in the morning sunshine. "You can't be old enough to be Mel's father," she blurted out.

"I'm two and thirty. She turned twelve years last month." An ache punched through his chest for the mere lad he'd been at her birth, so joyful, so proud, so certain his life held everything he wanted and more, despite not expecting to be a father that young. "I married her mither at nineteen, so you ken there's naught improper about her birth."

"I never—" Her cheeks turned from rose to cherry, and her hands flew to her face.

The brig slid into the trough of a wave. Without support, without the strength of leg muscles that seasoned sailors possessed, she lost her balance.

Rafe caught her beneath her elbows and held her until she steadied and the deck grew reasonably level again. She stood too close to him, close enough for him to smell the lavender soap, close enough that strands of her disheveled hair blew into his face like silk threads, close enough that a scar as fine as her golden locks glinted silver in the sunlight from her right temple to her ear. He raised one hand, tempted to trace the path.

He reached out and grasped the quarter rail. "You'd best hold on to something when you're standing. A midwife with a broken arm would be of no use."

"No, no use." She sounded breathless and kept her hands on her cheeks. "I'm so careful not to hurt my hands most of the time."

"Then stay careful with these." He drew one of her hands away from her face and curled her fingers around the rail. Slowly he pulled his hand away and shoved it into the pocket of his boat cloak. "You'll need to keep them safe, though we should not need your services on this voyage, no?"

"Yes, we may." She huffed out a breath, and her color returned to normal. "Belinda is only two months from her time, she tells me."

"Tells you? You cannot tell? I do not mean to be indelicate, but you are her midwife, are you not?"

"Not. I mean—" She compressed her lips. "I haven't yet had the opportunity to examine her."

"I see."

He saw too much. His gut twisted with the notion of Belinda Chapman going into labor at the moment he needed her, or worse, while they were still at sea.

"Which is another reason why I was so desperate to get you turned back to Virginia," Mrs. Lee added.

"Aye, so this is why you wished to speak to me? If so, the answer is no. We are nearly sixty miles from the coast, and I am not turning back, especially not in broad daylight. So if that is all you are needing, I have my work to do." He gestured to the men aloft, setting the studding and royals to gain every advantage of wind they could. At the last drop of the log line, they'd been making ten knots. He wanted eleven or even twelve while the wind lay in their favor. Too many of the men stood around in groups of three and four, heads close, faces intent. They needed more direction than they were getting with Jordy entertaining Mrs. Chapman.

And, Rafe hoped, questioning her over her loyalty to the mission.

He started past Phoebe Lee, intending to pick up the speaking trumpet and call orders.

She caught hold of his arm. "No, please, it's not." She gazed up at him with eyes so green he longed for land, for the sight and texture of moss that rich hue.

His mouth went dry, making his voice harsh. "What is it then?"

"I want to apologize." Her own words rasped as though she too spoke from a parched throat. "No, I wish to ask your forgiveness for—for last night. I was desperate. We're traitors now, or could be seen as such, and I lost my head a bit. But it doesn't make an excuse for what I did. So please forgive me."

He stared at her this time, but with narrowed eyes, scanning her face for signs she played some game with him. Her gaze remained open and clear, meeting and holding his eyes without blinking.

And something peculiar occurred inside him, a prickling, a plucking in his chest. He opened his mouth to speak, and no words emerged. He shook his head, walked to the binnacle, and stared at the compass without registering in which direction they sailed.

"Something wrong, sir?" Derrick asked in his deep, musical voice.

"No, nothing."

A flash of movement in the corner of his eye drew his attention to Mrs. Lee. She'd stalked down the ladder to the main deck, her head held high, her hair streaming out behind her like a banner. Mrs. Chapman and Jordy sat in the shelter of an awning the latter had rigged for the ladies so they could enjoy the fresh air without burning their skin, and Mrs. Lee stomped toward them.

So he'd lied about nothing being wrong. Of course there was. He'd just wounded her spirit. Her indignation radiated from her like that dreadful lavender scent, striking him, clinging to him.

"'Tis I who should be asking the forgiveness," he murmured too softly for the helmsman to hear.

If he spoke the truth, he should go after her. He picked up the speaking trumpet instead and crossed to the center of the deck. "Get you moving with those royals. I'll be sending up the ladies if you cannot move any faster."

Laughter drifted to the deck like autumn leaves, and the men moved faster, dropping the sail sixty feet above the deck, drawing the sheets taut so the wind caught the canvas. The *Davina* skimmed over the next wave, light and swift.

Rafe turned the speaking trumpet forward. "Jordy, drop the log line, if you can tear yourself from the ladies."

Jordy said something that brightened Mrs. Chapman's pretty face, bowed to Mrs. Lee, then strode to the bow.

Rafe turned his attention back to the ladies. Mrs. Chapman, young and plump and more courageous than people gave her credit for, Rafe figured, clutched Phoebe Lee's hand and talked, her lips moving swiftly, her dark eyes hidden behind thick lashes. The latter perched on the edge of her chair as though prepared to bolt at a moment's notice. He should go talk to her, explain—something. Mel's reason for being aboard, why he couldn't talk to her about forgiveness, how he wanted to at least be cordial on this voyage.

He set his foot on the quarter ladder as a shout dropped from the crosstrees to the deck like a stone. "Deck there. Sail off the larboard quarter."

Rafe sprinted for the side, caught hold of the shrouds, and began to climb the ratlines. In seconds, he squeezed onto the crosstrees and snatched the glass from the lookout.

"Couldn't see a flag, sir," the youth said. "She looks fast."

She did indeed. In less than a minute, her topgallant sails grew visible over the horizon, along with her flag.

Stars and stripes.

"Keep an eye on her, lad." Rafe leaped to a backstay and slid to the deck, shouting orders before his feet struck wood. "Alter course two points to starboard."

Derrick stared at him. "Don't you mean larboard, sir?"

"I mean starboard." He caught up the speaking trumpet again. "Clew the royals and topgallants."

That would make them less visible over the horizon.

Except no one moved. The brig maintained the same course of northeast by north, a course that would sail them across the American ship's bow if they maintained their current route and the men in the rigging didn't touch a single line.

"That was an order." Rafe addressed Derrick in a slow, calm tone. "If you wish to remain here, you will obey."

"Aye, sir." Derrick began to turn the wheel.

The men up top remained still, lounging across the yards as though enjoying a picnic. Others began to saunter toward the guns on the main deck.

Jordy had warned him. The men begged for a fight.

Rafe took a deep breath to calm himself before he shouted something to the men he would regret. "She isn't worth it. We want fat French merchants, not emaciated Americans."

The men near the guns looked thoughtful. One man in the shrouds turned toward the nearest sheet.

"And we have ladies on board to protect." Rafe pressed his momentary advantage before someone pointed out that, after twenty years of war, the French grew emaciated. The Americans seemed to be the ones growing plump—off of the British. "We have a duty to protect these weaker vessels."

Beneath the canopy, Mrs. Lee spun to face him. To glare at him, no doubt.

His lips twitched, and he continued, "We cannot risk their safety."

"Then no prizes while we have them aboard?" Ludlow, a young man who'd just joined up, asked from near the quarter ladder.

Rafe acknowledged the youth. "No, but they won't be here for long."

Mrs. Lee took a step aft, lost her balance, and grasped a shroud for support.

"Lookout, what's the status of the enemy?"

"Dropped down from the horizon, sir," came the faint response.

Good. He could breathe again.

"Must be slow," Derrick said from the helm. "Would have been easy pickings."

"If she was worth the effort."

"Might be slow because she's heavy laden."

"Might be." Rafe spoke into the trumpet again. "I said clew up the royals."

They went up, slowly, but the men obeying the command mattered more than speed—speed the *Davina* lost. It was a calculated risk—making themselves less visible and losing speed, or maintaining the speed and drawing every American in pursuit of a prize swooping down upon them. American vessels tended to fly across the water. For one to be slow meant a heavy cargo indeed, or perhaps they'd been dam-

78

aged. Either way, they were lost now. One battle averted. Only three thousand miles of ocean or so to sail through without encountering another enemy privateer, merchantman, or, worst of all, French or American Navy ship.

Surely he'd lost his reason to think he could manage this voyage. Even if he had, he was committed now with the two ladies aboard.

He replaced the speaking trumpet on the binnacle and nodded to Derrick. "Return to the original course."

"Aye, sir."

"I'll send Jordy up to replace you in half an hour." Rafe looked down at the main deck for his second in command.

Jordy had returned to the ladies. He stood too close to Mrs. Lee, with a forefinger pointed at her nose as though scolding her. Yet all three of them laughed.

No, four of them. Jordy shifted, and Mel, Fiona in her arms, appeared in the group, apparently having finished her chores and chosen to join the ladies instead of him.

A knot formed in his middle. Mel always sought him out when she was free to do so. She was only on board because she claimed to abhor the school for young ladies in which he'd placed her—the fourth school that had failed to hold her. Yet now she chose to join the females aboard. And the night before, she'd begged him to let her serve the ladies.

He needed to face the truth. Mel was growing up. Her disguise grew thinner with each passing month. Mrs. Lee had noticed Melvina's sex within minutes. The enemy could too, should a battle go poorly, and then—

He couldn't think of that. The visions of what could happen to her sprang from memories, not imagination.

Another reason to avoid fighting on this, his last voyage.

Avoid fighting with American or French vessels. Spats with Mrs. Lee he couldn't avoid, no doubt. They needed to finish their earlier conversation. No, not needed—should. She deserved a response. An explanation for why he walked away? No, a response was all that was necessary. She was an appendage to Mrs. Chapman, nothing more, and in that deserved no explanations, only courtesy.

He leaped to the main deck and strode forward to join the ladies, his daughter in trousers like a sansculotte French rebel, the other two in light muslin gowns that would have them freezing if not for Mrs. Lee looking rather fetching in his extra boat cloak and Mrs. Chapman in her own cloak of impractical blue velvet.

It was a sight he would never witness again, once his sailing days ended. Part of him warmed. Most of him trembled with an apprehension he hadn't experienced since his second battle.

The warmed part of him carried him to Mel's side first. He rested his hand on her shoulder. "Chores done?"

"Aye, they're done, and more. I was offering the ladies a look at our books."

"I was asking if such a thing as a Bible could be found aboard." Mrs. Lee cast her sister-in-law an annoyed glance. "She didn't think to pack anything but my midwife bag when she let your men abduct me."

"We have a Bible aboard." Rafe refused to acknowledge the barb. "Mel's, but she'll let you borrow it."

"We used to have two," Mel said, "but Captain Rafe—"

"Go fetch it," Rafe broke in. "I'll take them down to unlock the chest with the rest of the reading materials."

"What happened to the other Bible?" Mrs. Lee asked as they made their way aft to the cabins.

"It got wet." He descended the companionway ladder, then turned to lend Mrs. Chapman a hand. Above, Mrs. Lee remained on deck, one hand on the bulkhead, her face as pale as Caribbean sand.

"I—I'd rather stay up here. The air down there—" She spun on her heel and fled.

"She never has been a sailor, bless her heart," Mrs. Chapman murmured. "I do wish I could have found someone else to join me, but no hired woman would be as loyal as Phoebe. Why, she's so loyal to my brother, she went off to become a midwife rather than marry again."

Loyal to Gideon Lee? More like guilty for the manner of his death, if tavern rumors were to be believed. No doubt becoming a healer bringing life into the world alleviated her guilt.

And right now, she was paying for her choices in another way.

"Go make yourself comfortable, madam," Rafe told Mrs. Chapman. "I'll return in a moment."

"Where are you going?" Her lower lip protruded slightly. "I don't like being alone."

"Few people do, and right now Mrs. Lee should not be, I'm thinking." Rafe took the steps of the ladder two at a time and glanced around for the other lady.

She didn't appear on the main deck. He asked a sailor scrubbing the deck if he'd seen her.

"Aye, sir." The man gestured with the gnarled hand holding the holystone. "Behind the cutter, casting up her accounts."

Rafe made his way around the cutter lashed to the deck and found Phoebe Lee kneeling on the deck, her face against the damp gunwale, her shoulders shaking. He crouched beside her. "'Tis naught to weep about."

"I'm not weeping. I don't weep, cry, or snivel." Another shudder ran through her. "I also don't get ill. I've been ill only once before in my life." She looked up at him with her big eyes dark and red-rimmed. "If this continues, I'll be dead before we reach England."

"It does get better, I promise. But we'll be in Bermuda in two days or so if the wind holds. We can take some time there for you to recover a bit and . . . er . . . examine Mrs. Chapman to see if she's fit to sail further."

"She's not. A ship is no place for a child to be born."

"Many a bairn has come into the world at sea and survived bonnie and braw."

"Bonnie and what?"

"Strong. Which you'll be soon enough." He rose and held his hands down to her. "Come down to find a book to read. I expect Mrs. Chapman will be wanting you to read to her."

"I expect so." She made a face. "And she likes the cabin, whereas I feel better in the fresh air."

"Perhaps Mel can read to her. She's a canny lass and reads well." He clasped Mrs. Lee's hands between his, balancing her and himself between rail and cutter. "I've made certain of that despite her inability to stay at school."

"Her inability to stay at school? How is that?" She made no move to release herself.

"She runs away every time I place her in one. I get back to shore to find her skulking around the wharves, awaiting my return."

Mrs. Lee stared at him. "How could she? I mean, why would she take such a dangerous course of action?"

"I'm all she has, along with Jordy and Watt and Derrick too, of course. We're the closest thing to family she has, and she misses us." One corner of his mouth flicked upward. "I ken perhaps you do not understand this."

Mrs. Lee turned her face away. The wind snatched at her words, shredding them so he couldn't be certain he heard them correctly, but he thought she said, "Don't be so sure I don't understand."

The idea that she could indeed understand Mel missing him

warmed something inside him enough to twist it, an aching pain like fingers forced down on taut muscles.

"So I am not such a poor father," he said, pressing his advantage.

She gave him a sidelong glance. "You could choose not to go to sea."

"Aye, and I shall—soon."

"But not soon enough for my sake." She sighed. "Will you leave us on Bermuda?"

"No."

"But—"

"I need Mrs. Chapman with me."

"Why?"

"I will not discuss it." He used the same tone he used when Mel tried to wheedle some action out of him, and regretted it instantly.

He'd refused to discuss other matters with the widow today. It was unfair to her. The entire voyage was unfair to her. Her pallor, her tensed jaw, the white knuckles of the hand gripping the rail shouted out her frustration and anger. She'd offered him a chance to grant her forgiveness, and he had walked away. She wanted to talk about her "incarceration," for all practical purposes, aboard his brig, and he wouldn't compromise. Not compromising had kept him alive these past nine years, and he wouldn't change now that his goal lay in sight, not even for the sake of a lady whose skin resembled fine porcelain, whose hair shimmered like pirate's gold, whose eyes glowed or darkened with her moods, whose womanly form drew his attention, plagued his mind, distracted him. If only the scent of lavender oil didn't remind him of his mother, who had determined he should grow into a godly man. Every whiff made his stomach knot.

He swung away from Phoebe and the fragrant reminder

of the mother—nay, the parents—who would never approve of what he was doing. But Davina would approve. Surely she welcomed his mission for her sake.

And her daughter's?

"Melvina is safer aboard this brig than she was at any of the schools I put her in." He spoke to the gray expanse of the sea. "She is frighteningly resourceful, and no one could hold her behind locked gates."

"And would your wife approve of her here?" Phoebe Lee asked from close beside him.

Lavender. His mother. Davina.

He made himself face Phoebe. "Aye, she would approve. I am going about exactly what she asked me in her last minutes of life."

6

Phoebe decided dying would prove easier than suffering hours locked up in the cabin, with its low deck beams and dark-paneled walls. The second night in the cabin, though, Phoebe spent more time kneeling on the window seat with the windows open and Belinda whining about the draft than she did rolled up in Docherty's cloak on the deck. "I need to feel the wind."

"And I need to be warm," Belinda responded.

"And see the waves," Phoebe insisted.

"You can't see them. It's black as pitch out there."

But it wasn't. A nearly full moon sailed along with them, sparkling in the midnight-dark water like fallen stars and limning the edges of the waves with silver crests.

"How can anything so empty and stark make me feel so free?" Phoebe laughed with a breathy chuckle and pressed her hands to her cold, damp cheeks.

Odd that an image of Rafe Docherty would swim before her eyes at that thought. His features were too strong, too hard to call beautiful, and *handsome* sounded ordinary, dull to describe a man with such controlled and quiet power banked inside him. Pleasant—no, pleasurable—to look upon came close to describing him, rather like the fascination of the moon in the waves that drew her gaze yet chilled her to the bone, threw her off balance if she let go of a solid anchor.

He left her unbalanced, confused, aching with an emptiness she thought she'd banished with her midwifery studies, with friends, with other people's children like Tabitha and Dominick's two little boys. She could be independent, serve the women of her county, rich or poor—especially the poor—and not need a man's attentions, let alone anything else. Then Captain Rafe Docherty, an unscrupulous, probably criminal Scotsman, looked on her with kindness after she'd threatened to slit his throat, and a hole ripped open inside her. She tried to repair it with talking to him, asking his forgiveness, delving into his past.

He'd rebuffed her. He hadn't granted her forgiveness. He wouldn't discuss why he lived the kind of life that could do nothing but endanger his daughter or risk leaving her an orphan. He'd walked out on her, pulling on a thread that unraveled her carefully woven inner strength.

Or perhaps the sickness brought on by confinement in the cabin simply made her feel undone. Other than an occasional ague, illness had rarely been a part of her life. For the months she'd enjoyed her condition of being an expectant mother, those last months before her husband died, she hadn't suffered more than a twinge or two of discomfort in the morning for about a week. Now the idea of two more days, let alone two more months, of sailing left her shaken and convinced she could take a knife to anyone if it would get her onto dry land.

If only violence wasn't so against what God would want her to do, no matter how desperate she felt. He wanted her to trust in Him to take care of her, no matter what. She tried not to demand to know why He wasn't doing so.

"Just stop this sickness," she prayed again and again through the night. It was temporary quarters, a cabin at least ten by fifteen feet, not a clothespress of a room.

In the morning, Mel came down and offered to set up their breakfast on deck, and Phoebe murmured a Psalm of praise as the tangy sea air washed into her face like a cleansing draught.

"I'll simply stay on deck and enjoy the sunshine," she announced. "In fact, Mel, may I borrow your Bible for a while? If you don't need it now, that is."

"No, I do not. I did my reading this morning, ma'am, but 'tis going to come onto rain soon." Mel gestured toward the horizon. A bank of black clouds inked the line between slate-blue sea and ice-blue sky.

Phoebe moaned. "Don't tell me I'll have to go below."

"Why would you want to stay here in the rain?" Belinda upended a bottle of molasses over her bowl of oatmeal porridge. "I want to be warm and dry below."

"I feel better up here." Phoebe rose and touched the awning. "This is canvas. It should keep me dry."

"Aye, so long as the wind does not blow it down." Mel grinned.

"Minx." Phoebe scowled at the child.

Mel laughed and scampered away toward the quarterdeck and the man with dark red hair streaming in the breeze. He leaned on the taffrail as though he bore not a single burden.

But he bore a hundred of them, or Phoebe wasn't a lady born and bred. He bore them alone, forming a shield behind which he didn't always manage to conceal the gentle, kind man he must have been most of the time in the past.

She smiled at him. She smiled at the way he kept himself from smiling, at the way he kept his tone neutral or made it harsh, at an odd kind of joy over how much he loved his daughter.

Oh yes, she caught him looking at the child with that tenderness he'd shown when Phoebe first became ill. Even more so. He was clay in that child's hands, or he'd have found a place on land strong enough to hold her in place and not risk her life at sea. Dangerous for a man on what was probably an illegal mission. Most definitely illegal, treacherous, outright deadly.

If she remained aboard, Phoebe vowed to protect Mel. But none of them would remain aboard. As soon as they reached Bermuda, Phoebe would find a way to get them home to America. And she would take Mel with her. She would manage to keep the child from running off to a seaport and the danger of any number of horrors happening to her, incidents that would surely wipe the elfin smile from the child's face.

Mel wasn't that much of a child, or wouldn't be for long. Keeping her aboard, whatever the reasoning, was another black mark against Captain Rafe Docherty.

Yet watching him reach out and ruffle Mel's ragged hair, then stoop to pat the ubiquitous dog at the girl's feet, Phoebe experienced a tightening in her chest, a constriction of her throat. For a flash, such tenderness softened his features that longing tore at a once-buried wound in Phoebe's heart—the wish for a child of her own to love and a husband who would cherish both of them.

A husband and child didn't seem to be in God's plans for Phoebe's life. Her punishment, she supposed, after the mistakes she had made. She was to serve other women in their quest for motherhood, in being good wives.

She glanced at Belinda, round and pretty, robust in her health, and suppressed a twinge of envy. If Rafe Docherty did get George Chapman out of prison and safely delivered to his wife and child, Belinda would have everything, except for selflessness. She was as self-centered as her brother had been—most of the time.

Belinda rose from the table and wrapped her cloak around her. "I'm going to make sure Mel can stay in the cabin with us. She said her father makes her go below, and that has to be so dull for her. Maybe I can do something with her hair. And her clothes." Belinda shuddered. "A young girl in breeches is an abomination."

"But practical if she climbs the rigging." Phoebe smiled at her sister-in-law for her kindness to the child.

"She shouldn't be climbing the rigging. It's not safe." Belinda plodded toward the quarterdeck, her gait an exaggerated roll between her natural plumpness, her advanced condition, and the tilting cant of the deck.

"And sometimes she's surprisingly kind," Phoebe murmured to no one in particular.

Her gaze shot to the captain, also capable of unexpected kindness. She didn't like it. Life would be so much easier if people like them behaved one way or the other so she could know what to expect, could avoid errors of judgment as had caused her so much trouble the year before and three years before that.

Two times too many.

Belinda's voice drifted to Phoebe, high and sweet, the words indistinct. Mel turned from her father, and her face lit up. She ran to the quarterdeck ladder and leaped to the main deck. Belinda caught hold of the child's arm, and her tone took on a scolding note, though it was gentle at the same time.

"Don't jump down like that," Phoebe imagined Belinda saying. "A lady always walks."

Mel's laughter rippled forward. Fiona yipped in joyful response, and the three of them vanished down the companionway to the cabins.

The notion of going below to confinement disturbed Phoebe's breakfast. She must escape the ship to escape this illness every time she entered the cabin, this weakness born of the past she should have put behind her long ago. Surely

Bermuda would allow her enough of a respite to regain her strength and find a way back to America. Somehow.

Meanwhile, she survived on the deck, watching the sea, watching the band of rain draw nearer, watching the captain stride about the quarterdeck, climb the rigging, lounge sixty feet above the deck as though stretched out on a chaise on dry land, though the sway above looked more profound than the rolling of the deck. Phoebe couldn't look at him up there. The idea of climbing that high left her dizzy.

She shuddered and looked away to find Mel standing beside her chair. "I thought you went below with Belinda."

"I left Fi with her for company, but I forgot I need to finish a mathematics problem before I stay below." Mel perched on the edge of the chair and applied chalk to slate. "Jordy and Watt and Captain Rafe insist I know my calculations for celestial navigation."

"Do they think you're going to be a sailor?" Phoebe smiled.

"I wish I could be. I love the sea." Mel glanced at the angry waves piling up along the horizon. "Being up top is like flying, though Captain Rafe doesn't like me up there. He says it's too dangerous."

"I should think so. It makes me queasy to look at the men climbing." Phoebe took a deep breath of salty air. "I didn't know I was such a weak creature," she admitted to Mel. "Land is so substantial, it doesn't demand much of a body."

Mel balanced the slate on her knees and performed some complicated calculations before responding. "I don't like it, but Captain Rafe says we're staying ashore after this voyage."

"Indeed. I wonder how he intends to get us back to Virginia." Phoebe risked a glance upward.

A handful of raindrops spattered onto the deck.

"You'd best go below." Mel rose, tall for her age and

whipcord thin. "I need to show Jordy or Captain Rafe my calculations."

"Why don't you call him Father?" Phoebe asked.

Mel looked surprised. "No one's supposed to know we're related. He's afraid they'll harm me to get to him if they do."

"I guessed so."

And he'd told her. Confided that bit of information in her when he didn't need to. She wondered why.

"You have the same cheekbones," Phoebe added.

And Mel would be a stunningly beautiful young woman.

Phoebe glanced up again in time to see Docherty sliding down a backstay. She'd seen enough sailors doing it to realize it was a typical method of reaching the deck, yet it looked rather entertaining and carefree, something a boy did as a lark.

Rafe Docherty looked neither boyish nor playful as he stalked forward to Phoebe. "A squall's blowing up. You need to go below."

"And good day to you too, sir." Phoebe rose, curtsied, and gave him a sweet smile.

Mel giggled.

Docherty set his hands on his hips. "I said you are to obey me, did I not?"

"You'd best," Mel whispered loudly enough to be heard at the helm.

"I'm not one of your crew." Phoebe pushed her chair further beneath the canopy. "A little rain won't harm me."

"Nay, but a great deal will. Now go, or I'll carry you down."

The threat nearly worked. She didn't want him that close to her. His proximity made her insides feel odd, rather tense and tingly. Even at that moment, when more than a yard of deck separated them, she experienced a tugging to rise and step forward, as though he were the North Pole and she the compass needle.

She gripped the edge of the table. "I'll take the risk."

"All right. I dare say the weather will punish you enough. But you get below, Mel, either to the ladies' cabin or to your own."

Mel cast Phoebe a pleading glance. "Do come, Mrs. Lee. Mrs. Chapman says she is going to make me put on a dress."

"I think you'll look quite pretty in a dress," Phoebe said diplomatically.

"I'll look like a freak, won't I?"

"You'll look like what you are." Docherty touched Mel's cheek. "My daughter. Now scoot." He glanced at Phoebe. "Both of you."

"Aye, aye, sir. Whatever you wish, sir." The girl gathered up her things and dashed through the increasing showers to the companionway.

Watching her, Phoebe made two observations—Melvina Docherty spoke uncommonly good English for a child who had run away from four schools and spent more time than was prudent skulking in port cities or aboard a ship, and she was desperate for female companionship. Of course. She was twelve. Her femininity would soon be impossible to disguise well.

And she shouldn't remain around a ship full of sailors.

Not comfortable bringing the latter matters up to a near stranger, Phoebe addressed her curiosity about the former. "Who sees to her education?"

"I do, mostly." Docherty cast his daughter one of those heart-meltingly tender glances. "She's a canny lass. Her celestial navigation is nearly as good as Jordy's, and he's better than most."

"Not yours?" Phoebe gazed up at him from beneath her lashes.

He didn't look at her. "I do a'right, but I was not raised to the sea like Watt."

No, he wasn't. He spoke uncommonly well too. The accent was there, strong with rolling R's and musical cadence, but his grammar was better than hers.

What were you raised to? She thought the question, urged it onto her tongue.

He walked away before the words found voice. The rain pounded on the deck, creating a curtain between them. Just as well. She hadn't wanted him to walk away. Worse, part of her wanted him to carry her below.

She inhaled the briny freshness of the air. It worked on her system like an elixir. Not a bit of sickness while she huddled under the canvas awning, chilled, damp from the rain blowing into her meager shelter, but invigorated and well.

Until the wind increased. Within an hour, the waves began to raise as high as the deck and send rivulets of greenish salt water cascading over the boards as the brig canted, then back the other way when it twisted and fell into a trough. Phoebe braced herself, fearing the sickness might return in such heavy seas. It didn't. Cold air kept away the specter of sickness, cleared her head of anything but how she could free herself through their calling at Bermuda, how to persuade Belinda not to remain with a man who couldn't forgive a minor transgression.

All right, it wasn't so minor. But he could have subdued her in seconds if he'd chosen to do so. Why he hadn't she couldn't be certain. Maybe he, unlike her, couldn't practice violence against the opposite sex.

She sought him out, couldn't find him or anyone else on deck. They had to be there. Someone manned the helm. The rain had grown too dense to see through. She couldn't go below now if she wanted to. She'd take the wrong direction and possibly get swept overboard. She should have listened to him, should have risked her health and gone below. Now—

A gust of wind slammed into the canopy. With the drumroll rumble of tearing heavy cloth, the awning ripped from its moorings. Phoebe flung up her arms to protect her head from pelting rain and hail.

The canopy crashed down on her. It slammed into her hands, sixty square feet of sodden canvas. The weight knocked her from her chair and onto the deck. Seawater swilled into her mouth. She gagged on the saltiness, coughed to breathe, swallowed a scream with a quantity of the ocean.

And the canvas held her down like a soaked shroud. Like an angry man.

She did scream then, kicked and cried out, punched at the enveloping fabric with her fists. "Stop! Stop! Stop!" Blackness surrounded her. She was going to die because he was angry, because he couldn't forgive. Because she thought for herself and—

A hand grasped her arm. She struck out with her other fist. Another hand grabbed her wrist and pulled.

"No, no, you can't make me. You can't—" The cold rain and wind struck her face like a slap. She choked on her cry and went limp in the man's hold, the hysteria stopping as quickly as it began. She was aboard the brig again, drenched and cold and held by a man who had touched her only in kindness.

She sagged against him, too mortified to speak.

"I told you to get below." Half carrying her, Docherty headed aft. "Will you be listening to me next time?"

So he'd left her on deck to teach her a lesson.

She nodded against his chest.

He snorted. "I doot it. Now get you below and change your dress before you catch a chill." He left her at the top of the companionway.

She obeyed him this time. She stumbled into the cabin to

find Fiona snoring in the center of the bunk and Mel and Belinda reading *The Adventures of Roderick Random* and laughing over the scrapes the young Scotsman got into when he moved to London.

"Wait until he ends up at sea." Phoebe dropped the drenched cloak onto the bare deck outside the cabin. "It's not particularly amusing."

"Oh, but it is." Mel sprang up and retrieved the cloak. "You should have come down sooner. This will take a year to dry if the sun doesn't come out."

"You look like a drowned rat," Belinda added. "You'd better not get a chill and die on me."

"I wouldn't dare," Phoebe muttered through chattering teeth. "Will you help me find dry clothes?"

Belinda shook her head. "I can't risk moving around in these seas. But you'll find warm things in the bottom trunk."

Warm things that fit Belinda, who was wider and shorter than Phoebe. But the woolen stockings and dry gown felt too comforting for a poor fit to matter.

Phoebe wrapped a shawl around herself and joined Belinda at the table. "I'll read for a while." She read, trying to distract herself from closed door and windows, but the smells of dampness and bilge water overpowered her will. The sickness bested her. She curled up on the deck with ginger water laced with laudanum and escaped into sleep.

Quiet woke her. The deck no longer undulated beneath her but gently rolled like an oversized cradle. And everything was black—the cabin, the sea, the sky. Belinda's snores rose above the hiss of waves against the hull. Mel and Fiona curled up together at Phoebe's feet, as though they were both puppies. The entire vessel seemed to sleep except for the man who paced the quarterdeck above.

Did he never sleep?

He admitted to suffering from mal de mer, an odd condition for a man who chose to be at sea most of the time. Maybe being on deck helped him as it did her. The longer she sat awake in the cabin with Belinda's lavender oil cloying above the dank odors of mildew and a chamber pot that needed to be emptied, the more she wanted to join him for a midnight stroll.

Phoebe rose and stepped over girl and dog. She located her shoes, mostly dry, beneath the desk where she'd kicked them off, and slipped out of the cabin. Even Fi continued to sleep.

The binnacle light shone off tendrils of fog swirling across the deck like dancing ladies in fine gauze gowns. Dampness caressed her face, cleansing, refreshing, healing. She breathed deeply of the tannic air and climbed the quarter ladder. Her leather soles sounded like wooden clogs in the stillness, and she paused at the top of the steps.

Murmuring voices broke off their dialogue. "Who goes there?" A shadow loomed through the fog between lantern and Phoebe.

She held out one hand. "Phoebe Lee."

"Aye, I should have known." Docherty took her hand and led her up the final tread onto the deck. "The quiet woke you, no?"

"Yes." She drew her hand free. The deck tilted enough that she lost her balance and grasped his arm.

"Aye, hold on to something." He settled her hand into the crook of his elbow. "We're fair to being becalmed in this fog and need to be as quiet as mice, as sound travels in a fog, you ken."

"I do. I lived on the eastern shore for three years."

She liked the strength of his arm beneath her fingers and the fine wool of his cloak.

"I hope I'm not interrupting," she said belatedly.

"Nay, Jordy and I were simply discussing when this will lift." He led her to the far side of the quarterdeck, where he removed her hand from his arm and set it on the rail. "I'm used to Mel's company on nights like this. And in storms." He moved half a step away from Phoebe and spoke so softly she barely heard him. "Is she . . . well?"

"She's sound asleep with her dog. Reading to Belinda—" Phoebe stopped and wished she could see Docherty's face. She felt him, though, a tension radiating from him as palpable as the mist. "You didn't expect her to stay with us in the cabin?" Phoebe asked.

"The storms make her restless. I usually hear her lessons. And she does not like the quiet of the fog. But I expect she's growing up and needing females around her instead."

"Instead of you?" Phoebe smiled and touched his hand, a pale blur on the weather-smoothed railing. "We're new and interesting, that is all. She'll want her papa again soon enough."

"Aye, perhaps." Even the mere murmur of his voice sounded heavy, burdened, infinitely sad. "This is no place for a female alone."

"This is no place for a female at all."

"'Tis temporary, I assure you."

"So Mel says." Phoebe worried her lower lip, working out something to say, to ask, a way to make polite conversation. "What lessons do you possibly teach her?"

He snorted, possibly an attempt at laughter. "You think I know naught of history and literature because I am at sea?"

"Well, the sailors I've met haven't seemed precisely educated."

"And how many is that?"

Phoebe let out a breathy chuckle. "All right, only a few. The husbands of patients who happened to be home at the woman's confinement."

One husband who should have remained at sea for his wife's sake, for Phoebe's sake, for his own sake.

She suppressed the memory of that fateful night and tried again. "Did you attend good schools?"

"Aye, the University of Edinburgh. 'Tis not Oxford or Cambridge, but 'twill do for teaching Mel about her country, do you think?"

Phoebe flinched at the hint of sarcasm. "I did come across as a bit of a snob, didn't I?"

"A wee bit." His tone softened. "But I take no offense. 'Tis a normal assumption. But we prize education in my family, you ken."

"You still have family, besides Mel, that is?"

"I have an uncle."

An uncle and a daughter. Phoebe bit back the words of sympathy, and other remarks spilled out like water dumped from a bucket. "I have one of those. He's actually my mother's sister's husband. I was visiting them when I met Tabitha and Dominick. I watched her sew up a gash on his hand, though they didn't know I was watching, and I wanted to know more about her. How wonderful to heal instead of harm."

He said nothing. Tension radiated from him.

"And here I showed you and your men harm." Phoebe sighed. "You have a low opinion of me, I expect."

"Nay, Mrs. Lee, I do not." He spoke in a rumbling murmur that blended with the ship's timbers and sea. "If for no other reason than that you are kind to Mel and to Mrs. Chapman, who is not kind to you."

Phoebe's fingers flexed on the rail. "At least I've shown some Christian behavior. I've known Belinda all her life. She was spoiled by everyone and married a man who spoils her. His capture was difficult for her, and she's been quite brave about it. Sensible until—" She clapped a hand to her mouth.

Docherty emitted another one of his snorts. "Until she agreed to my plans for getting her husband free? Aye, 'tis not sensible, I ken, but 'twill reunite them faster than any other way. Whatever you think of me and what I'm about, madam, consider getting George Chapman free of a prison hulk as saving his life. 'Tis some good I can offer."

"Yes, I'll concede that." Phoebe took a deep breath. "And now that you've mentioned doing some good . . . Captain Docherty, I can't stay aboard. This mal de mer is hurting me every time I go below, and I can't live on ginger and laudanum for weeks. I need nourishment. I'm shaking, I'm so weakened already." She held up one hand.

He clasped it in his and returned it to the rail, warm and sheltered beneath his fingers. "'Tis steady now."

"Sir."

"Aye, I ken what you are saying. But you will improve, I assure you. Unless 'tis not a normal seasickness?"

"I—" She couldn't look at him, dim though his profile was. She stared at the pale blur of their clasped hands, then into the opalescent fog swirling above the water. "I'm all right on deck. But it's getting too cold to stay up here all the time."

"Aye, 'tis so. Perhaps if we get rid of the lavender?"

Phoebe laughed. "It is awful, isn't it? Usually women in Belinda's condition are sensitive to smells. Her sense of smell seems to be diminished. Could it have some accident in Bermuda?"

"Aye, I can arrange that. Jasmine or lily or lilac. Anything will be better than lavender."

"Odd you would dislike it so. That is, you can't smell it often aboard your ship."

"Brig. Nay, but it has an unpleasant memory to it."

She remained silent, waiting for him to continue.

"'Twas the soap my mither used to wash unclean words from my tongue."

"She didn't." Phoebe pressed her hand to her lips to stifle her amusement.

"Aye, laugh, but it worked for many years. And even now I remember her admonition every time I smell the stuff."

So lavender reminded him of a mother who wanted her son to grow up respectful and polite. How she would grieve over him now.

Heaviness settled around her heart. "Captain Docherty, even if getting rid of the lavender helps me not be ill below, I need to go home."

Even the home of her in-laws, where everyone thought she should live instead of in her own house in town, looked like warm shelter in her mind right then. She'd rather be back with Tabitha and Dominick in their cottage by the sea, full of laughter and joy and love—love for one another and their children, love for the Lord and all He'd done to heal their lives.

And reminders of how she'd nearly ruined everything for them?

Emptiness yawned inside Phoebe like an abyss. Though he was the enemy by political boundaries and by what he had done to her and Belinda, she ached to turn her hand over and curl her fingers around Rafe Docherty's, rest her head against his arm, feel, if only for a few moments, like she belonged somewhere again.

She pressed a hand to her chest as though she could reach inside and close the gaping wound. "Please let us stay on Bermuda. Surely we can get home from there somehow."

She would have a good excuse to return to Tabitha and Dominick.

"Aye, the British Navy could return you under a flag of truce, but—" He paused. His hand tightened around hers.

And he maintained silence. On the far side of the quarterdeck, Jordy shifted at the helm, the scrape of his boot a crashing cymbal in the fog. He coughed and fell silent. Along the main deck, someone sneezed, a forward lookout perhaps. The moisture dripped from shrouds and limp sails like raindrops from trees. Drip, drip, drip. Annoying. Mesmerizing.

And Docherty remained silent.

So did Phoebe. She leaned on the rail with the sea no more than a quiet, hissing flow below her and waited for his verdict like a condemned man in the dock. Hanging? Transportation? A pardon?

"Have you ever wanted something so badly you can think of naught else?"

Phoebe jumped at the low rumble of his voice and stammered out a truthful, "Y-yes."

A husband who loved her, children, the ability to practice her midwifery.

"Yes," she repeated more strongly.

"Then you'll be understanding when I say that I have had such a yearning for nigh on nine years." He half turned to face her. "I have mortgaged my life for this one purpose and sworn naught will stop me from getting it. That includes finding two ladies aboard instead of the one I need. Mrs. Chapman needs you. I need Mrs. Chapman, and that means you stay. Do you ken what I'm saying?"

"Maybe if you told me why—"

"Nay, lass, I will not. You already think badly enough of me. And to increase the loathing will make the voyage very uncomfortable, no?" He raised his hand and curved it around her cheek, turning her face toward him.

For a heartbeat, a heartbeat that remained captured in her

chest, she thought he intended to kiss her. She could loathe him then, slap his face and be done with the scoundrel.

But words formed on her lips, more truth spilling out. "I don't loathe you, Captain Docherty."

"Nay, I think you do not. I wonder why." He removed his hand from her face and tilted his head back. "And here's a breeze. Jordy is right as usual. The fog will be gone within the hour, and we must pile on more sail to make up for lost time. Good night, Mrs. Lee."

As she watched him stride away, a tall, broad silhouette against the binnacle light, she added one more reason why she must escape the *Davina* as soon as possible. She did indeed not dislike Captain Rafe Docherty.

She liked him far too much.

7

Rafe leaned on the taffrail and observed the cutter skimming over the water, which lay as smooth as a looking glass, reflecting the masts and spars of St. George's Harbour. A small merchant convoy, a frigate, and two sloops of war escorted them. Three other privateers rode at anchor, as well as an American vessel sailing under a flag of truce, likely on its way to Europe on a diplomatic mission.

Depending on the news Jordy brought back, Rafe must work out a way to get the ladies ashore for a respite while protecting himself. Whatever else he allowed them to do on Bermuda, he must keep Mrs. Lee out of the way of any British naval officers or whoever trailed them in the American vessel. He toyed with leaving her and Mrs. Chapman onboard the *Davina*. It would be the wisest course, and also the cruelest, to have them so close to dry land and kept confined to their little cabin.

They were certainly prepared to go ashore. Mrs. Lee stood at the rail amidships and gazed toward the land with the hunger of a starving man eyeing a banquet. Mrs. Chapman stood beside her, chattering and gesturing. And Mel stood between them, alternately looking thoughtful and shaking her head.

"But you looked so pretty in a dress, even though it was too big for you." Mrs. Chapman's voice drifted on the light breeze.

Mel must indeed have been pretty in muslin and ribbons. She complained to him about how the ladies had treated her like a fashion doll, but her eyes had glowed with remembered pleasure at the female attention. Even Fiona still strutted around the deck with a blue bow tied around her neck.

Mel was indeed already pretty. Even with her ragged hair, she showed signs of becoming a stunner in a few more years. She was pretty now in her boys' clothes. Boys' clothes that failed to disguise the fact that she was fast growing into a young woman.

He was losing his daughter. Since the ladies came aboard and he gave her permission to be near them, Mel spent most of her free time in their company. She'd hated the schools where she'd have been safe, schools full of females, but these two women, the enemy because of their country of origin—they stole Mel's company from him with Mrs. Chapman's inane chatter about hats and gowns and baby things, and Mrs. Lee's more serious discussion of novels and poetry and history.

"You'll be wanting a school after they're gone," he murmured to his daughter a dozen yards away.

He sensed rather than heard Jordy slip up behind him, caught a whiff of the man's tobacco, never smoked, never chewed, never snuffed, just carried with him like a pet. "She'll lose interest once they're gone, lad."

"Or be hankering after a mither." Rafe sighed. "I should see if I have any female connections who'll consider taking her under their wings."

Jordy joined Rafe at the quarter rail but leaned his hips against it so he faced the younger man. "Or find yourself a wife once you end this nonsense of yours and settle."

"I had a wife." Rafe didn't look at the master sailor half again his age—his mentor, his friend. "I won't put myself through that pain again."

"'Tis only the losing them that's the painful part. But you love again and forget—"

Rafe flung up a hand in a staying gesture. "Not this again. I know you've found another wife, one you seem happy enough to leave to seek your fortune, but losing Davina the way I did . . ." He gave his head an emphatic shake. "No more wives for me."

"I'm not seeking my fortune." Jordy removed his tobacco pouch from his pocket and began to toss it from hand to hand. "Aye, I've won one, or near as like, but you ken I am here to protect you."

"I do not need your protection."

The argument was old, nearly rehearsed.

"Someone has to watch your back," Jordy pointed out.

"I have Watt and Derrick."

Jordy snorted. "I'd watch my back around Watt if I were you, and Derrick is more likely to pray for your soul than lift a sword to protect you." Jordy inhaled the aroma of the tobacco. "Not that praying for your soul is not good."

"A waste of time."

"Prayer is never a waste of time, lad."

"I no longer have a soul."

"You have life. You have a soul, and God still wants it."

Jordy was too good a friend, too loyal a companion for Rafe to lash out at him over the sermon. He simply said nothing.

Jordy's craggy face stretched into somber lines. "You need to give this up, Rafe." His tone matched his countenance. "You've gone too far bringing the ladies aboard. Mel was bad enough—"

"Stubble it, Jordy," Rafe lashed out. "We have gone through this, and you went to get Mrs. Chapman too."

"Aye, so Watt wouldn't go alone."

"Because Watt is so untrustworthy?" Rafe snorted.

Jordy sighed. "Aye, lad, he's untrustworthy. You would think you kent that from long ago."

"My mither trusted him, and I can't shun everyone."

Unbidden, Rafe's gaze strayed to Phoebe Lee. A few golden hairs fluttered from beneath her hat, along with a spill of blue ribbons. Her muslin gown drifted around her, giving her a grace of movement though she stood still. That she was beautiful even a blind man could see. That she attracted him even he admitted to himself. She tempted him, urging him to touch her smooth hand, her soft cheek, her lips. Especially her lips. He'd come seconds from kissing her the night before last.

It wouldn't do, allowing himself to care enough to make such a personal contact. Too often he'd observed how women interfered with a man's judgment. And he needed all his faculties intact now, not focused on a lady who liked him a wee bit when she should have despised him, would despise him if she knew what he planned.

He spoke his thoughts aloud. "I can't afford to care."

"I presume we are not discussing Watt McKay now?"

Rafe started. "Nay, I will not discuss Watt. What happened in the past is gone. I have forgiven him that."

"But not James Brock? If you'd forgive—"

"I won't discuss my retaliation against James Brock in the same breath as my set-to with Watt thirteen years ago. They are not the same."

"Forgiveness is forgiveness—nay, lad, do not push me off the rail. I ken you are not interested, but God has done such a work in my heart, I want to share."

"Derrick's doing." Rafe gritted his teeth. "I should have left him in Edinburgh."

"He wouldn't have stayed any more than Mel did." Jordy glanced behind him to the three females, four counting Fiona

106

cavorting at their feet, her bow bouncing between her ears. "Ah, the lovely widow has your attention. I thought as much the other night. Not a female to trifle with." He rubbed his belly.

"I have no intention of trifling with her. What kind of a roué do you think I am? But—" Rafe clamped his teeth on the next words.

Too often through his thirty-two years of life, all of which he'd known Jordy McPherson, he had said too much to the older man. Jordy knew most of Rafe's secrets, alas. Yet if anyone could be trusted, it was the family retainer. And Rafe did need to trust someone. Being completely alone had never suited him. So he tolerated the lectures, the admonitions, the sermonizing, for in the end Jordy would do what Rafe wanted because he had served the Dochertys of Edinburgh, as his ancestors had for generations.

"Mrs. Lee is the sort of woman a man marries," Rafe said aloud, more to convince himself than Jordy. "Even if her past isn't pure."

"No one's is." Jordy grinned, showing a gap between his front teeth. "But you could still do worse for a bride."

"No more brides." He repeated it like an automaton making the same motion due to a broken spring. "Never."

"Do you fear 'twill turn you from your course?"

"Nothing will turn me from my course."

"Aye, I thought as much." Jordy gazed past Rafe's shoulder.

Rafe turned his head to see what held his supercargo's attention. Past two fat merchantmen, the American schooner gleamed with the grace of a racehorse.

"They do build beautiful vessels," Rafe said.

"Aye, and fast." Jordy squinted toward the schooner. "That one left the Chesapeake half a day after us and arrived half a day before us."

"What are you saying?" Rafe turned to Jordy. "Do they have aught to do with us?"

"They might." Jordy sighed. "I may as well tell you, Rafe. James Brock is aboard that schooner."

"Impossible." Rafe gripped the rail until his knuckles gleamed in the sunshine. "I've tried to run him to earth for nine years."

And to think those years could end in victory here, without the voyage to free George Chapman, without keeping Phoebe Lee against her will, without risking his daughter's life further. His heart began to pound a marching beat in his chest. His lungs tightened. Before his eyes, he saw another kind of vessel—a small, quiet boat, a narrow deck, men with savage blades and cruel spirits.

"Nay, 'tis no coincidence, I'm thinking." Jordy drew his graying brows together over a beaky nose. "I'm thinking George Chapman betrayed you from his prison hulk."

"And instead of running from me, Brock has decided to run after me while pretending to be a diplomat." Rafe spoke through gritted teeth, sending pain shooting through his skull. "Still a lying, cheating—"

He broke off. He and Jordy had drawn the ladies' attention. They turned toward the quarterdeck, faces tilted upward so that the sunlight spilled beneath their hat brims and glowed on their faces, so lovely, so sweet, so alive.

Mel ran aft and charged up the ladder. "What's wrong, Captain Rafe?"

"Nothing to concern you, little one." He brushed his hand across her mop of hair, glowing like a ruby in the brilliant light.

But it did concern her. Brock could use Mel as Rafe intended to use Brock's best henchman and his wife.

"I'm just thinking perhaps you ought to stay aboard until tomorrow."

"Oh no." Mel's lower lip protruded and her eyes glistened. "I want to go ashore and get my hair cut nice and help Mrs. Chapman buy some ribbons and Mrs. Lee buy some fabric, and we need stores and—"

"Hush." Rafe laid a finger across her lips. "You can go tomorrow. Today—" He rested a hand on her shoulder and gave her part of the truth. "There are bad men ashore I'd rather you didn't encounter."

"There are always bad men ashore. I always manage to avoid them." She clutched his hand. "Please . . . Papa?"

Rafe's heart twisted, melted just a little at her use of Papa instead of Captain Rafe. But he shook his head. "This man is different. 'Tis . . . personal."

Mel's eyes widened. "Did you take his ship or something?"

"Nay, lass, and enough questions. You go tell the ladies they may go ashore tomorrow."

If he wasn't dead. Well, if he were, they'd need to go ashore to get help from the Navy.

"Scoot." He tapped her shoulder.

With a sigh, Mel stalked off, head down, ragged ends of her hair swinging.

"Coward," Jordy murmured.

"Aye, that I am. 'Tis the privilege of being the captain—I do not have to deliver the bad news."

On the main deck, the ladies drooped at Mel's tidings. Mrs. Lee cast him a glance that should have withered him despite the distance between them. She would never accept that it was for her own good.

"I'll be going ashore now," Rafe announced. "Call the men to take me."

Jordy didn't move. The harbor seemed unnaturally silent for a busy port in the middle of the afternoon. No one shouted orders, no drums rolled. Timbers didn't creak in the near-calm winds. The scene seemed more like pantomime than port.

Then Jordy straightened from his lounging position with a clatter of boots on the deck. "You cannot. Brock is here under a flag of truce. If you challenge him, you will find yourself locked up in irons in a trice."

"Not if my meeting with Brock is private."

"It won't be. He's no fool to have eluded you for all these years."

"I'll take the risk."

"Rafe, lad—aye, I ken you're my captain and I'm to address you with respect, but I've kent you since you were christened, and I'd be doing your sainted parents no favors if I did not try to talk you out of this course of action yet again."

"Good, you've tried. And they're sainted instead of living happily in Edinburgh because of that man." Not waiting for Jordy to give in or concede, Rafe leaped to the deck and strode aft, shouting for the men to return to the cutter. It still bobbed alongside the *Davina*. Rafe grabbed the mooring line and climbed down the rope to the boat's deck. The two-man crew followed—Watt and Derrick.

"Cast off," Rafe called to the brig's deck.

He expected Jordy, Mel, or one of the other men. Instead, Mrs. Lee grasped the line and leaned over the rail. "Why are you keeping us aboard?"

A sudden tumult of shouts from one of the merchantmen nearly drowned out her words. Pretending not to hear her at all, Rafe glanced toward the nearby vessel. Two men in tight coats better suited to a London drawing room than the deck of a brigantine struggled to get a longboat over the gunwale and into the water.

"Why?" Phoebe Lee shouted down to him.

He couldn't pretend not to hear that time. "I cannot say,

madam." Rafe looked up at her and wanted to tell her—something.

If she'd been angry, pleading, petulant, he would have cut the line and sailed off to the wharf. But she looked confused, frustrated, a little sad. He understood confusion, frustration, and, above all, sadness.

"If my mission is successful, I'll see to it you find a way home from here."

The men had the boat in the water—capsized.

"And George Chapman?" Mrs. Lee pressed. "Will you leave him to rot in the hulk after your promise to Belinda?"

He should, if the American had betrayed him. But he kept his word.

"Unless I'm unable, I'll see him free," he reassured her. "I simply will not need Mrs. Chapman's assistance."

A woman had joined the men on deck. She wore a cloak too heavy for the climate and doubled over as though in pain.

"Indeed." Mrs. Lee's face tightened. "And if you are unable?"

He curled one corner of his lips upward. "I have not said this to anyone for a ver' long time, but perhaps you can pray for me, if you're a praying lady."

"If I'm—" She winced as though he'd shoved an elbow into her diaphragm. "I should have been praying for you all along." With that, she turned away from the rail and trudged back to Mrs. Chapman.

As much queasiness as he'd ever felt in twenty-foot seas ravaged Rafe's body. He folded his arms across his middle and glanced at Derrick. "Cut the line. We can't continue to waste—"

The cries and confusion from the merchantman rose like a fast-moving storm. The two men ran to the starboard rail, shouting and waving at Rafe. The woman followed them for two steps, then doubled over with a scream.

Phoebe charged to the rail and leaned so far over she nearly toppled into the harbor. "Go help them. Go."

The directive proved unnecessary. The cutter was already headed for the merchantman, single sail sending the small craft skimming over the water despite the light breeze. Shouts rang across the water, words indistinct, the tone of panic clear from the gentlemen aboard the brigantine. The woman had vanished from sight.

"What's wrong?" Belinda slipped up beside Phoebe, Mel at her heels.

"I don't know for sure." Phoebe kept her voice neutral, her words careful. She guessed what was wrong. She hoped she was right. Already plans formed in her head.

"Captain Rafe is going aboard." Mel pointed to the other vessel.

Belinda caught hold of the girl's hand. "Pointing is rude."

"Then how are you supposed to know where I mean?"

"You may nod your head in that direction or gesture." Belinda sounded like her mother, prim and tight-lipped.

Phoebe tried not to laugh as she kept her gaze on the other ship, the cutter, Rafe Docherty. Surely he needed her. Surely he would return to her . . .

Someone called out. Even over the intervening space of water and through other harbor noises of boatmen and ship clatter, Phoebe recognized the voice—Docherty had commanded his men to do something.

Return. The cutter turned away from the merchantman and headed back to the *Davina*. Waiting, Phoebe held her breath, praying one word. *Please, please, please.*

The cutter bumped lightly against the brig's hull. "Mrs. Lee," Watt called to her, "Captain Rafe wants you."

"Thank you, Lord." Phoebe knotted her shawl to keep it

from slipping off into the water and kilted up her skirt. Undignified or not, showing stocking ankles or not, she intended to descend the easy way rather than wait for a chair to be rigged to lower her to the other boat like a net full of fish.

"Can I go too?" Mel asked.

"May I," Phoebe and Belinda chorused.

Mel sighed. "I want to go."

"Nay, lass, you stay aboard with Mrs. Chapman," Watt said. "'Tis no place for a girl."

"If you wait just a minute, ma'am," Derrick addressed Phoebe, "I'll fetch you a chair."

"No thank you." Phoebe grasped the rope and, eyes closed, clambered over the rail.

"Phoebe, you can't," Belinda cried.

"It's better than the chair." Mel laid a steadying hand on Phoebe's shoulder. "The chair twists and turns and makes a body ill."

"I've had more than enough of that." Phoebe managed a smile, pushed away from the side of the brig, and slid more than climbed to the swaying deck of the cutter.

Derrick caught her in hands the size of dinner plates and eased the last few feet of her descent. "You shouldn't have done that, ma'am."

"Well, I'm here now." Phoebe took a long breath to steady herself. "Let us go. The woman is in her lying-in, I presume?"

A ruddy hue rose under Derrick's dark skin. "Yes, ma'am. Captain Rafe said you was the best person to come help. Of course, Captain, he's—"

"Cast off," Watt barked from the tiller.

Derrick grumbled something and tugged on the line.

Phoebe grasped the low rail and leaned toward the merchantman as though they needed to travel a far journey and her motion made them sail faster. The distance vanished in moments, the ships close enough she could have swum through the calm waters. Before she could speculate on the woman's condition or make any plans for her next bid for freedom, they reached the brigantine, where a chair already waited for her.

Mel was right—climbing a rope was better. Phoebe arrived on the merchantman's deck feeling sick and shaken from the spinning on the way up.

Docherty grasped her elbows and steadied her. "Are you a'right?"

"No, but I will be." She managed a smile.

"There's a good lass. Mrs. Torren is needing a steady hand." He smiled back at her. No, not smiled. He never smiled; he turned up one corner of his mouth in a softening of its usual grim line.

His fine mouth with its firm, full lips relaxed, and something inside Phoebe tightened, twisted, shivered through her. If she could get him to smile all the way . . .

She wouldn't be in his company long enough to think of that, of how else those lips could soften—

She jerked away from him. "Mrs. Torren?"

"Aye, one of the passengers. Her husband and his uncle are alone here on the brigantine while the crew fetches supplies and gets orders from their naval escort." Docherty reclaimed one of Phoebe's elbows and began to walk with her toward the aft companionway. "She's come to her time early."

"Oh dear." Phoebe shivered for an entirely different reason, her mind skimming to an incident with Tabitha when a patient went into her travail early. It had ended in tragedy. "How—how early?"

"She does not ken. I dare say she's no more than sixteen." His hand tightened on Phoebe's arm. "I do not like to think that this could be Mel in four years."

"Mel will have more sense."

"A tongue as tart as a green apple, I see. But let us hope 'tis true. Here we go." He ushered Phoebe down the steep steps and into a cramped but expensively appointed cabin complete with velvet curtains over the porthole.

A bunk filled most of the space. On the fine linen sheets lay a young woman barely older than a child, not much larger than Mel. Her pale hair spread out on the pillow like a silvery-gold cloud, and terror filled her wide brown eyes. As Phoebe stepped over the coaming, the girl clutched at her swollen belly and screamed.

Phoebe resisted the urge to clap her hands over her ears. The young man perched on a sea chest next to the head of the bunk possessed no such compunctions. His handsome features twisted as though he too experienced the labor pains. Phoebe glanced at him, glanced at the girl, glanced at the cramped space, and wanted to scream herself.

She couldn't help this woman. What ever made her think she was ready to practice midwifery on her own? The ladies of Loudoun County were right in rarely calling on her. Belinda might be better off without her.

Phoebe took a step backward and fetched up hard against Rafe Docherty's chest. For a moment, he closed his arms around her, held her close, his lips at her ear, his breath fanning her cheek. "You are a qualified midwife, no? You're wanting to do this all the time, no?"

She nodded.

"Then do not fail this lass now. She needs you." He released her and slipped away.

But his warmth remained, spilling through her, easing her fear. She could do this. She must.

She looked at the young man. "Out. Get me boiling water and clean cloths."

"How—how do I do that?" His lower lip protruded as though he were about to cry.

"Someone will show you. Now go." She stepped out of the doorway and swept her hand toward the companionway.

The man departed like she'd kicked him in the back of his nankeen breeches.

Phoebe closed the door. "What's your name?"

"T-Tess. Who are you?"

"I'm Phoebe. I'm a midwife."

"Ooooh." Some of the fear left the girl's eyes. "You can help me?"

"Yes."

We can always help, Tabitha had said. *Even if it's only by praying.*

"Let me examine you. No, wait." Phoebe opened the door. "I need soap and water now."

Derrick brought news that the young man, the husband, had settled in the bow with a bottle of rum. "And Captain Rafe has gone ashore with the cutter."

"And left us stranded here?" Phoebe pretended to be annoyed.

Getting away from Derrick would surely be easier than from Rafe Docherty.

"I righted the longboat." Derrick grinned. "These landlubbers don't know what they're doing."

"That's good anyway. Can you get me boiling water?"

"The other gentleman seems competent at that. He's the uncle."

"Then please fetch water for me. I can do nothing until I have clean hands."

He brought her soap and water from the elder Mr. Torren. She washed on the deck, then returned to the cabin and examined the young woman. And examined her again.

Then Phoebe sat on one of the sea chests and closed her eyes to pray.

She'd never delivered twins. She only knew they tended to come early. And the young woman's pains seemed extraordinarily fierce, or else she was uncommonly poor at managing.

After two hours, during which the spasms of labor grew closer and closer together, Phoebe began to suspect the latter. Tess Torren wept and protested and declared again and again that she couldn't go through with the birth.

"I don't want it like this," the girl sobbed.

"But it's how we get babies." Phoebe sponged the girl's face with cool water. "You'll forget the pain once you hold him or her in your arms."

Them in her arms.

Phoebe shuddered and prayed some more.

"How would you know?" Tess's lip protruded. "Do you have children?"

Phoebe didn't answer. She couldn't share that she had held her son for only minutes before he quit breathing, too young to hang on to life on his own. Yet in those moments, she had forgotten the pain of the preceding hours.

But not the reason why he'd come more than two months early.

Momentarily, her hands balled into fists before she managed to relax them, wash them, and examine the patient again.

"Only a little while longer."

Too soon for her to face whether or not she could truly manage on her own. Not soon enough to get it behind her and the best or worst exposed.

"It'll all be over with soon." She repeated the litany again and again until, with a speed that left her shouting for aid, the babies came, two tiny, perfect infants, a boy and a girl.

Derrick took the first one, washing him and wrapping him with hands that swallowed up the child in infinite gentleness. Phoebe managed the second child before the uncle appeared and lent his aid so she could finish with the mother.

"May I see him?" Mrs. Torren asked.

"It's them." Phoebe laid the boy in her arms. "He's perfect."

He was red and wrinkled and heart-achingly beautiful in his lusty cry. Not too early at all, but new mothers rarely knew when the first child would come.

And Tess Torren seemed to have forgotten her pain indeed. A beatific smile softened her pinched features, and her eyes widened with wonder. "Two of them. I managed to do even better than I'm supposed to."

Phoebe tried not to laugh. "Yes, you did well. Now how are you going to manage?"

"I don't know." Tess yawned. "I'm too tired to think of that."

"You'll need to." Phoebe glanced to the uncle and noticed the husband standing in the companionway behind him.

The young man's face was pale but composed, and he didn't reek of rum. He blinked several times as though stepping from blackness to sunlight, and his mouth worked without words emerging. Tears lent his blue eyes a glassy glaze.

"Come in, Mr. Torren." Phoebe offered him a smile. "If you're sober."

"I am." He flushed. "Rum doesn't set well with me. But Tess—" He blinked and the tears spilled unchecked. "Is she all right?"

"She's all right. But she'll need a woman to help her." Phoebe slipped past the uncle and beckoned to Derrick. "Let them be alone a while. I'd like to talk to you."

She led him on deck and inhaled deeply of air that didn't

118

smell like the blood and other effluvium of the birthing chamber. "I need you to take me ashore."

"I can't do that, ma'am." Derrick shook his head.

"But I need to find her a woman who's willing to sail with them."

"I can go."

"Do you know what to look for?"

"Some." He sighed. "Not much. My wife always managed on her own."

"You have a wife?" Phoebe asked, distracted.

"Yes, ma'am. She lives in Edinburgh——" He broke off on a laugh. "Didn't you think they have black folk in Edinburgh?"

"I'm sorry. I'm from Virginia." Phoebe's face grew warm.

Virginia, for all its beauty, wasn't a welcoming place for men like Derrick.

"I understand." As she had seen more often than not on this big, gentle man, Derrick's smile was warm, kind. "I almost ended up in Virginia. I was on a French merchantman nearly nine years ago. Captain Rafe captured it and freed me, then found my wife and babies on Jamaica and took them to his country to live."

A kind and generous act. Not the act of a man who had abducted—or abetted abducting—her.

"Then he'll surely understand why I need to go find a woman for this poor child," Phoebe insisted.

"He'd tan my hide if I let you go ashore right now."

Phoebe laughed. "I can imagine Rafe Docherty doing many things, but laying a hand on you is not one of them. Now please take me ashore, or that new mother is going to be at her wit's end within a day."

And surely God smiled on Phoebe's petition for freedom, with all this happening to support her bid to get ashore and to people who could help her.

Derrick tapped the toe of his boot on the deck. The wails of two babies rose up the companionway along with Mrs. Torren's exclamation, holding panic.

"Get the longboat ready." Phoebe tossed the words over her shoulder as she dashed back to the cabin.

She started issuing instructions the instant she stepped over the coaming. "We need cots for these babies. Crates lined with soft cloth will do. They need to be kept safe and warm. Now. Go." She looked at the uncle, who seemed the most competent of the two men. "Tess, you need to stay calm. You'll upset the babies if you get distraught, and your milk may not come in. Now let's work on this." She glanced at the husband. "She may be more comfortable with you gone for a bit."

Chin not quite steady, he fled.

Phoebe knelt by the bed, holding one baby while Mrs. Torren held the other. "Do you want to nurse or find a wet nurse?"

"I—I don't know. Which is better?"

"Finding a healthy wet nurse this quickly could be difficult."

No sense admonishing her to have thought of these things ahead of time before going to sea in her condition. She might not have had a choice.

Unlike Belinda, who could so easily be in a similar position should the rest of the voyage not go quickly enough. All the more reason to get them free.

"So let's see how you do. It's not very successful to start with . . ."

Things went better than Phoebe had hoped. Best of all, the love the young woman showed for her babies brought a rush of tears to Phoebe's eyes. She wanted to lay her head down and sob for all she had lost and never expected to have again.

She sighed with relief when the uncle returned with two

small crates lined thickly enough with fine linen to pad the sides and protect the infants from splinters. At last, as dusk began to fall over the harbor, mother and babies slept, and Derrick agreed to take her ashore.

"But you stick with me, you hear?"

She heard but didn't acknowledge so. She kept silent on the way ashore, mind racing, planning. Surely in a busy harbor she could get away.

After she found Mrs. Torren help.

She started at the market. Most stalls still stood despite the late hour. Torches lighted the wares of fruit and ribbons, seafood and costly fabrics, exotic spices and costlier jewelry—a pirate's treasure trove of goods and people. Phoebe began to ask after an appropriate woman.

Darkness fell, and the stalls began to close up. Every woman she asked for information sent her in another direction. Her feet dragged. Her stomach growled. For the first time in days, she wanted to eat. But she had no money. Belinda hadn't brought Phoebe's purse along, no doubt on purpose. She wouldn't ask Derrick for coin and be beholden to a man she could never repay, a man she intended to betray the first chance she found.

He walked along with her, his very size keeping the unsavory elements of humanity away. And he talked to people too, getting the attention of those who shied away from Phoebe's American accent.

In the end, he found a nursery maid for Mrs. Torren. The woman was young, spotlessly clean, and employed as a maid to one of the island's plantation owners. "But I'd like to leave this island," she admitted, shifting a basket of sweetmeats and fruit from one hip to the other. "Going to sea doesn't frighten me."

After that, slipping away proved almost too easy for Phoebe's comfort. While she and Derrick waited for the maid to give notice and pack her things, Phoebe asked for a necessary, then simply left the house and walked the mile back to St. George's. In all her questioning, she'd managed to learn of the diplomats sailing on the American ship and where they were staying. She headed straight for that inn, stepped into the light and noise and stench of spilled wine.

And saw Rafe Docherty on the other side of the taproom.

8

Phoebe stood in the doorway. Rafe caught sight of her over the heads of other patrons, sailors mostly. Several of those sailors drifted toward her, eyes intent upon her golden hair, her fine figure.

The sailor who should have been with her appeared nowhere in the inn. No one could miss Derrick if he stood anywhere near. Rafe would have him cleaning bilges for the next two months for letting her come ashore. He'd make Derrick clean bilges indefinitely if he'd allowed her to come ashore unaccompanied. If anything happened to her—

He began wending his way through the crowd, being careful not to jostle the elbows of men lifting tankards of ale and stronger spirits. He didn't want a fight or any distraction to keep him from reaching Phoebe before she vanished.

Men swarmed near her. She darted a glance around the room, her eyes wide, her lips parted. Her gaze clashed with Rafe's. Her head came up, her chin set, and she spun away. In a flash she vanished out the door and into the night.

Rafe forgot about care and shoved the imbibers aside. A chorus of protests followed him; a fist landed on his shoulder. He dodged and ducked and sped out the door. He slid to a halt. Which way?

Footfalls clattered to his left. He sprinted in that direction. "Mrs. Lee, stop! Phoebe!"

A flash of golden hair gleamed in the light of a torch. Rafe pressed forward. He could catch one small female.

One small, quick female. She slid between two buildings so close together Rafe needed to turn sideways to fit. The action slowed him. It didn't slow her. Her heels rattled on stones behind a building, then died away altogether, drowned in the tumult of another tavern's off-key fiddle. Rafe paused at the end of the close buildings, ears straining to hear, eyes straining to see. A crowd of gentlemen and brightly dressed women cascaded from the door across from Rafe. The aromas of roasting meat accompanied them with a spill of bright light from the candles inside. Other than the merrymaking crowd, the street lay empty. No sign of Phoebe.

He couldn't let her go. She mustn't find the Americans. If she told Brock where she'd been, he would vanish again, and no amount of manipulation of George Chapman could draw him out again. Nine years of searching, earning the wealth he needed and hunting the world for the elusive diplomat, would be wasted. He couldn't retire. He couldn't keep Mel ashore safe from harm, educated with females to become a lady good and proper.

He turned toward the harbor. She wouldn't go further inland, further from her goal of getting help. No Americans and few naval officers sought out the inns and taverns in the environs of the city. But a dozen streets and alleyways lay between Rafe and the wharves.

He slowed his pace, proceeded with caution. Every alleyway and intersecting street received his scrutiny. Most lay in darkness. Some sported lanterns or torches above the doors, and light poured through windows.

Movement in an alley smelling of rotten fruit and spilled perfume caught his attention. Then the gleam of gold sent him racing down an alley and into the back door of a shop.

Fabric surrounded him—silk like sapphires, brocade shimmering like Mayan silver, muslin shot with gold. It rustled and swayed in the breeze of his passing like the skirts of dancing ladies.

His running lady appeared nowhere in the storeroom. No flash of gilt hair, no flicker of her green gown, not a whisper of her dainty slippers on the wooden floorboards. He paused, listening for the sigh, the breath of another being in the room.

He heard the voice, the nasal tenor voice with the absent R of northeastern America. The voice he hadn't heard for nine years. The voice of the man he'd been trying to find all day.

He'd found James Brock without needing to free George Chapman from prison, without having to drag two females across the Atlantic, without having to face his growing attraction to Phoebe Lee.

Let her escape. If she could return to America, good for her ingenuity. He headed toward the sound of that voice, the man who had destroyed his life.

He flung open the door into the shop itself. Scents of sandalwood, bergamot, and patchouli assailed his nostrils. More brilliant fabrics from the Orient tiered before him for yards, filling the sight, the senses.

But not so much he missed the four men at the far end of the narrow chamber. Four of them, not one.

One man stood behind the counter, his face ashen, his hands trembling on a length of fabric he measured. Another man stood between two others. He was tall, slim, and elegant in a suit of deep blue wool with etched silver buttons and an enormous ruby in the center of a snowy cravat, his silver hair cut short and brushed forward. The men on either side of him stood at attention like soldiers on guard.

They were soldiers on guard. They wore the clothing of gentlemen too, but sported rapiers and pistols slung from belts beneath their short coats. And their dark eyes never stopped scanning the world around them.

They lighted on Rafe, and the men stiffened. "Sir," one said.

"What?" Brock turned his head.

For the first time in nine years, Rafe came face-to-face with James Brock and his cold, ice-blue eyes.

"Who are you?" Brock demanded. "You look familiar."

"I should." Rafe took a step forward, his hand dropping to his dirk. "You as good as killed my wife."

"You must be mad." Brock yawned and returned to his transaction.

Rafe took another step forward, his heart racing, the rest of him controlled. "Does the name Rafael Docherty mean anything to you? Or perhaps Davina Docherty?"

Brock dropped his purse. Coins chimed and rolled across the floor. He and his guards made no move to collect them. The shopkeeper dropped to his hands and knees and began to crawl after the money.

Rafe took another step forward. "Thirty pieces of sil'er, Mr. Ambassador?"

"I have no idea what you're talking about." Brock's face shone as white as his cravat. "Shopkeeper, get rid of this man. He's annoying me."

The shopkeeper remained on hands and knees.

"Go away, whoever you are, or my men will make you," Brock commanded.

"What's an American politician doing on a British colony during a war?" Rafe asked, still quiet, still calm—outwardly.

"No business of a Scot." Brock raised one hand encased in a cream leather glove. "Men, remove this foulness from my sight."

The men stalked forward. Rafe held his ground.

126

And a gentle hand dropped onto his arm like a feather. "Come along, Rafe," said Phoebe's melted-honey voice. "I can buy fabric in another store."

"Get out of here, Mrs. Lee." Rafe spoke in an undertone. "This won't be fit for a lady."

"I can't leave alone, my dear. I'm afraid to go into these streets on my own."

When she'd been leading him on a merry chase down alley after avenue moments earlier?

Rafe barely suppressed a snort of amusement. "They're safer than this store." He advanced another step toward Brock. "Call off your ruffians and pay what you owe me."

"Get rid of him," Brock growled.

"The lady—" one henchman began.

"If she's with this man," Brock drawled, "she's no lady."

Rafe closed the distance in two strides and slapped Brock's face with the flat of his palm. "You will be meeting me for that if naught else, and there's plenty else for you to—"

"Rafe, beware!" Phoebe cried his name, the warning.

Movement flashed in the corner of his eye. He spun, threw up his arm, blocked the cudgel swinging toward his head. His arm went numb. Pain seared through his ribs on the other side. He swung, landed a fist in the second man's face. Another to the first, a kick at Brock's knee.

Brock went down with a cry. The others charged at Rafe, one flourishing his sword, the other a pistol.

"Run!" Phoebe shoved between Rafe and the advancing guards. A roll of fabric flew through the air, sailed over the two men. Then she grabbed Rafe's hand and began to drag him from the store.

They darted through the piles of material, scattering them behind in fluttering clouds of color, a trap to coil around unwary feet. The alley received them with its noisome odors of rotting fruit. Another alley reeked of sewage, and a twisting lane carried them past shops and pedestrians, produce piled in pyramids, and ribbons flying from hooks like birds. They raced, twisting and turning around obstacles, never losing hold of one another's hands, gasping for breath in the cool night air. A glance back showed pursuit—a brute gaining on them, pistol in hand.

They reached the market square. Despite the hour, sailors, bawds, and fine ladies and gentlemen from the plantations swam around them, headed to and from vessels, to and from entertainments, heading home. They could no longer run. Neither could the guard on their heels. Nor could he fire his pistol.

Breathless, Rafe drew Phoebe between two booths and onto the harbor side of the vendors. A cool breeze off the sea fanned over them. Rafe stumbled to a halt in a pool of darkness between the lights of the market and the harbor. Phoebe collapsed against him, gasping, sobbing.

"Are you all right?" He touched her cheek, slid his fingers beneath her chin to raise her face.

She blinked up at him. "That was quite terrifying. I thought—" She paused and brushed his hair away from his face. "You're injured."

"'Tis naught."

Her touching him wasn't, though. Pleasure radiated from the contact. He grasped her hand in his, drew it away from his face, then brought it back to kiss her palm.

She no longer smelled of lavender. The delicate aroma of jasmine wafted from her skin. He inhaled, and something inside him gave way, snapped, dissolved. The raucous tumult of the market and harbor vanished. Phoebe stood before him with soft eyes and softer lips. Eyes meant for gazing into. Lips intended for kissing.

So he kissed her. He slipped his arms around her, drew her close to him, and covered her lips with his.

She tasted of apples, of ambrosia, of a future he didn't think he had. Yet he took it then in the sweet contact, and she made no resistance. She clung to his shoulders and kissed him back.

And his heart softened from a sharp pain to a dull ache in his chest. If he kept on kissing her, the discomfort might vanish forever, dissolved in the tenderness of a lady determined to take actions that could destroy him.

If he kept on kissing her, she might forget her intention to leave.

When she thought he might kiss her the other night, she knew then she would have slapped his face for his audacity. But this time he hadn't given her a chance to think, time to prepare for the contact. One moment they were running from men who wanted to harm Rafe. The next he held her in his arms and robbed her of breath, of reason, of everything but the need to stay where she was—safe and warm.

Well, maybe not safe. Wanting this man to continue to hold her seemed the antithesis of safe. She should run from attraction to him, run from the melting effect of his hands in her hair, his hair thick and soft beneath her fingers—contact like she'd never experienced from her husband, where a kiss meant power over her, not affection.

Surely Rafe Docherty didn't mean affection either. He couldn't. He was chasing her down to stop her from escaping to those who could get her home. He wanted, needed, to keep her aboard his brig, where she couldn't divulge information about what he'd done to her and how he intended to use Belinda to somehow free George Chapman from prison.

And what better way to keep her than to invite a liaison.

She planted her palms in the middle of his chest and pushed. "Stop. Stop. I can't breathe."

He freed her at once, but both corners of his firm mouth turned up in a near smile that tilted the corners of his eyes. "I was thinking breathing might not be necessary."

"No. I mean, yes. That is—" Her hands flew to her cheeks. They burned. "I shouldn't have let you do that."

"Nay, and I shouldn't have done it." His voice dropped to a purr. "But I do not regret it just the same."

Neither did she. With a glance, a touch, she might be tempted to kiss him again.

She took a step back. They were in public. Surrounding men and women came into focus, most of whom paid them no attention at all. A few grinned and called encouragement.

Phoebe's face would surely burst into flame at any moment if it grew any hotter. She absolutely must obtain transportation to the American vessel or British frigate, get far away from Rafe Docherty and temptation as fast as she could.

He caught hold of one of her hands and drew it into the crook of his elbow, holding it in place with his fingers laced through hers. "I cannot let you go, Phoebe."

He called her Phoebe. She couldn't object without sounding like a priggish hypocrite. She couldn't object to a number of things now that she'd let him hold her in his arms and kiss her.

"I have to go." Her voice held a note of desperation from the very fact that she wasn't angry, frightened, indignant. Quite the opposite, the true difficulty for her. "Please."

"Phoebe, 'tis not safe for you now that Brock has seen you with me." His voice, his face, his calm demeanor held no guile.

A chill ran through Phoebe. That man with the pistol had chased them both. He wasn't around now, or remained lost in the crowd running, strolling, stumbling around them, yet he'd been there, burly and too well armed. James Brock, George Chapman's primary investor, was Rafe Docherty's enemy.

"Why?" was all she could manage.

"I cannot say now. We must be returning to the *Davina*." He headed toward the end of the wharf. "Where's Derrick?"

"I don't know. I gave him the slip."

"That was unkind of you. By rights I could have him flogged for that."

"But you wouldn't."

The muscles in the arm beneath her hand rippled as though emotion so strong he couldn't contain it in his chest ran through him. He said nothing until they reached the place where the cutter bobbed, moored to a piling. Then he paused and faced her, his face soft in the yellow glow of the lanterns slung from boats. "Thank you for that. I am uncertain I deserve your confidence."

So he felt guilty for taking her with him against her will?

Phoebe's stomach knotted. She jerked her hand free of his and crossed her arms over her middle, a poor shield between her and the man who frightened her for the sake of her soul, for her heart, not her physical being.

"How did you give him the slip?"

"I—oh my!" Her hand flew to her lips. "My patient. Mrs. Torren. A nursemaid. Please, take me out to their ship."

"'Tis a brigantine, not a ship."

Phoebe screwed up her mouth. "It has masts and sails and there's a new mother aboard with too little help. Please take me."

"Aye, right away, madam, though I do not see Watt about. Can you handle a sail?"

Phoebe laughed.

"Nay, I suppose I did not think you could. A'right then, I'll get—ah, here's Watt."

Watt ran down the wharf, boots clattering. "Captain, Mrs. Lee, 'tis sorry I am not to have been here sooner. I saw Derrick with a lass and wanted to ken what he was about."

"Aye, I should think you would." Rafe eyed Phoebe.

"We hired a nursemaid for Mrs. Torren. That's why we came ashore." Phoebe lifted her chin, daring him to argue with her action.

He simply nodded, then picked her up and set her on the cutter's deck. Her skin felt cold where his hands had rested on her waist for only those moments. More proof she must get away. Only one man had caught her interest since her husband's death, and that had gone nowhere. His heart had belonged to another before she even met him.

Rafe Docherty didn't have a heart, or not one he would ever be willing to share. He would toy with her, use her attraction to his advantage, and leave her aching inside with longings she had no business feeling. Seeing him day in and day out could do nothing beyond harming her spirit, now that her heart had so carefully healed after the treatment she had received at the hands of a spoiled, selfish, and just plain mean man.

She moved as far away from Rafe as she could on the tiny sailboat and began to recite Scripture in her head to keep herself from hearing his voice, so rumbling and soft like a cat's purr, tingling from her ears to her toes.

"Nay, in all these things we are more than conquerors through Him that loved us." She murmured the thirty-seventh verse of Romans chapter eight. "More than conquerors. More than—"

He touched her shoulder. "Are you a'right?"

"Yes, yes, I'm well." She edged away from him.

"I'll give you a bit of explanation when we return to the *Davina*. Since you're now involved, you deserve it."

No, she didn't want an explanation, more involvement in his life. She said nothing.

He strode away from her to take control of the tiller. He and Watt talked over the minor work of hoisting the single sail and heading across the harbor to the merchantman.

"I saw Derrick getting into the longboat," Watt was explaining. "He had a pretty tale about taking the young lady to that merchantman. She seemed to trust him. But I do not ken what the true story is."

"Mrs. Lee concurs. 'Tis why she was on shore."

And to get away from him, another failed opportunity. And she'd neglected her patient to do so.

She sank to her knees and buried her face in her arms. "God, what are You letting happen to me?"

"Mrs. Lee, are you unwell?" Rafe asked.

He'd called her Phoebe moments earlier, the very sound of her name a near caress on his lips.

She shook her head and continued to pray, moving her lips in silent supplication. *I so want to serve You and have failed in this chance I've gotten.*

She needed forgiveness, guidance, release from her predicament, especially the way her ears, her eyes, her entire being strained toward a certain man, but those words of supplication would not come to her.

I don't want to care that way again. He seems to have no use for You. He's everything I don't want in my life.

The cutter bumped the side of the merchantman. Watt called up to the deck. A moment later, two sailors appeared to make the cutter fast and help the arrivals aboard.

"How is Mrs. Torren?" Phoebe asked the men.

They exchanged glances and grimaces.

"I think she's well," said an older man with a harelip, his words difficult to understand. "But those babies never stop their fussing."

"We'll never get no sleep," the younger one said.

"Not within earshot, that's likely." Phoebe smiled at them. "I expect quarters below deck will become more valuable."

"Ain't that the truth," the younger one agreed. "Can you maybe take 'em aboard your brig?"

Rafe laughed. "I am thinking no."

A good thing, as they might end up with their own wailing infant.

The thought gave Phoebe a certain satisfaction. Served him right for taking Belinda aboard.

"Go on aft," the older sailor said. "Your other man is here with the girl."

Phoebe went aft, Rafe trailing behind, dawdling at the top of the companionway ladder. Guarding the top of the companionway ladder. Phoebe kept her back to him, her distance from him, and looked in on her patient.

Mrs. Torren lay half propped up on her bunk, one baby in her arms, the other in the arms of the new nursemaid. Both infants were, for the moment, quiet.

"I'd like to examine you to make sure all is well," Phoebe said by way of greeting.

"I can't thank you enough for sending this girl along." Mrs. Torren glanced at the maid. "She had the baby quiet in a moment."

"I like babies." The maid glowed as though she were the new mother.

"You should have brought a maid along with you. Or perhaps a midwife. There are women who will hire themselves out, you know."

But of course the young woman didn't know or couldn't

have done so, or she might have taken the necessary steps to have company and help ready.

Phoebe began to examine the young mother, who wasn't in the least embarrassed by the intimacy with another female in the room. The babies continued to sleep. Phoebe began to gnaw her lower lip as she contemplated her own words and disliked them heartily.

Certain all was well—with the new mother at any rate—she bade mother and maid good night. "I'll return in the morning."

If Rafe Docherty let her off the *Davina* again. If she could bear to be near him long enough to ask.

Bear to be? No, she liked being with him. *Risk* being with him was more the truth.

Seeing him standing in the glow of a lantern, his hair burnished crimson satin in the flickering light, his face a silhouette of strong bones and smooth planes, she accepted she had two reasons to get away from the privateer as fast and as far as possible—she hated being at sea, and she was losing her heart to him.

And as much as she wanted away so badly she contemplated the idea of jumping overboard and swimming for the American diplomatic vessel, she had one major reason to remain within the danger Rafe Docherty could prove to her heart, her soul. She couldn't leave Belinda, a patient, to inexperienced sailors. Doing so went against every vow she'd taken when Tabitha accepted her as an apprentice and Phoebe moved into her home to be at hand whenever someone needed the midwife.

Phoebe stepped onto the deck and held her hands out to Rafe. "I'm ready to return."

"Are you now?" He didn't take her hands but stood with his fingers stuffed into the pockets of his breeches. "I do not think you ken what you are accepting. I will not—I cannot—give you the freedom of the brig after you tried to run to my enemy."

"I didn't know he was your enemy." Phoebe spoke each word with care to keep the panic edge from her tone. But panic clenched at her middle at the notion of confinement in the cabin, Belinda's whining, the stale air. The sickness.

She clutched at the folds of her skirt. "You don't need to make me a prisoner, Captain. I—" she swallowed against dryness in her throat—"I give you my word I won't run away again."

9

James Brock had eluded Rafe again. As he waited for Phoebe aboard the merchantman, he watched the activity aboard the American schooner. Too much activity for an evening in harbor. They were sailing on the outgoing tide, and because of the flag of truce, Rafe could do nothing about it.

"Coward." He spat over the rail of his own vessel two hours later as the sails of the schooner caught the wind and bellied out, sending the graceful craft skimming into the Atlantic. "You will not face your crimes."

Though he might try again to kill Rafe in cold blood. Or rather have one of his henchmen kill the man who could expose him for what he was—a liar, a cheat, a thief, a murderer. He'd tried before, in the early days after Rafe escaped the Barbary pirates with Mel and a rage so deep it still burned in his gut, burned so hot it dried any tears he might have shed for his wife.

It blazed again now, roared inside him until he feared his hands would rip the taffrail from the deck. He shook with it, with his inability to give chase and bring the man down once and for all.

But he wasn't going to lose Phoebe.

He caught a whiff of her delicate jasmine scent, soap from the merchantman, before he heard the whisper of her slippers and skirt on the deck blend with the sigh of rippling wavelets against the brig's hull. With all his will, he managed not to turn around and draw her to him and kiss her again. For those few minutes on the docks, he'd forgotten Brock and hatred and even Davina. With the fire of rage now ablaze afresh, the temptation to seek solace from the beautiful widow tightened every nerve in his body.

He would not disrespect her that way.

But she'd promised to stay. And now she'd come to him. For the past two hours she'd been below, soothing Belinda's histrionics over being left behind all day and knowing nothing of what was afoot. Now Phoebe glided up beside him within touching distance.

He continued to grip the taffrail so he didn't touch her. "'Tis late for you to be up and about. Should you not be in your bed?"

"When there's a caged lion pacing overhead?" She smiled at him in the blend of silvery moonlight and golden binnacle lantern glow. "I couldn't stay away."

"A braw lady to approach a lion in his lair." He allowed himself the luxury of one ghost of a touch on her face, the merest hint of his fingertips skimming across the curve of her cheekbone.

No more. No more. In harbor, no helmsman stood at the wheel to force him to propriety. The nearest watch stood halfway down the main deck and out of sight.

"And I've not paced this half hour or more," he added with the merest hint of a smile.

She'd been drawn to him as he wanted her to be, connected to his spirit because of those moments of contact on the wharf, those seconds of admitting their attraction to one another. Attraction without love or even liking and respect on her side. Something purely carnal and therefore wrong with a good woman like her.

Completely wrong regardless of the woman, a faint voice from his past reminded him—a past whose teachings he'd set aside for the sake of destroying James Brock.

She laid her hand over the cheek he'd caressed. "Nor have you spoken to me since I promised not to run off again."

"Perhaps I do not want you to change your mind. And if I do not speak with you, you cannot tell me otherwise."

"Do you think I'm that fickle?"

He quirked up one side of his mouth. "You're a female, no?"

She narrowed her eyes at him.

He laughed. Doing so felt like a rusty chain drawing the sound from the deep well of his chest. Yet once the sound spilled past his lips, breathing grew easier and he could speak truth to her. "I ken you have questions I do not care to answer."

"Don't you think I deserve answers?" She gestured toward the town, still bright with torches and lanterns and raucous with music and mirth. "He was chasing me with a pistol and a club."

"Only because you chose to be with me."

"And if I hadn't, you'd likely be dead now."

"You have no faith in my ability to fight." He tried to smile, to make light of her statement.

She pursed her lips. Instead of the tightness making them thinner, it emphasized their fullness, their ripe strawberry pinkness.

He turned his back to the rail and grasped it with both hands hard enough that a splinter drove into his palm. He welcomed the pain. "Aye, I ken you hear the talk aboard— I've lost my will to fight. I have. I never set out to become a fighting man. On the contrary—" He shook his head, erasing the memory of a life to which he could never return. "I found a way to draw out the man who has eluded me for nine years. 'Tis all I wish to fight. No more French merchantmen and certainly not Americans. I do not need more plunder. I need only to see James Brock at my feet, as his actions—" He broke off again. "Nay, lass, I will say no more."

"Then this will be a long night." She stood in front of him, the lantern light behind her creating a golden nimbus of her hair, an angel's halo. "I'm not going anywhere until I have more answers than that."

"You will grow mighty weary."

She folded her arms across her chest.

"I'll take you and Mrs. Chapman and Mel ashore tomorrow. Any danger has sailed."

"Can you be certain of that? He might have left his men behind."

"Perhaps. I'll have Jordy go ahead and make certain, but I doot he has. 'Tis a hostile place for a lone American."

"But two American ladies are safe?"

"Aye, with me you will be. The market is fine with goods—"

She shot out her hands and grasped his shoulders. "I may be a Carter by birth and a Lee by marriage, but I am no flibbertigibbet of a female more interested in fripperies than a man's life." Her voice dropped. Her eyes sought and held his. "Yours, for example."

"My life is doomed to the pit. Do not fash—um, concern yourself over it."

He worried himself over how he would manage not to kiss her again in the next half a minute if she didn't move away from him. It would work to distract her, perhaps even drive her into hiding.

And would cheapen her.

He tore his gaze away and stared past her to the line of foam creaming against the mouth of the harbor, and the vast, black ocean beyond. Once again his enemy had vanished into that endless sea. But not forever. James Brock couldn't run forever or hide beneath a flag of truce like a child hiding under his mother's apron.

"No one's life is doomed to the pit until it's over. Jesus is always ready to receive you if you—"

He laid a finger across her lips. "No more. I grew up in the kirk. I ken all the right words and actions, how to repent and save my soul from condemnation forever. But any desire to give my life over to God died with my wife on the deck of a Barbary pirate's boat. She died screaming for God to save her, but He did not. Instead, He's allowed James Brock to prosper when 'tis his fault Davina died with a knife across her throat. But not before they used her while they forced me to watch. All because James Brock did not keep his word, because he took every farthing my family possessed and lined his own pockets. And you want to talk to me about Jesus ready to accept me if only I—what? Repent of my sins? Give up my desire for revenge? Let a murderer go? Nay, lass, you can keep your God." Not until he ran out of words and the quiet of the brig settled around them did he hear the savagery of his tone, a savagery cultivated in nine years of nightmares and pain, in blood and the burning pain of hatred.

Phoebe had heard it, though. She'd understood his words and possibly more. Tears spilled down her cheeks in silent, silver ribbons. Her lips moved, but she said nothing. Her fingers flexed on his shoulders, and she laid her head against his chest. She wrapped her arms around him and held him.

No one had held him in comfort since his mother had also died beneath the relentless Mediterranean sun. His chest tightened. His throat thickened. The urge to hold Phoebe close, bury his face in her hair, and weep as she did sent barely suppressed shudders running through him.

He remained motionless. He wouldn't weep as she did, silently, gracefully. He would weep like a mountain cat deprived of her prey—with soul-deep, howling anguish. He must hold on to his pain. Without it, he knew nothing.

But he let her continue to hold him until her tears dried and her breathing grew steady. He couldn't have pushed her away had his life depended on it. She was too soft, too warm, too kind—everything he could not allow himself to have and yet longed for with every particle of his being.

"So you ken the truth now." His voice was rough, but not with anger this time. "'Tis not a tale for a lady's ears."

"Even the simplified version I suspect you gave me." She released him, leaving him cold. "It was worse, wasn't it?"

"I do not wish to say. You're a lady—"

"I'm a midwife. Birth is untidy and sometimes worse than usual. I watched a woman die before my eyes, with hemorrhaging we couldn't stop." She looked away, blinking. "And still what your wife suffered was worse. That woman was in her bed with her husband holding one hand and her mother holding the other."

"Davina's father remained in Edinburgh, but my mither—" The break in his voice left him speechless for a full minute. He took in more than one ragged breath before he could continue. "She was with Davina."

Phoebe's eyes widened. She gasped.

"And my father they made a toy of like a cat does a mouse." He couldn't stop now. The sluice gate had opened and the floodwaters descended. "James Brock was to pay a ransom for us. He was a diplomat for the Americans. They would not pay ransoms to pirates, and my own country was taking too long, but I got the money together. I took every pound, shilling, and pence my family had earned and saved for years of hard work and took it to Brock, but he sold me out. Me with my three-year-old daughter just trying to get our loved ones free ended up on the pirate's boat instead of Brock's. Brock expected them to kill me too, while he ran off with the money and my vessel. But they set Mel and me ashore on Naples after—after they'd killed my parents and wife. And you want me to repent instead of seeing this man receive justice?"

She clasped her hands before her and once again looked him in the eyes. "Yes."

"Ah, you dear, innocent lady. We'll see if your faith is ever sorely tested, if you feel the same."

"God doesn't test us beyond what we can endure."

"'Tis a falsehood, that. I am a living testimony to say my faith died on the deck of that boat."

"A true faith—"

"Hush now." He stopped her words with his lips this time, a swift brush of contact. "Go to your bed. I have no more patience for talk of true faith. My thoughts are straying elsewhere to how a man achieves forgetfulness."

He didn't wait for her to respond. He stepped around her and strode off to the main hatch. He would sleep belowdecks with most of the crew and let Jordy have his cabin back—a mere bulkhead from the ladies. Rafe needed rest.

Five minutes in his hammock told him he wouldn't get it. Even those brief words to Phoebe conjured the images, the sounds, even the essence of tar and sea, sweat and blood, and worse, so much worse. Every time he closed his eyes, Davina's sweet face swam behind his lids. She'd cried out for him to save her at first. Then she gave up on her husband and called on God, begged Him to take her, to forgive her. There, beneath the laughing, taunting corsairs, she had told Rafe she loved him.

Finally, the beautiful wife he'd adored for what felt like all his life had met his stare and admitted she loved him. He'd waited for her to say that for nearly four years of marriage, and it came too late to give him solace.

It contributed to his anger against the man responsible for her death.

He wished in those moments that he were a drinking man for the sake of forgetfulness in the loneliness of the night. But he'd seen what alcohol did to men, destroying their minds and willingness to work. He'd tried at first, but Mel needed him. He couldn't loll in a drunken stupor when his baby daughter cried in the night for her mama.

The company of women worked better. Not the sort who made a living on the docks, but women with breeding and education, who could talk and listen too. But they wanted marriage. He couldn't blame them. It was only right, the upright man he'd once been reminded him. But he could not make that kind of commitment until everyone responsible for the deaths of his wife and parents was gone to their reward.

And then what decent woman would want him, a man with blood on his hands, even if most of it had flowed from the enemies of his country as he killed in the name of serving his king? More truthfully, his actions stemmed from killing in the name of lining his pockets to seek out and destroy his personal enemies.

"Ah, but you are a despicable mon." He spoke to the man his mind conjured, his own image poised on the quarterdeck with Phoebe. "I did not deserve her tears."

Or her prayers. Yet he knew she prayed for him. As though he heard her voice, saw her person, he knew she knelt in his cabin and cried out to God for his sake.

"Do not waste your time with the Lord, *mo ghraigh*." The endearment *my darling* slipped out unbidden, unwanted, perhaps too much the truth. "He does not waste His time with me."

But Rafe could waste a great deal of time with Phoebe.

Aching like a man with an ague, he rolled out of the hammock and returned to the deck. He couldn't pace and keep others awake. The cutter and lights of the town lured him. What harm lay in a few hours of surcease, breaking his personal code amongst the lights, liquor, and ladies of the night? It was the least of his sins, so numerous a few more would make no difference in his eternity.

He strode aft to the boat—and found Phoebe waiting for him at the rail.

At the sight of her, calm and still save for the breeze flirting with her gown and the fringe of her shawl, a warmth kindled inside him, a sensation he hadn't experienced for so long he barely recognized it for what it was—joy.

He feared it more than any enemy he'd met over the hilt of a sword.

Phoebe watched Rafe approach, his strides long and easy, his hair lifting in the breeze above broad shoulders set with an easy straightness one saw in a man of self-confidence. And it was all posturing from Rafe Docherty. His outward calm and assurance hid a soul ravaged by grief and hatred, yet aching for love and full of honor and kindness.

She hadn't wondered what interrupted her prayers for him and urged her to return to the deck, to slip past the men on watch and wait by the rail. She knew. She'd urged him to bring up the past, to talk of his loss and the horrors vivid despite the few words he used to describe them. A body didn't sleep after an episode like that. She knew from the night she'd finally spilled the contents of her heart to Tabitha and

Dominick, who then stayed up with her as she wept for the first time in a year, held her, loved her, assured her that God didn't hold grudges. If anyone should understand that, it was Dominick Cherrett.

So she waited for Rafe, determined to go with him no matter what direction he chose. If he never came, she would sleep on the deck. But he would come, and he did, a formidable shadow gliding across the planks to where she stood.

He grasped her hands. "What are you doing here?"

"Waiting for you." Despite the warmth of the night, her hands felt cold against the warmth of his, cold and tiny within his encircling clasp. "I thought you might not be able to sleep."

"Does your training extend to predictions of the future then?" His grip tightened. His upper lip curled. "Or is that your faith?"

"Not my training, the prompting of the Lord." She smiled.

He snorted. "Do you intend to come to the fleshpots of the town then?"

"If that's what you want."

"Why would I want such a thing as that?"

"The fleshpots of the town, I don't know. I'd think a sick head and risk of disease in the morning would be a deterrent. As for my company?" She shrugged. "I'm better than the sort you'll find in St. George's."

He stared at her for a moment, his eyes silver in the moonlight. "You're a strange lass to be so bold in your speech."

"It's been my best defense against matchmaking mothers. They come to think that having my fortune and family connections for their sons might not be worth the embarrassment of a daughter-in-law who speaks outright of things ladies aren't supposed to understand."

"Aye, I can see that it would." He tilted his head and surveyed her through thick, dark lashes. "Are you rich then?"

"Quite. I was too young to understand the terms of my marriage contract, but apparently the money and property my father left me came back to me upon my husband's death, along with most of my dowry."

"So why did you not try to buy your freedom from me instead of holding a wee knife to my throat?"

"I—" She bit her lip and looked away toward the port city, leaned her ear to the poignant strains of a ballad strummed upon a guitar.

My love is like a red, red rose . . .

"Would it have worked?" she asked by way of an answer.

"I do not ken." He released one of her hands and curved his hand around her cheek, turning her face back to his. "I'm thinking perhaps 'twould be best for all of us, no? I can find a midwife in St. George's to come along for Mrs. Chapman and see perhaps if one of the British naval vessels will see you safe home."

"Why?" Her entire body chilled. Sickness cramped her belly as though they sailed through a gale instead of gently rocking at anchor in a harbor. "Why do you want rid of me now?"

He released her and shoved his hands into the pockets of his breeches, but his eyes held hers. "Because I want you to stay."

10

"You ken you will have no reputation left after this night."
Rafe gave her what passed for a smile across the table of the
otherwise empty coffee room of an inn whose name Phoebe
hadn't been able to read in the flickering torchlight.

Boisterous talk and laughter rose from the taproom across
the entryway, and outside the window an Irishman with a
Spanish guitar sang mournful ballads. But the coffee room
lay quiet and dark save for a candle burning on the table
between Phoebe and Rafe. Fragrant steam rose from a fresh
pot of coffee that an inn serving maid had just brought to
them with a knowing smile and wink for Phoebe, which had
likely prompted Rafe's remark.

Phoebe merely shrugged. "I have no reputation after being
aboard your . . . um . . . brig."

"You have Mrs. Chapman there as chaperone."

Phoebe raised her brows. "She is three years younger than
I am and about as good a chaperone as—as Fiona."

"Still, you should not have come with me." Even as he
spoke, he lifted the battered tin pot and poured the nearly
black liquid into their cups.

"I couldn't let you come alone."

The truth, but not the complete truth. She shifted on the
hard banquette, guilt stabbing her for the deceit by omission,
even if she meant it for his good.

"I told you I'd have not done anything so bad." He stirred cream into his coffee, gazing down at his cup as though the action took concentration. "Nothing worse than ruining the reputation of an otherwise righteous lady."

"My reputation is worth less than your soul." She took a deep breath, then added, "Rafe."

His head shot up. His gaze clashed with hers, his eyes wide, his brows raised far enough for the left one to make a question mark. "You used my Christian name."

"You called me Phoebe."

"I'm weary of Mrs. Lee."

"And I don't think 'Captain' sets well upon your shoulders." She smiled. "Now what do we talk about to make the night pass and its pain go away?"

"Nothing," Rafe said with quiet intensity, "makes the pain go away."

"I'm sorry. Of course it doesn't. That takes prayer and time."

But he didn't pray, and time hadn't healed his wound.

She laid one hand on the table, half reaching across the scarred wood to him. "How do you keep going without faith, Rafe?"

"I have faith in my ability to see James Brock pay for his crime." He too rested his hand on the table, but not close enough to touch hers.

"Will killing him and condemning yourself to a lifetime of running or a hanging bring your wife and parents back? What will happen to your daughter if something happens to you?"

"I expect there's a distant cousin or two who could take her in for enough sil'er."

"Then why isn't she with them now?"

"She has me to run to."

Phoebe stared at him for a full minute, then reached out her hand and touched his. "Don't you hear what you're saying, Rafe? Your daughter runs away to be with you regardless of the danger. She needs her father. She lost her mother tragically and now needs her father desperately. How can you be so selfish?"

"Mel will be a very well-off young lady." He didn't look at Phoebe.

She glared at him. "She wants her father."

"She has—" He sighed. "I have to do this. I want to die with peace." He straightened. "I will die with peace."

"Will you?" She met and held his gaze. "You only think you will. But believe me, you won't. I felt neither peace nor relief after my husband died."

One corner of Rafe's mouth tilted up. "No one thinks you grieved him either."

"No." Phoebe hid her face behind her coffee cup. The strong black brew rolled over her tongue, cream softening its bitterness. She inhaled the invigorating fragrance and sent up a prayer for strength from a power much greater than a robust brew.

Surely God would help her bring Rafe back to Him. Surely God would honor her sacrifice for the man there in the shop with the lovely fabrics and scented oils.

"I grieved the waste of a young life," she said.

"Aye, I have done that myself—my own. But Watt convinced me to come to sea with him, and Jordy came along because he has al'ays followed me, and eventually I worked out that destroying Brock was what I wanted to do. When he sleeps in eternity, I can sleep."

"In eternity, Rafe?" She moved her hand a fraction of an inch closer to his, wanting, needing to touch him again, feel his vitality and warmth, his life. "What sort of eternity?"

"Not now, Phoebe." His tone held an edge.

She opened her mouth to continue anyway, then closed it again, shook her head, and gave in. "What were we talking about before you began to concern yourself with my reputation—finally? Ah, yes, Melvina's education. She's remarkably well read for a child her age. Did you teach her?"

"Her maternal grandfather was a scholar." He lifted his cup but didn't drink. "She lived with my mither-in-law until she died. She was eight. Mel, that is. I placed her in the first school that year. But she ran off back to Edinburgh, and I was visiting. She did not like the separation after that."

"So you've been teaching her?"

"Aye, and Jordy. He's better at the mathematics than I am."

"And you read Aristotle and Hobbs and Locke where?"

"'Tis not all war and mayhem aboard the *Davina*, you ken. Most of the time we have naught to do but watch the sea and weather."

Phoebe shuddered. "Don't talk about the sea or I may break my word about not trying to escape again."

"Aye, there is that wee trouble of yours. We'll get a potion here in the market. 'Tis one reason why I set into port here— to give you a respite and buy more of the ginger." He sipped from his cup then, his head turned toward the window and their reflection in the glass.

It appeared perfectly innocent, the image of a man and woman on either side of a rough wooden table. Not so much as the toes of their boots touched. But the hour was later than they should have been together. Or perhaps earlier. The guttering candle had dimmed, their reflection faded. And the musician packed up and vanished along the wharf, his guitar tucked under his arm. It was a nearly empty wharf now, empty and devoid of light, as individuals, groups, and pairs slipped off to inns and homes and vessels.

Indeed, no time for a lady to be alone with a man to whom

151

she was not married, let alone barely acquainted with. Yet she spoke the truth when saying his soul meant more than her reputation. If through her actions she could show him God's love and forgiveness, His mercy and grace, perhaps she could dissuade him from his course toward destruction—his own destruction. She could start by being honest.

"Rafe, it's not the sea that makes me so ill, it's the confinement because—"

"Not now." He shot to his feet and sped toward the door.

Phoebe jumped up and followed. "Where are you going?"

He didn't respond. He continued to the front door and across the empty market square to the wharf.

A hundred feet behind him, struggling to catch up, Phoebe finally saw what must have caught his attention—Derrick and Jordy charging toward them. The three men met on the landward edge of the dock.

"Belinda." Phoebe broke into a run, her skirts gathered in her hands.

Something surely had happened to Belinda. For the second time in the past twelve hours, Phoebe had neglected a patient because of a man.

She stumbled to a halt beside Rafe, grasped his arm for support. "What's wrong?"

Derrick and Jordy glanced at her, then Rafe. Neither spoke.

"Belinda?" Phoebe demanded. "Mel?"

"They're quite a'right." A muscle bunched in Rafe's jaw, and the arm beneath Phoebe's hand felt as solid as a spar with tension.

"It's . . . not Belinda?" Her voice sounded small, squeaky.

"Nay." Rafe drew away from her. "Derrick, no, Jordy, take Mrs. Lee back to the inn. Get—"

"You shouldn't go out there," Jordy interrupted. "He's got the men aggravated."

"He who?" Phoebe demanded.

"'Tis my brig," Rafe said. "I am going to talk sense into the sensible ones and subdue those who cannot think for themselves and will follow—" He looked down at Phoebe. "Jordy, get her a room. I expect she'd like a rest and bath and so forth. Ensure the inn gives her whatever she needs. I'll send Mrs. Chapman and Mel ashore immediately." Without another word, he sprinted down the wharf to one of the bobbing boats secured to the pilings.

"Go to the inn." Jordy flung the words over his shoulder as he too raced for the boats.

"Wait." Phoebe followed. "I need to be with Belinda."

She spoke her sister-in-law's name. She knew that was right—her responsibility, whether or not she was willing to be at sea—but she fixed her gaze on Rafe, and her heart said, *I need to be with him if there's danger.*

"I said take her to the inn, Jordy McPherson," Rafe shouted. "'Tis an order."

"Aye, Captain, and your orders mean naught if they kill you." Jordy grabbed the painter to keep the boat from shoving off. "I am going with you."

"They are not going to kill me," Rafe said.

His face was set so hard that Phoebe believed him. No one would dare kill a man that cold. They'd be afraid to.

An ache started in Phoebe's middle, a longing to forever break up the coldness to find the man who loved so deeply he devoted his life to seeing his wife's death avenged, the man who adored his daughter, the man who calmed her when the deck canopy collapsed and sent her into a panic.

"I want to go too," Phoebe declared.

Rafe drew a knife from his boot and sliced through the painter. "Neither of you is coming with us. Derrick?"

Derrick hoisted the cutter's single sail.

Phoebe's heart sank into her stomach. "He can't go out there and leave us here."

"'Tis his brig." Jordy gazed after Rafe and the cutter. "'Tis the only home he has left himself."

"But—" She'd longed for this freedom from Rafe Docherty for days, but now that the prospect stared her in the face, she felt like weeping. She glanced at Jordy. "What has gone wrong?"

"Once Captain Rafe went ashore, some of the men began to talk." Jordy tucked his hand beneath her elbow and gently turned her toward the inn. "One mon in particular. He thinks himself in a position to say Rafe is no longer fit to lead the men. They say he has gone soft since letting his daughter come aboard and has no stomach for the fighting. So they need to take control of the voyage."

"But that's—"

"Aye, mutiny." Jordy's thin lips nearly disappeared, he compressed them so tightly.

"Who is it?" Phoebe demanded.

"'Tis none of your concern, Mrs. Lee. Captain will take care of it or—"

"Die trying?" Phoebe set her fists on her hips. "Jordy McPherson, I have a right to know what's afoot when my patient is aboard. And Melvina and her ridiculous excuse for a dog need protecting too."

"Captain Rafe will see to their safety, even if it means sacrificing his own. Now, if you please, Mrs. Lee, 'tis not good to stand about here in the middle of the night."

"Nor should Rafe—Captain Docherty be going out to meet a crew of mutineers. I mean, what if they kill him?"

And he held such anger in his soul rather than praying for redemption.

"His soul—" She couldn't speak for the pain in her chest.

"Aye, I ken what you are saying. He holds his sins to his heart like they're prizes to put in a vault." Jordy's face seemed to elongate with sadness. "Derrick and I have tried." He tried again to urge Phoebe forward, continuing to talk. "We thought perhaps having a Christian lady like yourself aboard might help, so we went along with the plans to not return you to shore."

Phoebe wrapped an arm around a stanchion and glared at Jordy. "If you're a man of God, how can you be aboard a privateer like you are and help Captain Docherty in his quest?"

"You cannot save the unbeliever by avoiding him." Jordy released her arm and scrubbed his hands over his face, his whiskers rasping beneath his calloused palms. "And I have kent him since he was a bairn. I'd been working in their household as a scullion since I was a lad of ten but I'd improved myself and gained the family's trust by the time Captain Rafe was born."

"So young?" Phoebe forgot her protest in her fascination and intrigue.

So Rafe came from a family well-off enough to have that many servants—a separate person to wash up the dishes and pots and pans.

"'Twas better than the workhouse." Jordy half smiled. "Aye, but they were good to me, the Dochertys. And he was a fine lad. I ne'er thought he would—" He sighed and shook his head. "So I went to sea with him to try to be a friend, even if I disapprove of what he is doing. If God wills, I am a light in the darkness Rafe sets around him."

Thoughts whirling in her head, Phoebe allowed Jordy to walk her toward the inn. Darkness huddled around them, but a starlit night, not the emptiness of a lost soul. Laughter and conversation drifted on the breeze, and somewhere a barbecue fire wafted fragrant smoke toward them. No shots rang out from the harbor. Few sounds at all floated to shore.

Most vessels lay in slumber, but a glance backward displayed a line of torches along the deck of the *Davina*.

"Why?" Phoebe burst out. "Why did they do it to him now? Surely they understand he can't fight battles with his daughter aboard."

"Most of them do not care." Jordy opened the inn door. A bell rang above it. From a far corner of the dimly lit entry hall, someone yawned and shuffled forward, and Jordy stepped up to meet the shadowy male figure. "The lady needs a room."

"Humph." The man glanced from Jordy to Phoebe. "She was with t'other one earlier."

"Aye, and what account is that?"

The innkeeper leered, and Phoebe's face grew warm. She'd been called some unpleasant names in the past four years. Patients in pain, her mother-in-law, a magistrate all found unpleasant sobriquets to pile on her head. Yet none had gone in the direction the landlord implied.

She took a step backward. "I'd rather return to the ship."

"Nay, the captain wants you here." Jordy loomed over the diminutive landlord. "Mrs. Lee would like a room to herself. In the morning, provide her with a bath and anything else she needs. Do you understand, mon?"

"I understand I need money for all that." The man jutted out a nonexistent chin.

Jordy drew a purse from his breeches pocket. It was woven leather and made a chinking sound. The landlord's eyes gleamed in the single candle's glow.

"Do not get greedy." Jordy drew out a handful of coins.

Phoebe didn't know British coinage but guessed the silver meant shillings. The landlord laughed and demanded gold. The men haggled and ended up with Jordy giving him silver.

"Aye, then, show the lady—" Jordy began.

The innkeeper shook his head of sparse gray locks. "The

room's not ready. A lady deserves clean sheets." He scurried off.

"I must have paid him too much if he is willing to give you clean sheets," Jordy muttered.

Phoebe came close to smiling, but a pop like gunfire from the direction of the harbor sent her spinning on her heel and racing for the door. "Rafe—I mean, Belinda. Mel."

Jordy grasped her hand and held her back. "You cannot help."

"I must. I'm a woman. Maybe I can talk them out of violence."

"You, Mrs. Lee?" Jordy touched his belly, where she'd kicked him.

"That was different."

"Watt will not understand—" Jordy grimaced.

Phoebe stared at him. "Watt is leading the mutineers? I thought he was the captain's friend."

"Nay, they have ne'er been friends. More like armed companions for the past thirteen years."

"What?" Phoebe tried to tug her hand free. The harbor lay quiet and sparsely lit again, but she wanted—needed—to go out to the *Davina*. And she wanted—needed—to remain and listen to Jordy, get more information from him. "How can they be when Captain Docherty has been at sea for only nine years?"

"'Tis his tale to tell, not mine. Now stay inside here where 'tis safe. I will go as soon as you are settled."

"And what can you do?"

"Pray all is well." Jordy offered her an encouraging smile, but the lines around his eyes appeared deeper and tighter than earlier.

"We can't stay here in comfort while anything could be happening out there." Phoebe strained toward the door.

Jordy held her back. "You cannot help out there. Once you are settled, I will be going out there, perhaps with a few men from that English frigate. The Navy does not take kindly to mutinies, not even aboard a privateer, you ken."

"I didn't know, but it makes sense." Phoebe's gaze strayed to the towering masts of the British warship. It belonged to her country's enemy, and yet it could be a symbol of help, an answer to prayer.

To more than one prayer.

"I believe the landlord is returning," she said.

Two sets of footfalls rang on the wooden floorboards. From the dim recesses of the hall, the innkeeper returned, accompanied by the maid who had served the coffee. "Bets will show the lady up," the man said.

Jordy emitted a long breath like steam escaping from a bellows and released Phoebe's hand. "Grand. See that she is comfortable and remains here." He flipped a coin to the landlord.

This time, gold glinted in the candlelight before the man caught it, bit it, and tucked it into his pocket. "Aye, she'll go nowhere."

"You," Phoebe ground between her teeth.

Jordy nodded and strode away, closing the inn door behind him with barely a click.

"Would you like a bath now, madam?" the maid asked.

Phoebe's skin crawled and itched with days of saltwater cleansings, and temptation lured her forward, up a flight of narrow steps, and onto a gallery. A half dozen rooms opened off the gallery, which overlooked a yard full of black shadows and scrabbling sounds like small paws. Rats? Cats? Phoebe appreciated being above the worst of the stench of rotting fruit and animal droppings. She wasn't glad about how difficult getting away would be. But then, perhaps she wouldn't have to. Jordy's instructions had been to give her whatever she wanted . . .

Phoebe reined in her impatience and accepted the offer of an immediate bath. "But I have nothing clean to wear afterward."

"I can find you sommit, madam." Bets opened the door to a small room and used a strike-a-light to ignite a branch of candles inside the door. "Guests leave things behind. Nothing'll be all that fine, but it'll be clean enough. I'll wash your dress for you."

"When will you sleep?"

The girl shrugged too-thin shoulders. "I sleep when I can snatch an hour or two."

"That's awful."

"It's better than walking the streets, if a fine lady like you understands me."

"I understand you." Phoebe shuddered. "I'm a midwife."

"Ah." The girl nodded. "Here's the bed. Have a rest while I prepare the bath. The water's nearly hot all the time, so it won't be long."

It was long enough for Phoebe to drift off to sleep half lying on the straw-filled mattress, but she roused when the innkeeper and maid arrived with a tin bath and then steaming water.

Left alone, Phoebe sank into the water with jasmine-scented steam billowing around her and focused on plans to escape. Getting Belinda away would prove difficult. Surely the frigate captain would help once she mentioned a connection to Admiral Landry, Dominick's uncle. Rafe and his mutinous crew could go on their way to pillaging for a fortune.

And Rafe might get his revenge. He might even survive in body. Yet he might lose his soul in the process.

If God wills, I am a light in the darkness Rafe sets around

159

him. Jordy's words rang in Phoebe's ears, in her conscience, interrupting her plans for escape back to Virginia.

She wanted to return. She yearned to sail west so badly her muscles ached with the effort not to run shrieking for help back to America, with promises to give her fortune to whomever helped her. But if Rafe did regain control of his vessel, he needed all the lights in the darkness willing to do God's work.

She yanked her mind away from the notion of leaving and set about washing her hair and scrubbing away an accumulation of saltwater residue from her skin. Refreshed, fragrant, and clean, she went to bed and fell asleep praying.

In the morning, with no word from the brig and sunlight streaming through her window, she asked the inn maid for a few items to make her morning comfort complete. The girl looked dubious, but she returned in a quarter hour with hot chocolate, bread, jam, and ink, pen, and paper.

Hot chocolate and food at her elbow, Phoebe dipped the pen in the ink and began to write:

Dear Tabitha and Dominick . . .

⟡

"Don't come no nearer." A youth named Tommy Jones leaned over the gunwale as the cutter bumped against the side of the brig. "No one's welcome aboard."

"I am your captain," Rafe stated.

"No more you ain't." Darkness hid the lad's expression, but the sneer rang through his tone. "We got a captain who'll let us fight."

"Or get you killed." Rafe made himself smile. "But if you want to be foolish enough to trust a man who got cashiered from the Navy for incompetence in sailing orders, at least allow me to collect the women."

160

"Can't. Hostages."

Rafe bit his tongue. He must not allow any of them to guess the rage boiling inside him. Rage and anxiety simmering like a vat of acid. He kept his smile in place, though it pained his face. "'Tis not wise, that notion, Jones. You ken the British Navy does not take kindly to mutiny."

"We all hold a share in this brig." Though the words spoke of defiance, Jones glanced toward the frigate bobbing a hundred yards away.

And Derrick struck. With a flash of a powerful arm, he sent a coil of rope sailing upward. It caught Jones in the face. He cried out and staggered backward. Before he recovered, Rafe grabbed the chains and clambered aboard. Jones surged forward and fired his pistol. It missed. With a lunge, Rafe grabbed the lad's wrist and twisted. The pistol sailed empty across the deck. Rafe kept twisting until Jones's hand rested between his shoulder blades and he was whimpering.

"Quiet," Rafe commanded. "I am not hurting you."

"You are," Jones whined.

"What is afoot here?" Watt called out as a crowd of men bearing lanterns swarmed along the main deck. "Jones, I told you—ah, Captain Rafe, have you come to join Mrs. Chapman and your daughter as our hostages?"

"Nay, I have come to take my brig back." Compelling Jones to the deck before him, Rafe glanced from face to face, meeting and holding their gazes, marking the names of those who wouldn't meet his eyes. He ended with Watt. "Do not do it. I could rightfully have you hanged for this."

Watt snorted. "Not if we are at sea."

"With Jordy and Derrick and Mrs. Lee left on Bermuda?"

"Mrs. Lee will do naught for you," Watt pointed out. "Indeed, she will like as not cheer as we sail away."

"Not with her patient aboard." Rafe released Tommy Jones and took a step toward Watt.

The older man drew his pistol from his belt. His gray eyes gleamed like honed steel in the flickering light. "Do not force me to shoot you, lad."

Rafe nodded. "I will not." He backed up and leaned his hips against the rail. "Why risk it? I said you could have the brig when we are finished with Brock."

"If Brock does not finish us," Watt grumbled. "You ken as well as I his position is protecting him."

"I ken he does not want me alive. Did he persuade you to this action, my old . . . friend?"

Watt's body jerked as though he'd been struck.

Rafe pressed on. "So quickly after I did you such a good turn—when was it, Watt? Fourteen years ago? Thirteen? When the Navy said—"

With a yell, Watt flung himself at Rafe, one hand fisted, the other brandishing the pistol like a club. Rafe leaped aside, and Watt hit the rail with an "ooph" of pain. His pistol dropped into the harbor with a gentle splash.

And Derrick yanked Watt into the cutter.

"Anyone wish to follow?" Rafe asked the motionless crew. "Or would you like to reissue your pledge to me?"

No one spoke for a full minute and then some. Rafe didn't know most of them well. Privateer crews came and went. Men grew weary of being at sea, or made enough money to give up the danger. The Royal Navy pressed some of them aboard, and others succumbed to battle or disease. More replaced them, ready to risk their lives for potential wealth. So Rafe stopped trying to know them all well. One couldn't care about the loss of men he knew little more about than their names and their ability to sail and fire a gun. Consequently, the men didn't know him either, except by reputation for fairness, justice rather than mercy, his ability to win.

The silence on deck stretched on. In the cutter, Watt growled as Derrick tied his hands behind his back. Below them, Fiona barked, and neither Mrs. Chapman nor Mel made her quiet down.

"So why would you be going back on your word?" Rafe broke the silence. "Are none of you men of honor?"

"We want more money," a topman named Riggs said.

Another man stepped forward, as rough-hewn as Riggs was slight. "We're jaded. There's nothin' to do, and the women are distracting."

Rafe's eyebrow twitched upward at the non sequitur. "We've seen only one potential prize since we left Virginia. That wouldn't have taken more than an hour or two to take, so you wouldn't have much more to do. That's life aboard any vessel."

"But we'd be richer for it," Riggs persisted.

"Or dead." Rafe smiled.

"We'd have had the cargo to keep us occupied," someone called from the back of the clustered men.

"True." Rafe nodded. "Would you like to go down to the hold and occupy yourself with the current cargo?"

Someone made a remark about the ladies.

Rafe clenched his fists. Before he thought what to say, a few of the crew rebuked him.

"You don't talk that way about ladies."

"Thank you, Farrell." Rafe nodded to the man. "I'm glad some of you have decency left. Now, about more money." Rafe set his jaw and fixed his gaze on Riggs. "I'm presuming you all are open to negotiations?"

"Maybe." Riggs took a step forward, hands on his hips, narrow chest and pointed chin thrust out. "Depends."

"It always does." Rafe returned to his nonchalant stance and said nothing.

The men began to shift from foot to foot. Their gazes strayed past him to the sight of St. George's. With dawn breaking over the eastern horizon, cries of vendors began to drift across the water, and bung boats paddled into the harbor to surround the vessels, bringing goods to sailors left aboard.

Several boats bumped against the hull of the *Davina*. Rafe nodded to Derrick in the cutter. He climbed aboard, quick and agile despite his size, and stationed himself behind one of the guns amidships. From his pocket, he took a length of slow match, and from beneath his loose shirt, a bag of grapeshot.

"What the—stop them!" Riggs shouted and charged toward Derrick. "Men, we gotta stop him."

"Why?" Rafe yawned. "The gun can't turn on you."

Riggs halted, and two men bumped into him in their rush. He seemed not to notice. "Maybe not, but he's up to no good."

"Just inspecting the gun." Rafe strode to the taffrail and glanced down at two bung boats pulling away. "Be off with you. My men are occupied at present."

One of the passengers waved to him.

He waved back, then faced the men again. "Do you want to stop Derrick from doing work you all should be helping with, or continue discussing taking over my brig?"

"We don't need to discuss nothin'." Riggs pushed through the other men, who stepped aside as though he were royalty, and stalked up to Rafe. "We are takin' over now."

"Are you certain that's what you're wanting to do? You ken I left Jordy ashore, and Watt is . . . indisposed." Four of Riggs's sycophants, Tommy Jones amongst them, slipped down the deck, heading for Derrick, and Rafe tensed, ready for action if necessary. "If you mutiny, Jordy will notify those frigates yonder, and they'll be after you before the cat can lick her ear."

Not that the *Davina* had a cat, only one frantically yapping dog.

Riggs laughed. "They won't do nothin' to us. We got your daughter and Mrs. Chapman as hostages."

"Do you now?" Rafe laughed and turned so he could wave to two of the boats rowing toward shore.

Mel waved back from one of them, having neatly slipped out of one of the stern windows and into the craft sent to fetch her and Mrs. Chapman.

Riggs and several others paled. By rights, Rafe could have all of them hanged.

"Just this once," he said in a voice barely loud enough to reach the quarterdeck, "I will be merciful. Now remember what you agreed to when you signed on, and get back to your duties—except for you, Tommy Jones and Sam Riggs. Do not you move."

11

Phoebe understood how Rafe had avoided her company during the five days they spent on Bermuda. She couldn't figure out how he managed it on a vessel the size of the *Davina*, but he did. She spent every minute she could manage on deck, where fresh air soothed her queasiness. For him to walk past her without even nodding made his avoidance obvious to everyone aboard. Why was more complex. She suspected she'd crossed a line of intimacy during their nighttime conversation over coffee. She couldn't explain that to anyone, though.

"What did you do to offend him?" Belinda asked after a week of Rafe striding past without the merest glance in their direction.

They perched on chairs beneath a canvas awning against the weather rail, enjoying breezes chilled by winter's approach. Belinda stitched miniscule garments while Phoebe read to her from a copy of *Evangeline*.

She closed the volume she found tedious but Belinda loved, and held her place with her finger as she glared at her sister-in-law. "Why do you think I did something to offend him?"

"He hasn't spoken to you since we were on Bermuda." Belinda paused to rethread her needle. "And there was all that nonsense about the men trying to mutiny."

"It wasn't nonsense." Phoebe glanced across the main deck.

Sam Riggs and Tommy Jones, apparently the ringleaders of the mutineers, knelt on the deck with a pot of reeking tar and a brush. They appeared to be engaged in the onerous task of caulking the seams of the deck. The previous day, they'd cleaned the slime from the scuppers. Before that, they'd scrubbed the decks from prow to stern. Apparently Rafe's idea of punishment was not flogging, hanging, or confinement, but the duties necessary and despised by sailors. As he worked, a muscle on the side of Sam Riggs's jaw bulged further, and his mouth thinned over his pointed chin. Occasionally he lifted his head, shook back his shaggy brown hair, and glared at Rafe, usually his back. Tommy Jones, on the other hand, kept his head down, the end of his queue often dragging in tar or bilge water.

"That one bears watching," Phoebe murmured.

"Which one? Oh, him? Riggs?" Belinda moistened her lips. "He was going to use us for hostages. I think he should be in prison. I think they all should be, including Watt."

"I don't think I'd have kept them aboard either."

But Rafe would have his reasons, perhaps keeping friends close and enemies closer. Watt apparently had been part of Rafe's life like Jordy, except not as loyal, even antagonistic. He maintained his old duties of helmsman and bosun when necessary, but he said nothing to anyone, and his dark gray eyes held a steely edge that sliced through Phoebe whenever she accidentally crossed their path of sight.

As she did too often, Phoebe allowed her gaze to stray to the brig's quarterdeck in the hopes that the captain would cross her line of sight. He stood at the binnacle, half turned toward Jordy at the wheel, Mel beside him and Fiona cavorting around their feet. Sunlight gleamed in his garnet hair, and the breeze flirted the ends of the strands against his cheeks. Phoebe's fingers itched to brush it back, smooth it to its normal satin texture, touch his face.

She snapped open the book and stared at the page without seeing the printed words. Instead, she saw other words, words written with a broken quill pen and poor quality ink. Words written in her hand and betraying Rafe's trust.

For his own good, of course. Of course it was. He must not continue on his mission. It would destroy him in spirit, if not in body too.

But they were words, words and actions that kept her from going to him and attempting to break down the barrier he had erected since the night she kept talking to him so he wouldn't do something foolish. She'd sacrificed her own reputation for the sake of his soul. Then she'd unleashed potential wrath upon him in the name of stopping him from becoming a man he himself could never respect—a cold-blooded killer.

Quite simply, guilt kept them apart. Phoebe's guilt stemmed from the letter she'd sent to Dominick Cherrett. And Rafe's? Guilt over bringing her along against her will. Kissing her. Or perhaps simply remorse over telling her too much about his past. Whatever his reason, an invisible wall lay between them no matter where either of them moved about the brig.

Her gaze strayed to the quarterdeck again. He and Mel faced Phoebe and Belinda now, faced the sun to take the noon bearings, identical sextants in their hands. Light flashed off the glass of the instruments, dazzled Phoebe's eyes.

Her heart squeezed, and she looked away.

"You're not reading," Belinda said.

"No, I'm not." Phoebe tried making sense of the words again, tried to transfer them from her eyes to her mouth so Belinda could continue to sew baby garments.

And Phoebe wondered if Dominick would get the letter. Would he or could he act upon it? That Rafe would never forgive her she did not doubt for a moment. If it spared his life, she didn't care.

At least she told herself she didn't care.

"Phoebe." Belinda heaved a sigh of exasperation. "You stopped reading in the middle of the sentence."

Phoebe closed the book. "I'm sorry. I can't read in this light."

The sextants had been returned to the drawer in the binnacle. Father and daughter bent over a slate, working out the calculations of longitude and latitude, no doubt. Their brows furrowed in identical manners of concentration. Fiona pawed at Mel's leg.

Phoebe rose. She needed to stop playing the coward and approach him, make him talk to her. She had thought they were developing a friendship, as much as a man and woman could be friends. At least a comfortable camaraderie. Approaching him should be easier with his daughter beside him. Surely he wouldn't be rude to her in front of his daughter.

"Where are you going?" Belinda asked.

"Aft." Phoebe set the book on her abandoned chair, ignored Belinda's protest, and set her feet on a path toward the quarterdeck.

Fiona set her feet on a path for the bow. She leaped down the quarter ladder and streaked past Phoebe, a blur of black and white fur. Mel shouted and charged after her, slate in hand. She shot past Phoebe, all gangling arms and legs.

Phoebe spun on the heel of her slipper and joined the chase. "The tar," she shouted.

Her words roused others—men polishing guns or repairing sails—to chase the dog. Fiona dove into the center of a sail, turned two revolutions, then slipped from beneath the sail maker's reaching hand and continued her quest, docked tail bobbing, lithe body springing—

"No!" Phoebe and Mel shouted together and dove for the dog—too late.

One of Fiona's leaps sent her flying right into the bucket of tar. The container overturned. Black sludge oozed across the deck. Cursing, Riggs bounded to his feet, grabbed a ratline, and hoisted himself onto the rail.

The dog sat in a puddle of congealing tar, her black eyes huge, her mouth clamped together. She shook as though suffering from a fever.

"Fiona Docherty." Mel reached for the dog.

Phoebe reached for Mel. "Don't. You don't want tar all over you."

"But it'll kill her." Tears sprang into Mel's eyes.

"Nay, lass, it'll not be killing her." Rafe reached them and crouched beside the terrier. "You silly wee beastie."

The softness of his voice, the gentleness of his hands as he lifted the terrified dog by her front shoulders set an ache deep inside Phoebe. Her own eyes filled with moisture. She blinked hard and turned away. "I'll go fetch oil or lard from the galley."

"You gonna drown her in it?" Riggs called down from the shrouds. "That's what she deserves."

Slowly, so slowly his movement was barely perceptible, Rafe straightened and looked up at the seaman. His features hardened like tar on a winter's day. "For that remark, Sam Riggs, you will be getting yourself down here and cleaning this muck off the deck. Now."

Riggs stared. "I didn't do it. I was minding my own business and—"

"Derrick? Jordy?" Rafe spoke the words in a normal tone.

The two men had moved up behind him, as no doubt he knew.

"Yes, sir," Derrick said.

"See that this man cleans up this mess, then confine him below."

"But I—" Riggs grew paler.

"Yes, sir," Derrick and Jordy chorused.

The former stepped to the rail in one stride and plucked Riggs off the shrouds as though he weighed no more than Mel.

As Phoebe turned away to fetch oil or lard from the galley, she caught Riggs's expression from the corner of her eye. It was cold, as cold and hard as ice-coated iron, yet his dark eyes blazed with hatred.

Chilled by that look, Phoebe hurried to the hatchway leading down to the lower deck. She thanked God for the fact that on the lower deck, even though it was low of beam and smelled of men who exerted themselves daily and lived in too-close quarters, the sickness didn't bother her as it did in the cabins. Quickly she entered the galley. The fragrant steam billowing from the chamber felt like balm on a wound. She paused to inhale it, to take a moment of comfort in the familiar aromas of peppercorns and potatoes, cinnamon and apples.

But the hard walnut shell of apprehension remained knotted in her middle.

She stepped over the coaming and called to the cook, a mere shadow in the steam and smoke of the room that needed better ventilation. "We need oil or lard, whatever you can spare. Fiona's got herself coated in tar."

"Silly wee beastie." The man Phoebe knew only as Cook surged out of the gloom.

Although his tone was just as gentle and affectionate as Rafe's had been, it didn't send that ache swirling through Phoebe as had the captain's words, his tone.

She hugged her middle, willing away fear of Riggs, willing away this ache for Rafe. "Riggs was caulking the deck and Fiona toppled over the tar bucket. Do you have what we need?"

"Aye, that I do." Cook produced a tub from behind a bar holding the containers on their shelves, and set it in her arms. "Can you manage it, lass, or shall I carry it up?"

"It smells like dinner needs your attention. I'll manage." She wanted to take it to Rafe, have an excuse to finally break the impasse between them. "Thank you."

The wooden tub sagged in her hold. She staggered a bit but hefted it onto one hip and crept back to the hatch, glad the sea lay in relative calm so she and lard didn't go tumbling across the lower deck like a child's hoop. Once at the ladder, though, she hesitated, not sure how she would manage the steep steps and lard. If she set it on the tread above her, she could balance it as she climbed. Once on deck, she could simply slide the tub across the planks.

She started up. One, two . . . The decks lay close together, barely more than five and a half feet. Three—

A shout rang overhead. "Sail ho. The Tricoleur."

A French ship. The enemy to this English vessel.

Feet pounded around her, below her, above her. Phoebe froze on the ladder, not sure if she should continue up or descend.

"Enemy in sight!" men cried. "A fight! A fight!"

Fiona began to bark. A female screamed—Belinda, no doubt. And a man hurtled through the hatch, tripped on the tub of lard. It slammed into Phoebe's middle. She folded like a fan, wind driven from her lungs. Her arms flailed in the air, grasping at—nothing. No rail. No rope. Her hands clutched space, and she fell.

Her back struck the lower deck, her head something harder. Lights flashed before her eyes. A scream echoed through her head—not hers then. She gritted her teeth against pain in her belly and back and skull. An old blow. Another scream. Another tumble down steps. Blood. So very much blood.

No, not blood. That was then, a different set of steps, a different floor, a different Phoebe. This was lard. Greasy, stinking fat oozing from a split in the tub beside her. A different man crouched over her, one with the kindness of an angel and a soul as empty as a broken glass.

And she loved him. God forgive her. She'd told Dominick and Tabitha she might, but the uncertainty had passed. She knew she'd lost her heart for the second time in her life, and to possibly the second-worst man she could find. Maybe even the worst one. Worse than Gideon Lee.

She doubled over, sobbing.

"Where are you hurt, lass?" Rafe stroked her hair away from her face. "Do you ken if aught is broken? Did you hit your head?"

Though his hand felt steady and warm, tension rang through his voice.

Phoebe held her breath in an attempt to suppress her gasping breaths, the flow of tears, the mourning for losing her heart so unwisely again. Around her, the brig had fallen into the relative quiet of normal activity, the tumult of potential action silenced as though someone had slammed a door. And Rafe hadn't been the man who ran into her. He had been shorter.

"I must have." She raised her head and blinked in the brightness of three lanterns held up by a ring of men with concerned faces. "I don't remember everyone coming."

"You lost consciousness then." Rafe cupped her chin in his hand and turned her face toward him. "Jenkins, bring that lantern closer. Yes, there. Shine it into her eyes."

Phoebe dropped her lids against the brightness.

"Nay, lass, let me look to see if you're concussed." He lifted one of her lids with a fingertip.

His face hovered mere inches away. His breath fanned across her lips in a light caress, his gray eyes gazed into her one open eye. She opened the other so she could gaze upon him so close, so concerned, so—

She closed her eyes again. "Why?"

"Your pupils will tell me if you have bruised your brain." He gave her that tilted corner of his lips that passed as a smile. "Are you seeing one or two of me?"

"One is quite enough, thank you."

"Aye, I thought as much."

"But I didn't mean why look into my eyes. I meant—" She remembered their audience and clenched her teeth.

He slipped an arm around her shoulders. "Are you in pain?"

"Not a great deal. But I don't know what happened."

"Watt the clod ran into you," Jordy announced. "I think he should be cleaning this muck off the deck."

"'Tis a day for muck on the decks," Watt grumbled. "But better the grease than the tar. I am sorry, Mrs. Lee."

"It's all right. It was an accident." She started to shake her head, winced, and barely resisted the urge to lay her cheek against Rafe's shoulder, so broad, so close, so tempting.

She stiffened her spine. "The French ship?"

"Sheered off, the cowards," someone grumbled. "Saw us and turned tail and ran."

"And when we didn't give chase," added another man, one back in the shadows beyond the circle of lantern light, "who's the coward?"

Silence. Stillness below deck. The arm around Phoebe grew as taut as a backstay.

"We have ladies and a child aboard," Rafe said in a quiet, even tone that nonetheless hummed with the tension of a steel wire in the wind. "There will be no fighting. I'll say naught more about it. Now get to your duties. Cook, I'm afraid we'll need more lard for the dog. And hot water for Mrs. Lee to no longer resemble a greased pig."

A ripple of nervous laughter ran through the men as they began to disperse around the lower deck and back up the ladder.

Phoebe glared at Rafe. "You don't speak to me for a week, then have the audacity to call me a greased pig? If that bite-sized excuse of a dog hadn't dived into the tar and—"

He brushed his fingers across her lips. "Hush. You'll be doing yourself an injury. Now then, do you need someone to carry you to your cabin?"

She thought she might. Her knees felt like water.

"I can manage."

She meant she should manage. She wanted him to carry her too much.

She allowed him to lift her to her feet. Her skirt slapped against her legs, sodden with lard. Her stomach rolled. She must look a fright. If she'd intended to attract the man with her good looks, she had failed.

No, not attract him. She must not. He was more wrong for her than Gideon had been. As she climbed the ladder to sunshine and fresh breezes, she listed the ways to keep her mind off of him close behind her. He came from an enemy country. He was on a deadly mission. He held no faith in God.

She could change all that. She had at least another month before they reached England. Surely in that month God would honor her prayers and bring this man to his knees.

But it hadn't happened with Gideon.

She shoved that memory aside. Gideon was dead, gone, her mistake paid for and then some.

She paused on the deck, dizzy from her aching head, queasy from the lard, heartsick with memory and knowledge. The sun beat down warm for October in the North Atlantic, so the sailor said. All lay quiet.

A chill ran through Phoebe for no logical reason. Belinda still stitched baby clothes beside the rail. Mel and Watt rubbed oil into Fiona's hair to remove the tar. Riggs scraped at the spilled tar on the deck, diligent despite his mutinous expression. Others performed their duties of adjusting sails, holding the brig on course, polishing the brass guns ranged along the gunwales. Peaceful for a vessel intended as a machine of war.

A war against one man. A vessel that existed to salve the hatred of another man.

No wonder cold seeped through her. She was more of a fool to love him than to have loved Gideon. If she couldn't change Rafe . . .

She'd been unable to change Gideon.

She bowed her head in case her despair showed on her face, and plodded aft. A glance back told her she had made a slimy mess on the deck. She paused at the top of the companionway and addressed Rafe without looking at him. "I'm so sorry for the mess. I'll help clean it."

"And risk your hands? Now go down, and we'll have hot water for you in a few minutes." He strode away, his footfalls firm on the deck planks, and she wished she had a serious injury so he would take care of her.

Odd she knew he would. Seeing to the sick and injured aboard any ship rarely fell to its captain. But Rafe Docherty seemed cut from a different cloth. He saw to everything aboard, from caring for the sick to navigating the vessel to ensuring the captive guests enjoyed every comfort the brig had to offer.

Within minutes of leaving her, he did indeed send down a barrel and men with canisters of hot water so she could wash away the lard. It was seawater that left her skin a little sticky, but better sticky than slippery. She smelled of the jasmine soap she'd purchased on Bermuda, heady and warm compared to Belinda's sharp tang of lavender.

No one appreciated it other than her. Belinda and Mel, seated on the deck with the latter now reading *Evangeline*, wrinkled their noses. A scrubbed and shorn Fiona sneezed, and Rafe appeared nowhere in sight.

Despite an ache in her skull where she'd landed on the deck, Phoebe climbed to the quarterdeck and leaned against the taff-rail behind Jordy once again at the wheel. "How big is this ship?"

"'Tis a brig. We have only two masts." He leaned toward the compass and turned the wheel a quarter revolution. "A hundred and seventy-five tons. Eighty feet long. Not so big, but big enough to get the job done."

"What job is that?" Phoebe stared at the Scotsman's gray-ing hair as though she could see the truth through his skull. "Killing men?"

He shrugged his massive shoulders. "We're a privateer, no?"

"Were, I think. But how big a brig or any vessel do you need to kill one man?"

"None, lass, but I'll not be talking of it further. Talking does no good. Only prayer."

Phoebe wanted to argue with him but guessed it would do no good. So she changed her tack. "Why did he take his family to the Mediterranean during a war?"

"It was during the Peace of Amiens. And Mrs. Docherty, the younger one, she—" Jordy's gaze strayed past Phoebe's shoulder. "You'd best leave the quarterdeck, Mrs. Lee. He's coming back and may not wish to find you here."

"I'm not afraid of him, Mr. McPherson."

So why had she let him avoid her? Not fear. On the con-trary—she wanted to stay with him, follow him around like Fiona followed Mel. She'd remained aboard the *Davina* in-stead of leaving when she'd had the opportunity because she wanted to block Rafe from his course, then she acted no differently than she had as a schoolgirl attempting to gain Gideon Lee's attention by avoiding him, peering at him over the edge of an open fan.

She remained on the quarterdeck as Rafe strode aft, paused to speak to Riggs and then to Mel and Belinda, and continued on. At the top of the ladder, he hesitated, his gaze falling on Phoebe. She waited, hand on the taffrail, half expecting him to order her away.

He merely inclined his head, then sauntered toward her, one corner of his mouth tipped up. "Mrs. Lee, you look a wee bit less greasy since I last saw you."

"I feel a bit less greasy." She gave him a full smile.

"And you are well?" Something flickered in his eyes—amusement, speculation, even warmth? "Your head is a'right?"

"Well enough." She dared touch his arm. "Thank you for the bathwater. I know it's an imposition."

"So is having you breaking a limb slipping on your own lard supply." He didn't draw away from her. "But I am thinking perhaps you should keep to your bed for a day or two to let the head heal."

Phoebe shuddered. "I fare much better on deck."

"Aye, an odd form of seasickness that is, to affect you only in the cabin." Rafe glanced at Jordy. "Do keep a watch on Riggs. Jones is well subdued, but Riggs is trouble in the making."

"'Tis a'ready been made, if you ask me." Jordy growled the words.

"I did not ask you."

"And Watt—"

"Nor about my—other senior crewman. Derrick will relieve you at the helm at the turn of the glass."

The hourglass, whose dripping sand measured time, appeared half full on its stand atop the binnacle.

She should have waited another quarter hour. Derrick never stared at her as Jordy did, as though she meant Rafe harm. She didn't. That letter was supposed to help him, protect him from himself if she failed.

She smiled up at him again. "Do you have a moment to walk with me, Captain?"

"I cannot think why you would wish to do so, Mrs. Lee." He did not smile back.

"Because I've missed your company?"

Jordy snorted.

Rafe headed for the ladder, Phoebe beside him. "He does not approve of you aboard, you ken," he said.

"I do know that. Neither does Watt."

"And neither do you?" He assisted her to the deck, then began to walk along the weather rail where salt spray touched their faces, cold but not too much to chill—enough to refresh. For the first time since meeting them, Phoebe understood why Tabitha and Dominick enjoyed walks along the beach in the morning mist. The swirling damp air felt like a cloak sheltering them both together.

"I'd rather not be here," Phoebe said, then wondered if she spoke the truth. "I prefer stable ground beneath me and a bath with fresh water."

"Then why did you stay?"

"Why have you been avoiding me since I stayed?"

He touched the back of her hand, which rested on his arm. "Because you stayed."

The deck rolled beneath Phoebe's feet as though a thirty-foot swell had passed beneath the bow. Never would she imagine him to be so open, so blunt. So vulnerable.

"You should have taken your opportunity to run, Mrs. Lee." He spoke nearly too softly for her to hear. The gentleness of his tone felt like a caress.

Phoebe tightened her hold on his arm. "I couldn't go after I knew what you're doing."

"Ah, you want to save my soul."

"I want to save your life. Only Jesus can save your soul."

"Why?" He paused and faced her. "What am I to you that you would do this?"

"I don't know." She met and held his gaze. "I just couldn't go."

"I am thinking you will regret it." He touched the tender lump on her head. "You have been injured a'ready. It could be worse next time."

"And you are almost certain to die if you continue. Rafe—" Her heart ached. Instinct prompted her to hold him close. A glimpse of Belinda staring at her and Mel grinning held Phoebe rooted like a garden statue. "How long do I have to work on changing your mind?"

He laughed. Chuckled to be accurate, a low rumble more in his chest than his throat. "You have nigh on four weeks, but Jordy has failed for nine years."

"That," Phoebe bit out, "is because Jordy talks of being a man of faith while fighting alongside you on the same mission. Can you believe in his sincerity?"

"Aye, but then he has been so all my life. Derrick, now, that is different. He fights with me out of loyalty and a sense of duty."

"As does Watt?"

"Not very subtle of you, Mrs. Lee."

"I was Phoebe the other night."

"Calling you Mrs. Lee reminds me you are a reluctant passenger, not my friend." He resumed walking.

"But I am your friend." The knotted end of a rope swung in her direction, and she danced aside to avoid it, noting Tommy Jones splicing lines twenty feet above her.

180

Had he swung the hemp on purpose?

"If you'll let me be," she concluded.

"I do not have friends, Mrs. Lee. But if I did . . ." Rafe paused, glanced up at the now safely coiled line, then faced Phoebe. "If I did—nay, I cannot say that. I am better off keeping my distance."

Phoebe opened her mouth to deny the truth of his words, then gazed into his gray eyes—eyes she once thought as cold and hard as quartz but now were something marginally softer. Marble perhaps, or at least flint. And she decided maybe he was right. Yet if she let him drift from her, her presence aboard the brig held no purpose. She wouldn't be with him in England if Dominick sent someone to help stop Rafe from his present course of action.

"Don't avoid me, Rafe." She released his arm and tucked her hands inside the boat cloak of his she still wore on deck. "Please."

"Now then, how can I refuse a lady anything?" He rested his hand on the lump on her head, allowing his fingers to linger in her hair a moment. "Do tell me if you have headaches or see double or are dizzy or faint. I am still thinking you might be concussed. No strenuous activity until we are certain you are all right, aye?"

Odd questions coming from a ship's captain. "Yes, but . . . does it mean I can't climb the rigging for fresh air as you seem to do?"

"Nay, certainly not."

"She cannot climb the rigging in a dress." Mel popped up beside her father. "'Tis why I prefer my breeches." And like a cat fleeing up a tree, with Fiona yapping and bobbing on the deck as though in futile pursuit, Mel leaped onto the shrouds and swept halfway to the crosstrees in seconds, then hooked her knees over a stay and released one hand.

Phoebe's stomach dropped to her toes.

"Melvina Davina Docherty!" Rafe shouted. "Do not dare let go."

Suddenly Watt poised beneath Mel. "Go ahead, lass. I will catch you."

"You will not." Rafe glared at Watt.

He shot Rafe a triumphant glance and held up his arms. "Come on, lass, you ken you can trust me."

For a heartbeat, Mel appeared as though she would take the dare. Then she laughed, wrapped her arms and legs around a stay, and slid to the deck.

Where Fiona and her father met her, the former wagging her body in joy, the latter stalking forward like a lion tracking down a tabby. His hands dropped onto her shoulders, and he spoke to her in a tone too low for anyone else to hear. That it was a severe scolding Phoebe didn't doubt. Mel paled, and her lower lip protruded, quivering.

"You don't think he'll hurt her, do you?" Belinda moved up beside Phoebe, puffing a little with exertion.

"No." Phoebe turned to Watt. "Why did you do that?"

Watt laughed. "We've done it before. She was a wee bit higher up, but I could have managed it."

"Or gotten her killed." Phoebe slammed her fists onto her hips and braced her legs to keep her balance. "If I ever catch you taunting the child like that again, I'll—I'll—"

"Blacken his other eye?" Rafe turned from Mel, who slipped along the rail as though avoiding everyone. "I think you had best leave the crew's discipline to me."

But he hadn't disciplined Watt after the attempted mutiny. From the smirk on Watt's face, he expected Rafe would do nothing to him this time either.

"We should go below and make sure she's not upset," Belinda said.

"No, leave her be." Rafe tucked a hand under Phoebe's and Belinda's elbows. "Come sit down and enjoy what mild weather we have left to us. I have duties to attend to."

"I need to rest." Belinda placed a hand on her belly.

"Are you feeling all right?" Phoebe sprang to Belinda's side and slipped her arm around the younger woman. "Any pain? Any—"

"Hush." Face reddening, Belinda clapped her hand over Phoebe's mouth. "Just because you have no sense of decency doesn't mean I don't."

"Sense of decency? There's nothing—" Phoebe sighed. "Of course."

She caught Rafe's glance and a glint in his eyes akin to amusement before he nodded and strode away.

"Let's go down to the cabin. I'm going to examine you," Phoebe said. "It's ridiculous for you to have dragged me to sea and then refuse to let me near you."

"You're here only to deliver the baby, should it become necessary," Belinda insisted. "I don't like being examined."

"And I don't like surprises like what might meet me when you go into your confinement if I don't know your condition ahead of time. Now, come below and lie on the bunk, or I'll ask you a lot of intimate questions on the deck here."

"You wouldn't." Belinda's color reversed to pallor.

"I would."

"No wonder none of the ladies in Loudoun County would let you tend them."

"It's the ones no one calls ladies I wanted to tend anyway." Phoebe clasped Belinda's hand in both of hers. "Endure this for the sake of the baby, if nothing else. Possibly George's heir."

"Well, all right." Head down as though she were heading to her own hanging, Belinda shuffled aft. In the cabin, she threw her cloak over a chair, then perched on the bunk.

"Lie down."

Phoebe washed her hands while Belinda flounced onto the bunk. Back at Belinda's side, Phoebe drew a sheet over Belinda to protect her modesty and made the examination she should have done weeks earlier. She followed all the procedures Tabitha had taught her. She ran through her experiences and lessons in her head, being without her books. She ignored Belinda's complaints about discomfort, embarrassment, and unnecessary invasion of her privacy.

When complete, Phoebe washed her hands again and slumped on the window seat. "You lied to me, Belinda, didn't you?"

"I don't know what you mean." Belinda struggled to a sitting position and rested her hands on her belly, emphasizing its size. "I told you right away I was increasing."

"You said four or five months. Then you said—" Phoebe took several deep breaths to keep herself from shouting. "Then you said seven. But that was a lie too, wasn't it? You were closer to eight months along when we set sail. That was two and a half weeks ago, and now I think you're closer to your time."

"Well, you're not that experienced—"

"Belinda!" Phoebe did shout this time. She sprang up from the window seat and leaned over her sister-in-law, her hands braced on the bulkhead behind her. "You've got to be honest with me about this. It could be a matter of life and death for you and the baby. I need to know if it's true labor or the false pains some women feel. Do you not understand?"

Belinda burst into tears. "I think the whole ship understands. And now he'll put me ashore and I won't be able to help George and—"

"Put you ashore?" Phoebe sank onto the bunk beside Belinda and slipped an arm around her shoulders. "My dear girl, there is no shore out here. You're going to have this baby either in England, if nothing holds us back, or in this very cabin."

"I think," Belinda said, clutching her belly, "it's going to be in this cabin."

12

"Captain?" Watt called from the quarterdeck. "You'd best come."

Rafe glanced up from amidships, where he'd taken to pacing so he wouldn't draw Phoebe's attention. The sails, close-hauled for nighttime travel, remained in good trim. The sea swished beneath the hull in gentle swells, and not a cloud marred the sky. Below, the men either slept or engaged in quiet activity, and on deck, a few others either stood watch or strolled about for exercise like their captain. One man crouched near the bow light reading a book.

Watt wasn't calling Rafe to the quarterdeck because of trouble with the vessel.

Gut tightening with suspicion as to where the trouble lay, Rafe headed aft. The scream reached him before he'd strode a dozen feet. He halted for a beat, then sprinted for the companionway.

The scream rose from the stern cabin. Something was wrong with Phoebe. She'd hurt herself after all. She was having a fit. She—

He slammed his hand against the door handle and shoved the portal open just as a glass soared toward his head. He ducked. The glass swooped past him, whispering through his hair on its trajectory, and smashed against the ladder.

Another shriek rose in the confined place, a banshee wail of rage or frustration. Rafe straightened as best he could beneath the low deck beams and flung himself across the cabin in time to grasp Belinda Chapman's wrist before she threw a glass jar of some red preserves at Watt, who now filled the doorway.

"Stop it," Rafe commanded. "You stop this nonsense right now."

"I can't." She tugged against his hold and kicked her slippered foot against his shin. "I'll go mad if I don't do something."

"You've done more than enough." Rafe removed the jar of preserves from her fingers and tossed it to Watt.

He caught it, dropped it into one of the capacious pockets of his coat, and otherwise remained motionless in the doorway.

Belinda smacked her other fist against Rafe's chin, not hard enough to even move his head more than half an inch to one side. "You can't hold me. I know that's wrong, even if you are going to rescue my husband. Phoebe, make him let me go."

"I don't think he should let you go," Phoebe said. "You're a danger to yourself and your baby right now."

She stood just out of Rafe's line of sight unless he turned his gaze away from Belinda, something he wasn't willing to do, but the widow's honeyed cream voice slid over him like warm silk on tender skin. Every hair on his arms stood on end, a reminder as to why he had been taking drastic and often inconvenient steps to be somewhere else on the brig from wherever she happened to reside.

Belinda punched Rafe again, and he caught hold of that wrist too. She clenched her teeth and growled like an angry kitten.

In the doorway, Watt snickered. Rafe shot his crewman a glare and caught hold of Phoebe from the corner of one eye. The pull to turn around and gaze upon her grew powerful within him.

Belinda began to cry.

Behind Rafe, the door clicked shut, Watt running away from feminine tears. Rafe braced himself against the lure, the heart-softening heat of a woman's tears—and failed. He released Belinda and stepped back. "What's amiss then, lass?"

"Everything." Sagging onto a chair, Belinda covered her face with her hands and sobbed. "I am as ugly as a porpoise. I don't think we'll ever get George free. And my midwife is incompetent, and I'm sure she'll kill my baby."

Phoebe sucked in her breath. If anyone should be throwing things, it should be her, not Mrs. Chapman. But Phoebe remained quiet and calm and still out of his sight unless he turned.

He turned. He couldn't stop himself. "What happened?" he asked Phoebe.

"A lack of understanding of her own condition and a lack of trust in my ability." Her voice remained steady, her face expressionless. Her hands shook at her waist.

"I understand enough to know that I'm going to have this baby soon, and she won't help me." Belinda's wail rang loudly enough to be heard all the way back to Bermuda.

Rafe clamped his hands against his thighs to stop himself from clamping them over his ears as he continued to address Phoebe. "False pains?"

"I have examined her and have every reason—" She broke off and narrowed her eyes. "What would you know of that?"

"I am a father. That plagued . . . Davina often near—you are not telling me she's further along than we thought, are you?"

"I wish I weren't." Phoebe glanced at Belinda. "Captain Rafe knows of these false spasms in the belly that make you think you're entering your confinement. So I am not making this up to—to get even with you."

Belinda turned to him with big, dark eyes like drowned pansies. "So it's true? I have to go through this for weeks, not just hours?"

"Aye, that seems the way of it." He took one of her hands in both of his. "Why do you not go to your bed and rest? I'll send for some tea."

"The galley fires are doused for the night," Phoebe pointed out.

"Then we'll light them again. She needs to drink. I do not think water from the butts will do."

"It tastes foul." Belinda had ceased weeping and now merely sulked, her lower lip protruding and the corners of her mouth turned down. "Will Mel come read to me?"

"I can read to you," Phoebe said. "No need to disturb the girl."

Bless her. She wouldn't be wanting to leave the cabin, following him onto the deck, drawing him further into wanting and enjoying her companionship.

"I like the way Mel talks better." One hand to her swollen belly, Belinda pushed herself to her feet with the other hand braced on the table and staggered toward the bed.

Rafe slipped his hand beneath her elbow and steadied her to the bunk. "And here I've been thinking—" Realizing he was about to compliment Phoebe's voice, he clamped his teeth together. "Mel is likely in her bed for the night."

Except she wasn't. Not a quarter of a minute after he uttered those words, his daughter burst into the cabin, hair tangled and eyes wide, Fiona clutched in her arms. "Is Mrs. Chapman all right?"

"Quite." Rafe eased the lady onto the bunk and patted her shoulder as though she were a child younger than Mel. "She had a wee bit of an upset."

And someone needed to clean up the broken glass.

"I'll fetch her some tea." Before anyone could naysay her, Mel darted off again.

"I believe I'll go with her." Phoebe followed at a slightly more sedate pace, her back straight, her head held high.

"I don't know what I was thinking bringing her along." Belinda snatched up a pillow and clutched it to her chest. "She doesn't know what she's doing."

"Aye, I'm thinking she does. She delivered twins in Bermuda, and the mither was doing well. That takes skill. But if you prefer, we can get you a different midwife when we reach England, should the necessity arise."

"That's the trouble." Belinda began to weep again. "I think it'll be too late."

"God, do please help me." The heartfelt plea for assistance slipped out unbidden. He ran his tongue over his lips, half expecting to taste the bitterness of mold, so long had the time been since those words had spilled from his mouth.

Phoebe influencing his thoughts again, talking about God and help and relying on Him, all through that night when he'd have killed James Brock in cold blood—or gotten killed first—if she hadn't intervened.

He backed to the door. "We'll manage just fine if it is."

Without God.

"Get yourself tucked into bed, and Mel and Ph—Mrs. Lee will be along in a trice."

He left the cabin and started up the companionway. Glass tinkled beneath his feet, and he stooped to gather it. He couldn't keep running away from Phoebe, neglecting duties simply to avoid her presence. Like now. He needed to clean up the glass before someone ran through in bare feet. Calling someone else just wasn't right. The men would begin to think Rafe considered himself above such menial duties, when he never had been in the past.

He wasn't in the present. He simply wished to end the visceral reaction he had to nearness to Phoebe. It was unwholesome and certainly unholy. She was a good woman, a decent woman. He would never dishonor her, even if she would do so herself, which she would not. Her faith sustained her, gave her courage and backbone, but she'd fallen for him. He'd read it in her eyes earlier when he picked her up off the deck, the wonder, the softness, the light of joy. He'd suspected that night she insisted on coming ashore with him, and his body yearned toward it, another chance to love and be loved.

And he pushed it away. He pushed it away every time he looked at her, heard her voice, wished for someone to talk to. She pulled him away from his mission, the only way he knew to give Davina rest and ease his conscience. No female must interfere with his plan, if it meant he avoided Phoebe for another two or three weeks.

But the glass needed to go.

He stooped and began to gather up the shards. Fortunately, Belinda had thrown a goblet of no great worth. It was well suited to shipboard life—solid and thick. The sturdiness of the glass made cleaning it up easier. Few slivers clung to the wood of the ladder. He could be done and gone before Phoebe and Mel returned.

He collected the glass in his kerchief and carried it onto the deck to toss into the sea. Then he returned to the quarterdeck, watching, listening, waiting to hear her voice. Three more weeks of this would be torture. The last two had nearly driven him to the bottle of rum he kept for purely medicinal purposes like numbing a man's senses before an amputation.

Laughing at himself, he crossed to the wheel to give the helmsman a rest. If he wasn't going to sleep, he may as well let someone else do so.

191

"Is all well, sir?" the man asked. "Watt called me to take over here, then went below."

"All is well." Rafe caught a whiff of smoke. "They've gone to restart the galley fire for some tea for Mrs. Chapman. Is all well here?"

The sailor—Hazelwood?—hesitated a full minute before saying, "Aye, sir, I believe so now."

"Which means?" Rafe pinned the man with his eyes.

Hazelwood moved from foot to foot, shifting his broad shoulders to keep his balance. "Now that you keep Sam Riggs and Tommy Jones locked up at night. Riggs is pure trouble, he is, and leads the rest along with talk of our own riches."

"You too?" Rafe didn't recall if Hazelwood had been with the would-be mutineers and had chosen not to make inquiries.

Hazelwood shrugged. "Do I have to answer that, sir?"

"No." Rafe laughed.

Hazelwood stood still. "I have six brothers and sisters who are counting on me making some money. I thought that's what a privateer is for."

"So it is, and you'll have your opportunity soon, I promise. Meanwhile, you have food and a place of shelter and wages coming to you. Now get to your hammock before you admit to too much."

"Aye, sir." The youth saluted and plodded from the deck, shoulders slumped as though he bore a burden.

Rafe took that possible burden into consideration. If another ringleader arose from the ranks, they would mutiny and go after a prize. If they did, he would have to step in and lead them. None of the men knew how to lead a fight. Watt thought he did, thought his years in the British Navy had prepared him, but the Navy had rid themselves of his incompetence, and only Rafe's loyalty to familial duty kept him aboard. Most of the other men were too green to war.

The ones who weren't would remain loyal to Rafe and not fight if he didn't. For all their sakes, he would have to fight, and he was tired of war, as much as it had served his purpose with prize money restoring his family's fortunes and then some.

"No battles, please." He gazed into the binnacle light but didn't know for certain to whom he spoke. "Not with the ladies aboard. And Mel . . ."

He shuddered to think of harm coming to his daughter because of his actions. Dear, mischievous Mel, all he had left—

"Please protect my daughter."

A hand landed on his arm, as light as thistledown, burning like molten glass. He started and glanced to the owner of the touch. The binnacle light had robbed his night vision and he blinked, but he didn't need his sight to know Phoebe stood beside him. Her jasmine scent, her stillness wrapped around him.

He removed one hand from the wheel with the intention of removing her fingers from his sleeve. Instead, he pressed her hand against his forearm and held her near him. Too weary from too many sleepless nights, he carried no strength for pushing her away.

"Who were you talking to?" she asked.

"I don't know. Whoever watches out for sailors and fools."

She laughed low in her throat. "You mean God? Were you praying, Captain Rafe Docherty?"

"It wouldn't matter if I were. He stopped listening to me a long time ago."

"Stopped listening, or did you stop talking?"

"I stopped talking when He didn't save my wife."

"Oh, Rafe, He was listening. He—"

"Had other plans for her." He removed his hand from hers and ground his teeth. "Aye, weel, I have different plans too,

193

and they do not include trust in a God who would let harm come to another person like that."

"He let His own Son be hung on a cross so we can be redeemed. Was that without purpose?"

"And who is redeemed by Davina's death? By my parents' deaths?" He intended the words to come out with anger. Instead, his throat closed and the binnacle light blurred.

Phoebe moved her hand to his face, stroked his cheek so the rasp of his whiskers sounded like footfalls tramping through dry leaves.

"I don't know." She dropped her hand to his shoulder. "We may never know, but the Bible promises that all things work together for good. We just have to trust—"

"I'll trust in myself and my skill with a pistol and sword."

"And sleep when your conscience is clear?"

"I don't know what you mean."

She snorted, a delicate, ladylike snort, but a snort nonetheless.

"What would you know of my sleeping habits?" he demanded.

"Or lack thereof? Ah, Rafe, you may pace on the main deck now, but I am aware of every step you take. My prayers and my heart follow you."

His own heart jumped and twisted. He knew exactly what she meant, except for the praying part. His heart followed her too. His heart, which wasn't dead after all. His heart, which he must guard until James Brock paid for his crimes.

"Don't, Phoebe. Stay away from me if you know what's good for you. I can't care for you the way you seem to want."

"Can't or won't?"

"Both."

"And we can't just be friends? I miss talking to you."

He missed her companionship too. But he shook his head. "I do not think of you as a friend, Phoebe."

"I don't think that's true. I think—"

He brushed his finger across her lips, quieting her, then replaced his finger with his lips. He held the wheel steady with one hand and slipped his arm around her waist, drawing her close against him so she'd know he wasn't thinking of friendly dialogue as mere acquaintances over a cup of tea.

Her response told him she didn't think of him as a mere friend either—giving him a reason to send her packing but a yearning to keep her close. She buried her fingers in his hair, murmuring something he couldn't hear above the sigh of the wind and the roaring of blood in his ears.

Oh, she tempted him, tempted him in ways far beyond the physical. She tempted him to abandon his mission and live a life of friends and family and the kirk on a Sunday.

As it had been with Davina—no, better than what they had known, more than the mere affection they'd had for one another. Before the consumption took her and all the medical advice said take her to a warm, sunny, and dry climate—where she died not of the disease that would have likely taken her within a year or two, but horribly, painfully—

He jerked himself away. "Go." He grasped the wheel with both hands as though it were an anchor to sanity instead. "I do not want you."

She laughed at him. He deserved it. She knew he was lying.

He felt like beating his brow against the wheel, a mast, something that would drive sense back into his head.

He took a steadying breath and smelled only the sea. She had left him as quietly as she'd arrived. A moment later, he heard a door slam, felt the door slam beneath his feet. Probably pretending it was his skull.

"Lord, please spare me from all females."

But of course he didn't mean that. He wouldn't trade away his daughter for anything. When she bounded onto the quarterdeck a score of minutes later, he welcomed her with a smile and a brief hug.

"How are you faring, lass?"

"Well. I think Mrs. Chapman will fall asleep soon." She slipped around to the other side of the wheel to lean against the binnacle. "Are all ladies in her condition so . . . hysterical?"

"Nay, not all. I think Mrs. Chapman has been spoiled and now her husband is in prison. She has a great deal to worry her."

"So do you, and you don't go all funny for nothing."

"I'm a sensible male." He winked.

She stuck her tongue out at him.

"Disrespecting your captain. I could have you punished for that."

"But you won't." She darted forward, executed a handstand, and landed on her feet again, her face sober. "Captain Rafe—I mean, Papa? Mrs. Chapman says I should call you Papa, if you like it."

He liked it too much to speak when she called him that. He merely inclined his head in acknowledgment.

"All right then, Papa, why did you let the men get away with mutiny? Isn't it dangerous?"

"I need them to sail this brig, child, and am counting on their guilt at their disloyalty to make them more loyal for not getting what they deserved. Understand?"

"I think so." She wrinkled her brow. "May I be lookout tomorrow? I'm not very good at sewing, and that's all Mrs. Chapman wants me to do now."

"No, you may not be lookout. I believe I'm the one who needs to be up there."

Where Phoebe would be too far removed by shrouds and ratlines to come near him.

Mel sighed. "What can I do then?"

"What may you do then," he corrected. "Tell her you have schoolwork you're neglecting, which I'm certain you are."

She grimaced. "But I want to do something. I'm tired of sitting still."

"You chose to come aboard, hinnie, so you may pay the consequences. Now get yourself to your bed."

"Oh, all right." She sighed but kissed him on the cheek before dashing off to her cabin.

Rafe occupied himself with creating lessons for her in his head. Should he start teaching her the principles of chemistry? Her mathematics were excellent, but females didn't usually learn the sciences. Mel, however, was far from a typical female. She would want to know science. But how to teach chemistry aboard a ship? Perhaps he would persuade Phoebe to teach Mel biology and explain womanly things to her.

It took no persuading. When he asked Phoebe the next day, she agreed in an instant.

"And I'll teach her how to embroider," Belinda added.

Behind Belinda's back, Mel grimaced, but said nothing more than, "I can make a coat for Fi."

And thus the next week and a half passed peaceably, if still with too little sleep for Rafe until Phoebe began to join him on his nighttime pacing. At first they said little. Then she began to draw information out of him, details about his growing up in Edinburgh, his interest in philosophy and the sciences, his family, his country, and God. He told her of things he hadn't thought about in years, harmless but naughty boyhood pranks. "I could not do my studies all the time," he said.

In turn, Phoebe talked of growing up in the foothills of

the Blue Ridge Mountains, where horses were king and her family next in line. "I got everything I wanted," she declared, "and it wasn't enough."

"Not very subtle of you, *mo leannan*." The endearment slipped out before he could stop himself, and he rushed on. "I ken you are saying I will get my wish with Brock and still not be happy."

"I honestly wasn't thinking that, but now that you mention it . . . What does *mo leannan* mean?"

"My annoying one." He drew her hand up, kissed her fingertips, and gave her a gentle push toward the companionway ladder. "Get your rest, Mrs. Lee. I am on watch now."

He climbed to the quarterdeck to relieve Derrick at the helm. His friend, the closest thing to a chaplain the brig possessed, lingered for a minute. "I couldn't help but hear, Captain Rafe, and Mrs. Lee be right in that. If you don't have the Lord in your heart, everything you have will be nothing."

"Go to bed, Derrick."

"Aye, sir." Derrick flashed him a grin. "I'll go to my hammock and pray for you." He chuckled all the way down the deck.

Rafe shook his head and couldn't be angry. Sometimes he wondered what he would do in the future. Finish raising Mel, yes, but she would likely marry in ten years or less, and then what purpose would he find in life after the first twenty-three had been devoted in one direction and the next nine in another? Where would the next thirty or forty go? He pondered the question without answers other than those he didn't want to accept. Focusing on the immediate goal rested more comfortably on his shoulders.

His relief helmsman arrived at midnight, and Rafe retreated to his bunk. He slept long and deep until he began to dream of Davina hauled away by the barbarians, the pirates plaguing the Mediterranean. Her screams filled his head and brought him jerking upright, his head fogged from sleep, screams ringing in his ears.

He should have found another way to ensure George Chapman would cooperate other than having his wife at hand. This screaming over nothing could not continue. They all needed rest, and she had surely awakened everyone.

Grinding his teeth, he tugged on his clothes. Not until he pulled his shirt over his head did he realize that daylight blazed through the portal. He shoved his feet into his boots and stalked out of his cabin.

"Rafe!" Phoebe flung herself against him. "It's Mel. She's fallen."

"Where is she?" He set Phoebe from him and raced for the knot of men gathered amidships. "Step aside."

They did, turning grim and pale faces toward him. In their midst lay Mel, crumpled like a discarded banner with her bright hair and white skin. His daughter, too pale. Too still.

Certain his heart had stopped, he dropped to his knees beside her and felt for a pulse in her neck. It was there, fluttering, weak, but constant.

Breath rasping in his throat, he glanced up at the ring of men and Phoebe. "How far did she fall?"

Jordy, as white as Mel, pointed to a dangling line and sagging spar thirty feet above the deck. "She was up top, and I told her to get herself down or I'd wake you up. She's as nimble as a monkey, but she just fell."

Rafe's gaze flicked to that dangling line, and he feared he would be sick right there on the deck. Swallowing the bitterness of bile, he began to run his hands over Mel in search of broken bones, especially her spine. If her spine was damaged—

He dropped his head to press his cheek against hers. "Be

all right, you disobedient brat. Dear God, please let my lass be all right."

A touch as light as spindrift brushed across his head. "May I help? I can do things other than midwifery, you know."

He didn't know, but Mel needed help, and Rafe would take it any way he could find it. He couldn't move, couldn't let go of his precious child long enough to finish looking for her injuries.

Apparently taking his silence as acquiescence, Phoebe finished looking Mel over for breaks, fractures, anything shattered beyond repair.

"I think one or two ribs may be cracked." Phoebe rested her hand on Rafe's shoulder, nudging, gently urging him to straighten. "But her head—"

He jerked upright and stared into her face, seeking the truth, the worst. She met his gaze, but her eyes held a hint of fear.

"I think her skull is fractured."

A collective gasp followed by murmurs rose from the men. Rafe closed his eyes and willed his heart to beat normally, not stop or gallop out of control. Mel needed him in control, needed special care.

Not that a fractured skull required care for long. He'd seen it before. Falls aboard ship were not uncommon. The lucky ones died on impact and didn't wake with their brains so scrambled they were good for nothing but taking up space in Bedlam.

Not that he'd put his lass in a hospital for the insane. He'd keep her with him, protect her.

Or do his best to heal her.

He clamped his teeth together and made himself look at his daughter's head. Behind her left ear, blood pooled on the deck, nearly the same color as her hair. Someone coughed and ran across the deck to be sick over the side. Rafe knew how he felt. Blood during battle was one matter. Blood oozing from a wound on a child was quite different.

"Let's get her below." He tried to be brisk as he began to issue orders. "Several of us, so we don't jostle her and cause more damage. I need bandages and seawater. It should be nearly as cold as ice this time of year."

No one moved.

He shot a glare around the circle of onlookers. "Now."

Phoebe sprang to her feet. "I'll get bandages. We have extra sheets that are still clean." She raced aft.

And started everyone else moving. Watt and two others ran for the line of buckets kept at the rail for water in case of fire. Others simply scattered.

Derrick crouched down and held out his massive arms. "I'll take her, Captain. Won't move a hair on her head. You just go on and get things set up for her."

"Yes. Yes, thank you."

Feeling as though he stumbled through a fog, Rafe descended to the miniscule chamber in which Mel slept.

Phoebe met him at the door. "Not here. She needs light and air, and we'll need space to tend to her needs. Put her in the stern cabin."

"But you and Mrs. Chapman—"

"Will manage."

Rafe's glance flew to Belinda. She stood by the table, gripping the edge for support, her face white. "Of course it's all right. Whatever the child needs from us she may have."

Someday he would ask her how she could be so kind to his daughter and so hateful to Phoebe. For the moment, he managed to nod in acknowledgment of her generosity and enter the cabin to ensure it would suit as a sickroom. Clean? Yes, as spotless as it could be after weeks at sea. Phoebe darted ahead of him and began to change the bedding for clean sheets reeking of lavender.

Rafe's stomach roiled. He couldn't be sick, not in front of

the women, not in front of his men, not when Mel needed him healthy and strong and able to pull up memories he tried daily to suppress.

"We need—we need bandages," he managed. "And cold water."

"And hot tea." Phoebe added.

Rafe stared at her. "She can't drink anything."

"Not for her." Phoebe smiled at him. "For you. Now, sit down before you fall down, Rafe. You can watch. If I do something wrong, let me know."

Her tone patronized him. A blazing retort sprang to his lips. He swallowed it. She didn't deserve him taking out his fear on her.

He sat on the window seat. Words reverberated through his skull. *Not Mel. Not Mel. Not Mel.* He realized he was praying again, begging the God he had rejected so long ago. *Don't punish me through my daughter. Weren't Davina and my parents enough?*

Apparently not. Derrick brought Mel in and laid her on the bunk. She didn't move. Her chest scarcely moved, so shallow were her breaths. With a head wound like hers, she couldn't live for long.

He dropped to his knees beside her and took one of her limp, white hands in his. "I never should have brought you aboard. 'Tis all my fault, lass. You ken I meant the best."

"It wasn't your fault, Captain." Jordy stepped over the coaming and loomed above Rafe. "I inspected that line. There was naught wrong with it."

Rafe surged to his feet. "There had to have been. Lines do not just break with no reason."

"I didn't say there was no reason." Jordy's eyes blazed. "I said there was naught wrong with the line until someone half sliced it with a knife."

13

During her apprenticeship with Tabitha, Phoebe had seen a concussion like Mel's. A farmer putting a new roof on his barn after a storm had slipped and fallen. The wife had called in Tabitha as the nearest person with any medical knowledge. Although she had applied cold compresses and tried to keep him from starving by spooning drops of broth into his mouth at regular intervals, no one could help the man. He needed a physician, but the nearest one resided twenty miles away and couldn't leave his patients to tend to one man, who was likely to die anyway.

And he had. One night he simply stopped breathing.

Phoebe sat beside the bunk, holding Mel's limp hand and stroking Fiona, who curled up beside her young master, keeping guard on Mel and refusing to leave for any reason. Phoebe prayed for Mel not to suffer a fate similar to that man. She was a mere child. A disobedient one, as she shouldn't have been in the rigging at all. But she was also warm and amusing, smart and loving.

"And if she dies, Lord," Phoebe murmured in the silent cabin, "Rafe will never trust in you or believe You love him."

Worse, Rafe thought he was being punished, perhaps for his quest for revenge. Phoebe wasn't certain, though, since he'd said nothing about abandoning his plans to destroy James Brock. The brig remained on her course. The sliced line had been repaired. Rafe was testing all of the lines for soundness after sitting beside his daughter's bed for nearly six hours without a break in the tedium.

Phoebe moved in and out of the cabin, resetting Belinda in Mel's box of a cabin, making sure everyone, including Rafe, had a decent noontime meal. Phoebe listened for complaints from Belinda, a dozen responses gathered on her tongue to shut up the younger woman, but that hadn't been necessary. Belinda simply took her sewing on deck, and when the skies clouded and threatened rain, she retired to the stern cabin, where she sat sewing and gazing out of the windows. Phoebe hoped she was praying too, praying for Mel, praying for Rafe.

"But why would you use this child to punish him? And his wife. Dear God—" Words failed Phoebe. She didn't know what to say, what she was saying.

She knew that Rafe needed to trust God regardless of what happened to Mel. But as she sat by the child's bed hour after hour with no change in her breathing, not a hint of movement, Phoebe felt a quaking in her middle—the shaking of her own faith.

She shot to her feet and paced the bit of open space in the cabin. God had a purpose in everything. Everything worked together for good for those who loved the Lord and were called according to His purpose. But what of those who rejected God? Surely this couldn't happen simply because Rafe was bent on his own revenge and not trusting in God to take care of James Brock in this life or the next. Surely God wouldn't mete out punishment by destroying a child.

He'd allowed Job's sons and daughters to die. But then, they'd been adults and, by implication, not particularly godly ones. Mel was trying. She read her Bible.

"Oh, God, why this little girl?" Phoebe cried aloud. She pounded her fists against the table, then pressed the heels of her palms to her eyes to stem the flow of tears that seemed ceaseless. "Lord, please heal this precious life."

Behind her, the door latch clicked. Phoebe didn't look. She smelled Belinda's lavender oil. If Belinda said one word of complaint about her tiny quarters now, Phoebe feared she would have no control over her reaction.

But Belinda slipped an arm around Phoebe's shoulders and just stood beside her in silence, save for a half dozen sniffs that suggested she wept too.

Phoebe glanced at her. Indeed, tears coursed down Belinda's pretty face. "You love her too, don't you?"

"I do." Belinda nodded. "She . . . well, she's made me want to be a mother. And to lose her—" Her voice broke into a sob.

"We need to pray for a miracle." Phoebe crossed the cabin to Mel's side.

The girl lay as motionless as ever, good for her cracked ribs, not so good for her future. She hadn't moved for nearly twelve hours. Darkness had fallen, and she made no reaction to the lanterns Phoebe lit. She lifted one of Mel's lids and shone the light directly into them. Her pupils neither contracted nor expanded. They remained pinpoints in her face, the irises more gray than green.

Phoebe dropped to her knees. Belinda stood behind her, her hands on Phoebe's shoulders. Phoebe clasped one of Mel's delicate hands and sought words that would break through the pain around her heart, the turmoil in her mind. She felt like a kettle with its lid pressed down and unable to let off the steam boiling up inside. If something didn't change, she might begin to shriek and not stop.

"Lord, we need a miracle," she managed through stiff lips. "I don't know how she will awaken now without one. Please, God, send Your healer."

"Amen," Belinda murmured.

Neither of them moved. Phoebe didn't open her eyes. Mel's hand remained limp in hers, her breathing shallow.

"God, did you hear me?" Phoebe cried.

Once again the door latch clicked. This time Jordy slipped into the cabin, his face grim, his eyes suspiciously red. "I can sit with the lass a wee bit. You two go on and fetch your dinner. Her da will be down in a moment."

"Then I'll wait for him." Phoebe shoved herself to her feet. "He probably shouldn't be alone."

"Nay." Jordy met her gaze across the intervening space. "He blames himself for not waking up sooner, though 'twas the best rest he'd had in weeks. And he is not responsible for the cut line."

"Who is?" Phoebe clenched her fists. "I might toss him overboard myself."

Belinda gasped. "Phoebe."

"Aye, I ken what you are saying, lass." Jordy's mouth hardened into a thin line for a moment. "We think 'twas Jones but cannot prove it. No one claims to seeing him up there. But if we ever can . . . weel, the captain will haul him up before a court on land, I'm thinking." For the first time, he glanced at Mel. "No change?"

"None." Phoebe bit her lip. "You're a praying man. Maybe your prayers will be heard. I fear for Rafe—for the captain—if anything happens to her."

"Aye, I already fear for his soul. And him such a godly lad." Jordy cleared his throat. "I am praying, but I'm thinking there may be more that can be done."

Phoebe and Belinda straightened. "What?" they chorused.

"'Tis an operation I saw once before." Jordy turned a bit green beneath his sun-bronzed skin. "'Twas a gruesome thing, but it relieved the pressure on the brain, like lancing a boil, the surgeon said, and the man lived."

"Not—" Phoebe's stomach rolled with the memory of a picture she'd seen in one of Tabitha's medical tomes. "Trepanning?"

"What's that?" Belinda asked.

"You don't want to know," Phoebe said. "It takes a man with skill and training, and that's rarely found aboard a ship, let alone the proper equipment needed. Maybe if we could keep her alive long enough to turn back for Bermuda, or perhaps sail into a port in France that might be closer? Under a flag of truce, of course."

"We do not ken if we can keep her alive so long." Jordy shoved his fingers through his graying hair, dislodging strands from his queue. "Two weeks at the least either way. But we do have a body aboard with the training and the equipment."

"You do?" Belinda grasped Jordy's arm. "Why wasn't I told? I wouldn't have had to drag Phoebe along as my midwife if I'd known there was a trained surgeon aboard."

"Aye, weel, he does not like to recall the fact, as 'twas long ago, but this is a special circumstance. If I can be convincing him."

"A trained surgeon?" Phoebe felt like shaking Jordy, not clutching his arm. "Who? Why hasn't he acted?"

"Not a surgeon," Jordy said, gazing past their heads to the stern windows. "He's a physician from Edinburgh Univer—"

Phoebe shoved past Jordy and Belinda and raced up the steps to the deck. Near darkness met her, and she slid to a halt on the smooth planks, blinking to gain her night sight, straining her ears to hear anyone around, letting her nostrils flare for a hint of ginger.

She found him between the rail and the cutter. He gripped the bulwark as though needing it to keep him upright or anchored to the deck. He didn't move, didn't even turn his head as she charged up to him.

"You're a physician?"

He jerked straight. "Jordy?"

"Yes, but I should have guessed. Your manner when I was sick. Questions you've asked." She shook him. "So did you train, or were you merely working toward it?"

"Aye, I was beginning to work with my father in his practice." He sounded fatigued. "You would ne'er ken it, would you now?" He gave her a tight smile. "Do no harm, my oath said, and I've spent nine years doing naught else."

"But you have the training to save your daughter's life."

"Or kill her in the attempt, aye." He rested one hand on Phoebe's shoulder. "I have been standing here wishing I still believed God cared enough to listen to me. But I am thinking He's taken everything else, why not my daughter too?"

"Oh, Rafe." Phoebe's throat closed. She swallowed. "I've been praying for a miracle. Your ability to perform the operation just might be the answer."

"I have not practiced in over nine years, my dear." He lifted his hand from her shoulder and held it in the faint light of phosphorescence off the sea. "Once upon a time, I thought naught of having the blood of my patients on this hand. I helped in difficult births using the forceps, I removed growths, and I sewed up gashes that nigh on severed limbs. It was all for the good, you ken. Most of the time my patients lived to thank me." He gave her a tight-lipped smile. "And pay me. Once I even performed the trepanning on a man struck in the head by a runaway horse. He woke up in a day and ended up as right as ever. Oh, aye, the pride I had. I was lauded the best young physician in Edinburgh. The best besides my father. But I could not heal my wife from the consumption. Nor save her from the pirates. And now my hand is covered with the blood of Frenchmen only trying to survive like anyone during a war. So how can I heal my daughter from the concussion?"

"Davina had consumption?"

"'Tis why we were in the Mediterranean. She needed sunshine and dry air, both in short supply in Edinburgh. But it was of no use. She was getting worse. I could not help her."

"You're not to blame for that. No one knows how to heal consumption, Rafe." She caught hold of his hand and cherished it between both of hers. "And trepanning is extremely dangerous, especially aboard a ship, I'd think, but you know as well as I—perhaps better than I—that her likelihood of staying alive is nearly nothing without some kind of help."

"And you have not been praying?" His tone held a blend of sarcasm and surprise. "No angels are coming down to rescue my lass?"

"Oh, I expect they will." Phoebe spoke through gritted teeth. "But to take her to heaven, not relieve the pressure on her brain."

Rafe flinched.

"Rafe, she hasn't moved a bit in twelve hours. I've seen this once before. He died in twenty-four hours."

"That does not have to be my lass. Some people wake up."

"Some, yes. How many do you know?"

"I've read of a few. A miner in Northumberland woke up after a month."

"A miner." Phoebe growled. "A big, strapping man, no doubt. Mel is a child, and a small one at that."

"She's in fine health."

"The healthy die. You know that as well as I."

Rafe jerked his hand free from hers, nearly sending her off balance. "I can do naught till morning. Let me think on it. 'Tis all I can promise."

"It's enough." Phoebe kissed his whisker-rough cheek and left him to ponder.

When she was a dozen feet away, he called after her, "The *Davina* is a brig, not a ship."

Phoebe laughed, her heart lightening. If he could tease her like that, he would make the right decision, maybe the miracle God intended.

Not until she reached the cabin to find Belinda sitting on the edge of the bunk, holding both of Mel's hands, did Phoebe pause long enough to think about Rafe being a physician. He'd been young to hold such a reputation. Not surprising with a father also a physician, a man with more training and education than a surgeon. Well, she held more medical training than most surgeons. But Rafe had been a true healer, a man with deep knowledge of the human body and how it worked and how to heal it.

Rafe was a healer.

She merely nodded at Belinda, too overwhelmed to speak. Seated on the bench below the stern windows, she clasped her hands beneath her chin and stared into a future she hadn't allowed herself to consider once in her four years as a widow—life with another man, life as a wife. With Rafe restored to his medical practice instead of his current mission—

She snapped herself to the present. His current mission lay in the opposite direction of healing. His soul lay in the opposite direction of the Lord. He'd rejected his training and vows and rejected his faith. She couldn't have him under any circumstances like those, even if he were inclined in her direction.

Oh, he cared about her. If nothing else, he wanted her. But he couldn't forgive those who had killed his wife. He couldn't turn his heart away from that great love of his youth.

Phoebe rose. "What happened to Jordy? I thought we were to go down to the galley to eat."

"He hadn't eaten either, so I told him to go." Belinda raised red-rimmed eyes to Phoebe. "I can't bear to leave her for long. How can her father stay away?"

"Besides still having a ship to run, he's suffering, Bel. She's all he has left."

Belinda jutted her chin forward. "Then he should be here."

"He's coming."

Footfalls on the companionway ladder told Phoebe of Rafe's approach. She recognized his stride, long, firm steps carrying him with speed and grace.

He opened the door and stepped over the coaming, then paused, fixing his gray eyes on the bed, on his daughter, without blinking for several moments, then he strode to her side and knelt beside the bunk. "Do not die on me, hinnie."

He seemed not to notice Belinda beside him or Phoebe a few feet away. He didn't acknowledge their presence as he continued to murmur to Mel.

Phoebe signaled to Belinda to follow her out of the cabin. Neither of them spoke until they reached the deck.

"He's a really bad man," Belinda said, "but we should pray for him too, shouldn't we?"

"Yes." Phoebe took Belinda's arm and led her to the forward hatch. "But I don't think he's a really bad man. He's misguided. His soul is troubled, but there's so much goodness in him, I—I—"

"Do you love him?" Belinda stopped walking and stared at Phoebe by the light of a lantern.

Phoebe said nothing.

Belinda's lips whitened. "How could you? How could you love a man like him after a man like my brother?"

Phoebe clamped her teeth down on the one-word response. "Easily."

"He—he's scum compared to Gideon." Belinda's voice went shrill.

"Quiet," Phoebe commanded. "He's not—"

"My brother attended William and Mary College and read the classics. He knew how to run a plantation."

"And how to drink himself senseless every night." The words slipped out before Phoebe could stop herself from saying them, nor from plunging on. "I've never seen Rafe Docherty take so much as a sip of spirits, nor allow it on this vessel, and he finished his schooling at a far more important institution of learning than that unimportant school in Williamsburg."

"Why, you—you—you murderess."

Although Belinda bunched her hands into fists, she didn't strike Phoebe. She didn't need to. Her epithet struck harder than her chubby little fists could. Phoebe staggered back, fetched up against the rail, and clung to the damp wood in an effort to stop the tremors shuddering through her.

"I—I'm sorry." Belinda reached out her hand, palm up. "I didn't mean to say that. Of course you didn't kill Gideon."

"It's just what everyone says." Phoebe spun around. She would have been sick except she hadn't eaten all day. "Go on down to the galley to get your supper. I'm not hungry."

"Phoebe, please."

"Leave me alone, Bel. You've said quite enough for one night."

"But—"

Phoebe hunched her shoulders against her sister-in-law. With a sigh, Belinda trudged away.

Phoebe took several deep breaths of the crisp, briny air, then turned aft again. She wanted to be with Rafe more than she wanted to eat. Rafe, more of a kindred spirit aboard this brig than anyone knew, including Belinda Lee Chapman.

14

Rafe set the chest on his bunk, the only place in his make-shift cabin large enough for the oblong wooden box. He hadn't touched it in months, not since their last battle with the protective frigate of a French merchantman, which had forced him to apply his medical skills for some musket ball extractions and even less pleasant uses of saws and scalpels. Those lay on the top tray, ready to handle. Below nestled his most useful medical books. Even deeper into the chest lay instruments he hoped to never use again, instruments that resembled something more like what the Spanish Inquisition might have employed to torture infidels than tools of healing.

Or death.

A shudder ran through Rafe as he lifted the trepanning saw out of its nest of silk. If he turned the handle a fraction too hard, if the saw blade guard slipped, he could kill his daughter in an instant. He would destroy her brain more profoundly than the blow possibly already had. Yet he must try. He knew the signs better than Phoebe, and her diagnosis demonstrated a measure of medical training beyond that of most midwives he'd met, a testimony to Dominick Cherrett's wife.

If Mel didn't wake up by morning, she was likely to not wake up at all. Already her breathing was shallow, her heart-beats thready. The water, tea, and broth they'd spooned into her mouth ran out again. She was too deep into her coma to so much as swallow involuntarily. A bad sign. A terrible sign. No one could survive long if she didn't swallow water at the least.

"God, how could You take my daughter too?" He murmured the query, though he wanted to shout it at the sky. "She's all I have left. I'd rather You killed me for punishment than her. Regardless of what I've done, please don't take my daughter."

He held the trepanning saw up to the light of the lantern swinging from a deck beam. A few spots of rust marred the gleaming Toledo steel of the teeth. He must scrub those off. The blade must be spotlessly clean, sharp enough to nearly cut glass.

He removed a whetstone from the instrument case and began to polish. He polished until the blade shone like pure silver. He then rinsed the blade in fresh seawater to remove any lingering flakes of rust and wrapped it in a fresh square of silk. Then he removed it again and tested the lock on the blade guard. No matter how much pressure he placed on the handle, the guard held.

Knowing this was the only preparation he could make, he returned the trepanning saw to its nest and left his cabin. He should sleep, but he wouldn't, not the night before he drilled a hole into his daughter's skull.

He opened the stern cabin door to see if Mel had made any change in the hour he'd been gone. Belinda sat beside her again reading in her sweet, rather childlike voice. Reading Psalms. Rafe hadn't opened a Bible in years, but he recognized the words for what they were.

"He shall cry unto me, Thou art my father, my God, and the rock of my salvation." Belinda continued to read as though he didn't stand in the doorway, until she concluded the chapter. "Remember, Lord, the reproach of Thy servants; how I do bear in my bosom the reproach of all the mighty people;

wherewith Thine enemies have reproached, O Lord; where-with they have reproached the footsteps of Thine anointed. Blessed be the Lord for evermore. Amen, and amen."

Mel didn't move. Rafe didn't move.

Belinda closed the Bible and smiled up at him. "The eighty-ninth Psalm. It always brings me comfort."

"Thank you for your care of my lass." Rafe swallowed against a tightness in his throat. "She thinks a great deal of you."

The only person on the brig who did. But then, Belinda Chapman treated Mel differently, as lovingly as a fond older sister or even a mother. That Belinda loved Mel lay in no doubt. Her devotion to his daughter since the accident brought a constriction to Rafe's chest, a lump to his throat.

"I've been praying for her and reading the Psalms to her for hours." Belinda rose and rubbed her lower back. "I don't mind in the least if it helps."

Rafe stiffened. "Where is she?"

"I don't know. Last I saw her she was leaning on the rail like she might be sick or something. Shall I go look for her?"

"It's not necessary. I'll be here." Rafe stepped aside so Belinda could pass.

She started to, then paused and laid her hand on his arm. "Is it true you're a doctor, Captain?"

"Aye, I was. I trained with my father and attended the University of Edinburgh. But I have not practiced for years."

"Aboard a ship that goes into battle?" She arched her winged brows.

He gave her a grudging half smile. "Aye, weel, you have me there. But I've done naught aboard this privateer that would not have been performed by a mere surgeon aboard a naval vessel or East Indiaman."

"But you can save Mel?" Her grip tightened, her eyes reflected eagerness. "A physician can help her, yes?"

"Perhaps. 'Tis a dangerous procedure." He held up his hand. "Do not ask. You do not wish to ken the details."

"But I want to help."

"You already have." He patted her hand and removed it from his arm. "Good night then, Mrs. Chapman."

"Good night, Captain. I will pray for Mel." She stepped over the coaming and turned back. "And for the day you call the Lord your rock and your salvation."

Rafe held off his snort until she closed the door behind herself. The only rock he was likely to receive from the Lord was the stone that marked his grave. As for salvation, he'd turned his back on that nine years earlier.

And was now paying for it with his daughter's life?

Not even God could be that cruel. Surely.

At the moment, he was the cruel one, the man to blame for Mel's condition. He should have climbed the shrouds. The slice was meant for him, not her. A traitor in his midst.

"Who are you?" he asked the plain teakwood bulkhead behind the bunk. "Which one of you should I not trust?"

Sam Riggs and Tommy Jones were the obvious ones, as they had urged the men to revolt, but they had been in irons when the line had to have been cut—the middle of the night. Besides, Riggs never went up top. He'd signed aboard simply to fight, not to man the ship. He was a landlubber.

Someone else wanted rid of Rafe. So they could be free to go back fighting for French prizes, even American prizes, or just to be rid of him?

"Whoever you are, you go on the list with James Brock."

He feared he knew who, one of the three men aboard he couldn't destroy even if he wanted to.

He smoothed back Mel's hair. "But I will be finding a way to bring you down. Especially if she dies."

Curled up beside Mel, Fiona lifted her head and looked

straight at him with beady black eyes as though she concurred.

"I'll do my best to save her, you useless cur." He stroked the dog's head.

As he ran his fingers over Mel's skull, his mind slipped back to his training, to the words of the instructors at university, and to his father. *In cases of head injury, we have found that blood pools beneath the dura and presses on the brain . . .*

Only one method released that pressure, a technique used as long as anyone knew. Ancient medical texts talked about the practice. People survived. More survived than didn't.

"My dear, dear lass, I should have found a place that would lock you up rather than bring you aboard."

"Would she have not managed to escape even a locked door or gate to be with you?"

Rafe started. "Phoebe, I didn't hear you enter."

"The door wasn't latched." She slipped her arm around his waist and rested her head against his arm. "Jordy said you brought up your medical instruments."

"Aye, I did."

"And you have a trepanning saw?"

"I do. 'Tis ready."

"Then sleep so you are. I'll stay with her tonight."

"Nay, I'm staying too." He pressed his cheek to the top of Phoebe's head. "I will not complain about your company."

"Then let me at least make you comfortable."

"I do not need—"

She waved him to silence and set about producing pillows and quilts from a chest. She wedged two sea chests against the window seat so he could sit beside the bunk yet lean back against the trunks with pillows for comfort, blankets for warmth against the chill of the night.

"Now rest," she commanded.

He looked at her, a question on his lips he wouldn't ask—for her to curl up beside him. As though she knew, she shook her head and retreated to the window seat behind him. "Shall I read? Belinda has left behind her copy of *Charlotte Temple*. She declares it's the best book she's ever read."

"Then is it safe to assume 'tis the worst I'll ever hear?"

"Probably. I believe the heroine dies in the end."

"Sounds like that book Davina liked so much." She'd been reading the seven-volume tome on the voyage to Naples—for the third time since he'd met her. "*Clarissa Harlowe*. Tedious and dull stuff to me."

"Then I'll read it so you go to sleep." Paper rustled behind him, then her creamy, honey voice began to intone the words, gliding over his senses like a soothing balm. "For the perusal of the young and thoughtless of the fair sex, this Tale of Truth is designed; and I could wish my fair readers to consider it as not merely the effusion of Fancy . . ."

Before the preface concluded, Rafe fell asleep. He remained asleep until daylight streamed through the stern windows.

Phoebe, her eyes rimmed by dark shadows, touched his shoulder. "It's time, Rafe. We dare not wait longer."

One glance at his daughter and Rafe understood. Her skin was drying before his eyes, as though she were a mere husk of who she'd been merely a day ago. Her lips were cracked, and her eyes stared into nothing when he lifted the lids.

"What all do you need?" Phoebe asked.

"Some coffee, but not too much. Clean clothes. A wash."

"Food," Phoebe added.

"Aye, that will not go amiss." He struggled to his feet. "Did you stay awake all the night?"

"I did. Someone had to watch over you both."

"Thank you." He headed to the door, then turned back.

"What sustains you? What keeps you going on when you must be worn to a thread?"

"My faith." She gripped her hands together in front of her and raised her chin, as though she were defying an argument. "I'd never have come this far without my faith."

"I thought you might be saying that. I cannot believe 'tis true." Before she argued with him, he left the cabin.

After changing his clothes and taking a little extra time to shave and wash, he made a circuit of the brig. Dying daughter or not, with a desperate attempt to save her in the offing, he still needed to remember that this was his brig, his responsibility along with the safety of every man and woman aboard. He inspected the course they were on, the barometer for signs of an approaching storm, the trim of the sails. He also looked into the eyes of every man he encountered, hoping for and fearing what he might see, searching for the one man who looked away.

He didn't. Even those he suspected specifically met his gaze without a flicker. Yet one of them wanted their captain dead, or at the least injured seriously enough to keep him from running the brig.

Rounds complete, Rafe gave orders to Jordy and Derrick and returned to the stern cabin. Phoebe had tidied away his makeshift bed and found time to pin up her hair and wash her face. Though the shadows remained around her eyes, the whites looked clear, as though she'd managed to sleep.

Mel hadn't changed.

"Jordy and Derrick are coming down to help." Rafe gripped the back of a chair, though the sea was as smooth as glass. Too smooth, as the wind was nearly calm. "You needn't stay."

"Of course I must."

"This could be gruesome at best." He took a deep breath to ease the pain in his chest. "She could die before I finish."

"I have more medical training than anyone else aboard, Rafe. I won't faint at the sight of blood."

"There could be a great deal."

"Do you know what happens to some women after childbirth? They—" She stopped with her hand over her mouth.

But he knew—they hemorrhaged and died.

The same could happen to Mel if he made one error, one fraction of an inch miscalculation.

"I can't do this to my child," he wanted to shout.

But he wanted her to slip away from him even less. At least with the surgery he would know he'd tried. He wouldn't betray Davina by letting her daughter go without a fight.

He took a deep breath and issued the first directions. As gently as though returning a fallen egg to its nest, Derrick lifted Mel onto a sheet of canvas with her head at the open end of the bunk. Phoebe produced a pair of silver shears and clipped Mel's hair close to her scalp. Rafe cringed at the strands of deep red hair falling onto the carpet. He'd chided her for cutting it off. Now it would be even shorter than she wanted.

"Where should I shave her?" Phoebe asked.

"That's always the difficulty—where to make the cut." Rafe ran his hands over Mel's shorn scalp again. Near the swelling on the side seemed most logical. But if the pressure lay elsewhere . . .

"Here." He must be decisive.

Phoebe nodded and applied a razor to Mel's head above and behind her temple. Then she bathed the area with vinegar.

Rafe gave her a quick glance, one eyebrow raised. "Why the vinegar?"

"Midwives are known for our cleanliness. This is part of it. When we use vinegar, strong soap, or even spirits to bathe a woman before and after childbirth, we have fewer incidents of puerperal fever."

"Hmm. I wonder why." He lifted the trepanning saw from its nest of silk and examined the blade yet again. "I like my instruments clean because I do not like the look of rust or blood."

"And did you not lose many patients?" Phoebe's gaze flicked to the saw, then darted away.

Rafe's lips turned up in a grim smile. "Not to the infection. And we can hope this proves true with—with Mel." He barely managed to speak her name.

"We can pray, sir," Derrick said in his rich baritone. "I've been praying since I saw her come down."

"A pity you didn't see who made her come down," Rafe muttered.

"Aye, sir, that it is. But that don't stop me from praying hard for our girl." Derrick laid a hand on Rafe's shoulder. "Or you. May the Lord provide you with a steady hand and calm seas."

"Amen." Phoebe also reached out and laid her hand on him.

A shiver ran through Rafe, partly a thrill, partly revulsion. His breathing slowed. His heart beat a tattoo against his ribs, but no longer one too fast for any kind of march. He would never be more clearheaded than he was at that moment.

"Let us begin." Rafe picked up a scalpel and cut to the bone. Blood spurted. "Forgive me, lass," he murmured.

Phoebe stood beside him, sponging up the blood. "She will, my . . . friend. She will."

A section of skin peeled back, Rafe picked up the circular saw and set it in position. Then he stood motionless, breath trapped in his throat, heart racing like a flock of gulls after dinner, arms paralyzed. He'd have shouted that he couldn't go through with the operation if his voice worked.

Then Phoebe rested her hand on his cheek, a mere ghosting

of fingertips across his jaw, and the tension fled. His lungs inflated, released. His heart settled to a normal rhythm, and his hands felt as steady and solid as the Cairngorm Mountains of Scotland. The handle moved beneath his fingers, though he remembered nothing of turning it on his own. Bone dust feathered the air. The blade bit deeper and deeper, mining toward permanent destruction or a hope of life. He could only hope, and perhaps pray a little, for the latter result. At the moment, the rest of the world could have stopped turning as the blade spun beneath his hand. He heard nothing of the sea, the wind, ordinary shipboard life. All that mattered lay beneath his hands.

A geyser of blood shot against the protective canvas. The blade caught on the guard, held. They were through. Now, only time would tell.

"If that doesn't relieve the pressure on her brain," Rafe said in a voice surely too calm to be his, "nothing will. Phoebe, will you help me clean up here?"

"Mrs. Lee and I can do it, sir." Derrick removed the trepanning saw from Rafe's hands. "You sit down and catch your breath."

"I need to stitch the scalp." Rafe looked at his hands. "After I wash, I expect."

"There are two basins of water on the table," Phoebe said. "But I can manage the stitching."

She appeared to not be affected in the least by the quantity of blood. Her face remained calm, her hands steady. A remarkable woman.

Her training or her faith, as she claimed? Training, of course, whatever she claimed. His training had taken over there. He'd been as calm without faith.

But with the support of Phoebe and Derrick's faith and, no doubt, Jordy's.

Still calm, he allowed Phoebe and Derrick to take over cleaning up. As he washed his hands, he watched her stitch up the scalp, her needlework as fine as anything on an embroidered gown. She then wound a bandage around Mel's head. Derrick removed the sodden canvas and placed a fresh sheet beneath Mel's head. Blood would still seep through for a while, but if she lived, the skull would heal.

If she lived.

The water in the basins was red, but his hands were clean. He carried the soiled water to the stern windows and poured it into the sea. It swirled away in the ship's wake, instantly lost in the creamy foam. Whether or not Mel lived, the memory of the surgery, of trying to save her, would live with him forever.

"I did my best to save our little girl, Davina," he murmured to the vista of sea and sky before him. "Wherever you are, I hope you know that."

He suspected Davina was in heaven. She had cried out to God to take her, and one of the pirates had slit her throat to shut her up.

"I think she'll live, Rafe." Phoebe stood close beside him. "You might not have noticed, but the blood that came out— much of it was old, clotted, like under a bruise. If the brain hasn't been damaged from the pressure, or not too much . . . You were amazing."

"Nay, 'tis only the training. I had a fine instructor in my father and others at university."

"But you were teachable and more. You were willing to perform this operation, and I've never seen steadier hands."

They weren't steady now. Rafe glanced down to find his hands trembling like those of an old man with palsy.

"I need to sit." He sank onto the window seat and covered his face with his hands. "One slip. One fraction of an inch too far. If the brig had rolled. My lass. She should not be here."

"You shouldn't be here. You should be back in Edinburgh with patients to visit and your daughter in school."

"Aye, and a wife by my side. If that had been so, I wouldn't be here." The surge of energy brought by thoughts of James Brock's betrayal sent him to his feet, steadying him, hardening his resolve.

If Mel died, he would hold Brock responsible for that too.

He dropped into a crouch beside the bunk and pressed two fingers to Mel's neck to test her pulse. Her heartbeats seemed stronger, more regular. Wishful thinking or reality? He leaned over the bunk and pressed his ear to her chest. Definitely stronger.

He wanted to shout for joy, for this flicker of hope. He remained silent, guarding hope close to him before it eluded him. He crouched again and took Mel's hand in his. "Does your head pain you, lass?" He touched her hairline, wincing at the shorn locks. He glanced up at silent, solid-as-a-mast Derrick, then at Phoebe. "Let us try to get some water into her. She's as dry as a desert island."

"I have some leftover tea here." Phoebe fetched a cup from the table.

"I'll fetch some freshwater." Derrick departed.

"I'll hold her up." Rafe lifted Mel to a half-sitting position as though she would break with the lightest touch. Phoebe held the cup to the girl's lips and dribbled tepid tea into her slack mouth, then rubbed her throat.

And Mel swallowed.

"Praise God!" Phoebe flung her arms around Rafe's neck, sending the teacup spinning across the carpet and causing him to reel off balance.

He closed his arms around her to right himself, to join in

this tiny victory. He couldn't speak. He pressed his cheek to hers and felt the dampness of tears. He raised his hand to her face. "Do not fash yourself, lass. 'Tis not a weeping matter."

"I'm not crying." She drew back and gazed at him from clear, dry eyes.

The tears were his.

15

Moisture dripped from the shrouds and limp sails like tears, the ceaseless patter nearly the sole sound aboard the brig. Everyone lay under the pall of the fog, the stillness, the orders to maintain as much quiet as possible. Belowdecks, men and women spoke in murmurs, dined on dried fruit, cheese, and stale bread so no smoke of fires drifted from the vessel. To move, they padded barefoot over the sanded planks. Sound traveled too well through the clouds that crushed the surface of the ocean into glassy calm. Many a vessel had been taken because betraying noise gave them away to an enemy who hovered close, then swept down upon the unsuspecting crew the minute the wind kicked up again.

Thus far, after two days, the wind showed no sign of honoring the *Davina* with its presence. Too restless to remain in the cabin at Mel's side a moment longer, so intent on the tiny signs of returning life that his body felt as taut as a backstay, Rafe prowled beneath the limp sails, the hulking gun barrels, the unwavering compass. Oh, they were drifting. With his years of experience, he felt the minute vibration of the movement, caught the infinitesimal sound of water rippling against the hull. Too many currents ran through the Atlantic for a ship to remain truly motionless. But the direction remained the same—east by northeast. Not northeast enough. On their current trajectory, they would end up too close to the Bay of Biscay, prey to any Frenchman and likely one or two Americans along the way.

His men would fight and fight well. They always had. That he remained alive and free attested to that. But he didn't want a fight with the ladies and his daughter aboard. His still-ailing daughter. A daughter who improved daily. She took in a diet of broth and tea. She squeezed their hands in response to questions. She'd even smiled once or twice. Her limbs weren't paralyzed. He'd pricked her extremities with a needle, and she'd whimpered in protest.

Those whimpers had been the only sound she'd made. His gregarious, lively child lay nearly silent and too still.

Because someone had tried to kill him, knowing Rafe had been the one planning to take the top watch that morning, but Mel let him sleep and went up herself.

Rafe paused at the rail and grasped the ratlines, then began to climb. Within moments, the deck lay no more visible than a suggestion of solidity beneath the gray blanket. So dense grew the cloud cover he had to feel for each handhold, each line onto which he set his feet. He tested the ropes too, leaned his weight on every one of them before trusting his body to their support. Again and again he performed this task, as he had every day since Mel's fall. Not a single line or cable, stay or hawser yielded more than it should have. The man had struck once and not tried another time, making catching him impossible. No one had seen, heard, or detected anything amiss. Yet a would-be killer lurked aboard the *Davina*.

Certain he was annoyed enough to chew nails into pulp, Rafe slid down a backstay and climbed to the quarterdeck. Jordy stood there, watching the compass, the barely drifting fog, the wheel for signs of turning.

"'Tis all quiet," he greeted Rafe in the murmur that didn't travel as far as a whisper. "Too quiet for my liking."

"'Tis inevitable this time of year. I'm thinking 'twill lift in another day."

"Aye, with an unpleasant storm."

Rafe studied his old friend, his mentor, one of the remnants from his carefree boyhood. "You seem blue-deviled today. Is it the fog or something more?"

"What do you think, lad?" Even in an undertone, Jordy's irritation rang through. "That precious lass was nearly killed, may ne'er be the same again, for what was meant to harm you. And we cannot for certain lay blame at any mon's feet."

"I have my suspicions same as you." Rafe allowed his gaze to drift forward with the fog, but he saw no one clearly, only walking shadows. "I should have tossed all the mutineers overboard or back onto Bermuda at the least. The British Navy would have been more than happy to take them aboard."

"But we cannot sail the ship without them."

"Aye, 'tis one reason why I kept them on." Rafe gave Jordy a tight-lipped smile. "And the old adage to keep one's friends close and one's enemies closer. I cannot watch them if they could be coming up behind me aboard another vessel, even if I could have replaced them."

"Humph." Jordy sounded dubious.

Rafe wished he could argue. Of course he should have put them all ashore. He should have remained in harbor until he could replace them. He'd waited nine years to lure Brock into his trap. He could wait another few weeks.

Brock had nearly sprung the trap too soon. Or perhaps intended to spring his own trap. Phoebe had foiled him with running away from Rafe.

Phoebe. Rafe should have left her ashore too, yet he was glad he hadn't. She'd been invaluable in caring for Mel. At the same time, the mere thought of her left him feeling as substantial as a cream custard in the region of his heart, a heart he thought he'd hardened against mankind—and women. He'd poured so much love into Davina as a youth who barely understood that women were a different and exotic species, the pain of losing her ripped apart any thoughts of caring about a female again. Then Phoebe Carter Lee landed on his deck—

He gripped the rail to stop himself from bolting below to join her in the great cabin. She needed time alone with Belinda, Phoebe had told him, to persuade her to undergo another examination.

"She's complaining of pains again," Phoebe had confided in him, more inclined to do so now that she knew his background. "I know this is normal, but how can one be quite certain without looking?"

"You cannot. But I admit I ken little more of childbirth than you and possibly less. We worked more with disease and serious injury than childbearing, though I have used the forceps upon occasion."

"Oh, do tell me about that." Her green eyes had glowed, her face animated.

Rafe slammed the door on that part of his life and left the cabin to the women and his daughter. He must, must, must not want Phoebe Carter Lee—in any sense of the word.

"I should have sailed straight back to Bermuda," he told Jordy. "Brock is likely setting a trap for me now, and we've a killer aboard and—" His throat tightened with confessions he didn't know how to make to the man who had helped raise him, to even himself. Certainly not to the God who had left him far behind.

"As soon as the fog lifts, lad, let us change course and sail for the Firth of Forth instead of the Nore. You can marry that beautiful lass below and return to your practice."

"As though nothing has happened? Take nine years of this

life and toss it away?" Rafe gripped the rail hard enough to cut his palms with the rough edges. "Let that man continue to get away with his lying and cheating and murdering? He's hiding behind investing in American privateers now, and they love him for his contributions to their cause. What if he comes after me? What if—"

The notion slammed into his head like a mallet. Stars danced before his eyes, an explosion of dawning light.

"Nay, nay, I'm mad to think it." He rubbed his temples, trying to eradicate the idea.

"Think what?" Jordy asked.

"Naught. It isn't possible." He strode away, his feet silent on the damp deck planks, his mind screaming with ideas. One idea shouted the loudest—talk to Phoebe. She was sensible. She would disabuse him of the knowledge in a heartbeat.

He descended the ladder to the great cabin and listened to gain an idea of what lay behind the door. No voices penetrated the thick wood. He scratched on the panel. No one responded. He turned the handle. The door remained locked.

"Phoebe?" He kept his voice low and feared she wouldn't hear him.

The door opened an instant later. She stood in the sliver of the opening, her face flushed, her eyes a brilliant glass-green in contrast. "What?"

"Oh, aye, I am begging your pardon?" The depth of the bow he gave her matched the sarcasm of his tone.

She smiled. Her posture and face relaxed. "I'm sorry. I shouldn't take my temper out on you." She stepped over the coaming and into the companionway, drawing the door closed behind her. "Don't ask me what's wrong. I'm sure you can guess it's Belinda. How George Chapman can love her as much as he apparently does doesn't speak highly of his character or judgment of people."

230

"Considering who one of his investors is, I concur about his judgment of people. But what of Mrs. Chapman?"

"She's as childish as a newborn kitten and as mean as a rabid dog. Except with your daughter. She's as kind as a—a—"

"Mither kitten with her bairns?"

"Something like that." Phoebe smiled.

Rafe clasped his hands behind his back to keep himself from reaching for her. "Is Mrs. Chapman giving you trouble then?"

"She's lied to me about her condition so often I don't know what to believe, and I doubt my own ability to say."

"And what does your instinct tell you?"

"That she could have this baby a week from now and not much longer."

Words crowded onto Rafe's lips. He caught a whiff of lavender from Phoebe, no doubt from her proximity to Belinda, and controlled his impulse to curse over the woman's lies to her sister-in-law and to him.

"We cannot have a newborn aboard this brig. You cannot be nursing Mel and Belinda both." He smoothed a fingertip across the groove forming between Phoebe's eyes. "Do not distress yourself, lass. We'll reach port as quickly as we can."

"Which is when?"

"If the fog lifts, not so long. Two weeks to Cornwall at the outside."

"Rafe." She caught hold of his hand and clutched it between both of hers. "I don't think we have two weeks. Is there nowhere closer?"

"Perhaps a channel island. Guernsey."

"Or you could set us down in France."

"Nay, lass, I cannot risk it. I'd never get you back."

"Then abandon your plan. Your daughter needs care on land. Belinda can't have this baby at sea. I'm not sure she's well. Her hands and feet are terribly swollen. And—please, Rafe, abandon this plan of yours. It's not worth the danger, the trouble, the—everything that comes with it."

Gazing into her big eyes, he felt himself tilting on the precipice of saying he would.

Which was precisely why he needed to stop himself from caring about her. Davina deserved to be avenged. His father and mother deserved to be avenged. Mel deserved to know that justice had been perpetrated on the man who had robbed her of her mother, her grandparents, and, for too much of her life, her father. And now—if Rafe was even remotely right in his assumptions—Mel's own ability to live a normal life.

"James Brock is trying to kill me," Rafe announced without preamble. "If I do not kill him first, he may succeed, and then who will see to Mel's well-being if she does not return to her normal self?"

Phoebe gasped. Her nails cut into the back of his hand. "What are you saying? You think Brock connived that accident?"

"Aye, that I do."

"How?"

"He got to one of my men while we were in harbor. Paid him, no doot."

Phoebe paled in the meager light. "But who?"

Rafe blew a long sigh through pursed lips. "I was hoping you would tell me I'm daft for thinking it."

"You're not. It makes a great deal of sense. I just don't know who it could have been. Who went ashore?"

"Mostly men I trust. Mostly, but one or two . . . I cannot stake my life on any mon."

"Or your daughter's life." Phoebe grasped his shoulders—hard. "Don't you see? This means you have to give up your pursuit of him. You have to get everyone to safety as soon as possible, or whoever this is will try again. And then where will we be, a ship without a captain? Isn't it enough that your daughter is so poorly? Rafe, please, you've got to stop this destruction."

Again he gazed into her fiery green eyes and nearly said he would. Ideas flashed before him. Asking Phoebe to be his wife. Taking her to Edinburgh with Mel to set up a house—nay, a home. More children—

Other images flashed before him. Davina ailing. His diagnosis. His father's diagnosis. Davina pleading for God to forgive her moments before the pirates slit her throat to shut her up.

"I'll be resting when that man is dead." He removed Phoebe's hands from his shoulders and turned his back on her.

She didn't try to follow. She gave out a tiny, hiccupping sob, then slipped into Belinda's cabin and closed the door without a sound.

Rafe stalked back to the quarterdeck. Noting Jordy still at the wheel, Rafe sucked in his breath, feeling the full impact of what he'd said to Phoebe, the near accusations he'd made.

Jordy and Derrick. Jordy had been with him all his life, teaching him to ride, showing him how to sail and fish, how to load a gun and hunt—when he could draw him away from his books. And Derrick? Derrick had been his friend for nearly nine years, humbling in his gratitude for Rafe freeing him and his wife and children from slavery. Neither of them would succumb to the lure of money or any other persuasion that led to killing him. Yet who else had been ashore? Half a dozen fetching supplies. He would find those six and question them.

A useless exercise. Every instinct pointed in one direction. But he could be wrong. Pray God he was.

He snorted at his thought of praying only for this. God wasn't about to listen to a man not interested in repenting.

Not even if it would restore your daughter to health? Phoebe's voice rang in his head. *Would you give up your pursuit of James Brock for the sake of your daughter?*

She hadn't asked that of him, but her voice sounded as loudly in his ears as though she had shouted the question from the crosstrees.

He knew the answer—no, he wouldn't. Letting James Brock go wouldn't change a thing for Mel. If she was going to fully wake up, she would do so whether or not the man roamed free and alive.

And what if you're not alive? Phoebe might as well have been standing beside him. *Will she want to wake up?*

He retraced his steps toward the great cabin just as the deck lurched beneath his feet and a gust of wind lifted his hair away from his neck. Glorious, glorious wind.

"All hands on deck," he shouted. "Topmen aloft." He raced for his cabin to shove his feet into his boots, then flung himself into the shrouds to climb and climb and inspect the approaching storm about to blow the clouds away and push the *Davina* to—not too far off course, he could only hope.

Mist lifted and shifted around him, swirling like the gauzy gowns of dancers on a ballroom floor. Men swarmed up the ratlines and joined him, streaming out along the yards to tighten sheets and secure them fast to the spars. Sails snapped and bellied out in the rising wind. Sun shone through a rent in the clouds, and someone began to sing in a rich, warm baritone.

"Sometimes a light surprises the Christian while he sings; it is the Lord, who rises with healing in His wings. When comforts are declining, He grants the soul again a season of clear shining, to cheer it after rain."

Derrick, of course. No one else aboard possessed the boldness to sing a hymn amidst a crowd of sailors. One of the men laughed—too close to Rafe. He shifted his hand from a line to the man's wrist and squeezed until he held the sailor's attention. "Do not laugh at him again. 'Tis far better for all than those drunken songs you favor. Understood?"

The man's features twisted in a spasm of pain. "Didn't know you was going soft with religion, sir."

"There's naught soft about Derrick, let alone God, lad, and do not forget it." Rafe released the man's wrist, swung onto the forestay, and slid to the deck in seconds. He began his inspection of the deck by daylight, checking every cleat and line holding boats and guns in place. No one needed a loose cannon in a high wind. And a high wind they were about to get. From the quarterdeck, Rafe caught sight of the waves swirling toward them, a mountain of water plunging across the sea to crash upon their deck. Yet the clouds shredded into nothing more substantial than puffs of wool left on thistles in the countryside. A windstorm, no more. Cold, biting wind that sheared straight through one's warmest wool coat and whipped the men's queues out like flying ropes.

And into the gale walked Phoebe. Despite her hair streaming around her like a veil and her skirts billowing hard enough to send her sailing above the deck, she glided toward him, her feet taking up the roll of the deck with practiced and graceful ease until she stood beside him at the binnacle compass. "Don't tell me to go below. I need to feel the wind."

He gazed at her, drank in her glowing face and flowing hair, and wondered why he shouldn't do what Jordy suggested and take her home to make a home. He loved her. Fool that he was for it, he couldn't deny it—except to her. He must deny it to her. He wasn't finished with Davina's ghost. Once that apparition of his last attempt at love and a family was sent away with Brock's lifeblood, he would be free to love.

And Phoebe wouldn't want him then.

235

He turned his back on her, shrugging. "Do as you like. Just don't get swept overboard."

Despite his rejection then, she sought his company later that day and the next. And he accepted her presence near him, her hand upon his arm as they talked, more often than not at Mel's bedside, watching for signs of her waking. He accepted Phoebe's probing questions about his past, even her talk of God's love and forgiveness. Each word from her landed on his ears, his senses, and was absorbed into his being like rain on the ocean until the ache, the longing to drop to his knees and beg her to marry him regardless, grew so strong he left the cabin in the middle of a sentence and slammed the door behind him.

And not five minutes later, Phoebe came charging toward him across the deck. "Rafe." She grasped his arm with both hands, her face glowing as brightly as the autumn sunlight. "Rafe, Mel is waking up."

"What? Truly?" He seized Phoebe by the waist and spun her around.

Her skirt flew up a wee bit too high, and she shrieked. "Set me down!"

"My apologies." He did so at once. "But the news . . . my daughter . . ." He grasped Phoebe's hand, his earlier annoyance with her shoved aside, and raced for the companionway. "Set the course for north by northeast," he shouted over his shoulder to the helmsman.

He didn't even notice who had taken the wheel. Watt or Jordy. It didn't matter. Nothing mattered at that moment except the possibility that Mel was waking up. He took the companionway ladder in one bound and burst through the cabin door to fall to his knees beside the bunk.

"Mel? Melvina Docherty?" He took her hand in his and squeezed. "Are you ready to wake up from your nap yet?"

She squeezed his hand, and the corners of her mouth twitched, relaxed, then turned up into a smile.

Belinda began to weep behind him and murmur a prayer of thanks. Phoebe rested her hand on his shoulder and applied a gentle, reassuring pressure. Across the cabin, the door flew open again, and Derrick and Jordy charged through the opening, Fiona yapping at their heels. Then she leaped past them and scrabbled at the edge of the bunk with her front paws.

And Mel turned her head toward the dog's frantic yips. "Fi." The syllable emerged more as a sigh than a word, but everyone heard it. The dog recognized it and took a flying leap onto the bed. "Fi," she said again, and her eyes fluttered open.

"Mel, my lass." Rafe's throat closed, and further words refused to emerge. He pressed his cheek against his daughter's, hoping the contact would say what he found he could not.

"Da?" Her hand moved in his, weak but restless. "You Papa?"

"You ken who I am?" For the first time since he was a lad, he wanted to leap up and down with joy. "You ken I'm your father?"

"Aye." She yawned, and her hand went limp again.

Rafe glanced up. If his face shone half as brightly as those ranged behind him, it could dim the sunlight.

"Glory to God," Derrick said. "I do believe that child is going to be all right."

"Aye." Rafe swallowed. "She knew me."

"And the wee cur," Jordy added. "Whoever means you harm will not have succeeded in hurting your lass."

"Nay, not completely," Rafe agreed.

"It's a miracle," Belinda said. "The Lord—" A look of surprise crossed her features, and she grasped her belly.

"Pains again?" Phoebe stepped to Belinda's side. "How bad? How often?"

"It's all right." Belinda's pansy eyes filled with tears. "It has to be. I tell you the truth, Phoebe, it's too soon. George will think me unfaithful if I have the baby now."

Rafe rose and exchanged amused glances with his two crewmen and friends. "Perhaps we should leave the ladies to ladies' matters. Mel may not wake again for hours or even days, I'm thinking."

"I'd like to pray for her first, sir." Derrick reached out his hand toward Mel.

"Aye, please do. I think if God listens to anyone, it's you."

"He wants to listen to you—"

Rafe held up a staying hand before Derrick. "No preaching. God and I have an understanding, and you—"

A shout rose from the deck above. "Sail. Off the larboard quarter."

"Och." Rafe speared his fingers through his hair. "We do not need this now. But I had best—"

Another cry interrupted him. "The Tricoleur."

"French." Rafe sprang for the door and slammed his hand down on the handle.

Nothing happened.

"What in the name of—" He shoved at the door again, then slammed his fist into it.

"Don't try to break out, Captain," Tommy Jones's voice piped through the panels. "We don't want to hurt you, but we will if you don't stay locked in there until we take ourselves another prize."

16

Belinda started to scream. Phoebe spun on her heel and slapped one hand across her sister-in-law's mouth. With the other hand, she grasped Belinda's shoulder and shook her. "Stop it. That kind of nonsense does no one any good."

"Neither does being locked down here." Rafe leaned his shoulders against the door and glanced from Derrick to Jordy. "We have to get out of here. If there is shooting—"

A boom roared across the water.

Phoebe gritted her teeth to stop herself from screaming. They needed quiet and calm now, not a bevy of hysterical women. But the boom hadn't come from the privateer's gun; it had come from the Frenchman, and the crew of the *Davina* hadn't responded with their own fire.

"This is no good. They have not run out the guns." Jordy gripped a chair back so hard he looked like he was about to rip it from the bolts that held it to the deck. "We cannot have a win without firing the guns."

Everyone in the cabin except for Mel looked at Rafe, Phoebe expecting him to have a brilliant solution, as likely the others did too, but he remained still and silent, his gaze fixed past their shoulders. His face looked as hard as a ship's figurehead carved of teakwood, and his hands bunched into fists against his thighs. Only a bulging muscle at the corner of his jaw indicated he felt any emotion.

239

Phoebe shivered. She'd never seen any man so cold in the face of an emergency. Gideon had been quite the opposite, red-faced and shouting, moving. Always moving, fists—

She jerked herself away from that line of thought and followed Rafe's gaze to the wall of weapons arranged behind their iron grill. A sword, two rapiers, several cutlasses and daggers, and a brace of pistols provided considerable protective or assaulting power. All of it remained useless with the six of them confined to the great cabin. They needed to get out, get Mel and Belinda below to relative safety, get Rafe, Jordy, and Derrick to where they could lead the men away from their current folly.

Surely Rafe intended to lead them away from the fight.

But presumably, armed guards stood behind the door with panels of teakwood thick enough that one could hear through it only if the interlocutors shouted—thick enough to stop a pistol ball. Likewise, the skylight's opening was too small for anyone larger than Mel to go through. Perhaps the stern windows? When opened, the gap looked large enough for a man, if he could somehow climb the stern to the quarterdeck without getting himself hacked down or shot the instant his head appeared over the edge of the deck.

But they wouldn't harm a woman.

Not sure what she would do once on deck, Phoebe opened her mouth to speak. A second blast of gunfire roared toward the brig. This time the *Davina*'s crew fired in response. The brig shuddered and tilted, rolling sideways into the trough of a wave.

"Aye, I taught them weel." Rafe's upper lip curled as he spoke into the ensuing silence. "They ken enough to fire on the up roll."

"But they do not have a leader," Jordy protested. "They ken how to fire the guns, but there's no one who can lead them, give proper sailing directions."

"Watt?" Phoebe glanced at Rafe, wondering why he'd let the man stay free after the last attempt at mutiny. "Can he—"

"A competent leader," Jordy growled.

Someone was giving sailing orders. The bellowed commands reverberated through the deck, directions to haul lines, to tack to starboard. The brig dipped and swung.

With a curse, Rafe lunged across the cabin. "The wrong maneuver. You fools, that's the wrong direction." He flung open a stern window. Frosty air swirled into the cabin, and Belinda staggered to the bunk to draw the quilts more tightly around Mel.

Who looked right at her and smiled.

"She's awake again," Belinda cried.

"And like as not ready for eternal sleep with these—" Rafe broke off and drew back into the cabin. He faced Jordy and Derrick, whose grim faces suggested they knew what he was about to tell them. "The Frenchman is trying to sail around us."

Jordy muttered something and dropped onto a chair. Derrick remained stolid, an immovable mountain in a gale.

"What—what's so bad about that?" Phoebe had to ask.

"'Tis one of the oldest fighting maneuvers in the history of using guns on vessels." Rafe spoke to them with his head out of the stern windows again. "Raking is what the maneuver is called. A vessel sails across the bow or stern of another one and fires a broadside. The shot flies down the entire length of the vessel." He drew his head in again. "Everyone on the deck." He spoke in an even tone bleak of emotion. "Derrick, get Mel."

"She can't be mo—"

Rafe grasped Belinda and dragged her to the deck. Derrick caught up Mel, quilts and all, and flattened them both along the side of the bunk. The crash of exploding gunpowder rumbled like thunder across the water, and Phoebe followed their actions, throwing herself between bunk and window

241

seat, Jordy crowding in beside her seconds before the windows exploded in a hail of splintering glass. The chair where Jordy sat moments earlier turned to kindling in a heartbeat.

Belinda screamed. Phoebe swallowed the cry rising in her throat along with a dose of bitter bile. But others wailed above them, the animal cries of men in agony.

"Lord, no, please." Phoebe choked on the meaningless prayer.

It was too late. Men had been wounded, possibly killed, men with whom she had probably talked, eaten, strode along the deck.

"I need to be up there. I can help." She scrambled to her feet.

Jordy caught her arm. "Nay, lass, stay down."

Something crashed on the upper deck, and the *Davina* listed leeward.

"I must be going out there regardless." Rafe rose from behind the dining table. Fragments of glass dripped from his clothes and hair, glittering teardrops in the still brilliant sunshine. Glittering like the cold light in his eyes that froze Phoebe's core. "Derrick, I need your help."

"Anything, sir, but we don't want you dead. They'll need a leader when it's all over."

"Not if we're all prisoners of war." Rafe glanced at Mel in her cocoon of blankets on the deck. "'Twill kill my lass."

"They'll kill you if you appear on deck," Jordy said. "Could we perhaps shoot off the lock?"

The door had escaped damage in the broadside, but the bulkhead beside it bore a jagged hole that surely led into the adjoining cabin, the one Rafe had been using.

"I don't think we can shoot off the lock without getting shot ourselves." Rafe fitted a key into the lock securing the grill over the weapons. "But a shot or two at the panels may distract them into thinking we intend to use the door."

Eyes fixed on the hole in the bulkhead, Phoebe pointed out, "If the ball does go through and hits a vital organ, it could kill whoever is on the other side."

"Aye, that it could." The lock snapped off the protective grillwork, and Rafe stroked one hand along the barrel of a pistol. "'Tis the risk they've taken on, thinking locking us in here is enough to stop us."

"You'd murder your own men?" Phoebe thought she might be sick then and there.

"He gets what he deserves." Rafe removed the pistols and moved on to the sword. "Derrick, a dagger or cutlass?"

"Both, sir."

"I'll take one of the rapiers." Jordy joined Rafe at the weapons array. "And a dagger. I like those best in hand-to-hand combat."

The two vessels exchanged more gunfire. Phoebe flinched with each shuddering boom, gagged on the stench of gunpowder blowing through the broken windows.

"We're all going to die," Belinda sobbed. "My baby. They're going to kill my baby."

"Maybe you can reason with them," Phoebe suggested. "They might be frightened enough now."

"Aye, of course a female would suggest talking." Rafe turned on her. "The time for talking is passed. I tried the talk in Bermuda and this is what's happened. Jordy, open the stern windows so I don't cut myself on the glass. Derrick, you can lift me?"

"Yessir, I can." Derrick's dark face tensed. "But, sir, they'll kill you the instant you appear on deck. You know they will."

"Only if whoever wants me dead is on the quarterdeck." Rafe gestured to the destroyed windows and ruined chair and bulkhead. "Nine years at this, and never once did I find myself aboard a vessel that got itself raked."

He stalked over fragments of glass and wood and a broken crate of preserves with red jelly oozing between the slats like blood. He poured black powder into the priming pan as he moved, a practiced action to perform such a delicate operation while walking. "And the two of you will come up right after me. Ready to go?" He pressed the barrel of a pistol to the door beside the lock. "One shot and—"

"Wait." Phoebe bounded across the cabin and grasped his arm. "You can't go up there. Whoever wants you dead probably is on the quarterdeck. He's likely one of the leaders of the mutiny."

Rafe smiled, but his eyes were cold. "Then he'd better be faster than I am." He cocked the pistol.

Phoebe grabbed his wrist with both hands. "Rafe, wait. You don't need to risk your life by going up."

Another roar sounded from the French vessel, and the *Davina* shuddered.

"I risk everyone's life by not going up." He tucked the pistol under his arm, gripped her wrist with his other hand, and tried pulling her hands away with a firm but gentle tug. "Now let go."

"No, there's another way."

"Indeed." He curled his upper lip. "I suppose you know a great deal about armed combat between two vessels?"

"No, but—" She licked her dry lips. "I—I'll go out through that hole in the bulkhead and distract the guards here. If I can get the door unlocked, you can come out with Derrick and Jordy."

"If you can get the door unlocked." His tone held doubt, but he released her wrist and his face relaxed. "'Tis a big risk on your part."

"And I need my midwife soon," Belinda wailed. "Don't get yourself killed."

"They're not going to harm me." Phoebe spoke with more confidence than she felt.

"The French will not hesitate," Jordy muttered.

"I'll have to be on deck for that."

Where, of course, she fully intended to go. She was a healer, capable of tending wounds or offering a moment of comfort for anyone whose wounds were beyond repair.

"Give me a chance." She lifted one hand to Rafe's cheek. "It's the best chance to keep you alive."

His eyes burned into hers like silver stars, then he gave one brusque nod. "You have twa minutes."

Too little time. Yet another booming crash of broadsides from both vessels sent her flying across the cabin and into the ragged hole blown into the bulkhead. Belinda began to weep behind her, and someone murmured soothing words. A soft, gentle voice too high in pitch to belong to any of the men—Mel.

Her heart and hands steady, Phoebe pushed herself through the opening. Her gown tore. Her hair snagged and tumbled from its pins. Near darkness met her, darkness filled with the scents of damp leather and ginger, bergamot and salt spray. Rafe's scents—heady, disarming, motivating her to climb over a sea chest and reach for the door handle.

She turned it with as little noise as possible, not that anyone would notice with shouts and guns blasting above, and the ominous creak of timbers below. For a heartbeat, the door stuck. If this one was locked too—

She yanked it hard. The door flew open, staggering her back. She gasped, and the guard in the companionway swung around and aimed a pistol at her chest.

"What are you doing?" he demanded.

"That raking shot blew a hole in the bulkhead." She groped for the man's name. "Pearson, I crawled through so I can go help the wounded."

"I can't let you." The pistol didn't waver. "Orders."

"From whom?" She smiled and took a step over the coaming, a step closer to the pistol, certain she would cast up her accounts onto the man's bare feet at any moment. "He couldn't have meant me. I don't know anything about weapons. I just know about wounds." She sidled around so her back nearly rested on the door of the great cabin. "You have wounded companions up there. I hear them calling for help."

Pitiful, whimpering cries that made her eyes tear and her throat close.

"Please." She held out her hands, palms up. "I might be able to save them."

Pearson's glance flicked from her hands to her face to the open cabin door. "Robbie's beyond help. That raking shot."

Phoebe sucked in her breath. She remembered the lad with silvery blond hair and a ready smile.

"I might have saved him."

"No, ma'am, a six-pound shot took his head off—"

Phoebe doubled over, retching.

Pearson shouted and leaped back. Phoebe followed, still bent over, and rammed her head into his middle. He collided with the ladder and folded, his gun clattering to the deck. Phoebe snatched it up and clipped him behind the ear with the barrel. He slumped sideways, and she spun to twist the key in the lock of the great cabin door.

The door flew open and the three men charged out. Rafe took a moment to lift her aside, and Derrick dumped the unconscious sailor into one of the cabins. Then they were gone up the companionway ladder, Rafe bellowing orders and Derrick and Jordy guarding his back.

Head and stomach reeling, Phoebe began to follow, then turned back to find the medical supplies in the cabin. "Stay on the deck," she told Belinda.

They would be safer belowdecks, but no safe way to get them there now.

"And cut some cloth into bandages," Phoebe added.

"But I need my cloth for—"

"Your baby can have a few less diapers to save a man's life." Phoebe snatched up the box of medical supplies and slammed the door behind her. For good measure, she locked it and pocketed the key. Then she raced up the companionway into a scene from a nightmare.

A pall of gray smoke lay over men black with gunpowder, crimson with blood. Wet sand marred the normal whiteness of the deck planks, absorbing water from the sponges for cleaning the guns and the life fluid of the wounded, the dying, the dead.

Telling who was whom seemed impossible in the swirling fog of smoke. Bodies lay sprawled between the guns, fetched up against the rails, and beneath an overturned cannon. Red hair shone in a flash of sunlight slicing through the cloud. Phoebe dropped to her knees beside the man, her heart and bile in her throat, her eyes stinging. He couldn't still be alive, not with the lower half of his body crushed.

But he was. When she touched his hand, his eyelids flickered. His lips twisted into a grimace of a smile, then moved in words. She leaned down and nearly touched her ear to his mouth so she could hear the utterance in a lull between crashing guns. "What I . . . deserve . . . for—for mutiny. Forgive . . ."

"God forgives you. Just ask Him." She touched his face, the side of his neck, not sure whether or not he heard her or asked for redemption.

Tommy Jones had died.

"Stupid men and their wars," she shouted.

No one reacted. The shriek of cannonballs overhead drowned out even thought.

In the seemingly silent aftermath, the groans and wails of

the wounded rose like tormented souls from the underworld. Keeping her head below the level of the gunwale in the hope a shot wouldn't separate her brainbox from her body, Phoebe began to crawl from man to man. She knew each of them, if not by name, at least by sight. She'd lived on the same vessel with them for a month. Even if she hadn't known them, she would have done what she could to help. She brought life into the world, and when necessary, she did what she could to keep it there.

For some of the men, she could do all too little except hold a hand and pray. For others, she let them lean on her until they reached the main hatch. "I'll be down shortly to look at that," she assured them. Or to remove a splinter of wood as thick as her forefinger, splint a broken bone until Rafe could realign the bones, or sew up a gash.

And as she crawled, staggered, and even rolled across the deck, the guns crashed and boomed, cannonballs flew, and men and rigging tumbled to the deck. After what felt like an eternity, she returned from below deck just as a cheer rose from the *Davina*'s crew. Every man capable rose and clapped and stamped, Rafe included from his position on the quarterdeck, Derrick and Jordy near, Watt at the wheel behind them, grinning like a jack-o'-lantern.

Watt, the ringleader Rafe had protected regardless. Watt, who wanted to be captain. Enough to kill Rafe?

No time to consider it. Across the yards of foaming seawater, the French vessel wallowed beneath a tangle of canvas, lines, and spars.

"Dismasted her, we did." The old cook leaped from beside one of the guns and picked up Phoebe, spinning her around. "We'll beat 'em now."

"Grappling hooks," Rafe shouted. "Prepare to board."

"Grappling hooks? Board?" Phoebe called after the cook.

She'd lost his attention. Along with every able-bodied man aboard, he raced for the gunwales. They brandished pikes and cutlasses, pistols and swords. With their smoke-blackened clothes and smudged faces, they looked like demons from the netherworld rushing to seize lost souls.

Which was exactly what they were doing.

Heat seared through Phoebe's middle, blazing white-hot, sending her insides coiling and lifting like a snake about to strike. "Stop! Stop! You can't do this!" she shouted at the top of her lungs.

Either no one heard her or they completely ignored her. They tossed grappling hooks to the other vessel, dragging it alongside the *Davina*. Frenchmen, ordinary sailors from this well-armed merchantman, struggled from beneath the fallen rigging. They brandished their own lethal weapons. Steel glinted in the sunlight. Shouts and battle cries rose like an oncoming storm. Deafening. Chilling.

Phoebe grasped the still-warm barrel of an abandoned gun and willed herself to remain where she was. She had patients to attend. She would have more. She must stop shaking and grinding her teeth in an effort to remain on the brig's deck. She would do no one any good racing after the men. She certainly couldn't stop them.

Then a man surged through the main hatchway, a second, a third . . . a dozen. They sported bandages on their heads and arms and legs. Those were bandages she had affixed with care, cloth intended for baby diapers and tiny garments, sacrificed to keep these men's wounds clean.

And they headed for the rail, stumbling, staggering, shouting. All bore weapons. Where but moments earlier they had gasped and cursed as she stitched up their wounds, they now acted with the same enthusiasm as their crewmates, vaulting the rail to walk the narrow plank bridge leading to the French vessel.

And Phoebe's control broke. She shoved off the gun as though launching from a catapult and flung herself onto the walkway. Twenty feet below her, seawater foamed and roiled. So did her stomach. She yanked her gaze forward and leaped onto the deck of the Frenchman, her only weapons shears, a scalpel, and a handful of needles.

"Rafe! Rafe Docherty!" Again the bellowing men, clash of steel, and occasional shot drowned out her voice.

She didn't see him in the teeming mass of men fighting hand to hand. She grasped a line attached to the remaining mast and pulled herself onto the rail. Above the heads of the throng, she managed to find him. For half a minute, she lost him for the red heat of rage blinding her.

He wasn't trying to stop the men; he was leading them.

"How dare you, you—you—" She broke off on a scream.

A diminutive Frenchman swung a hatchet at Rafe's skull. He ducked, spun. The Frenchman vanished amidst the feet of the fighting men.

The coiled snake inside Phoebe struck. Venom poured through her veins, burning, blazing, propelling her off the rail and into the fight like shot from a cannon. She thought she was shrieking something, likely Rafe's name. She knew she lashed out with her elbows, knees, and fists. Men fell away from her as though she were as deadly as a sixteen-pounder, fell back until she saw Rafe before her. He pushed toward the quarterdeck, Derrick ahead of him, Jordy beside him, Watt—

Phoebe screamed and lunged. Her foot tangled in tumbled rigging, and she crashed to the deck. Winded, she lay on fallen lines, struggling for breath, struggling to rise.

Her head rose far enough for her to see Watt plunge a dagger toward Rafe's back.

17

Jordy threw himself between Watt's blade and Rafe's back. The dagger plunged into Jordy's chest. Blood spilled across his shirt. He staggered back, rammed into Rafe, and fell, taking the younger man down with him.

Watt pulled the blade free in time to clash with Derrick's cutlass. Steel rang, a death knell even above the cries and clashes around the deck, those growing less furious, Watt and Derrick's conflict growing more fierce. Watt yelled in Gaelic, incomprehensible words that sounded like curses. Derrick said nothing, just slashed and parried with the single-edged blade of the cutlass.

Beside them, Rafe managed to extricate himself from beneath Jordy and kneel beside his friend, his mentor, applying pressure to the older man's chest with his hands. Ankle throbbing, Phoebe half walked, half crawled over tangled rigging to Rafe's side. She still held her bag of medicines and managed to produce a bandage. In silence, her throat too thick with tears to allow words to pass, she thrust the pad of linen toward Rafe.

He shook his head, his face an impassive mask. "Too late. He's gone." He took the cloth anyway, wiped a trickle of blood from the corner of Jordy's mouth, then draped it over his face. Without another word, Rafe gathered up his weapons and ran toward the French merchantman's quarterdeck, shouting, "To me, *Davina*s! To me!"

Phoebe stared after him, her breath snagged in her throat, that snake of outrage coiling and rising within her once again. A red haze blazed before her eyes. Blood roared in her ears. Only vaguely did she notice the cessation of exploding pistols, clanging blades, bellowing men. She held Jordy's hand so hard even this large man might have cried out in protest had he been alive to feel it.

But he wasn't alive. Rafe's friend, his mentor, a man who had been with him all his life, had followed him to sea though he strongly disapproved, had sacrificed his life for a man who didn't care about his life. A man who used people in his endless quest for revenge.

So why did she love Rafe Docherty so much her heart burst with the mere sound of his voice?

Dominick, I hope you have found a way to come rescue me from myself before I do something tragically stupid—again.

Another week of this. Maybe two. Too long. And with Jordy dead, who would rein Rafe in even a bit? Derrick, the former slave who owed his freedom to Rafe? Watt, who had betrayed and tried to kill him?

Phoebe's head snapped up. What of Derrick and Watt? She saw neither of them. The deck where their blades had rung such an ominous toll lay empty, splattered with blood and black powder.

Slowly, her ankle screaming as she put weight on it, Phoebe rose and looked around. The French had apparently surrendered. They stood huddled like cattle waiting for slaughter, a ring of men from the *Davina* holding them against the rail opposite the privateer. Rafe stood on the quarterdeck issuing orders to half a dozen of his men, amongst them Derrick. Watt was nowhere on the deck.

Head spinning, ankle throbbing, insides coiled tighter than a carriage spring, Phoebe limped to the quarterdeck and the captain who had seized victory twice—first from his own mutinous men, then from the French. His voice was clipped, his Scot accent thick, his eyes as cold as the North Atlantic beneath them.

Phoebe pressed her hands, her fisted hands, against her hips and waited for someone to notice her.

"Secure the prisoners below on the *Davina*," Rafe was directing. "And put a few of your own men in there with them. You all deserve to be flogged or hanged, but I will not do it, as I need to get to England. If you obey every one of my commands and keep your heads until we complete our mission, I will not turn you over to a civil court either and may even see that you receive the prize money. But a few of you are the ringleaders along with Walter McKay."

His voice held no inflection as he mentioned the unfamiliar name, but his eyes flicked toward the *Davina*. Phoebe followed his gaze and finally noticed Watt bound to the rail. His face appeared as pale as the canvas sails, a trickle of dried blood marred one shoulder of his shirt, and his lower lip quivered like that of a child about to cry or perhaps throw a tantrum. No other man stood nearby. Rafe had to mean Watt when he said Walter McKay.

Phoebe gripped the edge of the quarterdeck. Her arm shook. She should return to the brig, tend to those of her patients who hadn't made sudden recoveries when victory appeared. She should make sure Belinda was all right. And Mel. Mel had spoken.

She started to hobble toward the plank leading back to the *Davina*. Her ankle gave out on her and she slumped to her knees. If she tried to cross that narrow strip of wood, she would tumble headfirst into the sea.

"Lord, what have You brought me to?" Quietly she sobbed out the words. "I've been a good and faithful servant all my life. What have I done to deserve this?"

And everything else.

Her insides coiled and burned. She pounded her fists on the deck. When she raised a hand to her lips to stifle her desire to scream, she saw that blood and powder and sand covered her knuckles. Only the kind of will that kept her calm in the most frightening of circumstances in the birthing chamber kept her from being sick right then and there. She took several deep breaths and crawled toward a nearby gun to drag herself to her feet. She didn't know how she would return to the privateer. At that moment, she didn't care if she did, except she needed to be with her patients. She held responsibility for one expectant mother, one concussed daughter, and a handful of fighting men.

Let Rafe manage them. Rafael Docherty, physician turned killer.

The man she loved. Stupid, stupid, stupid her.

She leaned on the gun and took several deep breaths. They didn't help. Every inhalation snagged on the stench of smoke, sweat, and the effluvium of battle. After this, the worst situation in the birthing chamber would look tame, clean, peaceful.

She longed for hushed rooms with blazing fires and soft hands, soap and water and smooth, white sheets. She yearned for clear water to soothe her parched throat, a warm bath, clothes not stiff with salt. She saw them in her mind's eye.

She felt a calloused hand on her cheek, firm fingers gripping her shoulder. "Phoebe, are you a'right, hinnie?"

Hinnie, like he called his daughter. His voice held the same tenderness, his hands the same gentleness with which he treated Mel. Herein lay the reasons why she loved him, if anything in that most powerful of emotions made any sense.

"I seem to have twisted my ankle." She spoke with utter calm, matter-of-factly, as though they discussed weather on dry land. "I was afraid to walk back to the *Davina*."

"I will have to be carrying you then." He rounded the gun and slipped an arm around her shoulders.

She should tell him not to touch her with blood on his hands. She let him lift her into his arms before saying, "You can't carry me across that bit of wood. We'll both topple into the sea."

"Aye, weel then, we will drown together, no?"

"I'd rather not drown, thank you. And neither would you."

He didn't respond.

She lifted her head from his shoulder so she could see him. Though mere inches away, she read nothing in his face but caught his eyes flicking toward Watt again.

"Why did he want to kill you?" she asked since they weren't on the plank yet.

"What makes you think he wanted to kill me?" Harshness, a hint of anger, better than the coldness.

"I saw him aim for your back. I saw—" Her voice broke.

"I am sorry for that and so much more." His Adam's apple bobbed in his throat, as though perhaps he swallowed back emotions like grief. "Weel then, you may as weel ken that he is my uncle, my mither's brother. He has ne'er been fond of the Docherty family."

"Then why is he aboard your ship?"

Rafe gazed into the distance. "He is the only family I had left who was not a wee child who only wanted her mama. He gave me something to live for."

And fueled Rafe's hatred of James Brock for nine years? No time to ponder that now.

"I—" Phoebe blinked back the tendency toward tears. "I'm so sorry. What will happen to him?"

He said nothing as they reached the plank connecting the two vessels. With no effort, or so it seemed, he stepped up and strode across, then leaped onto the brig's deck.

At last he answered her when they reached the top of the companionway. "I have a complete right to hang him."

Phoebe gasped. "But you won't."

"Will I not?" Rafe's hold grew taut. "He mutinied, he tried to kill me. He murdered my first officer. Flogging doesn't seem like enough."

"But—" Phoebe decided not to argue. The man was understandably distraught. She would talk to him later, after he calmed himself.

After he measured the worth of his booty from the French privateer.

Her mouth thinned.

"Are you in pain?" Rafe asked.

"Only when I stand on that foot. It's probably just sprained a bit."

"I should examine it for a break."

"My ankle? You're not going to touch my ankle."

He gave her a gentle shake. "I am a physician, you ken."

"I know you were a physician." She ducked her head as he started down the companionway ladder. "Physicians take an oath to do no harm."

"You've a sharp tongue on you, don't you, lass?" He kicked open a cabin door—not the great cabin. "This one does not have the wreckage in it. You need a bath before you see Mrs. Chapman or Mel."

"But I should look in on them."

"Not looking like you've been mortally wounded. You are all over blood and smell like a charnel house."

"Perfume to you?" She tossed up the last word as he set her on a bunk.

His breath hissed through his teeth.

She cringed and shrank against the bulkhead, her hands raised. "It was a jest. A poor one at that. Please don't—"

"Shh." He brushed a fingertip across her lips. "I've ne'er harmed a lady in my life." He turned toward the door. "Not directly, anyhow." Then he was gone, closing the door behind him with the softest of clicks.

Phoebe drew her knees to her chest and wrapped her arms around her shins. She shivered in the tiny cabin with its porthole no bigger than a man's head and few furnishings. Throughout Mel's coma, Phoebe and Belinda had taken turns sleeping in here. It had belonged to Mel. Her books resided on a shelf built into the bulkhead and held in place by a wooden bar.

Mel had come awake as the fighting began. Bloodstained or not, Phoebe needed to see her, make sure Belinda was all right. She must make herself move, not cower in fear of blows that would never come. She must . . . she must . . .

She flung herself off the bunk and grasped the door handle. Nothing happened. She tugged and pushed. The door remained in place. She beat her fists on it. No one responded.

Rafe had locked her in. He'd made her a prisoner in a space not much larger than a dressing room. No, smaller. A coffin.

"No. No!" She heard the rising hysteria in her voice and stuffed a corner of the quilt into her mouth.

Though her voice was silenced, her heart raced, her limbs twitched. Her mind raced over a hundred scenes of locked rooms, her pleas ignored.

Calm. Calm. Calm. She cried the litany in her head.

The door popped open. Two sailors, who had obviously cleaned up a bit after the fighting, lugged in a bath too small for anything beyond standing in to pour water over oneself, and steaming water. It smelled of the sea and would leave her skin sticky, but she didn't care. To scrub away the grime of the battle looked like a taste of heaven.

"Cook's preparing some food, ma'am," one of the men assured her.

"Thank you." Phoebe didn't have room to stand with the two men and the bath in the cabin. "Please don't lock the door."

"Captain's orders, ma'am." The spokesman departed, and the latch clicked from the outside.

Beyond breaking the door down with the oversized tin washbasin, Phoebe was stranded, confined. The porthole opened, but the air outside proved too cold. Still, the gulp of fresh sea air helped. She would bathe, maybe even contrive to wash her hair free of the smell of powder smoke, and manage Captain Rafe Docherty later.

As she sluiced warm water through her hair a few minutes later, she realized the brig had grown quiet enough for her to hear voices in the adjacent cabin, one light and feminine, the other male. Rafe talking with Belinda or Mel? For a moment, picturing him with his daughter, his joy at her waking up after the great risk he took with the trepanning, Phoebe felt her heart soften toward him. The coil of anger loosened.

Then hammering began close at hand, and voices outside were loud enough for her to hear the words. They were repairing the wrecked stern windows and the hole in the bulkhead, wreckage from the battle—a great risk he had taken with his child and unwilling passenger—and the anger gripped her again. It gripped her so hard she could scarcely breathe. She yanked on fresh clothes and began to pound her fists on the door.

More hammering began elsewhere on the brig. Shouts rose. Metal clanged. No one would hear her, not even next door, unless she shouted.

If she opened her mouth and began to shout, she feared she would never stop. Surely she had lost her reason. She'd seen too much death, too much destruction that day. In earlier days.

"Lord, I can't go on like this." She returned to the bunk, huddled against the bulkhead. "Lord, where is my inner peace? Where are You?"

Around her, a cacophony of bangs and thumps and shouts rose. The cabin remained silent, empty of so much as a hint of the presence of the Lord she'd felt even in the bad years of her marriage.

Shivering, she wrapped a quilt around herself and sought Bible verses she knew. She fell asleep reciting the fifty-first chapter of Psalms. "Deliver me from bloodguiltiness, O God, Thou God of my salvation: and my tongue shall sing aloud of Thy righteousness."

"I have no bloodguilt" were the first words out of her mouth upon waking. "My heart is pure."

Gideon's face flashed before her eyes in the darkened cabin. She shook her head to dislodge the image. Another one appeared, one she had scarcely known, too distorted with rage, with pain, with grief, for her to recall features. Her bloodguilt.

No, no, no, she had done nothing deliberately. She had not willingly gone into battle, into any fight, led anyone into danger. Rafe had spilled blood, not her.

But she knew the truth and must not deny it, there alone in the dark as she had been too many nights over the past four years of her widowhood—and before. The quiet of the brig pressed down around her, each creak and groan of wave-tossed timbers emphasized by the lack of other noises around them—no talk, no laughter.

Only a solitary patter of footfalls striding back and forth. Back and forth.

Phoebe leaped from the bunk and shoved against the door, ready to shout the ship awake if it was still locked. But someone had unlocked the door. It opened so abruptly she stumbled over the coaming and into the companionway. At the top of the ladder, crisp, damp, star-laden air beckoned. She started up, limping as she put her full weight on her ankle. Little pain. Just a wrench. She certainly didn't need a physician to look at it.

She reached the quarterdeck. Light from the binnacle spilled onto the face of the helmsman. Expecting Jordy for an instant before she remembered his death, she started at the sight of another man, whose name eluded her. On the far side of the quarterdeck, Rafe had ceased pacing. He gripped the weather rail and gazed toward the horizon, his hair whipping around his face, his shoulders hunched beneath his heavy boat cloak as though he were cold.

A flash of tenderness plucked at Phoebe, a wish to take him in from the cold, serve him hot chocolate and bonbons—as though a hardened man like him would ever receive such gentle treatment. If he was cold, if he was in pain either physical or in his heart, he had brought it all upon himself.

But she went to him and touched his arm. "Why don't you go below, where there's less wind?"

"I do not dare leave my quarterdeck for more than a few minutes." He half turned toward her. "The men are calm now, sated with the spoils of victory. But the last time I turned my back on them, they . . . my . . ." Suddenly he unclasped his cloak and flung an edge around her blanket-wrapped shoulders, drawing her close to his side. "I can't get warm, Phoebe. I was beside the galley fire for a full turn of the hourglass. Aye, a full half of an hour, and I couldn't get warm. 'Tis a chill deep in my bones."

"Are you afraid?" She was quite warm beside him, maybe too warm. The temptation to lay her head against his shoulder and find her own peace in closeness ran as deep as the coil of anger now subdued but still present, twitching its tail. She remained upright and poised, as much as a lady could be poised surrounded by a man's thick woolen cloak, his strong arm, his scent. Her heart raced, and she pressed her hands against his chest, against his short leather jerkin as a further barricade, and let words build a stronger wall. "Do you fear your own men after this happened?"

"Aye, a wee bit. We're so close to England now, though, I have little doot they'll stay in line. Especially with the ring-leaders"—he cleared his throat—"dead."

Now the chill crept up Phoebe's spine, and her fingers curled around a button on the front of his coat. "Dead? All of them?"

"Aye, all of them." He clipped out the response.

"Your uncle?"

His chest rose and fell. His warm breath fanned her face with the merest hint of a hitch in it. "They put him in with the French prisoners of war. They . . . took any decisions away from me."

"The prisoners—the prisoners killed your uncle? Did you know they would do that? Did you order your men to put him there?" Her voice rose in pitch on each question. "Hadn't you seen enough death and destruction for one day, for one lifetime that you willfully—"

He pressed his fingers to her lips. "Hush. Mel sleeps right below us."

"I'm surprised you care." Phoebe stepped out of the pro-tective warmth of the cloak and planted one fist on her hip, the other on the rail. "This entire enterprise has risked your daughter's life, first with her accident meant for you, and then the battle itself."

"The battle was not my choice."

"You didn't try to stop it. You claim you love Mel, but you don't show it."

"Phoebe, please. You do not understand."

"Oh, I understand. I understand that a little girl who adores you nearly died again today because of you. I understand—"

He raised his hand again, as though intending to stifle her words, and she slapped it away. "I'll have my say, Rafael Docherty." She kept her voice low. "What I saw today is a man who has served you honorably and well, who has followed you through nine years of danger in the hope of protecting you until you come to your senses, and died today doing just that. Yet you stand here and worry about losing control of your ship again like a child who might have his favorite toy taken away, and talk about being cold inside. That's what happens when you have no conscience, no soul."

"Is it now?" He sounded calm, matter-of-fact, as though her words had rolled off him like raindrops over oiled cloth. "And you would ken this how?"

Phoebe drew herself upright, her chin a little elevated so she could look into his face, pale in the starlight. "I know this through my faith in God."

"Is that so? Your faith in God protects you from regretting your actions?"

"I—" Too late, Phoebe saw the trap. If he knew, if he'd heard one word . . .

She took a step backward.

He captured her hand beneath his on the rail, holding her fast. "So you are telling me, you sanctimonious prig, that being a Christian means you feel naught of the remorse for mistakes you've made?"

"No, I didn't mean—"

"So you act with impunity?" Though quietly spoken, his words lashed her across the ears like a cat-o'-nine-tails. "No matter what you do?"

"I didn't say that. I only meant—"

"That your faith in God keeps you warm despite sending your husband to his death and killing another woman's husband down in Seabourne, Virginia?"

262

18

Rafe regretted the words as soon as they left his mouth. The pain burning through his veins like poison gave him no excuse to lash out at Phoebe. And no words could take them back.

Silence hung between them like the layer of cold seeping beneath his cloak. Beneath his fingers, her hand felt as rigid as the weather rail, so stiff she scarcely seemed to breathe. But she didn't run from him. At any moment, she would open her mouth and give him the tongue-lashing he deserved.

Encouraged, he brushed his thumb against the satin smoothness of her cheek. "I expect you're wishing me in Davy Jones's locker now?"

"What—where?" The merest hint of a quiver began at that single word and reflected in a shudder through her.

"The bottom of the sea." He grimaced. "With the dead men."

"Is that—is that where you put them?" Another quiver in her voice, another shiver through her person.

Rafe sighed. "Aye. According to tradition, we had the service at sundown and slipped them over the rail."

"I would have liked to attend." Her voice grew stronger, steadier. "You didn't tell me, and I cared for Jordy too. But you had me locked in my cabin."

"Aye, for your own good."

"My own good? What good does it serve to treat me like

263

some kind of prisoner, a criminal, when I'm not—" She broke off on a hiccupping sob. "But you think I am a criminal."

"I do not ken the details to make that sort of judgment. But your locked door had naught to do with that. It had to do with the men after battle. They can be . . . irresponsible, especially if the drink is involved."

"I thought you didn't allow drink on your ship." Her tone held the hint of a sneer, a challenge, but still that tendency toward shakiness.

"I do not. But the Frenchman was not so inclined, and a few got ahold of it before I could put a stop to them. I didn't want you bothered, if you ken what I'm saying."

"Yes, yes, I understand. I suppose I should thank you then. It's just that being confined like that, in that tiny cabin . . ." She turned her face away. Her hair half tumbled from her topknot. It gleamed like spun silver in the starlight.

Rafe's fingers flexed, aching to touch those gleaming strands. "Phoebe. Mrs. Lee. Whatever I'm to be calling you, we cannot ignore what I said about you."

"Do you want me to talk about it?" She turned on him, her hands raised and fisted in front of her, her face ashen. "Do you want all the salacious details of violence and blood and how I really killed three people? The one life I saved—" She stopped as a sob more like a keening wail rose from her throat, and she twisted away from him.

He let her go. She couldn't get far on a brig with only eighty feet from stem to stern. She could hide below, but he knew her well enough by now to know she wouldn't.

His cloak secured around him against the brusque night wind, he paced to the binnacle, checked the compass heading, and turned the hourglass. "We'll be in England again in less than a week if the wind stays in our favor like this, eh, Hamish?"

"Aye, sir." The young man shifted his position behind the wheel from one foot to the other. "Is the lady a'right, sir?"

"Fighting distresses ladies." Rafe gave the youth a tight smile. "They like us coming home as conquering heroes, but they do not wish to hear much of the details of how we gained our sil'er. Remember that, lad, and you'll do fine with the lasses."

"Aye, sir."

Rafe clapped him on the shoulder and strolled away as though nothing of the day overset him. In truth, he thought he might have enough of the poison of rage and pain in his veins to tear all eighty feet of the mainmast out with his bare hands.

"You should have let him kill me, Jordy," he murmured to the night sky. "You had a soul worth saving."

The burning in his blood reached his eyes. He pressed cold fingers to them, forcing back any demonstration of emotion. Weeping like a woman wouldn't bring Jordy back, nor Watt, nor the others who had laid down their lives in the name of gaining quick wealth and in truth striving for his goal.

But he could hold the grief inside no longer. It came, tears as scalding as a spring from the bowels of the earth, as salty as the sea that had at last received the penultimate member of his family. All he had left was Mel, and he'd come too close to killing her too. She deserved a better father than he had been to her—sweet, loving, courageous Melvina Docherty.

To hide his weakness, he slipped behind the cutter and leaned over the rail, far enough for the icy salt spray to wash his face. He gripped the water-sanded wood and breathed deeply to get himself back under control, in command of his emotions and his future. He wasn't dead. He must go on, make the deaths of value.

He sensed Phoebe's presence beside him before he caught a

whiff of her jasmine scent still tainted with a hint of lavender. She said nothing. She didn't touch him. She simply stood beside him, her fingers curled around the edge of the rail.

"Am I to apologize to you, lass?" he asked at last.

"For speaking truth?" She shoved a handful of windblown hair out of her face and held it at the nape of her neck as though her fingers were ribbons. "I don't know how you found out. I thought only a few people knew. I hoped only a few people knew."

"'Twas gossip in the taverns and naught more. I had no business bringing it up as though I knew the whole."

"Gossip speaks truth this time—to an extent. I—" The *Davina* slid into the trough of a wave, and she released her hair to grip the rail again. Wild, shimmering locks cascaded over her face and shoulders.

Rafe gathered it in his hands this time and held it off her face, his thumb and forefinger acting as a hairpin to keep her face clear, a pale oval in the shimmering lights of stars and phosphorescent waves. Words to express how beautiful he found her rose to his lips. He swallowed them back and chose the less pleasant but far more intimate. "You do not need to tell me, but I'd like to ken the whole of it."

"I've told only two people the whole of it. About my husband, that is. Too many others had to know about the other."

Rafe waited, touching only her hair and the nape of her neck. If he told her that hearing of her transgressions might help him forget his own, she might run off again, avoid him like the plague she seemed to think he was.

She rubbed one hand over her face. "I wish there were someplace warmer and drier."

"The lady who wanted to stay on deck in a storm wants to go below on a clear night like this?"

"I don't like confinement. My husband—" She pursed her mouth. Her chin quivered.

"Did he lock you in the rooms?"

She nodded. "He said I flirted too much at parties, so he told me I couldn't go to any more. I was seventeen and missed my friends, so I went anyway. After that, he locked me in my dressing room every night."

Rafe kept his opinion of such a man to himself. "So your sickness when you were first aboard wasn't from the sea so much as the close quarters."

"I think that's likely."

"I'm so sorry." He propped one hip against the rail for balance and brushed the fingers of his free hand across her face. Finding moisture too warm to have come from a brief dose of sea spray, he brushed it away and kept his fingers curved around her cheek. "I had no ill intent in it, you ken."

"I know that now. But I was nearly angry enough that first night to use the knife on you."

"Perhaps you should have. The way the crew was feeling about me, they might have declared you a heroine and done whatever you liked, such as put you ashore."

"Jordy and Derrick wouldn't have let me get away with it. And Watt . . . Rafe, I thought he cared about you."

"Aye, weel, so did I until we were locked in the great cabin. But I ne'er thought he was wanting to kill me." His throat closed and he shook his head. "He was my blood kin, my mither's much younger brother. He went into the Navy, but he left at age thirty. He lived with us in Edinburgh for a year, then joined a privateer crew."

"So that's how you ended up here?"

"Aye, he made the suggestion, and I was game for anything in my rage and grief."

"But why would he turn on you?"

"Greed. He could claim to be captain in the event of my death and claim my shares. Who would gainsay him, when half a hundred men would attest that indeed he was the captain?"

"I can't understand that kind of greed, to kill one's own nephew for nothing more than gold?"

"I'd rather not talk about it." Or admit the rest. "What else did your husband do to you that prompted such a gentle lady to drive him to his death?"

She let out an unladylike snort. "I'm scarcely gentle. And by choosing to be a midwife, I am not much of a lady now."

"You'll al'ays be a lady, Phoebe Lee."

"Don't flatter me, Rafe." She stepped out of his reach, leaving his hands cold without her to touch. "As you not so subtly pointed out a bit ago, I'm not much of a Christian either. I'm a fraud, a hypocrite. I preach about God's love and forgiveness and accepting it. I talk about God's peace and healing. And all the while I have so much anger in my heart against my husband and . . . that other man, I wanted to hurt you myself today. Now I can never convince you that your path is wrong and following Christ is right, the only way." She began to weep in deep, harsh sobs. "I know that's the truth, but I don't know how to get there now that I realize I've lived a lie all these years."

"Ah, Phoebe, my dear." He stepped forward and gathered her to him.

She didn't resist. She laid her head on his chest, and the sobs exploded from her in shuddering bursts that made more of her words incomprehensible. After a few attempts, she gave up trying to speak and cried herself out, sheltered in his arms and warm boat cloak.

Rafe said nothing either. He remembered the platitudes of the pastor when Rafe had returned home broken in spirit.

The man had meant well. Perhaps they had been the right words under most circumstances of loss. But Rafe didn't believe even God could heal the kind of wounds dealt his soul in the Mediterranean. Phoebe's confession seemed like more proof that God's encompassing forgiveness was just not enough sometimes.

Yet Derrick forgave those who had held him in captivity and sold his wife and children elsewhere. Rafe had seen the man's back, a crisscross of scars from the lash. Derrick often tried to speak to Rafe about forgiving those who transgressed against him, James Brock in particular. No doubt Derrick would add Watt's name to the sermons. But Rafe had walked away. He didn't want to know.

Now he wished he did so he could give Phoebe advice, grant her words that would set her heart at rest for her past transgressions and those who had hurt her.

"It was bad, your marriage?" he asked.

She nodded against him, her weeping growing quieter, more shallow. "I thought I was in love. He was handsome and debonair and everything I was supposed to marry."

"Lots of land?"

"How'd you guess?"

"Things are not so different in America than England as you all would like to think, not when it comes to advantageous marriages."

"Did you make an advantageous marriage?" Her voice held an edge.

Rafe's lips twitched up at the corners. "Nay, Davina had only a passable dowry."

"But she was beautiful."

"Oh, aye, that she was. Like her daughter."

"Mel looks like you."

"Aye, she has some of my family's better traits, I'm glad to say. But I did not marry for land. I did not want it. I had my trade to support me and the house in Edinburgh. Davina was town-bred too, so we never hankered for the open spaces."

"Until you went to sea."

"Some things about a man can change." He stroked her tumbled fall of hair. "Did you take land to your marriage?"

"Four hundred acres of prime grazing land in the foothills of the Blue Ridge Mountains. Gideon wanted horses. More horses. He wanted that grazing land, and I wanted him. I always got what I wanted." She fell silent.

Rafe tucked his hand beneath her chin and tilted her head back. "You do not need to answer me on this, Phoebe, but did your husband beat you?"

She blinked. "How did you know?"

"The way you cringe sometimes. I knew someone had. The mon's lucky he's already dead."

"Rafe, you mustn't."

"Mustn't what? Despise a man who will harm a female? Watt—" He cleared his throat. "You need not talk anymore if you do not wish to."

"Or is it that you do not wish to listen anymore?"

"I will listen as long as you talk, but you're shivering even in my cloak, and the dawn is breaking over the horizon."

She twisted around and stared at the sky, where a line of pale pink curved between inky sea and gray-blue sky. "Let's go to the galley. I can make coffee."

"You can make the coffee?" Rafe didn't bother to disguise his surprise. "I ne'er knew a lady who could boil the water, let alone cook anything useful."

"Humph. I made myself learn after I was married. I thought if I got away—" She freed herself from his hold and headed across the deck to the ladder leading down to the galley.

Rafe followed her. In another turn of the glass, men would

270

stir, change the watch, and the closeness of their dialogue would end. And he didn't want it to end. He didn't realize how much he'd missed private talks in the middle of the night until Phoebe came along.

He didn't realize how much he'd missed a woman's company until Phoebe came along.

In the darkness below deck, they entered the galley. While Phoebe prepared the coffee, Rafe stirred the ashes in the stove until the embers banked deep beneath them flickered to life. He shoved sticks of wood into the stove, noting he needed to send a man into the hold to bring up more kindling. Heat began to radiate into the galley. He took a spill from the fire and lit one of the overhead lanterns swinging from a deck beam.

Phoebe set the pot for the coffee atop the stove. "I didn't realize I was so cold until I felt the fire."

"Aye, it can be that way." The galley offered no chairs, but a number of barrels of flour and oats provided seats. He patted one to indicate Phoebe should make herself comfortable.

She perched on a barrel of fine flour used to bake the occasional plum duff as a treat for the men, and glanced toward the dark recesses of the lower deck. "Won't we wake the men if we talk?"

"Not likely. A brig is too noisy all the time for anyone to be a light sleeper." Seated on a barrel of oatmeal, he took her hand and turned his back on the men sleeping a dozen yards away. "Do you have aught else to say?"

She gave him a half smile. "Yes, much more, if you're not to believe you have a common murderess aboard."

"Weel, not so common."

Her eyes widened for a moment, then a faint flush tinged her pale cheeks. "Are you teasing me, sir?"

"Perhaps a wee bit. I did not want you so sad. Fair breaks my heart to see a female weep."

271

She peeked up at him through her lashes. "It's good to know you have a heart."

Rafe stared at her for a moment, and something did indeed break inside him, but not his heart—a bit of the hardness around it fell away and lodged as a lump in his throat. He swallowed against it. "You cannot think so ill of me if you can flirt with me."

"Was I?" Her hands flew to her now bright cheeks. "I shouldn't. I can't. I think the coffee is ready." She leaped to her feet.

He drew her down beside him again. "'Tis not ready, lass. You can scarce smell it, so 'tis a poor excuse for running away."

"I don't—" She sighed. "I suppose I do. I was running away from Gideon, my husband, when I fell down the steps and—and—" She slid to the very lip of the barrel, her hands gripping the rim on either side of her as though she intended to launch herself upward and outward.

"Go ahead, lass, run from me like you have everything else," Rafe said softly. "But you'll still have to live with your own heart and conscience."

She whirled toward him so fast her hair flew out like a banner. "You talk to me about running and conscience? You? You?" Her voice, though quiet, rose a note on each *you*. "You've been running from your conscience for nine years."

"Nay, lass, you have that incorrect. I am not running from anything. I'm running toward something."

"Murder."

"Justice."

They locked gazes, held, while the coffee began to boil and hiss over onto the top of the stove, the combination of rich aroma and acrid scorching stinging to the nose. Her eyes took on the glow of stained glass with sunlight behind it, and Rafe braced himself for a poisoned dart of a word. But she bowed her head, hiding her face behind the shimmering curtain of her hair.

"The coffee's finished." Rafe rose to retrieve two pewter tankards from hooks and fill them with the hot liquid, black and strong in the dim light. He moved with slow deliberateness to give her time to gain her composure.

Or slip out of the galley without him watching her or barring her way.

He heard no movement behind him. Beyond the galley, a few men stirred. In moments, the cook would appear and want to know why someone, captain or not, had invaded his kitchen. Rafe and Phoebe would have no more privacy, and he still didn't know what had truly happened with the man in Seabourne. Then again, Phoebe didn't know the entire truth about him either.

19

Belinda wasn't doing well. Phoebe saw that the instant she walked into the great cabin two days after the battle, proud of herself for balancing a tray of coffee and porridge she'd managed to help the cook prepare. Proud of herself for how she'd evaded talking further with Rafe without running away. And now he was the one gone, having rowed over to the French vessel shortly after she walked out on their conversation in the galley, to ensure all was well aboard the prize. She had wanted to go with him. Because of her cowardice, too much lay unsaid between them. But besides the impropriety of her joining him, she needed to tend to her patient.

Her patients. Mel looked better each day, though pale and too thin. She was propped in a half-sitting position by several pillows and a bolster and managed a soft "Good morning" upon Phoebe's arrival.

Phoebe set her tray on the table and crossed to Mel's side. "You dear girl." She smoothed the rich red hair beginning to sprout around the girl's scar. "You've decided to join the living after all."

"I missed my papa." She curled weak fingers around Phoebe's hand. "I kept dreaming he was lost, and I had to wake up to find him."

Her father was lost, lost in his heart.

"I think he'll be down to see you soon. He'll be happy to see you doing so well. Are you hungry?"

"Yes," Mel said.

"I'm not." In contrast to Mel's burgeoning health, Belinda huddled on the window seat, her face a greenish hue, her arms wrapped around her middle. She did not smile at Phoebe. She glared at her from red-rimmed eyes.

"I've been sick all night and you weren't here." Her lower lip quivered like that of a distressed child. "Didn't get a bit of sleep."

Phoebe turned to kneel before Belinda. "You were sleeping peacefully a few hours ago. What happened?"

"It was the pickled watermelon rinds." Belinda groaned. "I ate all of them."

"Did you?" Phoebe swallowed hard so as not to laugh. "You must have been hungry."

"I wasn't. I just wanted them. They were so—" Belinda broke off on a groan.

"Perhaps you should allow me to examine you. Come into the other cabin."

"Can't leave Melvina alone," Belinda protested.

"If Papa is coming down," Mel murmured, "I'll be all right."

"He's coming soon." Phoebe listened as though she would hear his footfalls on the deck or ladder. "Right now he's aboard the French ship."

Mel's lips quivered. "I thought—why isn't he here with me?"

"Because—" Phoebe flailed for an explanation, since the truth wouldn't be acceptable. It wasn't acceptable that he would leave his daughter to avoid a woman. "We'll signal for him to come. He's—"

"He is coming now." Life sparkled in Mel's eyes, turning them bright green again.

Phoebe heard it then, caught the rap of footfalls on the companionway ladder, and knew Rafe descended even before he tapped on the door and asked if he could come in.

Given permission, he pulled open the portal and stepped over the coaming. "Mel, my dear lassie, you are looking well."

The sound of his voice, the light burr, the rich timbre, sent Phoebe's stomach somersaulting through her middle. If she turned to leave the cabin and their eyes even accidentally met, she might faint. Already the air seemed to have been sucked from the room.

She remained where she was, facing Belinda. An error. Belinda was often childish in her behavior, but she was not stupid. She had kept her husband's shipping interests going and organized for a year and a half by some means of intellect or human understanding. George was surely too savvy a businessman himself to have left his money in her care if he didn't find her capable.

Her eyes widened. "Oh my goodness." She rose with an alacrity that belied her advanced girth. "We'll be going then." She swept around Phoebe, who was still motionless on her knees, and sailed to the door.

"Yes, yes." Phoebe scrambled to her feet and swung around to follow.

Rafe glanced up at her from where he crouched beside the bunk. Their gazes met, held. "We've a conversation to finish, aye, Mrs. Lee?"

Mouth dry, Phoebe couldn't think what to say in response. She merely inclined her head and walked past him to where Belinda waited at the door, her face now alight with curiosity. Phoebe braced herself for Belinda to say something. Hopefully she would close the door before she began to talk.

She only closed the door to the great cabin before she

turned to Phoebe and demanded in a shrieking whisper, "What is there between you two?"

"Nothing." Which was basically the truth.

"Ha." Belinda flounced into the other cabin and flopped onto the bunk. "I don't believe that for a moment. The way you looked when he walked in . . ." She waved her hand before her face like a fan. "And the way you two looked at one another, why, I nearly blushed."

Phoebe definitely blushed. The heat of her cheeks emphasized the chill permeating the cabin, and she snatched up a quilt to wrap around her shoulders. Once again she'd left her cloak in the great cabin. "Lie back so I can make sure all is well with the baby."

"It was just the pickles. I feel well now. And maybe being in the cabin for too long. I want you to tell me about Captain Docherty. I mean, how can you care for him? The man isn't very nice."

Words to defend him sprang to Phoebe's lips. Before she made the mistake of using them, Belinda continued, "But that's not true. He's wonderful to his daughter, and he's been kind to me. But he acts like he doesn't care at all that his uncle and friend died the day before yesterday."

"He cares," Phoebe said. Her heart twisted at the memory of Rafe bent double in his effort to master his sorrow. "He cares."

"Maybe he does, if you say he does." Belinda drew a blanket over herself and slid back against the bulkhead. "But he's willing to use females to get to the man he wants to kill. That's very wicked."

"You're abetting his behavior."

"To save my husband."

"You think that justifies helping him murder someone?"

"I'm not helping him—" Belinda caught her breath. "I suppose I am. I thought only about seeing George free."

"And not George's baby. Do you think he'll thank you if his baby suffers because of what you're doing?"

"Phoebe, stop that. George loves me."

"Of course he does. And you're repaying that love by risking his baby's life on a whim, or is it a dare? Or do you want to be the heroine everyone will talk about so you can—"

Belinda reared up and slapped Phoebe's face. "Stop that. You don't know what you're saying. I'm a far better wife and mother than you were. I didn't—"

"Belinda, don't—"

"Kill my husband and baby."

"I didn't either. Gideon was trying to lock me up for the night, and I hit him over the head with a candelabra so I could leave. Yes, I said leave. I was running away from him."

"Unnatural wife."

"And he wasn't an unnatural husband for locking me away so he could drink and chase after loose women every night?" Phoebe knew she was shouting, but she couldn't stop herself, the volume, the flow of words. "I had a bag packed and started out. But I didn't hit him hard enough, and he came after me."

"So you were an oaf and fell down the steps."

"No, Belinda, he picked me up and threw me down the steps. He killed our baby and nearly me too. But he left me lying unconscious on the floor at the foot of the steps and rode off. If he hadn't gotten inebriated and thrown off his horse so the sheriff came to our house, I probably would have bled to death on that floor because he sent the servants away at night. I was alone and hemorrhaging because of your brother. He's the villain, no matter what lies your parents tell. Do you hear me?"

Belinda covered her ears with her hands and closed her eyes. "I don't want to listen to this about Gideon."

"You will." Phoebe bent over Belinda. "Your brother killed my baby and himself. Do you hear me?"

"I think," a soft voice from behind Phoebe drawled, "every-one on the brig heard you."

Phoebe's insides collapsed into a leaden lump in the center of her belly. As limp as an empty grain sack, she sank onto the bunk and crossed her arms over her face. "I'm sorry. I don't know why I'm behaving this way."

"Oh, I do." Belinda's voice held a vicious edge. "You're in love with this rogue."

If only a special hatchway would open up and swallow her right into the hold at that moment, it wouldn't be too soon. Phoebe couldn't even run. Rafe blocked the doorway, and the cabin barely allowed space for her and Belinda, let alone a place to hide. She may as well place a brave face on it. Slowly, as though she'd developed rheumatism in her shoulders, she lowered her arms and peeked up at Rafe.

He smiled. Not one of his uptilted corners of the mouth, but a full smile showing strong, white teeth. He wasn't look-ing at her; his gaze slid beyond to Belinda. "Aye, I believe your wee midwife has a fondness for me. 'Tis a pity the voyage is so near an end and we'll ne'er see one another again."

Slapped twice in one day.

"Since I do not share her faith," he added.

Except she'd begun to doubt the sincerity of her faith.

She could get away from the cabin if she knocked Rafe down and walked over his body. But she was a woman who didn't believe in violence, who had lashed out at him. She'd taken an oath to treat her patients with kindness and respect, and however unofficial that vow might be—given only in front of Tabitha, Dominick, and a handful of friends—she had broken it when she shouted at Belinda.

Twice a hypocrite—pretending to be a Christian while harboring anger in her heart, and claiming she was a midwife whose patients came first when she could have upset Belinda enough to send her into confinement.

"What you do share," Belinda responded, "is a penchant for killing off your fellow man. If she didn't knock him off his horse, then she may as well have. She drove him to drink and then ride like a wild man, he was so unhappy with her empty head. Or did you think he didn't tell us anything, Phoebe?"

"I do believe, Mrs. Chapman," Rafe said, "you have told us quite enough. Mel said you were not feeling well. Why do you not rest and allow me to get Mrs. Lee her breakfast?"

As if she could eat.

"Mel's alone, though," Belinda protested.

"I've gotten out a great bell the cook used to use to call the men to dinner. She will use it if she needs anything."

"Her breakfast," Phoebe managed to get out.

"Aye, she needs assistance with that. She is not so good at lifting the cup to her lips, but she will learn." His face twisted. "She will have to learn it all again like a bairn, but I ken she will. She is a braw lass."

"She is brave." Belinda's voice softened as she talked about Mel. "If I have a daughter, I hope she's as smart and brave."

"With you for a mither," Rafe said with a bow, "she'll certainly be as pretty. Now go about your rest, madam."

With Belinda spluttering over the compliment, Rafe grasped Phoebe's hands and drew her to her feet. "Mrs. Lee?"

Remain in the tiny cabin, go to the great cabin with Mel and Belinda, or go somewhere with Rafe for breakfast? She doubted she could eat, but she chose the latter option. "Where will we go?"

"To the galley. If you can mix up plum duff, Cook said he would leave us to the fire."

"Of course she can't," Belinda began.

Rafe drew Phoebe into the companionway and closed the

cabin door. "I understand why she hates you now, if she thinks you killed her brother, but I do not ken why she insisted you come along."

"She couldn't find another midwife to go with her." She preceded him up the ladder. Once on deck, they walked side by side between the hulks of the guns, and she added, "She thinks me cooking is even more vulgar than me delivering babies. Though I admit I don't know how to make plum duff, whatever it is."

"'Tis a boiled pudding."

"Is that what that cake is called? But it had raisins in it, not plums."

"We cannot keep plums aboard ship into November." He gave her a half smile. "'Tis simple to make, if a wee bit common. But isn't managing money vulgar?"

"Amongst the merchants of Virginia?" Phoebe shook her head and realized she'd never pinned up her hair. "In the cities, everything is money. In that, she has left behind her genteel plantation lady training. Except for the ability to manage accounts. We all learn to manage accounts."

"You ken how to manage accounts?" He stepped past her to descend the ladder first.

Phoebe followed, her skirt gathered in one hand. "The mistress of a plantation has to learn a great deal about managing income and expenses. It's not so different than in a business, just a bit more in the business—you hope. We have servants to clothe and feed, often an endless succession of guests to house, medicines to purchase or prepare, extra produce to sell or buy. The list is endless. I learned how, but now I have a manager to take care of matters since I hoped to be too busy delivering babies."

Rafe paused on the lower deck. "You weren't?"

"I was for a while, with the wives of some men in Middleburg and Leesburg, but then talk spread—" She glanced toward the galley. "Where's the cook?"

"I sent him away a'ready. We will leave the door open for the sake of propriety, but I wanted to be alone with you." He looked into her eyes, then his gaze dropped to her lips before he turned his back on her and entered the galley.

Phoebe pressed her hand to her mouth. He hadn't kissed her, but her lips tingled as though he had. Her knees wobbled as though he had embraced her.

She'd made too many mistakes for a once sheltered lady of six and twenty, but falling head over heels for Rafe Docherty was one of the greatest ones of all. Now was an appropriate moment to run, a time when few people would blame her for cowardice. Yet she couldn't run like that on a brig. Nowhere to run. Nowhere to hide. Unlike him, she couldn't flee to the French prize.

She followed Rafe into the galley, where indeed the largest bowl she'd ever seen sat in the middle of a work table, half filled with flour. A jug of molasses sat beside it, braced between two fiddle boards, its sides sticky with the sugary syrup.

"I'm supposed to mix batter in that?"

"Aye, it takes a wee bit of work. But first, you have not eaten your breakfast. Sit yourself down." He pushed one of the barrels up to the table.

Phoebe sat. The aromas of coffee and molasses filled the warm air, comforting. Homelike. Her heart ached for her own kitchen, children, a husband who would come home—

She cut the vision short. Especially after what had been said in the cabin, she didn't need that husband showing up in her daydreams with Rafe's face and easy, rolling gait.

"Coffee, oatmeal parritch." He set a cup and bowl before her. "I regret we have no butter."

"I'm not hungry." With him so near, her stomach knotted too tightly for food.

"If you are worrying about what Mrs. Chapman said there in the cabin, think naught of it. I will not, if 'twill please you." He tucked his hand beneath her chin and tilted her head up. "Unless 'tis what I said about ne'er seeing one another again that has you distraught." He smiled, perhaps to assure her that he teased her. Or perhaps to send a thrill through her.

She gripped the edge of the table. "I don't want to see you again. I want to get off this brig right now, take Belinda somewhere safe until we can get back to America, or until Dominick—" She snapped her teeth together—too late. The damage had been done.

Rafe's smile vanished. His hand closed on her wrist, not hard, but ensuring she couldn't slip away from him. "Until Dominick what? Dominick Cherrett, I presume."

"Ye-es." Phoebe ran her tongue over parched lips. "I wrote him. From Bermuda. One of the Navy ships took the letter."

"And what did you write?" His voice held that deadly quiet she would rather trade for one of Gideon's shouting rages. Gideon had been a boy having a temper tantrum. Rafe was a man in too strict control of his feelings. His face was a mask of indifference, his body taut. Only the faintest tremor in his hand on her wrist suggested the anger he held in check.

Phoebe picked up her mug of coffee with her free hand and held it in front of her mouth. "I told him I needed help because I'd been abducted and that you had to be stopped before you committed murder."

"Did you now?" He released her wrist and removed the cup from her hand to return it to the table. "Is that all you told him of my personal business?"

"Yes." The truth—strictly speaking.

"Are you certain of that?"

"Yes." She remembered every word.

"And what makes you think Lord Dominick can come to your rescue?"

"I was thinking more of your rescue than mine."

"Of course." Sarcasm dripped from his words. "How could I forget that? Nor can I forget that you think you know what's best for my life, my soul, my heart. So how do you think Lord Dominick is going to rescue me from three thousand miles away?"

"He'll find a way. He said if I'm ever in need, however great, he'd come to my aid."

"Why?"

Phoebe jumped at the abruptness of the question. "Because he and Tabitha are my friends."

"You will have to do better than that, bonnie Phoebe." His voice gentle, he caressed her jaw with his thumb. "What were you to Lord Dominick?"

Phoebe slapped his hand away. "I don't like your implication, sir. He's my friend, nothing more."

"That's a great deal to ask of a mere friend. Ask and expect to receive. So I'll ask you again, what are you to him?"

"Please." Realizing she was shaking, Phoebe held on to the table edge. "Please don't make me talk about this."

He said nothing. He wouldn't make her do anything. Except he'd implied something vulgar and improper, and now she must tell him the truth. Or at least part of it.

"I saved Tabitha's life," she blurted out.

"Ah, that makes a wee bit of sense. How?"

"I helped her through a rough lying-in."

Rafe nodded, then leaned one hip on the table as though ready for a long story. "Was that before or after you killed the husband of one of her patients?"

20

The lantern swinging from the deck beam shed a yellow glow over Phoebe's face, emphasizing its sudden pallor. Her knuckles gleamed white through the fine skin on her hands gripping the edge of the worktable.

And Rafe decided he should cut out his tongue before he said anything so cruel to anyone ever again. Regardless of his reasons for the unkindness, Phoebe had suffered enough. She didn't need to suffer by his hand—or tongue—also.

"I'm sorry." The words, so rarely falling from his lips, nearly choked him. "I had no right to say such a thing."

"No, you didn't." Gravel had gotten blended with the honeyed cream of her voice. Her eyes grew dull, like moss gone too long without water. "You talk as though I—as though I—I killed him on purpose."

"Some of the tavern talk implied as much. After your husband and all."

"And you believed the talk?" Phoebe pushed herself to her feet.

Rafe opened his mouth to accuse her of running away again, but wasn't that his intent, to keep her away from him, to make her hate him rather than . . .

He could scarcely countenance the notion that she loved him. She knew he was a reprobate, a man on a violent mission. She knew his past for the most part, and she knew what he intended in the future. She'd seen him in battle. Yet she looked at him with a tenderness that created a churning custard of his heart, and he had to be rid of her, for her sake. He would only hurt her.

For his sake, he wanted to stop her from walking away from him, hold her close, find a minister to marry them—

He snapped his thoughts closed on that notion and stared at Phoebe hovering in the doorway. "You are not going to stay and tell me the truth? Or am I to presume that the rumors, for once, are not false?"

She sank her teeth into her lower lip so hard Rafe expected blood to well forth. For a moment, her spine appeared stiff enough to crack at a touch. Then she collapsed. Her posture slumped, her head bowed. "Rumor is partly right." She spoke in a murmur barely audible over the crash of waves against the hull.

The sailor's corner of Rafe's mind, which he'd developed over the past nine years, realized the sea had grown rougher, indicating they drew near to the Bay of Biscay, an area fraught with storms and French vessels attempting to break the British blockade. There would be too many of them from the Navy and more gun power than his little brig could manage. He needed to be on his quarterdeck in the event of danger, especially now that Jordy and Watt were no longer around, and Derrick had gone to sail the prize into Portsmouth to sell to the Admiralty. But right now, Phoebe was more important. She had been more important for too long now, a dangerous distraction he could not resist.

He glanced at her dejected posture, thought about her last words, and reached out to take her hands. "You do not need to tell me, Phoebe. 'Twas cruel of me to mention a word of it after all you've found yourself saying about your husband."

Which had been his intent, to turn her from him, but he could not. And that spelled trouble.

She pulled her hands free, giving him hope that perhaps he had succeeded in sending her off, then she simply swallowed some coffee, set the cup on the table, and folded her hands in her lap. "It was an accident. That is—" She stared past his shoulder. Her face was pale with two spots of red high on her cheekbones. "He'd—he'd beaten his wife so badly she went into travail two months early. It was my second lying-in on my own. Tabitha was too near her own to go out. The woman survived, but the baby . . . it was too soon. Too small. It never breathed." Tears starred her lashes, and he rested one hand on her shoulder, whether to comfort her or stop her he didn't know.

She continued in a high, tight voice. "It was a son after three daughters, and the man was angry. He blamed me. He blamed Tabitha for not coming herself. He blamed his wife for being weak." Her voice rose. "She had a broken arm because of him, and he blamed her."

"Shh." Rafe kneaded the tension from her shoulder. "You ken 'twas not your fault."

"I know." She bowed her head. "I went home. And he followed me. He stormed into the house and up the steps. He was shouting." A shudder ran through her. "All I could think was to stop him from reaching Tabitha and Dominick. So I picked up a poker and caught him in the middle with it. He folded up and fell. He broke his neck. He shouldn't have. But he did."

"It was an accident, Phoebe."

"I know. Everyone said that. Everyone who mattered anyway." She sighed. "But others knew about my husband and decided I am a dangerous female to be around. So I fled back to Loudoun County and tried to start over. I thought I had. I thought I'd forgiven him and Gideon and myself. But when there was that fight and you and Jordy and Derrick ran into it like everyone else, it was like watching Gideon and that husband, and I realized I'm not the loving Christian I'm supposed to be. I want to save your soul, but now I see mine for the tarnished vessel it is."

"But isn't that the point of Christianity? Jesus forgives those who repent?"

"You're preaching salvation to me?" She glanced up at him, her eyes alight with amusement. "You who want nothing to do with God?"

"Nay, lass, He wants naught to do with me. I have not repented."

"If you did—"

"Have you then?"

"I thought I had. But there must be more bitterness inside me than I knew." She swallowed as though trying to clear her palate of the taste. "I'm so uncertain now. For four years I've been sure Gideon was behind me, but then there was this man, and now this . . ." She shook her head.

"Sometimes when a mon is shot, the ball carries cloth and other debris into the wound. I can remove the lead and what I think is all the cloth, and the wound may even seem to heal. But then days or even weeks later, the mon has trouble, a fever, pain—" He stopped before getting too gruesome. "I must open the wound site again and find what is the source of the infection. 'Tis more often than not a bit of cloth or wood, a fragment of lead left behind. Once 'tis gone, the wound can heal. I think—" He gazed at Phoebe's beautiful face with a warmth deep inside him, the glowing coals of wonder. "Perhaps God has used me to lance your wounds so they can truly heal."

"Maybe He has." She pursed her lips and half closed her eyes, pensive, calm. Then suddenly she smiled up at him. "And you, Rafe, how can we cleanse your wounds?"

"You do not wish to talk of that." He turned to the table and began to pour molasses into the bowl. "The weather has been cold enough we still have an egg or two for this, but there's no milk, so I use molasses to make it moist enough."

Phoebe was staring at him. "How do you know such a thing? I mean, how to make a pudding?"

"I didn't start out as captain of a ship. I was a lowly crewman, one of the lowliest, since I knew little about sailing. But that dried biscuit that gets weevils in it disgusted me. The captain then made some jest about me being too fancy for plain sailor fare, so I must be wanting pudding and I could make it for the crew." A chuckle rose in his chest. "So I bribed the cook to teach me how and did it. Now 'tis a tradition for me to make it once in every voyage. Will you fetch me the raisins?"

She rose and drew the tin of raisins from its shelf. "I didn't think you would go to sea when you knew nothing about sailing."

Rafe began to beat the batter. "I was willing to do anything to catch James Brock." He smiled at her. "I still am."

"I know." She slapped the tin onto the table with more force than necessary. "That's why I'm here."

"Phoebe?" Rafe began to stir raisins into the batter. "I wish you weren't here. I never intended for you to come along. Indeed, I would rather you had not. I did not want a lass who despises men to be aboard my brig."

"I don't despise all men."

Selfishly, he wanted her to.

"Only those who've hurt me." Her lip quivered.

"Did I not hurt you by bringing you with us?"

"No, not by bringing me. I had to help Belinda in the end. But the rest . . . You will hurt me, Rafe, if you continue on your current course."

"Then do not love me, Phoebe. I warned you straightaway what I am like, what I'm doing. I have no room for a lady or God in my life, telling me 'tis wrong to go after Brock. I cannot live with the knowledge that he is free, while Davina and my parents are dead. I hear her screaming in the night, and I ken I have to go after him."

"Would Davina and your parents want you going against the Lord?" The gravel had gone from her voice. Soft as it was, though, she may as well have boxed his ears.

He sighed. "Phoebe, nay, my parents would not approve. But Davina . . ." He braced himself. "Davina was the most beautiful, the most soft-spoken lass I ever met, but her heart was not with the Lord until the end. When she called on Jesus to save her, the pirates slit her throat."

Shock registered on Phoebe's face. "I didn't know. I just assumed—I mean, you married her and you said you followed the Lord then."

"Aye, weel, you make a number of mistakes when you are that young."

"Quite young for a man heading to university."

"Her father had a great deal of influence over who was accepted."

She narrowed her eyes. "You married her to get into university?"

"Nay, not as that sounds. I loved her since I kent what the word *love* meant." He took the last roll of dough and slid it onto its pan. "But she—"

His head filled with the memory of Davina weeping, still pretty in her tears, fragrant with roses and as soft as thistle-down in his arms as he tried to comfort her, his childhood friend with a broken heart.

"She loved someone else." There, he'd said it. For the first time in thirteen years, he admitted that Davina had not married him for love. "She loved someone who did not want a wife, just the adulation."

Phoebe's eyes widened, her lips parted. She said nothing. And he loved her in that moment. She offered him no words of sympathy, no foolish declarations that a silly girl of eighteen had loved the wrong man but had surely come to love him—all the nonsense he had heard from his minister at home, from Jordy, from Davina herself.

"I was her dearest friend," he continued, unable to stop, like a lanced boil releasing its poison. "But I was too much of a lad to her. Even in the end, she said if I had learned to fight instead of learning medicine, I could have saved her."

"So you learned to fight." She stretched flour-daubed hands out to him. His mother had done that when he was a child running in with some hurt needing tended.

He didn't feel as though Phoebe were his mother. She should be a mother—mother to many children. His children, in a softer, kinder world, where God still cared. Yet hadn't he just suggested that God cared about Phoebe, cared enough to want her wounds cleansed and healed? If that were true, perhaps his own—

But what did he have without a future based on destroying James Brock?

Phoebe stood beside him for the moment, watching him crack the last two eggs acquired on Bermuda into the batter, then toss in a handful of dried citron and begin to stir. She watched him with a softness, an intense, loving gaze he had seen on other women's faces directed at other men. If Phoebe, a mere human female, could still care after all his attempts to push her away, perhaps God would love him one day, when he let go of his need to destroy Brock. Destroy him and end his life of safety, because three people had died with brutality and a child had lost her mother. Destroy—

"Gently, Rafe." Phoebe curled her hand around the spoon beneath his and stopped his battering of the batter. "You're going to have half of it on the table."

"So I am." He began to search the shelves for a pudding bag, remembered he didn't have the water boiling, and lifted the bucket to fill the giant kettle. "This will take hours to boil. We will need to look in on it to ensure the water doesn't boil away." He turned from the stove to find Phoebe motionless, spoon in one hand, gaze still fixed upon him. "Stop your staring at me, Mrs. Lee."

"I cannot, Captain Docherty. The sight of you being domestic . . ." She released the spoon, closed the distance of the half dozen feet between them, and kissed him.

Though as cool and light as morning mist, the gesture blazed through him, melting, incinerating arguments and pain until it reached his core, where he managed to extinguish the yearning for her.

He set his hands on her shoulders and held her off at arm's length. "Aye, I wished to be domesticated once. That has been destroyed, and I am not certain I can get it back, no matter how much I—"

"How much you what?" Her words, her eyes, the hands with which she gripped his collar challenged him to finish.

The response burned on his tongue. He shook his head, biting it away. "'Tis unimportant if I do not change my course, and I will not."

Phoebe's lips quivered. "Because you still love her?"

"Nay, I do not love her. I have not loved her for over a decade. Not like a husband should. But I cared for the friends we were once."

"And as the mother of your daughter?"

He flinched. "Aye, that too. Mel has always been a joy despite everything else. But Davina . . ." He started to shrug, started to shake off the talk of his past and direct the conversation to Phoebe. But his shoulders weighed down too much to shrug off the sordid history. "Sometimes I think I despised her at the end. I tried to give her all the time I could between my studies and working with my father, but she complained all the time. No matter what I did for her, I—she—"

"It wasn't enough?" Phoebe lifted one hand and stroked the hair back from his face, as he'd seen her do to Mel, her touch spindrift light. "I do understand. And no matter how much we accomplish, it never seems like enough for anyone, even God. What I'm trying to tell you, Rafe, is that destroying James Brock won't be enough. At first I thought becoming a midwife and bringing life into the world would help me forget what happened to my husband. Then I thought giving up my happy life in Seabourne to give my services to the women in the mountains would be enough to help me forget that—that accident. But they haven't been. You will never forget your pain over your wife until you forgive. And you could destroy your life if someone else doesn't kill you first."

"Ah, yes, unless someone stops me first. Someone like Dominick Cherrett and his admiral uncle?"

"Would that be so awful?"

"Do you think having me thrown into Newgate as a pirate will save my soul?"

"Dominick wouldn't do that to you."

"But the Navy might. Or did you think they would take kindly to me removing one of their prisoners from the prison hulks? That'll get me hanged faster than the accusation of piracy. 'Tis treason, you ken."

"I want to stop you from either action, from either accusation."

"And leave Mrs. Chapman without her husband?" He gave her a half smile. "Few men live long in those floating coffins."

"I—well, I—" Her eyes grew round.

"You did not think, no?"

She shook her head, then looked away.

"You had the best of intentions, I have no doot, hinnie. You wanted to rescue me. But that stops me from rescuing George Chapman."

"If you could do both . . ." She shifted from foot to foot, gazing down as though she needed to see her dainty toes to perform the restless action.

She looked so chagrined he wanted to sweep her close and tell her not to concern herself. Instead, he injected an edge of hardness to his tone. "All good intentions have some kind of consequence, Phoebe. I know the possible consequences of my actions."

"And don't care?" Water from the kettle boiled over onto the stove top with a hiss. It may as well have been Phoebe expressing her annoyance with him. "You don't care if you're hurting me, hurting Mel, and most of all hurting yourself."

"Oh, Phoebe, I do care. I do not want to, but I do." He turned to the table. "And I care about my pudding, you ken. Will you hold the bag, or would you prefer to pour?"

"I'll hold the bag."

They said nothing as Phoebe held the pudding bag open and Rafe poured the batter in. He then pulled a needle and thread from his coat pocket and began to sew up the top of the linen, watching Phoebe gape from the corner of his eye.

"Aye, I can sew up more than people. And all the best cooks—"

A shout rang out from above. He raised his head to listen.

"Ice! It's raining ice!"

"Aye, but I do dislike sailing past the Bay of Biscay. 'Tis always the foul weather here."

"Is—is ice dangerous?" Phoebe had paled.

Rafe slipped the pudding bag into the boiling water. "Not if we take the right precautions and do not see the enemy." He turned back to her. "I must go, but thank you for telling me about what happened. I could not bear your hurt and ken I was partly the cause of bringing it back to you."

"Yet it helped. I feel . . . lighter."

And so, in a way, did he.

He cupped her face in his hands but refrained from kissing her with great willpower. "Keep your burden light, lass, and do not love me. If Lord Dominick received your letter, I am like as not headed for Newgate and a hangman's rope."

"Which would make me—"

"Captain?" Feet clattered on the ladder.

"I must go." Rafe released her and headed for the door, yet his feet felt too leaden to step over the coaming, leave the cozy realm of domesticity he and Phoebe had shared, a glimpse of a future that would never be.

Riggs, a quieter, most compliant crewman since the battle and Watt's and Jones's deaths, reached the galley. "We don't know how much sail to take in."

"Aye, I am on my way."

Afraid if he glanced back to Phoebe he would end up like Lot's wife, or at the least forget duty and responsibility, he charged up the companionway ladder as though she pursued him with shackles. Icy wind blew into his face, not strong, but crowded with needlelike shards of ice. Sleet would slow them, as it coated sails and lines and made handling the rigging dangerous.

"I want lifelines rigged," he called to the nearest men. "From hatchways to companionways and from bowsprit to quarterdeck. No one walks on the deck without using one."

Already the deck grew slick with freezing patches of water. As long as the wind blew, the sails should remain free of enough ice that would set them in danger of collapsing, but if the wind rose, climbing the shrouds to furl the sails for safety could prove treacherous.

"Aloft." He ran toward the quarterdeck as he issued the orders. "Clew up all but mainsail and spritsail."

Men leaped to obey. They knew the risks if they did not get the sails in.

On the quarterdeck, Rafe snatched up a spyglass and sought for the *Fleur de Nuit*, their French prize. It had proved to be a grand sailing vessel and kept on station without a hitch once the mast and rigging had been repaired. From the look of things, either the men had decided to take in sail too, or they mimicked what they saw aboard the *Davina*. Either way, they took in sail. If a gale blew up, they could be separated. He would lose his prize, nearly half of his men, and the French cargo. All he would have were the French prisoners and no-where to off-load them to another vessel so he didn't have to sail to the naval port at Plymouth or Portsmouth and risk being stopped if Lord Dominick had gotten word to his uncle. Rafe wanted to set in further east in Southampton. They knew him there. Few questions would be asked. He would be mere hours from the prison hulk in the Thames from there.

Southampton, by all his best estimations without sunlight for a noon sighting, lay another five hundred miles northeast. Five hundred miles, two to three days of sailing, until he reached the next step in his plans.

As long as no one from Dominick Cherrett arrived to stop him. The fool woman for writing such a letter. Rafe should not have sent Watt ashore to watch her after he tried to mutiny, but it had gotten him off the brig. Rafe wanted Watt away from the men he wanted to entice. Watt had likely delivered the letter himself, thinking it would destroy Rafe. And perhaps Brock's henchmen had persuaded Watt to go after Rafe then, persuading him to kill his nephew whenever and however he could.

If only the men hadn't put Watt in with the prisoners and they hadn't killed him. Rafe could have questioned him, learned why Watt had grown so murderous. Surely control of the ship wasn't the only reason.

"I will be asking Brock himself," Rafe muttered.

And even to his own ears, the declaration lacked much of its venom. His heart didn't clench quite as tightly with anger as it had for nine years.

Oh, Phoebe, what have you done to me? What's left if I don't have Brock to destroy? I will have failed Davina yet again.

A shriek drew Rafe's attention to the main deck. Phoebe had emerged from the hatchway and promptly landed in a heap on the deck, a patch of ice beneath her. Rafe started aft, then waited. Five men had already reached her, two practically yanking her in half in their endeavor to be the first to help her to her feet. Her trill of laughter rang through the wind and sleet and nearly yanked Rafe's heart from his chest. Although broad, calloused hands pressed her delicate fingers to the lifeline, a phalanx of men surrounded her on her careful way back to the cabin. Rafe watched her progress, wind blowing his hair into his eyes and stinging his cheeks, then she vanished down the companionway, and he returned to the wheel.

"I'll take over for a bit." He nudged the man aside. "You go get warm. There's coffee in the galley."

"Thank you, sir." The man—a youth of no more than nineteen years, in truth—saluted and started to turn away, then swung back. "Sir, I'm awfully sorry about what we did to you and—and Mr. Jordy. No wonder my mama always said that greed is a sin. It sure led to nothing but trouble."

"Aye, someone al'ays suffers when greed's involved." He tried to give the youth with the guileless blue eyes a smile, but failed. "But you've got prize money now to take back to that mama."

"Yes, sir, she'll appreciate it." The boy grinned. "After she tans my hide for how I got it."

Rafe did smile at that. "I had a mither like that myself. Run along now. You are turning blue with the cold."

The boy saluted again and did just that, leaving Rafe to shiver inside his woolen cloak and coat and linen shirt. He wanted Phoebe tucked beside him. He'd been warm with her close.

But Phoebe had betrayed him to Dominick Cherrett, though nothing was likely to happen. The Navy was too occupied with the French and Americans to fash themselves over one privateer, but she'd divulged his plans to others, and that struck a blow to his soul.

She'd done it to save his soul because she loved him, the misguided, wonderful, infuriating female. At that moment, he wanted his soul to be worth saving. If she came to him and said she wanted him to repent so she could spend her life with him, he might have given in, given up.

But she didn't appear, and the moment passed. He wasn't suffering cold and deprivation of comfort in order to sacrifice his plan to destroy the man who had deprived him of his family. God had abandoned him when Rafe needed Him most. He wasn't about to crawl back without his mission accomplished. The world would be a better place for it.

So why did that declaration sound as empty as words hollered down a well?

He squinted into the rain and wind until Riggs, his left arm in a sling, came to relieve him at the wheel. Then he descended to his cabin for dry clothes. He had to brace himself for seeing

Phoebe, but he couldn't avoid Mel to avoid the other female, so he tapped on the great cabin door.

Mel was alone, sitting up with her Bible on her lap and tears streaming down her face. "I can't read, Da. I know the letters, but they make no sense to me now." She gazed up at him with trusting, innocent eyes. "Why can't I read?"

"'Twas the blow to your head." He stroked her head, his fingers seeking the indentation in her skull, assessing how well it healed. "A blow to the head can make a body forget his own name."

"I'd rather forget that than how to read. I—I'm stupid."

"Oh, lass." Rafe perched on the edge of the bunk so he could hold her head against his shoulder. "We will teach you to read again. Your brains just got a wee bit scrambled is all."

"But I want to read now," she wailed.

An echoing cry rang through the bulkhead.

Rafe snapped his head up, listening. He heard nothing save for the usual shipboard noises and turned his attention back to Mel. "We cannot al'ays have what we want now, lass. You ken that. Sometimes we can have naught that we want."

Like the revenge that had eluded him for nine years.

"But sometimes we can get things back when we lose them."

"We never got Mama back."

"Nay, she's gone to heaven."

"Has she?" Mel raised her head and gazed at him with tear-drenched eyes. "Uncle Watt said he did not think Mama believed in God that way."

"She did at the end. She called on Jesus to save her and begged for His forgiveness. I have told you this."

"Aye, but it helps to hear it. If it was not too late."

"It was not." Rafe picked up the Bible and flipped through the pages. Once he could have found the passage in moments.

Now it took him a full five minutes of searching first in the Gospel of John, then to the eighth chapter of Matthew, to the parable of the man hiring workers for his vineyard. "So when even was come, the lord of the vineyard saith unto his steward, Call the labourers, and give them their hire, beginning from the last unto the first." He glanced up at Mel's pale but still beautiful face. "I am thinking that means 'tis never too late."

"Not even for you?" She grinned at him.

"Only if a man accepts the work, bairn." He kissed her brow. "I'll make certain you learn to read again, a'right?"

"But who will read to me until then? Mrs. Chapman isn't well, and Mrs. Lee is never here." She tilted her head. "She's always with you, isn't she?"

"Aye, much of the time." He rose and backed to the door.

"Don't you think she's very pretty?"

"Aye, she's beautiful." He laid his hand on the handle. "I will be sending up—"

"She has a *tendre* for you, you ken."

"Aye, lass, I ken she does, and I ken 'tis of no use, and I ken 'tis time you had a rest." He flung open the door to find Phoebe with her fist upraised.

"Are you going to strike me or knock?"

"Knock. I heard you." She glanced past him. "May I enter? I need a moment."

"Mel's awake."

"That's all right."

He stepped aside, and she swept past him, graceful aboard the vessel now.

"What is it?" he asked, closing the door.

"Belinda." She glanced at Mel, then back to him. "Rafe, we need to get her to land as soon as possible. She's going to have that baby within the week."

300

21

Soon. That was all Rafe had said to her about when they would reach land. Soon, if all went well aboard the brig, if a French naval vessel didn't stop them, if the British Navy didn't stop them.

For Phoebe, soon wasn't good enough. Belinda wasn't quite at her confinement, but Phoebe had examined enough women in Belinda's condition to recognize the signs. The fact that Belinda didn't fuss about Phoebe examining her told its own tale—Belinda suspected the nearness of her time too.

"I'm going to die," she had murmured before falling asleep the night before.

Of course Phoebe responded, "No, you won't."

Aboard a vessel somewhere outside the Bay of Biscay or perhaps in the English Channel? Phoebe didn't know. The worst conditions under which she'd delivered a baby had been aboard the merchantman in St. George's Harbour. Although cramped, that cabin had been clean and the deck steady.

They did their best to keep the cabins aboard the *Davina* clean, but they had to use seawater, so all felt sticky or even grainy. And damp. The only time Phoebe had felt warm and dry in the past five weeks had been in the galley.

Walking on the main deck in the early morning after a restless night of little sleep, Phoebe struggled with the pain now bubbling to the surface, the lanced wound releasing its poison and the fragments causing that poison. Rafe the vengeful privateer captain trying to drive her away. Rafe the physician unwittingly beginning the healing. Unwittingly solidifying her love for him.

Not what he wanted to do, but willingly admitting the defeat of believing he could never care for another woman.

"He loves you." She whispered the words to the edge of dawn breaking along the horizon. "He loves you, but he won't give up his quest even for you, let alone God."

He was right to push her away under those circumstances.

"But I want those circumstances to be different, God. I want . . . him."

Who was she to want, to pray, to think she deserved anything from God? She had hidden behind a shield of self-righteous superiority, condemning Rafe for his actions while harboring anger and bitterness to two men who had damaged her life—Gideon, for making her existence miserable and contributing to the loss of her baby, and the man she'd known only by his surname, Kenyon, for making life in Seabourne so uncomfortable she had fled from her friends.

Now, with Rafe less than seventy feet away on the quarter-deck scanning the horizon, Phoebe examined her heart and wondered if she had written to Dominick for help to save Rafe from himself, or to get even with him for keeping her aboard—being alive and open to her own form of revenge. If that were so, she was more despicable in her action than he was. He made no secret of his intentions or his knowledge that what he did went against God's will for the lives of His people. She, on the other hand, spoke of peace and love and forgiveness, and plotted to bring him down in the name of saving him.

"Don't let Dominick come," she prayed. "Please."

If God chose to let her suffer the consequences of her

behavior, she would have to find another way to save Rafe. She would do nearly anything to keep him out of prison, away from James Brock, free to find peace and forgiveness and a future.

Free to love, even if it wasn't her.

She turned from the rail to see that he had lowered the spyglass and watched her instead of the horizon. A smile tugged at her lips. An invisible cord yanked at her heart. As though it were a lifeline stretched taut between her and Rafe, she traversed the main deck and climbed the quarter ladder, then paused at the top while he slipped the spyglass into its holder on the binnacle, said something to the helmsman, and closed the distance between her and himself.

"You look cold." He took her hand not holding the rail and chafed it between his, his gaze soft on her face, a sweetheart's caress with the eyes. "What were you doing down there all alone?"

"Praying." She gazed into his eyes and smiled. "For you."

"Good. We need all the prayers we can get here in the Bay of Biscay."

If she had a ruff like a wolf, it would have risen at that moment. "What do you mean?"

"Storms, Frenchmen, Americans, English Navy." He smiled. "Which would you prefer?"

"None."

"Indeed?" He clasped her hand, lacing his fingers through hers. "But you sent for their aid, did you not?"

"And prayed they don't arrive."

His fingers flexed. "Why?"

"Because I don't want you thrown into prison regardless of what you do." She shook her head. "No, I don't want you to do anything you shouldn't, and I don't want you in prison either, especially not because I was wrong in the decisions I made. Because I want you free to find your own way back to the Lord. Because Mel needs her father."

"Ah, yes, Mel." He glanced back at the helmsman, who wasn't even pretending not to listen, then turned back to Phoebe and lifted her hand to the crook of his elbow. "Let us walk."

They walked in silence. Icy wind buffeted their faces, the sky clear now but with more clouds on the horizon. The sea swirled away from the hull in waves the color of tarnished pewter rimmed with white froth, not high but low and choppy and empty of any vessel save for them.

Near the bow, with the men at watch on deck and in the rigging, Rafe paused and scanned the horizon instead of looking at Phoebe. "How would you feel about Mel needing me if I told you that she's not my daughter?"

"Not your—" Words eluded Phoebe. She stared at his profile, chiseled and strong enough for a figurehead.

"Aye, I have been trying to tell you for days now, perhaps weeks, but the time has ne'er been right. 'Tis true, nonetheless. I married Davina to spare her shame."

"Her father asked you to." Things he'd told her came rushing in. "And you loved her."

"Aye, I thought I did. I think that died when I learned what she had done. And then she told her father he could compel me to marry her." His tone was flat, his arm rigid.

Phoebe hugged his arm close to her side. "If you didn't, no place for you at the university?"

"Aye. 'Twas not quite said that way, but we kent what he meant. Everyone would think 'twas I who dishonored her."

"But—but, Rafe, she looks so much like you. She could be. That is—"

"There is a family resemblance? Aye, indeed there is." He turned to Phoebe then. "Watt McKay was her father."

304

"Rafe." Phoebe's hand flew to her lips. "Is that why—"

"He hated me? Aye. He'd gone off privateering before he knew. We were wed before Watt returned."

"I thought he was in the Navy."

"He was." Rafe grimaced. "They court-martialed him for running his sloop aground from sheer incompetence. But he can manage the guns—could manage the guns, so a privateer was happy to have him."

Phoebe glanced from bow to stern of the *Davina*. "This one?"

Rafe nodded. "When the captain was killed, the crew voted on a new captain. Watt wanted it, but the men were not fools. I was good at the mathematics and learned celestial navigation quickly, so they elected me, and I changed the brig's name. I was not so quick to learn the fighting, but it has been learn or die, and I have had a powerful reason to live."

"With Watt fueling your hatred all the time." Phoebe's eyes burned. "And now he's dead. Haven't there been enough deaths?"

"I ken you wish me to say yes, but I cannot."

"It won't bring Davina or your parents back, and the risk to you—"

"The risk to me, Phoebe, is keeping Brock alive. He tried to kill me on Bermuda. Watt tried to kill me and nearly killed Mel. That Brock was even on Bermuda when I was says someone has betrayed me, and I ken of no other man to do this but Watt."

"Yet you protected him for Mel's sake." As she spoke the words, Phoebe knew nothing could ever keep her from loving him, and she would do anything to keep him safe until he made his heart right with the Lord. In doing so, maybe she could find the way back herself.

His hand covering Phoebe's on his forearm, Rafe headed

back toward the quarterdeck. "Mel does not ken the story of her parentage. I will tell her one day, though by law she is my daughter." He gave Phoebe a smile so gentle and sweet her knees turned to porridge. "Aye, and by my love too. But there were rumors, and she may hear them again one day. I do not want her to have to live with me having killed her true father."

Phoebe's heart felt so full she feared if she began to speak, she would gush forth nonsense words of love and admiration.

Rafe paused at the top of the companionway ladder. "'Tis too much to ask, I ken, but will you look out for my lass if something happens to me?"

"Rafe—"

"If 'tis not too much to ask."

"No." Phoebe shook her head. "It's not too much. But you can't go on, for Mel's sake. Now more than ever she needs you."

"Phoebe." He faced her, holding both her hands, his face bleak. "I have ne'er been enough in all I have done. I was too bookish for Davina to be happy with me. I was not a good enough physician to heal her sickness. I could not save her from the pirates, and I could not keep Watt from hating me enough to keep him alive for Mel. In destroying James Brock, I ken I can succeed and do the world a service."

Heart shredding in her chest, Phoebe gazed up at him. "In the man you are beyond the hatred for James Brock, you are enough for Mel and for me."

"Aye, perhaps, but 'tis the rub of it, no? I do harbor the hatred."

"God can take it from you."

"As He has taken yours?"

Phoebe flinched.

Rafe touched her cheek. "That was unkind of me. Forgive me?"

"Yes, of course."

Forgiving him for all he had done to her was so simple. Why could she not forgive Gideon and the man who had stolen the new life she'd built?

Because she had never loved Gideon, and the other man was a stranger. Yet forgiving them was no less important.

"Then we will speak no more on this. Let our last days together be as friends and not opponents." Without waiting for her assent, he leaped down the ladder, then held up a hand to steady her on her way down.

On deck, the clatter of feet and pewter plates rang out as breakfast was served. Below, the cabins lay quiet with Mel and Belinda resting and Phoebe sitting beside Rafe at the table as he read *Robinson Crusoe* to Mel. Phoebe etched the scene in her mind, wishing she could draw, and sought for a way to make the domesticity continue. If she couldn't change Rafe's heart, if God didn't change his heart, this would be the last of it. She would say goodbye in a few days, and he would likely go to his ultimate death, preferring to die as a hero to a woman who had never deserved him and had been dead for nine years.

Another person for Phoebe to forgive.

I'm not very good at this, Lord, so how can I persuade Rafe of its virtue? she prayed.

What she was good at was tending to people. Her sailor patients were all doing well. Mel would live. She couldn't hold a spoon well or read, she remembered nothing about being in the rigging the day she fell, and she complained of headaches and dizziness. But she lived, she was eating, and her color improved with each day.

Phoebe treasured every minute with Rafe and Mel and

even Belinda. Part of her wished they weren't so close to their destination, but a day, then two, slipped by. They entered the English Channel on the third day, and with only a hundred miles to go to the coast, the cry rang out, "Sail off the starboard quarter."

In a heartbeat, Rafe dropped the book onto the table, snatched weapons from the array on the cabin bulkhead, and charged onto the deck, calling out, "Call to stations."

The race began, the drill Phoebe had seen a dozen times in the past five weeks. Someone began to beat upon a drum, a rapid, martial cadence. Men swarmed from along the rails on deck and up from below. They pulled canvases off the guns and hauled out barrels of water. Ammunition appeared on deck, but no one lit the slow matches.

Phoebe followed Rafe up the ladder, then remained frozen, flattening herself against the rail to stay out of the way, her hands locked onto the wood as though she were an off-center figurehead molded into the brig and only an ax would remove her. She knew she needed to get below, gather up Belinda and Mel, and get medical supplies and foodstuffs they could eat without cooking. Her hands refused to unstick from the rail.

"Phoebe." Rafe's voice rang clear and sharp through the frosty air. "Get below."

She meant to shake her head, but only her hair, free in the wind, moved.

"Mrs. Lee." Rafe again, sharper. Closer. He strode toward her. "Get below. Now. That's a frigate sailing toward us, and if we can't tack and outrun it and it's French, we're in for an uncomfortable fight."

"You want me below." Her voice emerged barely above a whisper. "I can't go there."

"You have been a'right with me lately. You will do a'right

now." His hands as gentle as his voice now, he grasped her shoulders and turned her from the rail. "I'll take you down."

"Belinda. Mel."

"We'll fetch them."

"But if it's a battle . . ."

"We run from frigates. With this much warning, we'll likely manage to get away. We can maneuver in shallower water if we can reach it in time. But it could be close."

"And if we don't get away?" She gazed up at him, trying not to show how badly she was shaking.

Of course he knew. His face softened, and he drew her against him. "Then we lose and they'll likely guillotine me."

"They wouldn't dare." Tears starred her lashes and spilled over.

"Shh." He brushed the tears off her cheeks with his fingertips, then tilted up her chin. "But if the worst happens . . ."

He kissed her, a silent reminder that no matter what the future, he loved her. The knowledge gave her the impetus she needed to break away from him when someone called for clearer direction, then slip aft and gather her charges together. Two sailors appeared to carry Mel and Belinda to the lower deck, dark now with lights and fires out. Mel talked more than she had in the days since she'd regained consciousness, but Belinda sat in silence, a state more unnerving than her histrionics.

Phoebe huddled between the two, one arm wrapped around Mel's frail frame and the other around Belinda's shoulders, not quite as plump as they had been at the beginning of the voyage. Phoebe concentrated on breathing slowly in and out, in and out, while her ears strained to hear the orders given above.

Those proved to be few, mostly for sailing instructions. More sail, haul to larboard, to starboard, full and by. Voices remained indistinct, the lookout's reports incomprehensible. Every time Rafe's voice rose loudly enough to penetrate the deck, Phoebe's heart leaped. He'd kissed her instead of saying words. He'd helped her forget her fear of the dark confinement below. She'd drawn on his strength. Yet he believed he'd weakened her faith. He had simply shown her the weaknesses in it.

The ugliness of her bitterness loomed before her like a sea monster, a hideous creature ready to devour her with a truth she didn't like. A sob racked through her. She gulped it back. She wanted to cry out in protest. She'd been a Christian for years. She'd claimed to be a Christian before she married Gideon. A warning had sounded in her head about marrying a man of whose faith she was uncertain, but she'd ignored it. Phoebe Carter wanted what she wanted, and her parents gave it to her.

Marriage to Gideon Lee had shaken her faith. She couldn't understand why God would allow her to be so mistreated, why her life, intended to be perfect—an enchanted existence of being adored, pampered, and protected—had turned into a nightmare. But when her baby died, stillborn in a labor too early after Gideon had shoved her down the steps, Phoebe reached out to the Lord for strength, for another chance at life. When her mother came to tell her Gideon had died, indeed that he had been buried while Phoebe lay delirious with fever and loss of blood, she had turned her heart fully back to the Lord.

Because Gideon was dead.

Self-loathing rose in Phoebe's throat like bile. As a rumble like distant thunder reverberated overhead, Phoebe faced a monster far more frightening than a French man-of-war. The shaky foundation—no, the despicable foundation—upon which she had built her façade of holiness.

"Dear Jesus, where do I go from here?" She didn't realize

she'd spoken aloud until her words fell into the otherwise silent brig.

"Then—then it was a gun?" Belinda whispered. "Phoebe, tell me it was thunder."

"I don't know." Phoebe assured herself she didn't know for sure. Just because the day started out bright and sunny didn't mean a storm hadn't blown up. The English Channel, someone had told her, tended toward stormy weather.

"It was a gun." Mel rested her head on Phoebe's shoulder and gripped her hand. "But we're not going to die. I don't think God would save my life so I would die like this."

"My baby," Belinda moaned. "I can't have my baby down here and see him fall into French hands."

"You won't." Phoebe spoke with more conviction than she felt. "And the French aren't at war with Americans. They—they'll take care of us."

Belinda wrapped her arms around her middle. "But my back hurts. What if it's my time?"

"Of course your back hurts," Phoebe said in a bracing tone. "It's not comfortable down here. The deck is cold and hard, and the air is foul."

"But my back hurts," Belinda persisted.

And it could mean her travail had begun.

Phoebe laid a hand on Belinda's abdomen. It was distended and firm with a hint of movement from the baby. She detected no contractions, not the merest hint of tightening. Of course, it could begin in the back . . .

"You're all r—"

Another rumble sounded from above. The *Davina* lurched to larboard. All three women shrieked.

"We've been hit." Belinda began to sob. "I'm going to die so close to George. Oh, I've been so wicked, I'm going to kill our baby."

"They'll cut off Papa's head," Mel whimpered. "'Tis what the French do to people like him. He'll go under that blade and—and he doesn't believe in God."

"Hush, both of you." Ashamed of herself for coming so close to an actual scream, Phoebe snapped at her companions. "Belinda, Captain Docherty will surrender before he endangers our lives in a futile fight." She hoped. "And, Melvina, your father does believe in God."

"But he doesn't follow Him. Uncle Jordy and Derrick tried to convince him he should, and so have I, but he doesn't like God because of what happened to my mither."

That was part of the truth. Phoebe didn't think she should tell Mel the rest, how her father didn't follow God because Rafe wanted to get revenge on the man who had caused Davina's death.

Gideon had chosen not to follow God because he preferred his wild ways, the drinking, the gambling, the women. Phoebe had thought she could change him once they were married. Instead he changed her, turned her into a woman with bitterness buried deep within her, so deep she found striking another man with a poker far too easy, and not regretting her action even easier.

She should have learned her lesson. Instead, she thought she could accomplish the same thing with Rafe. She thought staying with him instead of getting herself and Belinda to safety would lead Rafe back to the Lord. How vain of her. How arrogant. How sanctimonious. There she sat with an expectant mother about to deliver and a child barely recovered from a trepanning, huddled on the lower deck of an English privateer, being chased by a French frigate half again their size and with three times the men since their own prize crew was aboard the French merchantman, because she thought herself so spiritual she could sway Rafe Docherty from his course. Instead, she'd poured out her anger and bitterness against the male gender and shown him how much of a hypocrite she was.

"Lord, can You ever forgive me?" She surged to her feet and began to pace, stumbling in the darkness.

Above, men shouted and wheels rumbled on the deck. She'd witnessed the drills. She recognized that sound—the guns being run out.

"They can't fight." The cry burst from her lips, and she raced for the ladder.

Behind her, Belinda cried out—not a scream, not a whine, but a wail of fear and pain.

Phoebe swung back and reached Belinda's side before she toppled sideways. Even before Phoebe set her hands on Belinda's belly, she knew her time had come.

Above, a line of guns bellowed as though saluting the oncoming child.

22

Phoebe appeared on deck. Darting between recoiling guns and water barrels, gun smoke wreathing her tumbled hair like a halo, she raced aft toward him, and Rafe's heart leaped with joy at the sight of her, then clenched with fear for her.

"Phoebe, go back," he shouted through the speaking trumpet. "'Tis not safe—"

A crash of gunfire from the French frigate rolled across the water. Iron shot sailed above the waves toward the *Davina* like fat, deadly birds. Most dropped into the sea yards short of the brig. Two struck the bulwark. Splinters flew, and two men tackled Phoebe, dragging her out of harm's way.

They loved her too. Even the ones who wanted Rafe out of the way respected and adored Phoebe. Fearless or foolish, her actions didn't matter. She ran onto the deck and into the path of danger to help others.

Sickened by the sight of blood—a gunner's arm lanced by a six-inch splinter—for the first time in a life at first dedicated to stopping bleeding then dedicated to spilling blood, Rafe leaped from the quarterdeck and stooped to lift Phoebe to her feet. "What are you doing up here?"

"Belinda." Phoebe gasped for air. "It's her time. We've got to get to port."

"We are heading there, lass. 'Twill be no more than a

quarter hour to Guernsey, Lord willing something stops the Frenchman before he stops us."

"Lord willing?" She widened her eyes at him. "Since when do you care about the Lord's will?"

"Since I have only half my crew. Now get below. You will do your patient no good if you have your head shot off." He gently turned her toward the hatch.

She ran back, paused beside the wounded man, then dropped down the hatch, the man following. As he returned to his quarterdeck, Rafe guessed at the dialogue. She would help the man remove the knife-sized splinter from his arm, but he had to come to her. Belinda needed her. She had treated Phoebe awfully for the most part, abducting her, accusing her of killing Gideon Lee, being demanding and rude. But Belinda needed Phoebe's aid, so she went. Duty called.

If someone needed him, perhaps he would set duty before his own desires to for once accomplish what Davina wanted for him. Not that she would know. But he would. He would know that he had succeeded at something.

At that moment, he needed to succeed at reaching the island of Guernsey before the French drew near enough to damage his vessel into surrender. Along the horizon, Derrick sailed the French prize out of harm's way, as instructed. Two cable lengths off his starboard quarter, the Frenchman, who was still the enemy, drove a diagonal path through the water, guns blazing, rigging white with all sails crowded onto the yards, a full bloom of canvas to catch every gust of wind. They would think a privateer on the way home would be full of cargo. Instead, they would find French prisoners, a lady about to deliver a baby, a sick child, and a midwife who would fight every French Navy man to protect Belinda.

If the Frenchman caught them.

"How far to port?" Rafe shouted to the masthead.

A roar of gunfire from the frigate drowned out the answer.

Too far. Half a dozen rounds of shot slammed into the *Davina*'s hull. The brig shuddered. In the aftermath of the silence from guns, brig, and crew, a scream rose from below.

Belinda in travail.

"Lord, for her sake, let us reach harbor in time." Rafe didn't realize he'd prayed, let alone aloud, until half a dozen men spun toward him and stared.

"Amen," one said.

Riggs curled his upper lip. "Since when did you get so holy?"

"Since when did you decide you want to be in the hold with the French prisoners?" Rafe responded.

The men laughed. Riggs ducked behind his gun and snatched up the swab for the already cleaned weapon.

Rafe glanced to the frigate. It was gaining. They had more men, more sail power. Guernsey and safety lay no more than a quarter mile away. It might as well have been a quarter of the globe away. The Frenchman held all the advantages despite the nearness of British land. No ships could sail out of harbor in time to help send the enemy packing, and Guernsey possessed no shore battery. Rafe saw the harbor, the masts of ships anchored there, the steeple of the church.

He leaned toward them as though he could increase the brig's momentum. "Just a wee bit more speed. Just enough to—" He broke off, realizing he was praying again.

Perhaps he hadn't addressed God directly, but he had been praying for the past nine years, calling out in need, and there he stood, alive and well and loved.

Phoebe loved him. Mel loved him. Jordy had loved him enough to die for him.

Jesus had loved him enough to die for him?

No time for that. The wind shifted closer to the island.

They must tack or founder. He shouted the orders to the topmen. Yards squeaked as halyards dragged them around. Sails flapped, hung, then caught the wind. The brig lurched forward, swung to larboard seconds before another round of gunfire erupted from the frigate. Round shot sailed harmlessly past and died in the sea.

And the harbor mouth appeared. Three cable lengths. Two. One.

The Frenchman tacked, drove up on the *Davina*'s stern. If the frigate swung sideways, she could rake them, kill half the crew. More. The wrong placement of a ball could blow them all up.

Including Belinda, Mel, Phoebe.

Because he had selfishly brought them along.

How had he ever thought he had killed his conscience? It must have merely been dormant. Now it reared its head, ready to strike in a vulnerable moment.

No vulnerable moments, not this close to the prize.

They needed speed. More speed. He gazed down the deck, up to the sail, back to the deck. Something other vessels had done—

The last broadside from the French had stopped against the superstructure, ripping away a section of bulwark and rail. It gapped along the side like a mouth with a missing tooth. If they fired the adjacent gun, it was likely to fall over the side and into the sea.

And lighten the brig by a ton. If they did the same with another . . .

"Send guns two and eight over the side," he shouted through the speaking trumpet.

The crew straightened and stared at him.

"Now," he commanded.

The men glanced to the French vessel gaining on them

yard by yard, then leaped into action. Chocks slid across the deck. Tackles were sliced from cleats. A rumble like thunder drowned out Belinda's next cry as the truck wheels rolled the heavy guns to the gap in the side and sent them careening over the edge and into the channel. One geyser of water. Two. The guns vanished. The *Davina* leaped forward, a runner who had discarded a burden.

Rafe had discarded a burden. Firepower wouldn't have beaten that size vessel. Even Watt had run from frigates. Victory lay in speed now, outwitting or outrunning the enemy.

They outran them. At first the frigate seemed to have stopped in the water, hanging suspended between sky and surf, then she slipped behind by a yard, then two, then a dozen. She tacked in an attempt to rake the brig. Her shot landed harmlessly in the sea.

And the *Davina* slipped into St. Peter Port.

"Lower the topgallants." Rafe gave the first of the orders for taking in sail, then dropping anchor.

"Sir," the helmsman exclaimed, "there's our prize."

Indeed, the French merchantman rode at anchor a hundred yards away. Men crowded against her rail, and two of them, including Derrick, lowered a boat over the side.

"Please get out the cutter." Phoebe had reached his side. "Belinda's not doing well. We need to be on land."

Rafe turned to her and grasped her hand. "What's amiss?"

"I think the baby is breech." Phoebe was pale.

"Can you turn it?" Rafe looked down at Phoebe's small hands, perfect midwife hands, slender and long-fingered. "Under better circumstances?"

"I've done it once before." Phoebe bit her lip. "Or it could turn on its own, but she's scared, Rafe. I think she'll feel safer on land."

"Does not everyone?" He managed a smile for her, then

issued the orders to have the cutter prepared, the bulwark repaired, the men fed and rested. "We have more work to do."

"You aren't staying here?" Phoebe's eyes shone deep green with her anxiety. "I don't know this place. Do they speak English?"

"'Tis an English island, for all 'tis closer to the coast of France than to England. Most will speak English."

"Where will we go?" Her voice and face were calm, but she twisted her hands together beneath the cloak of his that she had made her own.

He drew her hands out and held them, warming them. "Do not fash yourself, lass. We will find a place for Belinda. She is precious to me too."

"Of course she is." Phoebe yanked her hands free. "I must go to her." She turned her back on him and stalked down the deck.

Rafe didn't try to speak. He understood her anger. He felt her anger slicing through him. He simply followed her like Fiona followed Mel. And like Fiona, he would break away, blacken himself in the tar of his mission.

"Cutter's ready, sir," a man called from the rail. "Do you want us to fetch up the ladies?"

"I will bring them." He dropped down the ladder and approached the huddled group of females. Mel lay on a pallet, too still, too pale in the lantern light, Fi tucked up in a ball at her side. They would have Phoebe if he didn't return. Had things gone differently, Mel would have had Watt, and one day perhaps he would have admitted he was her father. Now he was all she had. He knew Phoebe was right and he should cease his plans and stay with this child, help her recover from her injury. But if one day she learned he had let her mother's killer go free? She adored him now. She might despise him then.

He couldn't let her down either.

He stooped and stroked her temple, where wisps of red fuzz sprouted. "You will have your bonnie hair back again, lass. But 'twill grow on land. We are going up top and ashore."

"For good?" she asked in her now quiet voice.

"Aye, mostly."

Belinda let out a wail, and he patted Mel's shoulder. "Let me get Mrs. Chapman settled in the cutter first and I will return for you." He rose and crossed to where Belinda huddled against the bulkhead, doubled over as far as her middle would allow, whimpering and sobbing, responding to Phoebe's soothing voice and words with one coherent phrase. "I want my husband. I don't want to die without my husband."

Rafe exchanged a glance of concern with Phoebe. He couldn't free George Chapman and sail back to Guernsey in less than three days. Belinda wouldn't be in travail that long. She would have delivered the bairn or be dead by then.

"I will bring him just as fast as I can," Rafe promised recklessly. "But you will not die. 'Tis only a wee bairn."

"But something's wrong." Belinda clutched at him, her hands surprisingly strong. "Please help me. You're a physician."

"Aye, and in your situation, you need a midwife. All I can do different is use the forceps, and I have none."

"Get some. There are doctors here, surely," Belinda pleaded.

"Aye, and Phoebe will fetch one if she thinks she must." He stroked Belinda's sweat-dampened hair away from her face. "I am off to fetch your husband."

"Oh, yes, yes, I want my husband." Belinda began her keening again.

"Let's get her and Mel ashore as quickly as possible. Both will be better off." Phoebe scooped up Fiona and muttered, "If you bite me, I'll throw you into the harbor."

Fiona gazed at her with adoring eyes.

How much had changed in five weeks.

Rafe stooped and lifted Belinda into his arms. She was heavier than her voluminous gowns suggested, and he staggered beneath her weight. "I am going soft in my old age." He tried to make a jest of it.

"Let me, Captain Rafe." Derrick came down the ladder and lifted Belinda as though she weighed no more than Mel. "There, there, Mrs. Chapman, nobody's goin' ta die, so you just hush that talk." His deep, melodious voice continued to blend with Belinda's whimpers up the ladder and across the main deck.

Rafe lifted Mel into his arms. She felt no heavier than that frightened three-year-old girl he'd carried home from the Mediterranean, both of them grieving, confused, him outraged as he had never known he could be. "We will be finding him," Watt had said when he learned of the murders. "We cannot have Melvina growing up to be ashamed of her father."

Had Watt meant himself or Rafe? Rafe never knew for certain, but he took it upon himself to lead the way to avenging Davina's death. Mel turned to him for comfort and love. She needed to know he had done all he could to see that justice had been carried out.

She had nearly died because of him. Surely he owed her that much, a purpose behind his voyages, his absences, her nearly fatal fall.

"I love you, Melvina Docherty." He kissed her shorn head.

She smiled up at him. "Aye, I ken. 'Tis why I decided to wake up. You were weeping over me."

"Aye, weel." He cleared his throat. "Sometimes even I have a heart."

"Then do not go away again." Animation rang in her voice

321

as he climbed the ladder. "Please, Papa. I know you love Phoebe. Marry her and be done with this. I can't take care of her."

"Phoebe needs no one to take care of her, I am thinking, wee one."

"Someone else will get her if you do not."

And she was better off.

He said nothing, simply delivered Mel to the cutter and dropped into the small boat beside the ladies and Derrick. He discussed with Derrick where to go. St. Peter Port was familiar to them, a haven they had sought in the past. They knew the inns. It would have to be an inn.

"The George is the nicest," Derrick said.

"Oh, please, the George," Belinda cried out.

Rafe refrained from snorting. If it gave her comfort, he would find rooms there.

Enough gold ensured that the finest inn in St. Peter Port would accept their somewhat bedraggled and decidedly odd cavalcade. They certainly collected enough stares and catcalls along the route from harbor to street. Sailors, military men, and ladies of questionable repute laughed and pointed and asked rude questions in five different languages. Mel giggled, apparently recalling her French, Spanish, Portuguese, and Italian, even if she didn't remember her letters. Phoebe blushed over compliments to her looks. Belinda continued to whimper or cry out in Derrick's arms.

The George faced the harbor and welcomed their gold, if not their party. A sturdy country girl with an accent somewhere between English and French showed them up the steps to two rooms at the far end of the gallery. Rafe placed Mel in one, with a request accompanied by more coins that the maid stay with her as much as possible, and Phoebe and Derrick took Belinda to the other.

"Come back, Papa," Mel murmured from the bed. "You are all I have."

"You have Phoebe now. She will take care of you if aught goes wrong with me." He kissed her cheek, then left without looking back. If he did, if he got even a glimpse of her bright green eyes, he knew he would stay.

Unease rustled through him like stalking footsteps in the grass. A premonition of his death? He'd expected that every day for nine years. This mission was no different.

He shoved the thought aside and knocked on the other door.

Derrick emerged, shaking his head. "I can see why women keep us out of the birthing chamber. They turn into something other than our sweet wives."

"Davina kept screaming that she hated me." Rafe blinked in the torchlight bright along the gallery. "I just remembered that. Peculiar."

She had forgotten he wasn't the bairn's father. Watt was gone, back to sea, and Davina had claimed Rafe.

"Maybe it is peculiar," Derrick said. "She just keeps asking for her husband."

"Then let us go fetch him for her." Rafe started to turn away.

The door opened and Phoebe slipped out. "I want to say goodbye." Her smile didn't waver. Her eyes were steady on his. Even her hands rested on opposite forearms without fidgeting. But two tears coursed down her cheeks.

"I'll be on the cutter." Derrick glided away into the dark beyond the torches.

"Stay," was all Phoebe said.

"I cannot. I have to get George Chapman." Rafe tried to smile. Failed.

Phoebe shook her head. "You're still going after Brock."

323

"Mel deserves to have one of her fathers do something good in his life."

"Often 'good' is giving up what we want for the sake of others." She took a shuddering breath. "Jesus didn't want to die as He did, but He did it for our sakes. For yours, Rafe, if you'll just give up this desire to destroy."

"You destroyed for the sake of others."

"Yes, but—"

He laid a gentle finger across her lips. "Hush, lass. Naught but death will stop me from what I'm about."

"Rafe, no."

"I intend to stay alive." He kissed her, then stepped away. "I love you, Phoebe." Before simply standing near her bound him to her and away from what he believed he must do, he spun on his heel and strode away, to the *Davina*, to the destruction of one who had lied and cheated and robbed innocent people of life.

23

"I'm going to die." Belinda's claim had been going on for so many hours, Phoebe didn't believe it, but sometime in the middle of the night, after twelve hours of her travail, Phoebe began to wonder if her sister-in-law spoke the truth.

The baby wasn't coming. It hadn't turned. Phoebe's attempts to manipulate the baby into a head-down position had failed so far. And Belinda grew weaker.

She clutched Phoebe's hand. "I want to see George before I die."

"Then you'd better stay alive." Phoebe smiled at the younger woman with lips that felt stretched out of shape from so many forced smiles. "He'll be back soon, but the Thames is a long way from here, at least a day's sailing."

"I know." Belinda started to close her eyes, then cried out with another pain. Her fingers convulsed on Phoebe's, crushing the bones until Phoebe sucked breath in through gritted teeth.

Phoebe tried to extricate her fingers. "I should look in on Mel. The inn maid is with her, but she's a stranger."

"Mel doesn't know strangers." Belinda smiled. "She talks to everyone. Such a kind child. Even if her father—" She groaned. "Even if her father is a reprobate."

"He's not. That is—" Phoebe wished she had an excuse to groan, to weep, to beat her fists on the wall and scream.

325

Of course he was a reprobate. He had taken loyalty too far, was taking loyalty too far. The memory of a dead woman who neither knew nor cared what he did drove him to commit an act of treason and murder. She should despise him, never want to see him again.

She would do anything to keep him safe and whole. She would fight his battles for him, if it would save him.

But she would not abandon Belinda now, even if she knew how to help Rafe.

"Don't leave me." Belinda stared at Phoebe with big, dark eyes like pansies. "Please."

"Just to make sure Mel is all right." Phoebe rose from her stool beside the bed. "I can hear you if you yell."

"Please," Belinda repeated.

Phoebe hesitated. Belinda didn't often say please. She must be desperate, frightened.

"Rafe asked me to take care of his daughter," Phoebe said. "I'm not keeping that promise if I don't at least ensure she's all right."

"All right." Belinda bit her lower lip. "But hurry back."

"Of course." Phoebe slipped next door, where the inn maid slept on a pallet by the fire, and Mel lay with her eyes closed and her breathing even. But she opened her eyes the moment Phoebe flipped the coverlet back into place. "How is Mrs. Chapman?"

"She'll be all right." The Lord willing, that wasn't a lie. "How are you?"

Mel sighed. "I have bad dreams about Papa every time I close my eyes. He—he—" Mel reached out a fragile hand. "He's not going to come back, is he?"

"He has to bring Mr. Chapman back." Phoebe sounded too cheerful, too enthusiastic even to her own ears.

Mel frowned. "You do not believe he will either. I thought

326

perhaps you could stop him when you stayed. He loves you, I think."

"I thought I could save him too." Phoebe clasped Mel's hand in both of hers. "Only Jesus can help him now, child. I failed him with my own weakness and inability to forgive."

"Have you forgiven now?" Mel asked.

Phoebe opened her mouth to say yes, but she knew that wasn't the truth. She saw Rafe walking away from her and knew she hadn't forgiven him for not staying, for not giving up his dream of carrying out justice, for not loving her and his daughter enough. And if he didn't return to her, or at least to Mel, Phoebe thought she might never find the strength to forgive him.

"Please." Mel's voice was so soft Phoebe had to lean over the bed to hear the child. "Please don't be angry with him. My mither didn't love him, and he is still trying to make her."

"How do you know a thing like that? I mean—"

"Uncle Watt told me. He didn't like Papa either." Her fingers moved restlessly in Phoebe's hold. "I just want my father home. Do you know I can't read?"

"I do. We'll teach you again."

I'll teach you again, Phoebe amended in her head.

"Thank you." Mel's voice faded. Her breathing grew deeper and more even, and her hand went limp.

Phoebe backed away, nodded to the now wakeful maid, and slipped from the room.

Not hearing any whimpering or moaning from Belinda's room, Phoebe leaned against the railing of the gallery and gazed out over the harbor. Torches and lanterns lit the scene in a carnival atmosphere of commerce and raucous merry-making, from the street to the wharves to the vessels in the harbor. The French prize rode at anchor out there, a fat prize Derrick would sail to England the next day so the Admiralty court could decide on the value of the vessel itself. The cargo would go to market, an English market starved for French goods. All the men aboard would have extra money in their coffers in a few months. Rafe, as captain, would get the lion's share. Or Mel in his place.

"Because you're such a fool," Phoebe ground out to the night, "you likely won't come back." She shook the railing in her frustration and anger. It creaked like ship's timbers. "How could you do this to me?"

To her? Was that all she cared about? How Rafe and Gideon and Kenyon—that angry, hurting husband—treated her, how their behavior hurt her?

It wasn't an easy admission to swallow—the truth of her selfishness. She didn't think how Belinda missed the brother who had always been kind to her. Or how Mrs. Kenyon felt losing her baby and her husband in the same night. Or how much pain Rafe suffered having an uncle ruin a girl Rafe loved, then toss her away for him to gather up the pieces, being constantly told that he was not the one she wanted. Rafe had wanted a family and healing work like his father. He got a wife who didn't love him, another man's child, and a career his bride despised.

And all Phoebe had done was tell him in one breath that she loved him, and in the next breath how wrong he was. Like Davina, then Watt, Phoebe told him he wasn't good enough, his decisions were inadequate. He needed to be some kind of fairy-tale hero slaying dragons. He would rather die accomplishing that than live being a mere father.

"And all I did was take out my anger with others on you." Phoebe sank to her knees and dropped her forehead onto her hands still clasping the rail. "Lord, please be with him. Keep him safe. Heal his heart." She took a shuddering breath. "And mine. I don't care if he doesn't come back to me. Just please bring him back to You." Her voice broke as she prayed.

Fear, anguish, and the remnants of old anger spilled out in a silent torrent of tears. She didn't know if she continued to pray anything coherent. All she heard in her head was, *Lord, break my heart of stone.*

When the tears dried and a cry from Belinda's room prompted Phoebe to return to her patient, she felt broken, or at least like a log someone had hollowed out to use as a drainpipe. She prayed that maybe, just maybe, she was a vessel through which God's love would flow, cleansing, healing, and spilling over onto others.

But her deep repentance had come too late to help Rafe, to convince him of his need for the same. She'd ruined that with her anger and bitterness spilling over instead.

Shaken, aching with regret, she returned to Belinda's side. "I'm sorry I was gone so long. How are you doing?" As she asked the question, she went to the pot of water keeping warm by the fire and poured some into a basin to wash her hands.

Belinda shifted in the bed, sheets rustling in the quiet room. "I don't think I'm doing well. The pains are worse."

"That's normal, Bel." Phoebe returned to the bed and lifted the sheet. "Let me look."

"If you must." Belinda squeezed her eyes shut, her mouth in a grim line.

Phoebe smoothed her hands over Belinda's belly, then gave a more intimate exploration. Belinda sucked in her breath, but not from pain—from humiliation. Phoebe ignored the wordless protests and continued, touching, stroking, going back to the basin to wash.

"I think the baby is finally turning the right way, Bel."

"But it's—" She gasped, and fabric tore.

Phoebe whipped around to see Belinda gripping the sheet so hard she'd ripped it.

"I'm . . . sorry." Belinda began to cry. "I'm sorry I brought you along. I'm sorry I let this happen to me. I want my husband here so I can cuff him."

Phoebe didn't succeed in hiding her chuckle.

"I mean it. I can't do this."

"You don't have a choice right now, and you'll forget once you hold your baby." Phoebe took a damp cloth from a second basin and wiped Belinda's face. "Every mother does."

"Not me. This had better be a boy. I don't want more children."

"I do." Phoebe stared at the knotty paneling on the far wall without seeing anything other than half a dozen children with hair as red as garnets. "I always have."

"Oh, Phoebe, I'm so sorry." Belinda clasped Phoebe's hand in both of hers, relaxed now. "I never thought about you. I'd rather die than my baby."

"I would have too. But God has other plans for me."

If only they were clear.

"I'm sorry about all those things I said about you." Belinda squeezed Phoebe's fingers, but in reaction to the pains of labor this time. "I didn't know things were so awful for you."

"Your brother was good to you."

"Yes, everyone is." Belinda wiped tears from her eyes. "I don't deserve it."

"What are you saying?" Phoebe moved across the room to pour a cup of tepid tea for herself and a glass of water for Belinda. "You don't deserve the other—people being unkind to you."

"No, but—oh, Phoebe." Belinda cried out, clutching at her belly. "I've done a terrible thing."

"I can't imagine that to be true."

Other than forcing Phoebe to go along to sea with her, but Phoebe couldn't think that too awful now.

"It is, I tell you."

"Hush. Getting agitated won't help you or the baby." Phoebe carried the water to Belinda. "Let me help you sit up straighter."

Belinda pushed the glass away. "No, no, don't try to placate me. You must listen to me. I can't die without telling you."

"You're not going to die." Phoebe spoke with conviction. Now that the baby was finally turning head-down, Belinda was indeed likely to live. "No more of that talk."

"But it happens. You've seen it happen, haven't you?" Belinda's eyes darted from side to side as though seeking death lurking in the corners. "I've heard talk."

"Yes, it happens more often than we'd like. But you're young and strong, and everything will be as it should."

"But just in case." Belinda focused her gaze on Phoebe's. "Please listen."

Phoebe sank onto her stool. "All right. What did you do? Spend too much of George's money? Lose his business money?"

"Certainly not," Belinda snapped. "His company has done well. His partners are happy—or will be once he's free."

"Then I can't think what it could be, since I already know you lied about how far your condition was advanced. I'd have kept us on Bermuda if—"

"Stubble it, Phoebe. It's about being in Virginia." Belinda struggled to turn on her side and prop herself on one elbow so she could look into Phoebe's face. "James Brock came to see me there. You know he's one of George's investors."

"I know." Coldness seeped through Phoebe's bones despite the roaring fire. "It's why Rafe will help him get out of prison, to persuade George to tell him where Brock hides."

"Yes, well—" Belinda sank back onto the mound of pillows behind her and flung her arm over her face. "It's not George who knows where Brock is. I just told Captain Docherty that so he'd get him out of that prison. But I've known all along where to find Brock when he's this side of the Atlantic."

24

The following night was as dark as a new moon and cloud cover could make it. With lanterns extinguished, the prison guards would not be able to see three rowboats bobbing downstream a hundred yards away. Though the guards, underpaid and mistreated themselves, had been paid not to see anything out of the ordinary that night, men waiting for the tide to carry three prisoners toward freedom would be all too much for them to ignore.

Downstream and downwind. The stench from the dismasted ship turned into a floating prison for Frenchmen and Americans sucked the air from Rafe's lungs. Every man in the boats attempted to breathe through his mouth and not cough.

"How does they bear it?" one man whispered.

Rafe elbowed him in his ribs gently, a reminder to keep quiet. Whispers traveled over water like shouts. Guards could claim they saw nothing on a dark night, but not to hear anything stretched credulity.

Rafe strained his ears for the sounds he wanted to hear, a faint splash no louder than a wave from the outgoing tide tossing against the hull. He gripped the gunwales, ready to lean the opposite way the instant other hands grabbed for the side of the boat, ready to signal the men to haul in the prisoners. They had practiced in Southampton Harbor the night before, after taking the Frenchmen ashore at Portsmouth for the Admiralty to take care of. But his crew was strong, well-fed, and exercised. These men would be sick with hunger and cold, weak from confinement. They might not get away, might fall on their way down the side of the hulk, might drown during the short swim.

Tension radiated through Rafe like the moments before a battle. He expected no fighting. He feared Chapman might not arrive for rescue. Rafe could never go back to Belinda and tell her he had failed to save her husband. He wouldn't have Brock either, and his mission would have failed. But more than the moment he anticipated—facing James Brock with the odds in favor of Rafe Docherty instead of the unpleasant surprise of the ambush on Bermuda—he kept seeing Belinda's drawn countenance and her pleas for her husband. For him to bring back her husband.

And Phoebe. Rafe couldn't put Phoebe's face out of his mind—calm and tear-streaked, her sweet, smooth voice pleading with him to stay, to not commit treason. But he had left her. He wanted Belinda to have her husband, if she had survived childbirth. Her husband was American. Rafe and his crew could be hanged for rescuing Americans from prison. Even if he got away, he could never stay in England. He would have to go to America.

And James Brock divided his time between his homeland and other parts unknown. Unknown to Rafe. Not unknown to his business partner George Chapman.

George would be able to go home—home with his wife and bairn, a good deed for Rafe to have accomplished at the least. Perhaps God would show him some mercy for that. But not likely. Rafe would have shown James Brock no mercy. Only justice.

A justice that saddened Phoebe. A justice she wanted him to leave to God, along with his hatred. But he couldn't let Davina down again. He must see this to the end.

He tried to conjure Davina's face growing ravaged from her lung disease but still holding much of its beauty. It blurred before his mind's eye as though behind a gauzy veil. But he heard her cries, her begging for mercy—mercy from the pirates and from their mistreatment, mercy from God for her sins. Mercy . . . Mercy . . .

So why did he think she wanted justice in the form of Brock's death? No matter now. He wanted it so he could set his memories to rest.

He gripped the gunwales hard enough to score his palms on the edges. *Do not fail me, Chapman*, Rafe mouthed.

The hulk of the prison rose against the horizon, a blacker shape against the blackness. Wind, damp and chill, ruffled the Thames estuary, sending up the sparkle of saltwater phosphorescence, splashing against the Kentish mudflats, the prison, the rowboats. One, two, three. Men slipping down the anchor chains, or mere waves. Four, five, six. More waves? Too many escaping prisoners for the *Davina*'s men to haul away.

The rowboat rocked, tilted to windward. Rafe leaned the opposite way. Men grabbed the swimmer and hauled him aboard.

Despite the swim, the stench of the river came with the man. His saviors released him and moved as far away as possible, which wasn't far enough.

"Sorry." The murmur was distinctly American. "Maybe you could haul me along behind."

"Quiet," Rafe commanded.

More splashing. A few rank odors indicated others joining them.

"How many?" Rafe asked.

"Six." The escapee sighed like the night wind. "We couldn't leave them behind to rot in there."

"No, of course not. We'll do our best not to sink."

Or still be in the estuary dragging along their boats when dawn struck. Once seen, they would be pigeons for the plucking if anyone from the prison or Navy saw them. The Americans couldn't disguise their accents. Nor could the French. Especially the French.

"Any Frenchmen?" Rafe inquired.

"No, sir. We didn't have truck with the French."

"Chapman?" Rafe couldn't stop himself from asking.

"He was beside me swimming," the American said. "Expect he made it."

"You'd best pray he did." Rafe bowed toward the men with the oars. "Shove off. We need to be back—"

Flashes of light upriver preceded the bark of gunfire. The guards giving a show of force, a pretense of trying to get their prisoners back or drown them.

"Row," Rafe commanded.

He didn't try to maintain silence now. More shots rang across the water. A splash louder than their oars hissed down the river. The guards had lowered a boat. They would come after the escapees and rescuers.

"Row, lads. I ken you don't want a fight," Rafe called out.

"I want a fight," the American growled. "I could strangle every one of those—"

"Quiet," Rafe barked.

The man obeyed, but he emitted a whistling breath through his teeth like steam escaping from beneath a kettle lid to keep it from exploding.

Rafe knew how the man felt. He caught up an extra pair of oars and bent his back to the work of rowing. The tide was with them, tugging them toward the channel. The guard boat pursued. Muzzle flashes lit the night, growing fainter and fainter, then vanishing behind a spit of land.

The guards wanted their lives preserved or respected the

word they'd been given with the gold they'd received to let the prisoners escape. They hadn't pursued any longer than necessary to save their necks from court-martial.

A grim smile touched Rafe's mouth. It might be the first fight he'd won without bloodshed and against the English— and he was supposed to be on their side, not the Americans'. Calmness flowed through him even before he caught sight of his brig riding at anchor with but one light showing. He didn't need to keep fighting.

The boats bumped the side of the brig. Instantly a line of men appeared. "Who goes there?"

"'Tis I and the men," Rafe responded.

He waited to board until the last prisoner and crewman climbed or had been hauled aboard. Then he drew himself up the line and took a knife from his boot to cut the mooring lines. The rowboats drifted away.

Rafe faced the men, his own upright and hardy, the prisoners stooped, ragged, pale, with lank greasy hair hanging in their faces, obscuring their identities. "George Chapman?"

"Here." He shuffled forward on bare feet, his torn breeches showing legs like gnarled sticks. "I know you've done this because you want something from me, but I still thank you on behalf of all of us."

"Amen," the others murmured.

"If we'd've swum, we'd likely have ended up stuck in the mud," Chapman continued.

"We saw it happen often enough," another man said. "The men would get stuck and drown when the tide came in. The guards would leave 'em there to remind us what could happen."

Rafe cringed inwardly with disgust. He couldn't blame the behavior on the English. Plenty of Scots served in the British Navy and Army. They were supposed to be civilized. How could they be so barbaric?

How could he be so barbaric?

He fixed his gaze on Chapman. "After the men find you some soup and hot tea and warmer clothing, have them bring you to my cabin." He addressed all of the Americans. "You are not prisoners unless you show any hostility toward my men or try to take the ship. You will be losing a fight, I am thinking."

Uneasy laughter rippled across the deck.

"Ver' good. Riggs, you serve these men. The rest of you, up anchor and set sail." He turned and strode aft to his cabin.

It still smelled of a combination of lavender and jasmine, remnants of Belinda's and Phoebe's presence. Now, however, ribbons and thread, bits of fabric, and tiny feminine shoes no longer littered table and seats. The cabin was spotlessly neat and clean, save for his cloak, his dress cloak, draped over a chair as though its temporary owner would retrieve it at any moment.

Unable to resist, Rafe picked it up and raised it to his face. It smelled like jasmine, like Phoebe. He imagined her warmth, her soft hair blowing against his cheek, the salt of tears and seawater on her lips. His heart ached worse than any wound he'd ever received, as empty of Phoebe as the cloak.

"Oh, Lord, I'm a fool to love her." He tried to thrust the cloak from him. The end caught on the chair back and wrapped around his arm. His fingers lingered for a moment on the soft wool as though it was her smooth cheek. "Where is my sense of victory at being so close to the end?"

He didn't need to ask how it had died. He knew—in a pair of moss-green eyes shining like sunlight behind stained glass. In a voice like honeyed cream. In a lady so sincere in her belief in God she understood when and how her faith was weak. She didn't reject God for her pain, she mourned her lack of faith and how it might have damaged Rafe. He had pressed his advantage against her to push her away, to weaken her faith further so she would stop pricking his long-dormant conscience. But she admitted to her failures as a woman of God and wanted Rafe to forgive her. And all the while she never stopped loving him. She loved him as no one ever had.

And he was willing to toss it away for the sake of a woman who would never know. And even if she did, Davina hadn't asked for vengeance. She had asked for mercy. She had asked for forgiveness and mercy, yet he had spent nine years determined to give neither.

"But surely my sins are too great, Lord. I've taken lives. I've cost others their lives. I've rejected You. Surely it's too late."

He disentangled the cloak from the chair and wrapped the warm wool around his shoulders. Phoebe's scent enfolded him like loving arms. Her voice glided through his head, echoed in the recesses of his brain by the minister at the kirk of his childhood. God wanted a broken and contrite heart. It was never too late, as long as he still lived.

"Lord," he murmured as the deck tilted and the *Davina* got under way, "my heart is surely broken. The fully contrite may take a wee bit of time, but Phoebe says You will help me if I ask." Feeling the flush of embarrassment creeping up his face, he continued, "I am asking for that help."

And at that moment, someone knocked on the door. "George Chapman," an American voice called.

Rafe strode to the door and pulled it open. "Come in. You look a wee bit better, but do you not want some supper?"

"It can wait." Chapman, a man with a broad-shouldered frame and too little flesh on his bones at present, stepped over the coaming. "I want to know about my wife first. How is she?"

"She has likely delivered her bairn by now." Lord willing she wasn't dead. "Her sister-in-law was with her."

Chapman's blue eyes widened. "Phoebe came along?"

"Aye, that she did. Why does it surprise you?" Rafe stepped back so Chapman could come fully into the cabin. Realizing he still wore the cloak, he started to remove it, then changed his mind. He liked holding this memory of Phoebe close. "Do sit down. You look ready to fall over."

"I am." Chapman strode over to the table and dropped onto a chair. "Is she all right? Belinda, I mean?" He slumped forward, his elbows on the table, then straightened, sniffing. "Lavender. She was here."

"Aye, I let her have this cabin until my daughter was injured." Rafe joined Chapman at the table.

"Your . . . daughter? You had your daughter aboard?"

"Not by choice, so do not give me the lecture Ph—Mrs. Lee did."

"I . . . see."

"Nay, you do not, but 'tis of no importance. We have business to settle, do we not?"

"Yes, we do, but I want to make certain Belinda is well first. In fact, I need Belinda well to help you." Chapman met Rafe's gaze, his own eyes red-rimmed but still clear in their sky color. "You see, Belinda is the one who knows where Brock hides out, not me."

Rafe sat motionless, feeling like one of those hot-air balloons without its fire—deflated, an empty sack upon the ground. He should be outraged with the Chapmans. He'd had his answer all along. He hadn't needed to alienate himself on British shores by freeing six American prisoners. He could have simply gotten the information from Belinda.

But he simply responded, "'Tis no matter who has the information, mon. I am not going to go after him after all."

"You're . . . not?" Chapman stared. "Then why all this?" He waved his hand around.

"'Tis a recent revelation. Or perhaps I should say a recent rep—"

The roar of a gun shattered the night.

Rafe sprang to his feet and charged up the ladder to the deck. He didn't need anyone to tell him what was afoot. Bearing down on his starboard bow was a ship of the line, ablaze like a ship on a nighttime parade.

"But we're English," one of his crew cried. "Can't they see we're English?"

Rafe looked at the naval vessel, recalled Phoebe's admission of her letter sent from Bermuda, and sighed in resignation. "Aye, they ken we are British. Signal our surrender and prepare the boat to take me across."

"They're already preparing one," someone reported.

And so they were. Rafe strode to the side to meet the envoys from the seventy-four. "Bring more lanterns."

By the yellow glow, he could see they had sent two marines, two lieutenants, and a midshipman. Grinning, the lieutenants made the midshipman go up first, though the marines, broad and stolid, followed closely behind the youth.

"Are you Captain Rafael Docherty?"

"Am I Captain Rafael Docherty, sir," Rafe corrected him. "Aye, I am."

"Yes, sir. Sorry, sir." The boy blushed. "Will you come with us, sir?"

Rafe's men and the Americans grew silent and still.

"Am I being arrested?" Rafe asked, suddenly feeling like laughing at the irony.

"I don't know, sir." The midshipman glanced at the two marines behind him. "We were just told to make you come with us."

"Make me, eh? Then I have no choice?"

"No, sir."

"Then I call that an arrest." Rafe glared at the marines. "I give you my parole if you will let my brig go without trouble."

He felt the men arrayed behind him draw in a collective breath and hold it. He held his own. Chapman needed to get to his wife, and Phoebe needed to know where he was.

The older of the lieutenants clambered through the entry port and stepped forward. "I'm the first lieutenant, sir. I can safely say that our interest is with you, not your brig or your men."

Or six American escapees.

"Thank you." Rafe removed a dirk from his belt and handed it to the lieutenant hilt first. "You have my word I will go without a fight and not try to escape."

At least until his men were safely away.

He had to escape, had to get back to Phoebe and tell her, if nothing else, that God had finally begun to remove the anger from his heart. But he wanted to tell her more. So much more, if she would listen.

And if the Navy didn't see fit to hang him for piracy or treason, or both. He didn't fear that. He didn't welcome the prospect, but his heart remained steady, his spirit calm. For the first time in his life, he didn't fear death.

"I must give my crew instructions," he told the marine. "They will not assault you or your party."

Not with thirty-seven guns glaring at them over a mere cable of water.

He turned to the men. "You will find instructions in my cabin."

Chapman would know to sail them back to Guernsey. The crew would believe him.

He descended the rope to the gig and settled on one of the thwarts. The officers joined him, and the coxswain gave the oarsmen instructions. Six men made short work of the distance. In moments, for the first time in his misadventures as a privateer, Rafe found himself aboard a man-of-war. Acres of deck and throngs of men stretched out before him. This vessel could have taken his own small craft aboard and barely dropped on the waterline. He scrutinized the faces he passed. He read no hostility, no contempt, mostly simple curiosity.

But the men meant little. He had to reckon with whomever resided over the great cabin.

That too could have housed most of his crew in comfort. Brass lanterns swung from deck beams high enough Rafe could stand upright. The dining table seated twelve and didn't have to serve as the chart table too, and the sleeping cabin was separate.

Despite the capacious chamber, only one man was present. He lounged on the cushioned bench below the stern lights but rose at Rafe's entrance with the two marines and another redcoat at the door. "The three of you may go." He spoke with the precise, clipped tones of an aristocrat. He also wore a plain, dark blue wool coat and fawn knee breeches instead of an officer's uniform, and Rafe experienced the stirrings of uneasiness in his middle.

The door clicked behind him. The gentleman sauntered forward, tall and elegantly built, with dark hair lying on his shoulders like some seventeenth-century cavalier. He smiled and held out his hand. "Good evening, Captain Docherty. Am I correct in presuming I need not introduce myself?"

"Nay." Rafe shook the proffered hand, probably a good sign. "I ken who you are, Lord Dominick."

25

Phoebe had never left a woman in labor to the hands of someone else. She had sent an inn servant to find an island midwife. After the woman arrived—a storklike woman somewhere over sixty with a long neck and long fingers, the latter impeccably clean—Phoebe had kissed Belinda on the cheek and run for the harbor.

Though it wasn't possible, she thought she heard Belinda's cries all the way to the water. No need for such histrionics. All should be normal now. The baby had turned.

Phoebe was the one who had been stifling her own hysterics since Belinda's announcement that she had known all along where to find James Brock.

"He isn't a diplomat," Belinda had explained. "He lives in France and funds American privateers to harry the English. Certain men in the government like his money helping to support the war, so we let him sail under a diplomatic flag."

"Tell me where he is," Phoebe commanded, her hands behind her back so she didn't shake the baby out of Belinda. "Where?"

Belinda had told her. Phoebe took action, and the next day she found herself in Dieppe, a bustling port city in Brittany on the coast of France, Derrick beside her like a quiet mountain of bone, sinew, and muscle.

"Captain Rafe is goin' ta kill me," Derrick said not for

the first time as they paused at a baker's stall. They bought loaves of hot, crusty bread, then stopped at another booth for strong, milky coffee. "Me sailing his lady to France like this. It's too dangerous."

They had arrived in a sailboat that felt no larger than a canoe, with a strip of canvas instead of paddles, and it tossed about on the channel waves. Phoebe determined to learn to swim before she set foot on anything smaller than a brig.

Which would make leaving France difficult. If she could leave France. The day and a half the arrangements and journey took left her too much time to think about the folly of what she was doing. Brock had shown no compunction over having his henchmen go after her too, because she was with Rafe. What would stop him from killing her there in Dieppe?

The answer was simple—nothing. From what Belinda told her and what they had learned thus far in the French city, Brock was a powerful man everyone feared and no one wanted to say much about.

The fact that he would learn she was a fellow American, a woman from one powerful family and related through her marriage to another, might give him pause before he tried to strike out at her again.

Might. But she had left letters with Mel. One for Rafe, one for Tabitha and Dominick, and one for the governor of Virginia telling them where she had gone, with whom she intended to meet, and what to do if she did not return. At least, the letters to the Cherretts and Governor Randolph said that. The letter to Rafe said to let the true diplomats manage James Brock. It was out of his hands. She begged him to use his hands to heal, not harm.

She doubted Brock would harm her. Perhaps confine her until he got away again, but if he did, she would have served her purpose in seeking him out—keeping him out of Rafe's sphere.

So, to find James Brock in Dieppe before Rafe did. A difficulty, since Phoebe spoke too little French to matter. Her schoolgirl attempts at the language left the listeners shaking their heads and laughing at what she was certain they were calling an American bumpkin, or some French equivalent. Derrick wouldn't tell her.

Derrick spoke West Indian French, oddly accented to these Bretons but comprehensible. He asked questions of shopkeepers and servants passing through the street, urchins living on the streets, and sailors. Whether due to his size or his kind, gentle smile, most of the people talked to Derrick. None of them laid claim to having more than a passing knowledge of an American living in Dieppe, until nightfall.

Phoebe thought her feet would fall off and stay behind from sheer exhaustion. She was cold and wet from a light rain, yet she stubbornly refused to stay in an inn and wait.

"I don't sit still well," she admitted.

"You like to manage things yourself, I'm thinking." Derrick patted her shoulder, then snatched his hand back. "I do apologize, Mrs. Lee."

"Don't." Phoebe took his hand in both of hers. "I know that could get you into trouble with other ladies, but not with me. I appreciate your care and kindness."

"I appreciate all you did for the captain."

"I didn't do enough, but if we can find Brock . . ." Phoebe turned away and huddled inside one of Belinda's shawls that smelled only faintly of lavender now. She wished she hadn't left Rafe's cloak behind. It always made her feel protected, safe. Oddly close to him.

Her heart ached for him, for herself, for them.

"Do you know yet what you're going to do once you find

Brock?" Derrick paused beside a vendor selling a spicy-smelling fish stew. "Let's have some supper and talk on that a bit."

She ate the savory stew along with more crusty bread and fresh cider, though she would have declared she wasn't hungry if Derrick had asked her. He probably knew that, so he hadn't asked.

Food gone, they continued along the wharves of the port, busy despite the English blockade. Plenty of small fishing boats and other craft slipped in and out, as she and Derrick had.

"About Mr. Brock, if we find him, what do we do with him?" Derrick asked.

"It's not a very good plan." Phoebe paused to gaze over the choppy water of the harbor, slate-gray beneath a sky only a shade lighter. "I inherited a great deal of money when my father died. By the terms of my marriage contract, it came back to me upon my husband's death since we had no children. I've spent little of it. So I'm going to offer it to Brock to buy up his shares in the privateers if he'll disappear."

Derrick leaned against a half-stone, half-wood structure that looked old enough to have been built by the ancient Celts, and crossed his massive arms over his chest. "What will you do if he says no?"

"The same thing I'll do if he says yes—we'll take him to England to have a little voyage on one of those prison ships to Australia." She smiled.

"And what makes you think that'll stop Captain Rafe from going after him?"

Phoebe's smile faded. "I don't know that it will. I can only pray that once he realizes his bird has flown and is several more years out of his reach, he'll remember that Mel needs him, especially now."

Or realize it wasn't what he was supposed to do and turn his heart back to the Lord. For she needed him.

"He needs to be healing men, not harming them," Phoebe added.

"He needs to heal himself, or let the Lord do it."

"I'm hoping . . ." Phoebe shook her head. "Let's keep looking."

"I'm going to ask ten more people," Derrick declared, "then take you back to the inn to sit down before you fall down."

He needed to ask only three. A matelot, coming off a fishing smack that lay low in the water with either an excellent catch or smuggled goods, proved to be an American.

"I've done business with him." The man, a youth really, grimaced. "Not the kind I'd like. He says I'm too young or some such nonsense." He glanced sideways at Phoebe. "But I can't see him minding himself over a pretty female wanting to do business with him." He told them where Brock lived. "Like a king the French fear more than Napoleon around these parts."

Night was falling, too dark and too late for a journey by sea or land to the inlet and house that James Brock had called his home for six years.

"Tomorrow," Derrick said. "You should be rested before you meet with him."

"Yes." Phoebe doubted she would rest. Her heart raced. Her stomach knotted and twisted and doubled back on itself.

Now that seeing the man face-to-face was so near, she recognized the complete folly of her actions in coming to Dieppe.

"It's too late to go back now," she muttered.

"I could get us back to Guernsey tonight," Derrick offered.

"No, I can't do that." Phoebe took Derrick's arm to give her strength for their walk back to the inn.

As she'd feared, she slept little. The wakeful hours she spent on her knees praying about what she was doing, praying for Rafe, praying for Belinda, for Mel, for everyone she knew, then for Rafe again.

"Lord, I should have prayed for him more and condemned him less."

Daylight arrived at last. Cold and stiff, she rose, washed, and donned her once elegant but now sadly limp gown despite the ministrations of an inn maid. All she could do with her hair was comb it, braid it, and wind the plait into a coil to anchor with the few pins she had left. She wouldn't look much like Phoebe Carter Lee of Loudoun County, Virginia, but she had learned how to act like a lady no matter what the circumstances.

Her breakfast tray barely touched, save for the fine, rich coffee, Phoebe opened her bedchamber door as a servant was about to knock.

"*Un monsieur est ici vous voir*," the girl said.

Phoebe stared at her blankly. "A gentleman here . . . ?"

"*Oui, oui.*" The girl bobbed her head, sending dark curls dancing. "*Ici. La café.*" She tugged on Phoebe's arm. "*Vite. Vite.*"

Phoebe didn't remember the word, but she got the idea that the girl wanted her to go in a hurry. So she went, her heart leaping into her throat, one name screaming through her head like cannon shell: *Rafe. Rafe. Rafe.*

The maid opened the door to the little coffee shop on the ground floor. "*La dame americaine, monsieur.*"

"*Merci bien.*" Not Rafe's accent. Not his voice. Not him.

Phoebe stood paralyzed in the doorway as James Brock strode forward.

Rafe felt like a prisoner. He wasn't. He enjoyed the freedom to roam about the seventy-four as he willed, except for going onto the quarterdeck without permission. He'd even been given fine quarters amongst the ship's officers once Lord Dominick Cherrett finished with him. But he wasn't on his own vessel, giving his own instructions to the crew, making his own decisions as to the destination and how they would reach it.

"The respite from command will be good for you," Cherrett had said the night before.

Leaning on the weather rail, watching the English coastline slipping out of sight at least two knots faster than his two-masted brig could sail, Rafe didn't agree with Cherrett in the morning any more than he had the night before. Rafe needed to return to Guernsey, needed to see Phoebe.

Which was why he found himself aboard a ship-of-the-line instead of the *Davina*.

"Why have you taken me into custody?" Rafe had inquired of Cherrett, as though he didn't know.

"Phoebe asked me to stop you. And here I am." Unhurried in his movements, Cherrett returned to the window seat. "Do sit down. No, wait." He rose again. "Hot coffee?"

Rafe didn't sit. He gripped the back of a chair and raised one eyebrow. "I ne'er thought the day would come when an English lordling would be serving the likes of me."

"I spent time as an indentured servant, don't forget." Cherrett smiled with surprising warmth and proceeded to pour coffee from a silver pot in the center of the great table. "For my sins."

"And for mine I am here?" Not sitting would have been churlish, so Rafe slid onto one of the chairs and wrapped his cold hands around the warm china cup.

Cherrett laughed. "To stop you from carrying out at least

one act I am here." Cherrett took an adjacent chair. "We received a rather odd letter from Phoebe a month ago. She seemed to think you were about to commit a serious crime and wanted you stopped."

"I was going to." Rafe gazed at the reflection of the lantern lighting his coffee. "I cannot think that ridding the world of James Brock is such a bad thing, but 'tis not my place to do it."

"Indeed?" Cherrett leaned forward, his face intense. "What are you saying? This mission to go after Brock is over?"

"Aye, for me." Rafe shifted on his chair, avoiding Cherrett's eyes. "I have had a change of heart, you ken."

"I don't know. Do tell me more."

Rafe shrugged.

"Would it help," Cherrett asked, his voice suddenly losing its aristocratic drawl and oddly more gentle, "if I tell you I will be the new pastor of the church in Seabourne when I return?"

"I have had naught to do with parsons for nearly a decade," Rafe interjected.

"I understand. It was a calling I devoted my life to running away from." Cherrett snorted. "No, spent my life fighting so hard I hurt a lot of people in the process."

Rafe flashed him a swift, questioning glance, and this man, who could have enjoyed a life of privilege and ease, told a tale of rebellion, death, and servitude.

"But I found forgiveness from the Lord in the end." His eyes seemed to glow for all their dark coloring. "And of course I found my beautiful wife too."

Rafe said nothing. He couldn't find the right words, nor the voice with which to express them.

"It hasn't been easy," Cherrett added. "And those we've hurt may never forgive us."

"Like Phoebe," Rafe managed.

"If she truly does love you, she will."

"Aye, the great question, no? If she truly loves me. I am thinking she might add me to the men who have hurt her beyond forgiveness."

"I wish I could say she wouldn't do that. But we can pray for her."

And he had prayed for Phoebe, for Rafe, and for James Brock, citing the verse in the fifth chapter of Matthew that said to pray for those who wronged you.

Rafe knew that verse. He'd read it one day because Mel wanted him to, and in a fit of anger that he now realized was the calling of his conscience, he'd thrown his Bible into the sea.

"Are you done with your quest to bestow justice on Brock?" Cherrett asked at the end of his prayer.

Rafe examined his heart and found only a sense of hope, of promise for a different purpose in life than destruction. "Aye, 'tis behind me."

"Then I'll pray that God shows you what's before you." Cherrett rose and held out his hand. "And I'll tell the captain we can safely go to wherever you've set Phoebe and Mrs. Chapman on shore."

"Guernsey." Rafe stood and shook the proffered hand. "But why would you or the British Navy do that for me?"

"Not for you, for me. And perhaps so they can capture Brock for themselves."

"But how did you know I had set the ladies ashore?"

"One of your crew isn't as loyal to his captain as he should be. When you sent a few of your lads ashore with the French prisoners, he sent a message to the Admiralty regarding some escaped American prisoners."

Rafe wasn't about to admit to that.

Cherrett laughed. "Officially, we've seen none aboard your brig. And Guernsey is neutral territory, despite being English."

They'd parted on amicable terms, and now Cherrett was gone, set ashore at Poole in the early morning to see his father for the first time in nearly five years.

"And I was right to fear him," Rafe mused aloud. "He has powerful friends and family." The highest being the greatest power of all—his heavenly Father.

God would have to be great indeed to change Rafe's heart. He smiled to himself and began to pace the weather deck.

Another eight to ten hours to Guernsey with nothing to do didn't please him, especially when rain began to fall. He retreated to his cabin, a canvas-sided box off the wardroom, but with a bed and chest and washstand. Someone had given him a clean shirt and shaving gear. And Cherrett had left him a Bible with a simple note saying, "We will meet again. You can return it then." As though they were friends. The idea rested a bit askew on Rafe, a man who had avoided friendship for far too long.

"I will be doing that," Rafe murmured, then sat down to read, to sleep, to pace the deck again once the rain ceased. The captain's own steward brought Rafe meals, and eventually they reached the island.

"You're free to go," the captain told Rafe. "But Admiral Landry has revoked your letters of marque."

"No matter that." Rafe drew a handful of paper from the inside pocket of his cloak. "I already destroyed them."

The captain's personal gig crew took him ashore, and he ran up to the George, and Phoebe.

"She's not here," Mel explained, hugging him. "She left with Derrick day before yesterday."

"With Derrick? Where's our French prize?"

"In harbor."

Rafe hadn't seen it in his haste to reach the inn. He didn't look for it now. He left Mel's room to bang on the door of the adjacent chamber.

Chapman opened it. "Hush. Baby Phoebe is sleeping at last."

"Phoebe?" Rafe stared at him. "You named your bairn Phoebe?"

Chapman sighed. "Belinda wanted it."

"It's the least I could do after bringing her along." Belinda's voice drifted from inside the room. "Even if now—"

"'Tis good to hear that your bairn is well, mon, but I want to ken where the adult lady Phoebe might be found."

"Phoebe?" Chapman's eyes darted from side to side. "I—I don't know. She's not here. Wasn't here when we arrived. Abandoned my Belinda during her lying-in."

Rafe's gut clenched. He couldn't believe Phoebe had abandoned a patient in the middle of her labor. "What are you saying? Where did she go?"

"She's gone to Dieppe to find James Brock," Belinda called out. "She abandoned me so she could fight your battles for you. It wasn't right, but—"

Rafe didn't wait to hear any more. He spun on his heel and raced back to the harbor in time to catch the captain's gig. "Dieppe," he said, breathless. "How can I get to Dieppe?"

<hr>

Phoebe took a long, deep breath. She would not scream. She would not pound on the walls. She would not be sick. She could bear the confines of a prisonlike room. Her heart and spirit were free of her past.

But that didn't free her from Rafe's past. Nor her own stupidity of meeting with Brock alone. While he reminded her of their previous meeting and asked her what she wanted with him, another man slipped up behind her, lifted her over his shoulder, and calmly walked out of the inn with her. Her attempts to call for help failed. Her French was inadequate to the task. If anyone spoke English, he pretended not to. They wouldn't go against a man with so much money he spent with a lavish hand.

So she paced what appeared to be a larder. Its stone walls were certainly cold enough to keep meat fresh. Her fingers and toes were numb. More of her grew numb with cold if she sat. So she paced like Rafe on his brig—back and forth, repeat. Repeat. Repeat. Her slippers whispered on the flagstones. And her heart slowed. As darkness closed in on a window too high and small to help her, a fetter inside her snapped away. She no longer felt imprisoned by the walls. They embraced her, sheltered her. Her body could be imprisoned, but God held her heart and soul, and nothing imprisoned Him.

She opened her mouth to pray aloud, then heard footfalls on the other side of the door, the heavy footsteps of a man. She hoped it was dinner or at least a glass of water.

It was the man who had carried her from the inn then dumped her into a carriage. It was the man who had chased her and Rafe through the streets of St. George's.

"Mr. Brock will see you now." He sounded like someone from Massachusetts or maybe New York.

"I hope he'll see me over supper." She smiled.

The henchman grunted and took her arm in a hand large enough to surround her bicep. He guided her through a kitchen, then down hallways of a house with wood paneling and crystal sconces, fine furniture and velvet draperies, but not a single painting, statue, vase, or anything moveable. By the time they reached a library with no books on the shelves, Phoebe guessed what was afoot.

"You kept me locked away until you had everything moved out?" she asked, smile still in place.

"I came back to France to pack everything up that's worth shipping home," Brock responded. "Sit down."

"I'd rather—" The henchman pushed her into a chair. "Stand."

Brock glared past her shoulder. "I'm not going to hurt you, Mrs. Lee."

"No?" Phoebe rubbed her bruised arm.

"Leave us," Brock commanded.

"But, sir—"

"Keep an eye out for Docherty," Brock directed.

Phoebe drew on her training to show no reaction to Brock, conjured Tabitha's voice in her head, telling her to remain calm in the face of the direst situation. *Never let a patient or family member know if you're flustered, scared, distraught—anything.*

Tabitha had seen her share of taxing situations in the twelve years she had been a midwife. Not once in three years did Phoebe see her teacher become flustered in the birthing chamber. "You may have hysterics afterward," Tabitha admonished.

The desire for hysterics roiling in her middle, Phoebe smiled at James Brock. "Why do you think you need to look out for Captain Docherty?"

"Because you're here." Brock smiled. "Or do you think I abducted you because I think you're charming?"

Phoebe laughed, though she felt like screaming.

"Indeed, Mrs. Lee, you are merely the means to an end." Brock gestured to the room, empty save for a few pieces of furniture. "I have decided to retire and wish to return to America permanently, but before I can do that, I need to put an end to Rafe Docherty. He's proved a difficult man to catch or kill."

Phoebe turned on her best lady-of-the-plantation drawl. "I expect he'd say the same thing about you, sir."

Brock laughed. "*Tres bien*, madam. But whatever reason you have for looking for me, you've done me a good turn." He paused.

Phoebe could have filled in the momentary silence with what Brock would say next. She feared if she opened her mouth, she would start screaming, railing against her stupidity, her carelessness, her need to manage every situation the way she wanted it to be.

"With you here," Brock concluded, "Docherty is sure to follow."

26

Rafe found Derrick a quarter hour after reaching Dieppe. He was haggling with a fisherman for the use of his boat to go up the coast. When Rafe strode up to him, he broke off his negotiations and flung up his arms as though about to embrace his captain. He shook Rafe's hand instead.

"I knew you'd come," he said. "I've been—"

"Where's Phoebe?"

"He's got her." Derrick's face crumpled. "She just disappeared from the inn, but she was talking to him before she did."

"He came to her?" Rafe clenched his hands into fists. "If he's harmed her—" He stopped himself from making the threat, from even thinking it. "Where?"

"Ten miles up the coast, but, sir—"

Rafe turned to the gaping fisherman and addressed him in French. "I need your boat. How much?"

A gleam in his dark eyes, the fisherman named a price that was likely more than he would make from his trade in a year.

"That's robbery," Derrick protested.

Rafe drew his purse from his pocket and paid the man. At the clink of the leather pouch, the fisherman looked like he wished he'd asked for more.

"Do not be greedy," Rafe admonished him. "My friend here and I could have taken your boat without your permission, had we a mind to be dishonest." He turned to Derrick. "We are going to be followed, I have no doot. Do not fash yourself about it. They are friends."

"Friends? Who?"

"Let us be off first." Rafe dropped into the fishing smack and, choking on the reek of fish, set about hoisting the single sail. "Do you have any weapons?"

Derrick loosed the painter and leaped aboard. "I got a brace of pistols and stickers. Now then, who's goin' ta be following us?"

"A few lads from the British Navy."

"Did I hear you right? You said the Navy?"

"Aye." Rafe took the tiller. "Which way?"

"East. What are you doing having truck with the Navy?"

Rafe told him as they navigated the fishing boat along the rocky coast of Brittany. "They'd like to have an excuse to lock Brock away," he conceded. "When I learned Phoebe came—Derrick, why did she come? And why did you let her?"

"She would have come whether I came with her or not." They tacked further east, and Derrick hauled the line to better catch the wind in the single sail. "I thought it better to come with her, not that I did such a good work of taking care of her. I should have stood guard outside her door."

"Brock would have found a way to get her even if you had." Rafe fixed his gaze on his friend. "What better way to lure me in than to take Phoebe."

"Yes, sir, we be sailing right into a trap."

"'Tis not a trap if we ken 'tis one." Rafe scanned the coastline, ash-gray against the charcoal of the sea in the darkening twilight, a rocky landscape not easy to defend. "We'll set in here."

They steered the tiny craft into an inlet not much larger than the boat itself. No one challenged them as they used a rocky outcropping for a mooring post. No one challenged them as they climbed onto the rocks despite inevitable noise from falling pebbles and the scrape of boots. Lights blazed in the near distance, and no one challenged them as they stalked toward them, toward the aroma of wood smoke on the frosty air.

"I don't like it," Derrick murmured.

Rafe nodded. His gut felt like someone had crushed it beneath the wheels of a two-ton carronade. No challenge to their presence meant they were supposed to get inside without a hindrance, then the trap would spring. Brock's men would surround them, capture them, probably even kill them.

A copse of stubbled pine rose up along the path from water to house. Rafe slipped into it, motioning for Derrick to follow. Derrick blended with the darkness beneath the prickly branches. Rafe drew the edge of his boat cloak over his face so its paleness would not shine in the approaching night.

"We've got to find them before they find us," he said in the undertone he'd learned traveled less distance than a whisper. "What do you suggest?"

He knew nothing about land tactics. One couldn't hide on the ocean if one encountered another vessel. One fought or prayed to outrun a larger enemy.

Prayed. Of course he'd prayed, to get away from an enemy, to stay alive for Mel's sake if nothing else, to keep his daughter safe. Those prayers had been answered, and he hadn't even acknowledged either that they were prayers or that God had listened. Yet there he stood, ready to finalize what he'd wanted and never prayed for because, unlike what Phoebe had accused him of what felt like a lifetime ago, he did have a conscience, one that knew his quest for vengeance was wrong.

"If Phoebe wasn't there," he told Derrick, "I wouldn't go. But she is there, and I don't have a choice but to rescue her.

Will you—" He sought for the right way to ask his question through a dry mouth. "Will you pray for our safety and Phoebe's?"

"I have been all along." Derrick squeezed Rafe's shoulder. "Welcome back to the Lord, my friend."

Rafe shook Derrick's hand as though they'd been separated for years, and the tension inside him uncoiled. Peace descended, and he knew what to do.

"They want me, not you. Go back to the boat and get back to Dieppe for aid, or direct the Navy lads here."

"I'm not letting you go in there alone." Derrick's gentle voice held steel. "I'm going to set up a decoy while you slip in."

"Nay, that will not do. They might kill you, and I will not have anyone else's blood on my hands."

"They'll have to catch me to kill me." Derrick's voice held a smile. "I know how to get around in the dark. Did a lot of that back on Jamaica when I wanted to see my wife."

Rafe suppressed a chuckle, then sobered. "You do not ken this territory."

"I can find the house and the sea. That's enough."

"You could trip."

"And I could've been shot all these years fighting. Now let's go. Time's a-wasting."

It was. Short of tying Derrick to the tree behind him, Rafe couldn't stop the other man from doing what he liked. He was no longer a subordinate, no longer one of the crew. Rafe had given up being a captain.

"God be with you," was all he said.

"He will." Derrick slipped from the copse and strolled toward the house, his footfalls nearly silent, his tall frame a mere shadow against the now cloud-blackened sky.

Rafe followed, his movements deliberately slow to minimize noise, his ears alert for the sound of others. He kept his hand on his dirk, ready to defend Derrick in an instant. And he prayed for the Lord to keep his friend safe to go home to his family.

The closer they drew to the house, the more tension threatened to wrap Rafe like a shroud. He fought it back, kept his breathing slow and even, willed his heart to remain at a steady beat. If blood roared through his ears, he wouldn't hear the approach of another man.

But he saw them first, shadows flickering against the light from the house. He hissed a warning through his teeth, then ducked into the vegetation along the track, ready to surprise the men if they assailed Derrick.

They did. With a shout in American English, they charged Derrick. One grabbed his arms. A glint of light flashed on steel that rested against Derrick's chest.

"Don't move," someone commanded.

"No, sir, I'm not stupid." Derrick spoke in a tone that sounded like he was.

The man behind him cursed. "This isn't Docherty."

"Where is he?" the other man demanded.

"I don't know." Derrick didn't lie.

"Where is he?" the other man repeated.

Rafe rose from the shrubbery behind the man holding Derrick's arms. "I am right here." He held his dirk to the man's throat. "Release him."

"I'll skewer him," the other man cried.

But he didn't have time. With Rafe's blade against his neck, the first man obeyed. Freed, Derrick leaped to the side, light and agile as a cat, and twisted the other man's blade out of his hands and held it to his chest.

"How many are you?" he asked.

Neither man spoke.

Rafe applied a bit of pressure with his blade. "How many of you are there?"

"Enough to kill you," the man beneath Rafe's blade responded.

Rafe admired his mettle and, because of it, began to search him for weapons. He confiscated a knife, a rapier, and a pistol and threw them into the bushes. "How many?"

"Four," the other man said in the voice of a sulky child.

"Besides you?" Rafe pressed.

"Including us." The man spat on Derrick. "And Mr. Brock. Who's got your lady."

"Yes, and for that alone—" Rafe stopped himself. "Where are they?"

"Stop talking," the first one said.

"Why should I?" the second one said. "I'm not going to die spitted like a pig."

"A wise man," Derrick said. "Now you two jus' take us into that stable I see over there so we can make sure you don't cause us no more trouble."

"I'm not going without a fight." The first man lunged toward Derrick and away from Rafe's blade.

With the grace of a ballet dancer, Derrick spun and slammed a ham-sized fist into his jaw. The man dropped like a stone. And his companion raced for the house, shouting for aid.

"Maybe I shouldn't have done that," Derrick said.

"Oh, nay, you should have." Rafe smiled as he stooped to secure the fallen man. "Take off his stockings and tie his ankles. I'll use his belt on his hands. And by the time we're finished, we will have company, I have no doot."

A hundred yards away, the front door of the house burst open. One man charged out, shouting for another one to be quiet. Then footfalls thudded toward Rafe and Derrick.

"Company," Rafe muttered, yanking the belt tight.

The bound man grunted and tried to roll away.

"I'll just be dumping him into the bushes." Derrick did just that with a crash that brought the other men racing toward them, only to halt out of arm's reach.

They glanced around, seeking Rafe and Derrick, who crouched in the shrubbery, weapons drawn. Rafe didn't want to shoot. He would use the pistol for a club first. If he'd had rope and time, he'd have affixed a snare across the track. No matter. He'd come up with something else.

With his left hand, he yanked off a branch of the pine boughs, wincing as the needles pricked his fingers, and tossed it along the path. In the dark, it could pass for the flickering shadow of someone darting an arm or leg from the bushes. Perhaps.

The men didn't fall for the old trick. Rafe tried again. Still nothing. Then Derrick on the other side of the path yanked up an entire shrub and sent it sailing toward the men.

Brock's men charged. Derrick rose and met them, one man against two, not a fair fight with most men. With Derrick, almost unfair to Brock's men. Still, Rafe leaped to enter the fray.

"Go," Derrick commanded. "Go get Miss Phoebe free."

Rafe didn't argue. He didn't want to distract his friend. Hearing grunts and the thud of blows, then the crash of breaking branches suggesting one man had ended up in the bushes behind him, he raced for the still-open front door and the one man left inside, provided the man outside hadn't lied.

He hadn't, at least from the first glance. The guard stood tall and tense in front of a door on one side of the marble-floored entry hall. He brought up his pistol. It clicked as he cocked it. Rafe darted to one side, then the other, a moving target hard to strike. Still the man fired. One shot. His only shot. Rafe dove to the floor, hearing the whine of the ball streaking above him, then tackled the man's legs. He dropped with a floor-shaking boom and lay gasping for breath.

Rafe didn't take time to secure him; he grasped the handle to the room. Locked. He stepped back and kicked the door near the latch. The portal sprang open and slammed back against the wall. Light blazed from several candelabra and reflected in Phoebe's spun-moonlight hair.

For a moment, Rafe felt as though he'd been knocked half senseless onto the floor. She smiled at him, and he couldn't breathe.

Then Brock rose from behind his desk, a pistol in his hand. "How did you get in alone?"

"Sorry, sir." The guard wheezed the apology from behind Rafe. "He just . . . came out of nowhere. Shall I secure him for you?"

"No." Brock's face tightened. "Since you've failed thus far, you may leave. I can manage him myself."

"But, sir—"

"Go."

Before the guard could protest further, Rafe grasped the door and slammed it in his face. Setting his shoulders against the panels, he faced Brock, his own pistol in hand. "I wonder which of us is the better shot. Or do I get my duel?"

"Rafe, no," Phoebe protested.

He dared not so much as glance at her. He kept his gaze fixed on Brock's face, his eyes, as he took two strides farther into the room. "What will you have, thief, murderer, wife killer?" He took another step closer. Though his eyes remained steady on Brock's, his hand holding the pistol shook just a little from the tautness of his grip.

Prayers for all to go well, for repentance for the desire for revenge, evaporated from his head with Brock so close. Blood roared through his veins as it did before battle. Only Phoebe halfway between him and his enemy stopped Rafe from charging the other man.

But Phoebe was there, quietly weeping.

Rafe shut his ears to the rebuke of those quiet tears and pressed forward. "Why did you do it, Brock? Why did you let my wife and parents die for your greed?"

Brock swept out his right arm as though shooing away a fly. "Your wife was dying anyway."

"But she didn't deserve to die like she did. And my parents were well. They had years of life left in them, years of taking care of the sick, lost because of you." His chest tightened, his throat threatening to close. "You robbed the world of a great physician."

Brock grinned. "Seems I robbed the world of two, Dr. Docherty. But I dare say you're richer for it, just as I am."

"Have you no conscience?" Power surged into Rafe's hand. He raised the pistol and cocked it.

"Rafe, don't." Phoebe choked out the protest. "He's not worth your life. He's not worth your future."

"Get onto the floor," he said without looking at her. He caught a gleam in Brock's eyes and understood his intent. Now was the time to fire, put an end to a man who had caused so much misery. His finger tightened on the trigger. Now, now, now the time lay upon him.

And crushed him. He couldn't breathe. He couldn't see. Through the roaring in his ears, he heard Davina asking God to forgive her, then his own feeble prayers.

He threw the pistol aside. It hit the wall and went off with a blast that silenced the roaring, the cries, everything but Phoebe's quiet prayer.

Until Brock began to laugh. "Coward. You waste all these years trying to catch me, and now that you think you have, you can't do it. I should shoot you where you stand."

Rafe crouched beside Phoebe and stroked her hair away from her face, its silk tangling in his fingers. "'Tis a'right, lass. I will not kill the mon in cold blood or otherwise. 'Tis not my place to take a mon's life."

"All the easier to take yours." Brock rounded the desk and stood over Rafe, his pistol pointed. "Why shouldn't I pull this trigger?"

"Because even you cannot get away with shooting an unarmed mon."

"You're in my house without invitation."

Rafe shrugged. "I cannot stop you. I will not. Just do not harm my lady."

Phoebe shot a glance up at him, her green eyes as bright as stained glass. Then she straightened and faced Brock. "I'd rather you used that pistol on me than him. Let him live. He has a daughter to raise."

"He hasn't cared about that all these years, so why should I?" Brock asked.

"He's changed." Phoebe stood, and Rafe rose with her. "Or just let us walk out of here. As you can see, we're finished with hunting you down."

"No." Brock shifted the muzzle of the pistol from Rafe to Phoebe and back again.

They smiled at him. Rafe looked into Brock's eyes, judging when the man intended to pull the trigger so he could push Phoebe out of the way. Intent on Phoebe and Brock, he didn't hear the shouts and shots from outside until Phoebe gasped, darted around Brock, and raced for the door.

Brock spun and fired. Phoebe fumbled at the door handle and turned to look back.

"Stay in here." Rafe grabbed Brock's wrist and twisted. The gun fell. Rafe kept twisting Brock's arm back and up between his shoulders. The man cried out and tried to kick. When he raised his leg, Rafe pushed him off balance. He fell with a thud, Rafe holding him down.

"Phoebe, I need your sash," he said calmly.

She smiled, albeit tremulously. "My dress will look a fright without it."

"Perhaps your dress, but not you." Rafe smiled back. The tension inside him melted in a glow from his core outward. "Stay in here, lass. 'Tis safer."

Brock said something vulgar, but his struggles to free himself proved too feeble to so much as dislodge Rafe's little finger, let alone his hands.

Rafe looked down at his captive, noted the gray hair, the thin body inside the fine clothes, the gray tinge to his skin, and realized the man was old, aged beyond the five and forty years he knew Brock to have.

"All your thieving has done you no good," Rafe murmured. "You are dying, are you not?"

Phoebe knelt beside him and began to tie the ribbon sash from her gown around Brock's hands. "Consumption?"

"Or worse, aye. Let us get him up. He will be hurting no one else, I'm thinking."

The door burst open, and three British sailors plus Derrick crowded into the room. "Is all well here, sir?" the lieutenant in the lead asked.

"Aye. Quite a'right." Rafe rose to shake their hands. "You can take him away if you like."

"You'll take care of him for us?" Phoebe asked.

"He's a prisoner of war, ma'am," the officer said. "He's committed crimes against our country."

Rafe drew her away from the bustle of sailors, a protesting James Brock, and Derrick with his eyebrows raised high enough to stick to his hairline. She went with him without a struggle, and they circumvented the others and slipped into the hall. The front door stood open, allowing the cold night air into the house. Rafe glanced around and picked a door at the back of the hall. As he hoped, it led into the kitchen, warm from a still-burning fire. Warm and empty for the moment.

"Are you a'right? He didn't hit you?"

"I'm well." She smiled up at him, her eyes glowing with wonder. "You didn't kill him."

"Nay, 'tis not my place to do so." He drew her against him and kissed her. "Perhaps 'tis not my place to do that either, but I can hope."

"You can more than hope." She buried her face against his shoulder.

"I have so much to tell you, about my wee talk with the Lord and a bit longer one with Dominick Cherrett."

Her head shot up. "Dominick? Here?"

"In Dorset now. He has gone to see his father, since you dragged him across the sea to save me." Rafe smiled at her. "Quite unnecessarily, you ken."

"I don't know enough. Tell me everything."

"Aye, I will." A thousand words crowded into his throat, words about finding his faith, words about forgiveness, words about his future wishes. All that squeezed its way out was, "I love you."

"I know." She buried her fingers in his hair. "I love you."

"You must. You were prepared to die for me. You—" His voice broke, and he held her more tightly.

She laughed. "I left Belinda for—" She pulled free. "Belinda. How is she? Do you know?"

"She is well. She delivered a wee lass safely and is with her husband."

"Thank God." Phoebe set her hands on his shoulders. "You're not good for my patients. I keep neglecting them for you."

"Then I'm thinking I can't ask you to marry me." He started to step away.

She held him fast. "You certainly may. Except . . . Rafe, will you go back to Scotland?"

"I thought I might. Does it matter to you?"

"It doesn't, except I'm not sure I can be a midwife there as your wife."

As his wife. Those three words made his heart sing.

"I expect you can, though city women want physicians. But I'm thinking—" He held her hands so he could look into her lovely, delicate face. "What would you think of going back to America, perhaps beyond the mountains? 'Tis a new land for a new life. I'm thinking they can use a physician and a midwife in the settlements there."

"If I'll cross an ocean with you, I'll cross some mountains for you." She glowered at him. "Just don't be interfering with my patients."

"Nay, never."

They laughed together. He kissed her again, and with her close to his heart, Rafe saw their new life blazing before them like the sun rising over the peak of a mountain.

Epilogue

Virginia, 1819

"You're the worst patient I've ever had." Phoebe delivered the complaint with a smile. "Just do as you're told and let me do my job right."

"When this is my fifth child—" The words died on a groan.

"Good. I see the head." Phoebe's hands shook only a little. More than ever, she wanted this birthing to be perfect.

Not that she expected anything to go wrong. The mother, at thirty-four, was healthy and strong, the labor progressing normally. Still, this patient was special. Phoebe had traveled over three hundred miles through spring rains and mud to arrive in time for the lying-in.

"Push," she directed. "It's time."

"I'm pushing."

"Not hard enough."

"It's another boy." Weariness colored the mother's voice. "I don't have the strength for another boy."

"You only have four of them."

"I want a girl." Another contraction robbed her of speech. "Always . . . wanted . . ."

The baby slid into Phoebe's hands. For a heartbeat, she stared at the perfection of limbs and fingers and toes before clearing the mouth and nostrils and giving it a gentle slap to start it breathing. Her assistant tied off the umbilical cord and snipped it, then took the baby to bathe and wrap.

Wonder still warmed Phoebe all the way through her heart as she turned back to her patient to finish up the aftermath of birth. She knew she should speak to the mother, tell her the baby's gender, but her throat felt tight and raw with a desire to weep with relief and joy.

"A midwife never weeps at the birth," Tabitha had taught Phoebe.

She couldn't cry now, not in front of the woman who had given her that admonition.

"You're forgetting your lessons," Tabitha told her with a hint of irritation. "If you aren't going to tell me I have another boy, at least let me have my baby."

"I can't tell you that you have another boy." Tears trickling down her cheeks, Phoebe took the baby from the apprentice and laid the bundle in Tabitha's arms. "Meet your daughter, Lady Dominick."

"Don't be absurd. I hated being called that in England. I'm just plain—" She gazed up at Phoebe, all fatigue lifted from her clear, blue-gray eyes. "Is it really a girl? You're not playing a cruel joke on me?"

"No." Phoebe shook her head. "'Tis a wee lass, as Rafe would put it." Phoebe wiped her eyes on her sleeve. "I'll go fetch Lord Dominick."

"Stop that." Tabitha was half laughing and half crying while gazing into her daughter's wrinkled face. "She's beautiful."

"Just like her mother." Phoebe smoothed hair back from Tabitha's face. "Do you know what you'll name her?"

"We decided on Esther for a girl long ago." Tabitha emitted a gentle laugh. "After all those boys, she's likely to be the queen of the household."

"I expect Lord Dominick will spoil her."

"Not if I can prevent it." Tabitha yawned. "And don't call him that to his face. He detests it."

Phoebe had been calling her old friends by their English titles since they had journeyed to England following the end of the wars. Dominick's father had died shortly after his youngest son's visit in 1813, but his brothers welcomed Tabitha and her offspring as part of the family. They credited her with keeping their brother from destroying himself and blessed her for producing so many boys. Neither of them had produced anything other than daughters, and the family needed heirs, of course.

"I expect we'll have to take her to England one day to meet her cousins." Tabitha stroked Esther's cheek. "Will you like that?"

The infant's mouth moved as though she spoke.

Phoebe laughed, wiped her eyes again, and headed for the door, motioning the assistant to follow. "I'll tell Dominick."

She didn't have to go far to find him. He paced the front hall of the parsonage while Rafe leaned against the parlor door frame, watching. Rafe straightened at Phoebe's approach, his eyes lighting. She paused on the steps, fighting the urge to run to him. Duty first.

"Dominick?"

He spun mid-step. "Yes? Is she all right? The baby?"

"You would think you would not fash yourself so much after all those bairns of yours." Rafe strode forward, his eyes asking the question.

"All is well." Phoebe ran down the rest of the steps and hugged Dominick. "You have a daugh—"

Before she finished saying the word, Dominick raced up the steps three at a time and burst into the master bedroom. A faint wail and soft voices drifted out.

Rafe took Phoebe's hands. "Is all well?"

"Yes, easiest delivery I've ever tended, except for her treating me like an apprentice every step of the way."

"You are no different when 'tis your bairn, you ken."

"I know." Suddenly weary, Phoebe rested her head against his shoulder. "Speaking of babies, where are our three?"

"In the yard tending a new litter of puppies."

"Poor puppies. They'll want to take at least one apiece home with us."

"Aye, to add to the three dogs we already have."

"And the—how many cats is it now?"

They exchanged grins, loving the animals as much as the children did. Dogs, cats, horses, children . . . They'd add as many to their lives as they could manage.

"Maybe Tabitha and Dominick's daughter will marry one of our sons," Phoebe mused aloud.

Rafe chuckled. "Give her a few hours to at least be christened with a name before she makes up her mind on which of the scamps she will be wanting."

"And speaking of the scamps . . ." Phoebe yawned. "Do I get a rest before I have to collect them?"

"Aye, rest all you like. Mel's looking after them."

"Dear Mel. She's so good with children I expect she'll be wanting to get married—"

"Do not remind me of how old she is."

"And pretty."

"Worse."

Mel had healed from her injury and surgery aboard the *Davina* and, though a bit quieter and sometimes still struggling to read with her former facility, showed no other lasting effects of nearly dying. Especially not in her beauty and kindness. Soon Phoebe would have to draw Rafe's attention to the young men already beginning a path to the Dochertys' door so they could see Mel. For now, however, too weary and too comfortable in her husband's arms to concern herself with the future, Phoebe kept more comments on marriages to herself. She and Rafe had learned so much about the joy of being wed that she couldn't stop herself from matchmaking now and again.

The joy of marriage and of children. She heard the shrieks of children at play, Dominick and Tabitha's four boys plus Phoebe and Rafe's three. Three boys in six years of marriage, thanks to a set of twins, still amazed her. Her life amazed her, as different as it was from that of a pampered plantation princess. In the New River Valley beyond the Blue Ridge Mountains, she still delivered most of the babies born. Rafe took care of every other medical need and the difficult births. Together, they formed a formidable couple, healing bodies as the Lord had healed their hearts.

Acknowledgments

Without the help of many people, this book would not have come into being. Here are the ones who stand out the most for having read those early chapters with which I have so much trouble, who lent me moral and prayer support along the way, and who gave me research assistance.

Those amazing experts on the Royal Navy Sail and Steam Listserv. Who else would be able to give me the dimensions of an early-nineteenth-century brig?

That person whose name I no longer recall, who long ago suggested I'd be interested in a book called *Seafaring Women* by Linda De Pauw. I think the concept for this book started while I read the story of the seafaring midwife.

Patty Hall, Gina Welborn, Louise Gouge, and Marylu Tyndall, who were early readers and cheerleaders.

Carrie Fancett Pagels, for having the instinct to call me just when I needed it.

My husband, who rescued my computer from the brink of death. He gets the 2010 Husband of the Year Award for doing so, not to mention putting up with slapdash meals and my brain sailing off to parts unknown when he was trying to have a conversation.

Last, but far from least, the wonderful team at Baker Publishing Group, for making the Midwives series happen.

Award-winning author **Laurie Alice Eakes** wanted to be a writer since knowing what one was. Her first book won the National Readers Choice Award in 2007, and her third book was a Carol Award finalist in 2010. Between December 2008 and January 2010, she sold thirteen books to Barbour Publishing, Avalon Books, and Revell, making her total sales fifteen. Recently, she added two novella sales to that collection. Her first book with Revell, *Lady in the Mist*, was picked up by Crossings Book Club, and three of her books were chosen for large-print editions by Thorndike Press. She has been a public speaker for as long as she can remember; thus, she suffers just enough stage fright to keep her sharp.

In 2002, while in graduate school for writing fiction, Laurie Alice began to teach fiction in person and online. She lives in Texas with her husband, two dogs, and probably too many cats.

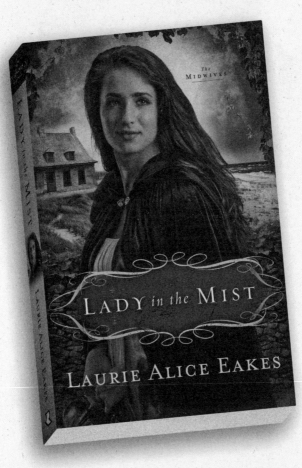

"An adventure that will leave readers breathless."

—Louise M. Gouge, award-winning author of
At the Captain's Command

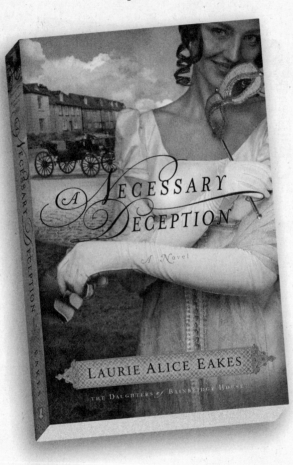

Laurie Alice Eakes whisks readers through the drawing rooms of London
amid the sound of rustling gowns on this exciting quest to let the past stay
in the past and let love guide the future.